The assassin needs an ally... on the inside.

SWALLOW

Kindred Book Two

SCARLETT FINN

Also by Scarlett Finn

NOTHING TO...
NOTHING TO HIDE
NOTHING TO LOSE
NOTHING IN BETWEEN: ONE
NOTHING TO DECLARE
NOTHING TO US
NOTHING IN BETWEEN: TWO
NOTHING TO SAY
NOTHING TO GAIN
NOTHING IN BETWEEN: THREE
NOTHING TO YOU
NOTHING TO THIS PREQUEL: ONE WILD NIGHT
NOTHING TO THIS
NOTHING IN BETWEEN: FOUR
NOTHING TO DO
NOTHING TO FEAR
NOTHING IN BETWEEN: FIVE
NOTHING TO DENY

GO NOVELS
GO WITH IT
GO IT ALONE
GO ALL OUT
GO ALL IN
GO FULL CIRCLE

KINDRED SERIES
RAVEN
SWALLOW
CUCKOO
SWIFT
FALCON
FINCH

EXILE
HIDE & SEEK
KISS CHASE

THE EXPLICIT SERIES
EXPLICIT INSTRUCTION
EXPLICIT DETAIL
EXPLICIT MEMORY

THE FORBIDDEN NOVELS
FORBIDDEN DESIRE
FORBIDDEN WANT
FORBIDDEN WISH
FORBIDDEN NEED
FORBIDDEN BOND

WRECK & RUIN
RUIN ME
RUIN HIM

MISTAKE DUET
MISTAKE ME NOT
SLEIGHT MISTAKE

THE BRANDED SERIES
BRANDED
SCARRED
MARKED

TO DIE FOR...
TO DIE FOR TRUTH
TO DIE FOR HONOR
TO DIE FOR VIRTUE
TO DIE FOR DUTY
TO DIE FOR LOVE

RISQUÉ & HARROW INTERTWINED
TAKE A RISK
FIGHTING FATE
RISK IT ALL
FIGHTING BACK
GAME OF RISK

FORBIDDEN PREQUEL DUET
ALL. ONLY.
ONLY YOURS

LOVE AGAINST THE ODDS STANDALONE COLLECTION
SWEET SEAS
HEIR'S AFFAIR
RESCUED
MAESTRO'S MUSE
GETTING TRICKY
THIRTEEN
REMEMBER WHEN...
RELUCTANT SUSPICION
XY FACTOR

LOST & FOUND
LOST
FOUND

ONE

BRODIE MCCORMACK HAD told her that she wasn't allowed to leave his property, but he had done little to welcome her into his home. Zara Bandini chose to view his indifference as acceptance because he hadn't banished her after commanding her to stay. The truth was he'd given up caring about everything since his Uncle Art had been murdered, so she couldn't be insulted by his inattention.

With every new demonstration of apathy, she became more worried about her love's mental state. Grief was a dangerous beast that could consume and contort a man until he became unrecognizable. Brodie, the man she'd fallen in love with, was still in there, he was just struggling to navigate the path back to her.

At thirteen, Brodie McCormack had lost his parents. Now at thirty-three, he'd lost his guardian and mentor. Since his life was torn apart by the death of his mother and father in an explosion on their boat twenty years ago, Art had been his rock. After that tragedy, Brodie had lost his way, and it had been up to Art to guide his nephew through the trauma.

Three months had passed since they'd watched the Kindred Chief succumb to the gunshot wound delivered by Albert Sutcliffe in the Atlas warehouse. Since that day, Brodie had locked himself in the manor he'd inherited from his parents and shunned the world.

The task of keeping the sniper alive had fallen to her and Zara had done her best to look after him, but she feared that wasn't good enough. He just didn't seem to want to liberate himself from the darkness that was his perpetual companion.

During his long periods of aversion to company, she had been afforded the chance to explore McCormack Manor and learn the quirks of the building. What began as a way to entertain herself grew into a bigger project. She tended to forgotten rooms, welcomed the light, and put her own touches around the place, taking the harsh masculine edge from the home that had once been a palace meant for Brodie's mother.

Living in a large city, in an apartment without exterior space, she hadn't had a recent chance to test her yardwork skills. Zara had been raised in the country and was no stranger to getting dirty. When she waded out onto the grounds, it struck her that she'd missed toiling in the sunshine.

Maintaining such a vast estate wasn't a task meant for a single person. Zara embraced being tossed in at the deep end because she needed the distraction. Broken objects could be repaired with time and attention. Her lover was broken too, fixing him wasn't as simple as a new coat of paint or a few soft furnishings.

So much of McCormack Manor had gone to ruin with Art and Brodie as its distracted caretakers. The Kindred had abroad missions to focus on, meaning uncle and nephew were rarely here for any more than a few weeks at a time. Hence how the place had fallen into disrepair. Since Art had pulled a teenage Brodie out of his parental bereavement funk, no one had spent such an extended period of time here.

On that particular day, Zara Bandini was just finishing up with her checks in main security in the basement of the grand gothic manor house. It had become her daily duty to inspect the systems, to make sure the perimeter was secure, and that all the cameras were unobstructed. In the months since losing Art, she'd become efficient through necessity more than desire. At first, filling the chief's shoes was daunting, but it had become clear that no one else was going to step up to the plate and these routine duties wouldn't perform themselves.

Glancing at the clock, she registered the time. If she wanted to be punctual for the funeral, she would have to speed up. The last thing she wanted to do was arrive late. Her entrance would be conspicuous given that she was expected on the front pew.

While typing in the last commands to the computer log, she stood up. Rolling the seat away with her locked knees, Zara remained bowed over the keyboard to conclude her work. With a final keystroke, she adjusted one of her diamond earrings with two fingertips and straightened to scan the bank of monitors in front of her once more.

Satisfied that she'd completed her duty, she hooked her purse over her head to let it rest across her body and headed for the exit. Thinking about the grim day ahead, she went into the blackened basement corridor. Funerals reminded her of the day they'd buried her mother. Pity had surrounded her and at fourteen, she should have been thinking about boys and makeup. Instead, she went from caring for her withering mother to caring for a home she did not intend to die in.

Her father and brother would have been happy to keep her in the family home, cooking and cleaning, and never again thinking about the future. But she wouldn't repeat her mother's mistakes. Zara wanted to make something of herself, and while her life hadn't followed the path she might have projected, she had made a difference in the world—albeit with Kindred help and guidance.

Zara would much rather blend into the background today. But she'd agreed to sit with Grant McCormack, CEO of CI, who was grieving the loss of one of his youngest VP's. Losing a vibrant man, full of such potential, was a shock. As a victim of a mugging gone wrong, they'd lost him to murder, which distressed the high society members he moved amongst.

Since meeting Raven, which was Brodie's professional alias, she'd become more accustomed to death and wasn't so surprised that these kinds of things could happen. Bunking in with a professional marksman would do that to a girl.

Especially when he had a habit of putting bullets in men who got too close to her.

Zara would be happy to avoid memories of her mother and the other more recent losses she'd suffered. If she could, she would limit her time at the wake. After showing her face, she should be able to sneak out early. Grant would have plenty of hands to shake, giving him plenty of distractions.

Hurrying along the basement corridor toward the stairwell at the end, she came to an abrupt halt when the door to her left opened. Brodie startled her from her thoughts when he emerged from the gym, damp from the shower, wiping a towel over his jaw. His brown hair was wet and because personal grooming wasn't high on his to-do list these days, it hadn't been cut in months.

She hadn't been aware that they'd occupied the same floor because she hadn't sought him out this morning. These days he didn't surface from his bedroom until closer to noon—if he came out at all.

Giving her the once over, his expression registered no change in his thoughts. "What's with the getup?" he asked, still examining her demure black dress and conservative heels. "You going to a costume party?"

It didn't surprise her that he didn't know what time of the day it was or what season they were in. It was just another example of his lack of focus. The outfit she was wearing had been typical of her daily wardrobe before Brodie came into her life. Now, she spent more time in casual or workout clothes, or items that she didn't mind getting dirty in the yard when she went out to work in the muck.

There wasn't any affection or joy in his features. Brodie had become a shut in, and there were times she feared she'd never be able to reach him again. "I'm going to a funeral," she said, edging closer to curl her fingers around the waistband of his shorts.

Any glimmer of conversation spelled a good day. Savoring every chance to connect with him, she wouldn't give up on him or let him be lost forever. He needed a constant, a touchstone, and she wanted to be that beacon for him.

By the way he was looking down his nose at her, she

could tell he was considering possibilities. "Anyone I know?"

"I doubt it," she said, trailing a fingernail up the center of his vest. "He was a VP at CI. He was killed by a mugger. Random shooting."

The story didn't interest him, she could tell by how his attention cooled. Nothing seemed to interest him anymore, except brooding solitude. Sometimes he drank into the night, sometimes she wouldn't see him for days. Other times, he kept her locked up with him so he could gorge himself on her body. Those times were physical. He wouldn't talk to her, not about anything but sex. But there had been times she gleaned his inner needs in the way he touched her.

One of the less enjoyable tasks that had fallen to her was arranging for the engraving of Art's headstone. With Tuck's help, they'd affixed the granite slab to Art's plot. Tuck took off as soon as the job was done. He hadn't opened up to her, but she could tell that Art's death was taking its toll on the hacker too.

Dirty and tired, tears had stained her face when she'd come back inside to find Brodie waiting on the stairs for her. It was nights like that one which kept her love for him alive. He hadn't said anything, he'd just taken her hand and led her up to his bedroom where he made quiet love to her before holding her against him all night.

Later on, she discovered that he'd watched her and Tuck working from one of the high manor towers that gave him a partial view of the headstones through the treetops.

Thinking of that day always made her crave his devotion. "Do you need anything before I go?" she asked.

Slowly, his head angled to the left. Zara clung to him during these rare interactions and always took the opportunity to touch him when she got close enough. The physical connection spurred on her desire to stay at the side of this man who was floundering.

Whipping the towel off his neck, he dropped it to the floor then groped for the zipper under her arm. He slid it down. As it descended, her heart rate ascended. She didn't have time for games. Didn't have time to sate his wants now, but if she said no, Brodie would only want her more.

"I'm late," she said, but he grabbed her ribcage and rushed her against the wall with a thump that expelled the air from her lungs.

The strap of her purse slipped from her shoulder to her elbow and encircled her upper body until she straightened her arm and let it fall to the floor in a wide loop around her feet.

With narrow eyes and lips, his gaze drilled into her. "Sorry, baby, you won't be going to that party," he murmured.

A funeral wasn't a party and she didn't know why he would object to her going. It could be he didn't want her being around Grant, which she would be if she went to any CI event. Maybe he was worried about her well-being and didn't want her to go to a solemn occasion without him there to support her. It was more likely that he was just horny and didn't want her to stray when he required her attention.

The shadows beneath his eyes betrayed that she'd been wrong. He wasn't awake early as she'd thought, he hadn't gone to bed yet. He'd emerged from the gym, so she guessed that he'd worked out before taking his shower, which was something he did when he was frustrated. It was possible he'd tried to exorcize his arousal through physical exertion or maybe he'd had a rough night of grief. Either way, she wished he'd sought her out sooner.

"What you got going on under the dress?" he asked and stepped back to pull her straps from her shoulders, though they only fell as far as her elbows before the dress caught on the apex of her breasts, hiding from him what she wore beneath. He wasn't patient. Grabbing the neckline, he tugged it down and seemed pissed off to find her bra there blocking his view.

But he leaned away to get a look at her legs beneath the hem of her dress. When his lit eyes landed on hers, she felt exposed. She didn't have to be naked for Brodie to know her habits. "Let me see 'em," he grumbled and, although he was tense, he did seem to be enjoying this game.

With the heels of her hands on her hips, she gathered up the fabric of her dress just enough to let the lace tops of her stockings peek from beneath. She knew how to tease him, knew what he wanted to see. His gruff single laugh made her shoulder blades press deeper into the wall at her back as her pelvis rose toward his. Coming a step closer, he took her hips, but only long enough to give them a brief squeeze before he let go.

"Take off your panties," he said, and she was sure he was going to take her here, against this wall in this darkened basement hallway.

She'd already given in to one of his commands, and his attention was enough to arouse her into forgetting about the plans she'd made. Picking her skirt higher, Zara found the elastic of her thong and pulled it down, past the lace summits of her hold-ups. Bending at the waist, her face was in his crotch when the fabric got to her ankles. He got closer, close enough that when she looked up, her nose brushed the solid length of him that was throbbing beneath his shorts.

Stepping out of the panties, she left them on the floor and grabbed the waist of his shorts with intentions of freeing him, but Brodie had other ideas. He intercepted her wrist, and while she was still bent over, he turned and dragged her toward the stairwell.

This was his house, they were alone, not even Art was around to happen upon them, but that could've been why Brodie chose to hurry her up to his bedroom. Screwing her in the hallway, without any concern of being discovered, was another reminder of what they'd lost.

Brodie got her up to his bedroom and didn't slow when he reached the door, he got them inside and dragged her over to the bed. Her dress was still hanging on her arms, but when he flung her face first onto the mattress, he grabbed the hem of it and tugged it down to expose her. Zara pushed onto her hands to look around, the first thing she noticed was the blackness of the space she'd once considered a haven. The room was a mess, beer and bourbon bottles were on the bedside table with empty glasses and dirty plates beside them.

When she got the chance to come in and clear up, she did. But his erratic moods sometimes left her feeling unwelcome. Often Brodie flat out demanded that she leave him alone and get out.

His fingers skimmed down between her ass cheeks and

around until he made contact with her feminine threshold. Plunging the digits deep into her, he circled and spread them to expand her inner passage, testing how her body would yield for his cock.

"Your pussy's all juiced up, baby," he grumbled.

She always got wet when he talked, whether it was dirty words about what he wanted to do to her, or commands meant to put her in her place, Zara gave her heart and her trust to the man she loved without reservations.

Brodie worked her for a few seconds and when he pulled her hips upward, she knew he was going to enter her from behind. Zara let herself be contorted, let herself be pushed and pulled for his pleasure because she gave him something no other woman did, he had everything he needed right here. Zara was his and although he hadn't spelled it out yet, she knew that Brodie belonged to her. She gave him what he needed whenever he needed it and the possessive nature of his rough hands were enough to show her how grateful he was for her sticking by him.

Once he had quenched his desire in her body, he would need sleep, meaning she might still have time to show face at the wake. But Brodie had been her priority since the day that Art died and that wasn't going to change now. She'd stay here, in his room, in his bed, for however long he wanted her there. Everything was secondary to her love for him and once he emerged from the isolation of his grief, their connection was going to be stronger than ever.

He massaged inside her, curling his fingers to explore her g-spot and twisting his hand to abrade her with his knuckles. His actions made her tense and relax all at the same time. Brodie was a combination of contradictions that proved how complex his character was, he wasn't a killer who reveled in the scent of blood. He was a good man with morals of his own, even if they didn't match the morals of the masses.

Preparing herself for his entry, she began to sway forward and back, using his wide fingers as a tool for her release. But while one hand was delivering pleasure to her, the other grabbed her arm and flipped her to her back, then with his shins over her thighs and his weight pushing into her shoulders through the heels of both hands, he growled down at her.

"You want out of here so bad?" he asked with a sneering smile that reeked of menace. "Prove it."

This was his sport. She never refused to play these role play games with him because for every second she tried to get away from him, she'd spend twice as many seducing him or lying in his arms when they were done.

Taking a moment to build up air in her lungs, she kept her expression tight. When her eyes pinched, he lunged down, trying to snag her bottom lip, but she turned her head away and began to struggle.

"Get off me," she said, trying to lift her legs, but she couldn't kick out, the solid mass of his powerful thighs gave her as much room as a concrete block would. Still, she wriggled, turning her face away from his every attempt to kiss her.

"You've got something I want," he said and bit her earlobe.

The pain was pleasure. There was no fear here, only stimulation. Brodie was strong. He worked hard on his body to make sure it was a weapon able to protect her. Trying and failing to free herself from his control was a reminder of how resolute he was to have her. His potency intoxicated her.

His weight came down to pin her pelvis onto the mattress and the pulsing proof of his intentions pressed itself into her. On feeling him so near, she began to writhe against that pleasure, but he surged forward making it impossible for her to move.

Releasing his grip for long enough to tear the strip of fabric between her bra cups, she shrieked. That was one of her favorite bras and if she'd known this was going to happen, she wouldn't have worn it. But her chagrin was erased when his stubble tickled her cleavage and moved deeper until the rough hair on his face scratched on the sensitive skin of her breasts.

Using the tip of his tongue, he licked his way to one nipple, circled it, and then crossed to the other. She expected the same delicate touch, instead he stole her nipple into his mouth and sucked it so hard a spear of pain shot through her and settled against the heat of her engorged center.

"I have to go," she said, but her resistance was lessening.

"You give me what I need," he said. He chose that moment to elevate his hips to free himself from his shorts. She sensed, or maybe hoped, that he meant those words because that admission would mean more to her than any game. "You're my horny little plaything."

The game wasn't over, and she was pulled back into it when Brodie rose to grab her inner thighs, he pulled her legs apart and leered down at the swollen pink flesh of her glistening vulva. Zara was ready for him, her body was on fire, her nerves fizzling, she wanted this, wanted his hands, his mouth, his dick, all of it. Being intimate with Brodie was a rollercoaster, there were ups and downs, and just when you thought you had a handle on what he'd do next, he'd flip her upside down in a loop-the-loop.

"That's what I need," he murmured and curled his fingers around his shaft.

His hand moved up, then back down. He squeezed himself from hilt to head. Watching him pleasuring himself while remaining fixated on her body was a new kind of thrill. Even though it seemed like he was committing a private act, she wanted to be a part of it.

Sitting up, she barely got her balance before he seized her throat to pin her against the mattress. He came down over her so their upper bodies were parallel. Her knees made contact with his thighs, so she rubbed her legs up and down his, but the fabric of his shorts was still around his thighs and made complete skin-to-skin contact impossible. But she wasn't disappointed.

Her throat was uncomfortable, but he wasn't squeezing, just using his hand to keep her right where he wanted her. From how his other arm moved, she knew he was still pleasuring himself. But the intensity in his eyes, that wouldn't leave hers, was a connection deeper than the one they were going to make with their bodies.

"Baby," she whispered and stroked up his torso. "Talk to me."

His brows snapped down. His frown was always an

indicator of his annoyance. He widened his knees to spread her legs farther and she gasped at the burning ache in her upper thighs, but he pushed forward and impaled her with the organ he'd been caressing.

Because he was fucking her so fast, she couldn't breathe right. His frown was still there, fixed on her, pissed off that she'd let a moment of intimacy creep into their game. Brodie didn't shy from intimacy, but he liked to be the one who initiated softer moments. Somehow, he'd known she didn't mean she wanted dirty words from him. She wanted to know his heart because until he confessed his grief, there was always a chance it would consume him.

Her eyes closed as he shunted her body up with his powerful thrusts. His frame receded from hers, she relaxed for a beat, then tensed to rise up and meet his plunges with her own. Being a part of his body, for these precious unions, cleared her head and centered her thoughts in a way no other exercise or meditation could. Brodie was her rock and when she was with him, she never doubted her decisions.

All she needed from him was this commitment, and given what he'd recently lost, it meant a lot that he trusted her. It would have been easy for him to reject everyone. He could've retreated inside, canceled all security clearances except his own, and disappeared from the radar forever. Instead, he was sharing his life with her. It just so happened that at the moment, his life existed inside the McCormack Manor walls.

Hot, wet bliss burned her veins and she had to grab his shoulders, to use him as traction, because she was losing her ability to keep up. Brodie batted her arms away and grabbed her hips, holding her at the angle he needed to increase his pace further. Just as she screamed out his name and the meteors of orgasm shot through her body, Brodie cursed, surged forward, and released his liquid into her.

Seconds of silence flitted between them. As soon as he made eye contact, she opened her mouth to talk, but he scowled again, let her go, and got off the bed to head for the bathroom. He slammed the door and she heard the click of the lock. He was done with her and now she'd been dismissed.

TWO

IN THE END, she didn't get to the funeral. She'd learned Brodie's signals and locking the bathroom door meant he didn't want to interact with her anymore. For weeks, she'd been trying to break through his barriers, but he was still too affected by the loss of his mentor to allow her to make any meaningful progress with him.

Grant hadn't been happy when she'd appeared at the wake, flushed, apologetic, and late. Still, he kept her near while making the rounds and shaking hands. After Atlas, and Art's death, she hadn't intended on going back to Cormack Industries. The whole mess still upset her, the senseless loss of a good man and the deal Grant had been going to make with a person intent on murder made her sick. She was sorry to have been involved.

But a couple of weeks into her stay at the manor, Grant McCormack—Brodie's brother and her former boss—had called and begged her to come back to work. Without any sense of obligation, she intended to refuse him. But after discussing it with Tuck, who was also known as Swift, they decided she should go back, at least for a few months, until they were sure that Grant had gotten over his notion of illegal justice. So far, so good.

The funeral passed and she went back to her juggling act of trying to keep an eye on Brodie, while maintaining her own apartment and her job at CI, which was just cover for her role as Kindred spy. She knew her future was not in that company.

Over the last three months, Zara had learned the rhythm of the manor and of her man. As tough as it was being everything to everyone, she valued Brodie's need, and his trust. She could roam free in a space he'd always kept private. The manor was so highly restricted that only six people had set foot on its floor for over a decade. Now, it was becoming her home.

Tuck had grown to be her closest ally. She could call on him day or night for anything and he would always help her as quickly and thoroughly as he could. Zara wasn't sure she'd have gotten through this quarter without him.

Tuck's expertise was needed in the manor that day, about two weeks after the funeral. When she'd called for his help, he'd been close enough to get there quickly. Sitting in the main security room in the basement of the manor, Zara stayed as quiet as possible while Tuck typed, fixing the issue that she'd called him about. Tuck knew everything there was to know about computers and had programmed most of the manor system himself. It was impossible for this network to stump him, as it had done her.

Tuck rolled his chair to the side and opened his palms toward the trio of keyboards indicating she could take her place at the central one again. "Thanks," Zara said, using the desk to pull herself to the middle position of the control panel where Tuck had just been.

"No problem," he said.

She could feel him watching her. He'd been looking at her in the same way for three months, and just as usual, she did her best to look anywhere except at her friend and colleague. So Zara examined the timestamps on the monitor bank above her as each screen rebooted. The last one flickered up and she exhaled, pleased that she had a clear and present view again.

Still scrutinizing the screens, Zara was aware of Tuck waiting for her to say something. "I think it crashed last night," she said. Staying on topic didn't give him the explanation he wanted, but it was all she could volunteer. "Everything was all screwed up when I came down this morning."

"Zara," Tuck said in such a way that told her, he wasn't going to let her skirt the issue any longer. The hacker was too astute for his own good sometimes. "How is he?"

Pasting on a smile, she did her best to sound breezy. "Oh, you know, some days are better than others."

The feigned cheer in her voice was fooling no one, let alone the man who knew Brodie better than she did. "You can talk to me," he said in the same soft voice most people used when broaching a difficult subject.

Exhaling, she accepted that her avoidance wasn't going to hold up. Shouldering all of the responsibility for Brodie and his mood was as selfish as it was selfless. She was protecting the Goliath that this man was and he wouldn't take kindly to people discussing him behind his back. The trouble was, he didn't talk about himself or the dark place he'd descended into, and so she was left to soldier on without any idea if she was helping him to progress or just facilitating this holding pattern.

Just because she understood that she had to be honest and share, didn't mean she could look Tuck in the eye as she did it. So she spread her fingers on either side of the middle keyboard and traced the outer edges of it.

"For the first four weeks he didn't come out of his room," she said. "He locked himself up in there. It was hit or miss whether he'd eat, let alone shower or shave. For the next four weeks, he threw himself into working out. He'd be in the gym for hours sometimes. I would leave in the morning for work at CI and he'd still be in there when I came home, lifting weights or running. I thought it was an improvement, you know? At least he was taking care of his body and he was drinking and eating again."

He rolled his seat closer and his hand came into view near her elbow. "And for the last month?"

She sighed. "He's been back and forth," she said. "Sometimes I almost see glimmers of his old self coming back, then just when I think we're getting somewhere, he locks himself in his room again and I don't see him for days."

"It's a process," Tuck said, pulling his chair close enough that he could take her hand. "You're not going through this alone. If there's anything I can do to help—"

"You've been amazing," she said, turning her hand over to link her fingers with his. "Every time I call, you pick up… I can't say the same about Brodie."

"He's lucky to have you," Tuck said. "You've kept him alive for the last three months."

"Sometimes I come into the house and I can't find him, I have no idea where he is."

"You won't have that problem now that I've shown you how to access and control the motion sensors. You'll be able to look after him no matter where he is."

"He can take care of himself… I've just been helping out."

Sometimes while sitting at her desk in CI, she wondered how Brodie would have dealt with Art's death had he not had her. Maybe she wasn't helping at all. Maybe if she hadn't been there he'd have been forced to carry on and to look after himself. There would have been no alternative. But abandoning him had never occurred to her because if he didn't pick himself up and move on, the alternative was too horrific to even entertain.

"Are you two still…?"

"I stay over most nights," she nodded. "But I'm… I moved my things into one of the guest bedrooms because you know… he needs his space and I don't like to intrude."

"Are you telling me that since Art died you haven't—"

"Oh no, we've had sex," she said. "When he wants it, he seeks me out. Sometimes he's waiting for me as soon as I arrive. Other times he comes to me at night, you know? But he hasn't left this house. I still have my apartment where I stay when I'm not here and he hasn't visited me there. He's still so angry about what happened. He blames himself and sometimes he needs the vent."

Tuck sucked in a breath. "What about your needs?" he asked. "The guy needs a good punch to the gut. He can't just breeze into your life any time he wants to take out his frustrations with some angry sex… Not that I'm one to talk about healthy relationships."

"How is Kadie?" she asked, referencing the girlfriend Art had told her about.

"I haven't seen her in a while. All of this it's just… it reminds me how dangerous what we do is. If I had been the one to take that bullet… she would never have known…'

"It's not too late to change your life," Zara said. "Art told Brodie not to be like him… I'd guess that goes for you too."

"I wouldn't know how to change," Tuck said. "My life has been like this for as long as I can remember. I met Brodie and Art in Thailand when I was twenty-two… just a few weeks before my twenty-third birthday. Art planned a huge party for me when he found out I had never celebrated a birthday before"—his smile grew more distant as he turned it away—"I didn't know half the folks there, but… I've been knocking around with them on and off for ten years. Art taught me a lot about control and indulgence… Man, I was an idiot back then."

Concerned that Tuck was dealing with his own torture alone, she wanted him to confront what he was dealing with. Repressing it could lead to further damage. "He was like family to you too," she said, slipping a hand under his jaw to make him look at her. "You need to grieve the loss as well… And there's always a place for you here. You're still family and I'd have been lost without you these last three months."

It was obvious he was trying to deflect her worry by the way he squirmed. "Everyone grieves in different ways," he said, taking her hand away from his face.

"Do you want to stay tonight? I'll cook and we can watch a movie or something?"

"You cook now?"

Raising a shoulder, she took her turn to look away. "I'm trying my best… I'm learning. I'll never be a substitute for Art, but if I was to feed Brodie nothing but microwave meals, he'd be worse off than he is."

Laughing, Tuck pushed out his chair and stood up. "Thanks for the offer, but I have things to do, places to be, you know?"

She didn't know whether to believe that or not, but she didn't push him. She got up and pushed in her chair "It wouldn't hurt you to go home for a little TLC from your lady… Why don't you tell her what happened?"

Tuck was already shaking his head and took his jacket from the back of his chair. "Kade isn't a part of this part of my life. It wouldn't do either of us any good to upset her."

That he wanted to protect the woman he loved was admirable. But if Kadie was as strong as Zara imagined Tuck's woman would need to be, she wasn't made of glass and probably wouldn't appreciate being shut out when Tuck was so obviously dealing with distress. "Compartmentalizing your life like that is the quickest way to drive her away."

"She's put up with me for years," he said. "She knows what the script is. Besides, I like her the way she is: innocent of all of… this." He looked around the room as though it was the first time he was seeing the place. Then as quickly as it appeared, the expression vanished and he smiled at her. "Call me if you need anything, okay? Anytime. I'll be here as soon as I can."

"Thank you," she said, bowing her head to let him kiss the top of it. He stroked her back and looked into her eyes once more before he disappeared from the room and the house.

After Tuck was gone, she took the time to return an email to Art's sister, Bess, and go over everything Tuck had taught her about the system. He'd been teaching her during his frequent visits, though he never stayed and she had no idea where he went when he left here. Brodie and Art had told her not to ask too many questions and she stuck to that out of respect for them all.

She had tidied up in the kitchen when she arrived because she'd had groceries to put away. Keeping this house stocked was more important to her than looking after her own apartment. If Brodie decided he wanted something to eat then she was going to make sure he had a choice. Sometimes he came downstairs to grab something, but she had never seen it happen, she only knew it did because things disappeared.

As much as she was loathed to admit it, she had been guilty of checking the trash to see what he was up to. She did it because she cared. She did all of this because she cared. Love was not just about the good times. Brodie was facing the greatest trauma he ever would in his life. By losing the uncle he'd idolized since birth, he'd lost his mentor, his roommate, and his best friend.

Cooking had been her idea of hell, but she'd started giving it a go in an effort to reach Brodie. It hadn't worked. But he ate what she put down, though not in front of her. He ate alone… just like he did almost everything else.

The steak she'd cooked was resting, so she went over to the plate of salad she'd arranged and was about to pick it up from the lower portion of the central island in the kitchen when something startled her. It wasn't a sound or a touch, it was just a prickle on the back of her neck, and sure enough, when she spun around Brodie was there, just inside the kitchen door.

"I was about to bring up your food," she said.

Bringing a finger up to his lips, he indicated she should be quiet, though he himself didn't make a noise either. Rolling her eyes from one side to the other, she was about to carry on with preparing the meal when he came toward her. He kept on coming until his body was against hers, and from the protrusion in his jeans now digging into her, she assumed something else was about to be on the menu.

Relaxing, she stretched out her arms and brought them around to the back of his neck. "Does somebody want to say hello?" she asked.

One of his hands came up between them. He grabbed the front of her neck, spun them around and forced her back against the tall kitchen cabinet next to the door.

"I told you to shut the fuck up, plaything," he grumbled.

For one second, they remained immobile. His lips came closer, and just when she thought he was going to kiss her, he bypassed her mouth to push her head aside with his to suck the tender flesh on her neck beneath her jaw.

Zara let him take from her what he needed because she had complete faith that he would desist if she told him to.

Except she loved this. Running her hands down his back, she dragged her nails up and kept on going until they were embedded in his hair, in his scalp. Scratching back and forth, she relished his hiss of gratification. Being with him, when he was physical with her, it reminded her of how close they'd once been. He could leave this house and get what he wanted from almost any woman. But he chose to indulge himself in her and she would not discourage that anytime soon.

The grate of him dragging his zip down razed the air, crackling in the space between them. He crouched and drummed his fingers against her flesh to take the hem of her dress in his grip. Keeping his eyes on hers, he raised her skirt and let it gather at his wrists.

Beneath the fabric, his hands sank around her butt and hoisted her off her feet. On reflex, she grabbed his shoulders and found her stability by securing her legs around his hips. Hooking her underwear out of the way, Brodie plunged into her without warning. He went all the way, deep inside. At the same time, as if he'd known it would come, he covered her mouth to conceal the gasp that answered his penetration.

Out he slid, then he drove back into her. This man's covert skills knew no bounds. He stood here in the kitchen, pinning her to the cabinet, with his dick buried to the hilt within her trembling passage, and he didn't even blink. He kept on moving in her, teasing the flesh of her ass with his fingers and the skin on her neck with his mouth.

All of their woes and heartache were forgotten when she came all over his dick. Her mouth was still covered by his hand, but when she climaxed, he stopped moving in her and the wicked tilt at the corner of his lips told her he had felt the explosion in her loins.

When he slid back, her nails dug into his shoulders through his shirt. Loosening the clamp of his hand from her mouth, Zara nabbed his middle finger with her teeth. The growl in his eyes betrayed that his tolerance was at a tipping point. Most of the time they were together, he tried to prolong the experience for both of them, but he could only go so far before she would topple him into his own release.

Dragging out, he slammed into her, and he was already

back out and in before she caught her breath. The fire in his dark eyes soaked her, giving him easy undulating access inside her, she grew slicker with every thrust.

She tasted blood when her teeth clamped in sync with her inner muscles, which were desperate for the scream that joined the sparkles of heat that exploded in her womb. Forcing himself deeper, Brodie's palm slapped the wall and his curse stuck in his throat.

Tremors still racked her when he stayed in place corking his seed within her. His hand slid away from her mouth, but she took it in hers and kissed the wound she'd caused, hoping apology conveyed in her eyes.

When he slid out of her, she gasped at the remaining frisson of pleasure he delivered. His knuckle grazed her clit when he dragged her underwear over the intimate opening he'd just violated. He lowered her back to her feet and ensured that she had her balance before he put himself away.

Something about the moisture of their union now dampening her underwear strained her already aching nipples and didn't help her wobbling legs. Catching his arm for balance, he only let her hold him for half a second before he pulled himself away from her. They hadn't spoken, but that only heightened the power of the moment they were in. Every experience she had with Brodie was sexier than the last and the contorted expression of satisfaction on his face almost mocked her, as though he could read her mind and knew that he was the most intense lover she'd ever had.

Still plastered against the kitchen cabinet, trying to quell the panting that wracked her body, Zara shivered when Brodie left her to cross the kitchen and snag a beer out of the fridge. Walking back, he grabbed the cooked steak from the counter she'd left it on and took a bite.

"Go home, Zar. No one needs you here tonight," he said, taking his steak, his beer, and leaving her alone all over again.

THREE

CI WAS THE SAME as it always had been. If Grant had succeeded in selling Game Time to Albert Sutcliffe, cult leader and criminal, the domino trail would have led straight back here, and the company would have been irrevocably changed.

Thanks to the Kindred, the near miss had escaped everyone's notice. Grant was probably quite pleased that no one had figured out his intentions because he got to carry on in his role of authority without answering questions that could only lead to the implosion of his cushy existence.

Before Brodie came into her life, she'd been unaware of Grant's agenda to sell the Game Time device. But because she'd missed those signs in the boss she'd had for five years, she was now hyperaware of indicators that might imply he hadn't gotten over his warped ideas of vigilantism.

It served the Kindred's interest that she didn't criticize or question Grant about Game Time, Sutcliffe, or Art's murder. She played nice, so she and Grant had fallen back into professional step with each other without disruption.

A knock on her office door made her look up from her desk. When she saw Grant entering, she shot to her feet and took off her glasses. Her office was right next door to her boss's and he typically called her to come to him if he needed her to do something. This impromptu visit could be cause for concern.

Subduing her surprise, she kept her cool. "Is there something you need, sir?" she asked, hoping for a quick and simple explanation for this appearance because it was Friday night and past time for her to go home.

Grant wanted her back at CI and seemed to just accept her lack of questions as though they'd come to an unspoken truce. Neither discussed what had transpired in the Atlas warehouse and Grant was fine with that. He'd never suggested anything to the contrary.

In the times her thoughts had meandered back in time while working here at CI, she fizzed with anger. They lost Art because of Grant. Albert Sutcliffe, his buyer, was only a part of their lives because Grant had been determined to make the deal and sell Game Time. Her boss hadn't been the one to pull the trigger, but none of them would have been in that warehouse if it wasn't for him. Avoiding discussion of those events prevented her from blowing her cover and releasing that pressurized rage.

Though from the tilt of his head and his furrowed brow, she feared those days of business as usual might be over. "No. I wondered if you needed a shoulder," he said, and she couldn't quite figure out what he meant. The McCormack's sure knew how to do cryptic, though the younger McCormack did brooding better. "I've seen how distracted you've been recently. You zone out at meetings, come in looking tired, sporting new bruises."

His pointed look at her neck made her raise her hand to the mark Brodie had left on her. Pulling up the collar of her shirt, she cursed herself for not reapplying the makeup she had used to hide the hickey that morning. She'd had a conversation like this with Grant months ago, except she'd been the one to highlight his erratic behavior, now it was his turn to call her out.

Having avoided any personal conversation of late, she could only assume that this was a dressing down, so she responded with appropriate contrition. "I'm sorry, sir. I'll get more with it. I've just…" There was no acceptable end to that statement without mentioning the topic they'd so far avoided.

Grant took care of that awkward transition for them. "You know," he said, coming in and closing the door behind himself. "I know what he's going through."

Diverting her eyes to the work laid out on her desk, she wasn't sure of her footing. Her relationship with Brodie had been another taboo subject. So far, that had worked out for her as thoughts of the fraternal relationship aggravated her already agitated wrath.

Aware of her covert role of observation here at CI, she couldn't lash out at the CEO or he might realize she wasn't as pliant or forgiving as he assumed she was. What she wanted to do was beat the crap out of him, to scream at him for what he'd done and for how selfish and senseless his apparent motivation was. Art was gone, Brodie was lost, and Grant had suffered no punishment.

But she was here to play it meek and get inside information, so she pulled her lip into her mouth and let her eyes drop portraying that she was uncomfortable with them broaching this previously off-limits topic. "I, uh…"

Grant wasn't interested in her response. He was focused on getting out what he wanted to say. "When Frank died, it was like losing them all over again," he said. "I didn't think that anything could hurt more than losing our parents, especially in the way we did… Then with Frank, he was… he was my father, my confidante, my support and when he was gone… I suppose if I had any excuse for what took place, losing Frank would be it."

In implicit terms, he'd brought up Brodie, the loss of Art, and the Game Time deal all in one swift release. "I know it was difficult for you," she said. Once she'd revered her boss, now when she looked him in the eye all she felt was betrayed, which was funny because technically she was the one who'd betrayed him by giving her loyalty to his younger brother. But her anger didn't completely overtake her compassion. Frank had been Grant's guardian through his latter teenage years and his death just over a year ago had hit Grant hard. "I remember how you struggled."

His solemn expression warmed. "I wouldn't have gotten

through it without you. You kept this place together and fended off every meeting that might have made me lose it. I was angry, so angry, and I tried everything to control it. Anger can consume a man. It distorts his thinking. The world becomes skewed and you believe you're handling things until… you're not."

Zara had gotten so used to consoling herself that she played the same platitudes for Grant. "He'll be fine," she said, nodding and trying to believe that Grant's concern was genuine. "He's getting better."

She had been telling herself these things since the day they lost Art, but Brodie didn't seem to be getting any better. Still, she had to believe that there was hope.

Grant didn't accept her appeasement and excuse himself. "So much better that reports are being missed? So much better that you've been late three times this week?"

She couldn't figure out what it was that he wanted. Having gone from awkward to understanding to commiserating, he'd now landed on subtle reproof. She didn't know if she should apologize or explain. Given that she didn't want to reveal anything of her private life to him, she went for the former. "I apologize for—"

"No," he said, walking across the room. "I am not looking for an apology. I don't mind, I just…" He sighed and surrendered to the direct approach. "It's Friday. Don't you go to Purdy's on a Friday night?" Not in the last three months. Usually, she went straight home after work or she got errands done before she went over to McCormack Manor. "You look like you could use a drink. How about you let me buy you a glass of wine and we can talk about whatever you want? I promise not to mention his name if you're worried about how he'll react to us socializing."

The last thing she wanted to do was get cozy with Grant, who had proved he wasn't as tame or humble as he was trying to appear. Whatever his reason for wanting to make friends with her again, Zara couldn't ignore the opportunity that this occasion presented. She wanted Grant to think that she was warming toward him, that she considered his perspective and cared about him.

Grant hadn't mentioned Brodie before today, not once, and Zara always assumed that was out of respect. She'd been protective of her love for him and hadn't denied it once the truth was out. But maybe if Grant thought her feelings for Brodie were wavering since his descent into depression, it would make her boss believe she was more susceptible to his suggestions.

She had no errands to run tonight and she could be at the manor all weekend. Brodie wouldn't notice her tardiness. He didn't keep a check on her schedule. So she exhaled and nodded. It might be good to get out of her routine of fretting as well. She was getting good at being in a constant state of anxiety. Now she had the chance to test her skills as an undercover operative.

Grant collected her coat from the hook beside the door while she shut down her computer and grabbed her purse. He helped her into her coat and then curled her fingers around his elbow.

"Let's see if you remember how to have fun," Grant said and took her out of the building.

***

FUN MIGHT BE pushing it. But she was certainly having something at Purdy's. The bar was the same as it always had been, that was the first thought she'd had after coming inside. With everything that had gone on in her life in recent months, she expected everything and everyone in the world to be somehow changed. Yet Purdy's proved her wrong. The same décor and generic affluent professionals still characterized the unchanged space.

While Grant ordered the drinks and got them a table, she considered whether or not it was reassuring or terrifying that so many profound things could happen while so many other things remained entirely the same.

Conversation had remained neutral, they spoke about CI, about projects going on, and Grant told her about the remodeling he'd done at his apartment. There was nothing difficult about small talk, but she was beginning to lose patience. She had better things to do than sit around shooting the breeze with the man who had caused her lover such pain.

"Another?" Grant asked her, wearing a smile that betrayed his ease.

They'd been here for almost an hour, and she had just finished her glass of wine. His loose form and pleasant demeanor exasperated her. Grant's life was just the same as it always had been. He hadn't been close to Art, hadn't seen him for years, so he couldn't care that his uncle was dead. Having her here enjoying a drink with him, while his brother grieved, must have given him an ego boost because his arrogance had been on eleven since they sat down.

Swallowing the cool liquid, she shook her head because she didn't intend to encourage his superiority. "I should get going."

Raising his brows, Grant spread a hand on the table and met her eye to enhance his condescension. "If the last three months have taught you anything," Grant said. "It's that he's not going anywhere."

Squirming in response to such a patronizing platitude, she rolled her tongue in her mouth and lowered her volume. The patrons surrounding them weren't eavesdropping, they were more interested in their own conversations, but dropping her tone to a growling whisper helped to emphasize her displeasure. "You promised not to mention him."

If the topic of Brodie came up—while there was alcohol in her system—she couldn't trust herself to keep her annoyance in check. Using the professional setting of CI as a smokescreen, she'd managed to restrain her desire to ream Grant out. In this social environment, the professional shield wasn't as reliable.

Beyond the fact that she wouldn't betray or discuss Brodie, and couldn't see how they could talk about him without Grant discovering her true loyalty and motivation for returning to CI, she hated Grant talking about his younger brother with familiarity or superiority because he hadn't earned the right.

He laid a suited forearm onto the table to huddle closer. "I know and I'm sorry," Grant said. "But sometimes a little tough love is what's required. He has to know that you won't always be there. He has to learn to take care of himself."

Hearing him dishing out advice in relation to her love was too much for her to tolerate. The wine boosted her adrenaline and she had been keeping a lid on so many emotions for months that she was beginning to worry about her grip on them.

Ire and impatience made her lose the will to maintain this charade tonight. "I have to go," she said, thrusting up from her stool and hooking her bag up over her head across her body. "Thank you for the drink."

Pouncing onto his feet, he snatched her arm to impede her retreat. "I'm sorry. I shouldn't have said anything. It's just difficult for me to see you like this. You're a special person and you deserve more than he gives you."

Leaning closer, she allowed her anger to thrive. "You don't know what he gives me," she hissed. "You haven't cared about him for years. He's your baby brother and you couldn't care less if he was dead or alive. Yeah, things have been tough on us recently, all of us, we are our own family and we don't turn our back on each other just because things get difficult."

Yanking her arm away from him, she prepared to spin and storm out. But the thrum of automatic gunfire made her tense in shock while others screeched and furniture fell. Dropping into a crouch, she turned and saw through the screaming people and scattered furniture that there was a gang of masked men storming the bar.

For a second time, the lead man aimed his gun at the ceiling and let out another blast of bullets that left a trail of holes in the ceiling. The unexpected and threatening display led to further screaming and furor. Most people were on or near the floor in submissive positions cowering for their lives.

One suited patron tried to rush the first guy, but he never reached his target. Another member of the gang aimed his weapon and fired, killing the businessman without hesitation.

Whatever this was, it was no joke. There were six gang members and all held similar machine guns. The leader was on route to the bar, one man stayed at the door, blocking the exit, while the others herded patrons to the wall, shoving tables and chairs out of their way to clear space and pen people in.

"Oh my God," Grant said. She glanced around to see that he was crouched under the table behind her. "What do we do?"

Already her hand was snaking into her purse, but she didn't answer his gutless question. She pressed and held the speed dial programmed into the lock screen numbers by Tuck who'd tweaked the tech, then prayed that Brodie would answer. Risking a look in her bag, she saw the call cut off, he'd diverted.

"Damn you," she whispered.

Another round of bullets joined the pattern of holes in the ceiling, and the head of the gang jumped onto the bar using a stool as a stepping aid. The staff and patrons were being herded into the corner beside where she and Grant already were.

Full of swagger and arrogance, the blond man smiled as he spoke. "Ladies and gentleman, if you would just give your wallets and jewelry to my colleagues as they go around, we won't have any problems."

The other four masked men went to each of the huddling patrons in turn offering an open black trash bag for the victims to drop their valuables. They waited patiently and said little but shook the bag to hurry those who were too slow in emptying their pockets.

Time wasn't on her side. She needed to call for help while there was still confusion and while the gang members were distracted by their spoils. Giving up on Brodie, she bypassed Art's speed dial on her phone, and pressed in Tuck's. He would never abandon her. He would answer. He always answered. She needed a sure bet.

Keeping one eye on the men who weren't yet closing in on her position, she waited for the line to connect. "What are you doing?" Grant hissed from behind her. "You're going to get yourself killed."

Taking action when others cowered was part of the Kindred job description. She didn't have the skills of the others, but she could call in reinforcements then distract these guys long enough for the cavalry to arrive. The Kindred gave her strength, even when they weren't with her. Imagining that Art was there, looking over her shoulder, she was determined to show him that she had the mettle Brodie's woman should have. Priority one for the Kindred was to watch each other's backs and she needed someone at hers now.

What she didn't need was Grant second-guessing her or getting involved in her actions when his words wouldn't alter them. "Rather that than sit here like a pussy," she whispered back, glad she had the chance to demean Grant in his cowardice.

He chose not to hear her contempt and instead judged his brother's culpability. "You've been spending too much time with him. Don't be a hero."

Grant blamed Brodie for her confidence, but if Brodie was in her ear now, he'd tell her to keep her head down and her mouth shut. The funny thing was she'd been making decisions for herself, the manor, and for Brodie every day for months. That had prepared her for this. She was ready. She'd been using the manor facilities to train and was in better shape now than she'd ever been before in her life.

Physically, she was quick and used her supple flexibility and speed to dodge rather than attack because she didn't have the strength to launch an assault. The Kindred did. They gave her direction, they gave her support, and she was one of them, which meant inaction was the only wrong thing for her to do in this scenario.

"That's what he would say," she said.

When something had to be done, she did it; to procrastinate would drive her nuts. In the past, Brodie had told her not to be the hero and to call him in times of need. Well, she'd tried that and struck out. Brodie was too busy wallowing in his grief to remember the lessons Art had taught him about self-pity. It was an indulgence not meant for them. That thought spurred her anger, not aimed at Grant or these criminals, but at Brodie for failing to fight for his own sanity. A surge of potent emotion gave her the excuse to show Grant her impatient fury.

Glaring at her nervous boss, she cooled her regard. "But

he's not here, is he?" she said.

An alien voice interrupted their interaction. "Hey! What's that light in your bag?"

Spinning back to face the room, Zara saw one of the gunmen standing over her with his firearm aimed at the floor, only a few inches from her. He was trying to peer past her at the dull light emanating from her bag.

"It's the way to paradise, why don't you come here and check it out," she growled at him while thinking of the gun she had in her purse. Taking on a room full of automatic weapons with her handgun would be foolish, but if the guy got too close or she felt threatened, she would use it. Otherwise, carrying it around made no sense. She'd never killed before but had witnessed lives being taken by Brodie.

The thug lunged down, grabbed her hair to haul her up from her crouch onto her feet, and managed to smack her head off the underside of the tabletop in the process, sending the table into a wobble before it crashed onto its side. Drinks had been scattered when furniture was tipped, nudged, and kicked aside. The floor was sticky and glass crunched under her feet as he pulled her across the room toward the bar.

Holding his gun aloft, she was aware of his finger resting on the trigger guard, close enough to do damage in a hurry if he was spooked. "She's got a phone!" the gunman said, shoving her toward the leader who was still standing on the bar.

Their masks were little more than plastic costume faces of dead musicians held on with a strip of elastic that went around the back of their heads. Buddy Holly secured the exit. John Lennon came over raking through a black treasure bag with his gun hanging on its strap off his arm. Jim Morrison and Jimi Hendrix must still be watching their hostages. Frank Sinatra had a hold of her and Elvis was standing on the bar, commanding them all.

"They've all got cellphones, dummy. That's the point! If the cops come the media come, then we get to hold these rich fucks for ransom," Elvis said and crouched closer to her. "Who are you calling, sweetheart? Your boyfriend. How much would he pay to get you back?"

Logging everything that these men were saying to each other, in case anything turned out to be important later, she locked her eyes onto the boss. "I'm calling his best friend," she said and he laughed then looked in the direction she'd come from to register that she'd been at a table with Grant.

Elvis's eyes lit and the mask shifted to accommodate a smiling mouth. "And you're here with another guy? Good time gal, are you?"

Showing courage was the only way to get through this, she wouldn't be intimidated. If she could stand up to Brodie then dealing with this guy would be a breeze. "I'm whatever the hell I want to be," she said, invigorated by this chance to vent her own grief and frustration. Using those negative emotions, being open about her resentment was freeing and so therapeutic that a weight lifted from her shoulders. "Why do you want cops here? You want a shootout?"

Elvis hopped down onto a stool and jumped onto the floor beside her with his gun in hand at his side. "Why don't you hand over your phone? Let's see how much your buddy would pay for your life?"

Putting her hand in her purse that hung on a long strap across her body, she took out her phone and he opened a palm to accept it. But there was no way she was handing over Kindred tech.

"Treason terminate," she said in a clear, concise tone, just as Tuck had taught her.

The voice command made the phone spark and fizzle, destroying itself. Just for good measure, she dropped it onto the floor and smashed it with her heel. Training the innovative system to recognize her voice had taken time, but it learned her signature and she was glad she'd spent the time doing what Tuck told her.

Elvis's angry eyes pounced up to hers and she had to smile in triumph. "Oops… clumsy me."

Now she had his attention. It felt good to get one up on the men who had terrified so many innocent people. "Who the hell are you?" he demanded, having lost his good humor. "I thought this was a bar filled with rich, dumb as fuck yuppies."

With a half-shrug, she let him know she wasn't as easily scared as the others here. "You're almost right," she said. "There's them"—she nodded to the side without breaking eye contact—"And then there's me."

He sneered and examined her figure. "You think I'm afraid of you?"

No, she didn't, not with so many others here backing him up and significant firepower at his disposal. "I think you should be more afraid of what my boyfriend will do to your men when he hunts every one of them down, which is what he'll do if you don't let me and these people go now."

Elvis threw back his head and laughed. She expected that reaction. But she wasn't braced for his fist to fly at her face. He smacked her a beauty that sent her backwards, but Sinatra caught her shoulders, and forced her back onto her feet.

Coming near, he scanned each side of the room. "I don't see him," Elvis said, taking another look. "Does anyone see the big scary boyfriend?"

Trying to contain the automatic tears caused by his hit, she maintained her gumption. With an inhale and a gulp, she lifted her chin to prove her sustained defiance. "You'll never see him coming," she said, every bit as sure of what she said as she portrayed. Except she underestimated what it was not to have Brodie there to backup her disobedience.

Snatching her arm, Elvis pulled her toward the restroom at the back of the bar. "Take what you can off these pricks and wait for the cops to roll up. Come find me when they call, don't forget I'm driving his party bus!"

Pointing his gun upward, he was laughing as he fired at the ceiling. The screams of patrons joined the shower of plaster that rained down. Dragging her around the tables, Elvis shoved her through the swing door that led to a back corridor. Aiming for the men's room, he propelled her inside. It didn't matter that she stumbled, he gave her another push, and she slipped on the tile floor.

Her arms shot out in a desperate attempt to break her fall, but she fell against the row of sinks face first, hitting her head on the porcelain, and dropping onto her knees. Dazed by the impact, she knew she couldn't stay down so groped for the sink to use its stability to pull herself up onto her feet again.

"You want to know what I think?" he said while she was still blinking and turning, holding herself against the steady strength of the sink, trying to bring him into focus. "I think you've made up the crazy boyfriend. See that thing with the phone, that's a party trick, and God knows what tech company you probably work for. It's a toy, isn't it? You're full of shit."

As sure as he seemed, she knew she wasn't bluffing, so didn't mind him testing her resolve. "Are you willing to risk finding out?" she asked, securing her footing, though she stayed by the sink just in case she lost it again.

Unhooking the strap of his gun from his arm, he hung the weapon on the condom machine behind the door and started toward her. "With a pretty face like that, yeah, I think it might be worth risking the wrath of your imaginary boyfriend. This is gonna be a long night. My men and me might need a distraction like your clever mouth. You're a good time gal, right? I can give you the best time of your life."

Her fingers curled around the lip of the sink behind her when his hand went to his fly. One agonizing tooth at a time, he pulled down his zipper. "You don't want to do this," she murmured.

Sauntering toward her, he put his hand into his jeans and pulled out his thickening member. "My dick says different," he said, proud of himself. "I don't see your scary boyfriend yet. When is he gonna come to your rescue?"

This was going to get real fast, he was already erect, and there wasn't much space left between them. Sexual assault was every woman's worst nightmare. Some women froze and didn't put up a fight in hope that their attacker would leave them alive. She couldn't be one of those women. How could she possibly look Brodie in the face and tell him that another man had put his hands on her?

"I'll give you one more chance," she said, increasing her grip as panic and adrenaline began to impede her breathing. "Stop this now."

He stopped walking but kept jerking his dick in his fist.

"Why?" he asked, smug to the point of almost laughing again, and that arrogance gave her strength. She wasn't going to fear a man who took pleasure in tormenting others. He was a bully and she would never back down for one of those. "What are you gonna do about it, sweetheart?"

She had only one chance to save herself. The potential of threats against her body was why Brodie had taught her how to defend herself. "What my big, scary boyfriend taught me to," she said and thrust her hand into her open purse to pull out the Sig Brodie had furnished her with.

The sound of her chambering a round made him blanch and his swagger ebbed as she took aim. "You're not gonna use that," he said, but she recognized the nerves flavoring his tone. "It's probably not even loaded."

Confident, she set herself against the sink and held the butt of the gun with two hands. "It's loaded all right," she said

When he tensed to leap for her, she squeezed the trigger.

Zara didn't see him go down but she heard the familiar slump of a lifeless body hitting an unyielding floor. Her eyes stayed shut for a few seconds after the gun recoil made her blink. Her hands were shaking as rationale warred with instinct. The danger wasn't gone yet, and she needed to confirm the Elvis threat had been neutralized.

On opening her eyes, she saw him sprawled on his back on the sterile tile of the bathroom floor. His open eyes were fixed and vacant. He was dead. Yelping out her horror, she lost her cool and stifled her mouth with a hand to block any other sounds that might come out of her.

Noise from beyond the bathroom shocked her out of her daze. Stuffing the gun back in her purse, she leaped over Elvis's corpse on her tiptoes and avoided the quickly growing pool of blood beneath him.

Grabbing his gun from the condom machine, she needed a weapon that could match what the other gang members were carrying. Being that she had never used anything as powerful as this weapon before, she wasn't convinced of her ability to wield it. But common sense dictated that her measly pistol wouldn't hold up to the might of this criminal invasion. Already she was outnumbered; she didn't want to be outgunned too.

Leaving the men's room and her victim behind, she approached the swing door that led back out to the main bar. She couldn't loiter because the wooden door would never protect her from a bullet. So pressing her spine into the wall beside the door, she closed her eyes, and tried to come up with a plan.

Killing Elvis was a necessity, if it was that or be raped, she didn't have to ponder the choice for long. But killing him didn't save her from the hot water. His colleagues were between her and freedom, but she couldn't burst out of here and open fire when there were innocent people still in the bar.

"Hey, Elvis! You okay?"

Sinatra's voice came from the other side of the door. From its volume, she'd guess he was close and could come through the door at any second. They must have heard the gunshot, the kill shot, and come to check on the boss. Even though Elvis was probably only a pseudo name, she wished she didn't have a moniker for the man she'd just murdered.

There was no time to languish in the emotional turmoil of what was going on, she had to focus on the new threat, which was Sinatra. If he was just outside the door and alone, this could be her only chance to take another man out. Eliminating them one at a time would be easier than taking on the five remaining guys by herself, especially when she didn't know what ammunition was left in this gun or how to check it. Elvis had shot up the ceiling and would be packing fewer bullets than the rest of his group would be.

Sucking in her bottom lip, she sent a silent request to Brodie for some of his fathomless courage. Determined, she spun around and shoved through the door, gun barrel first. Sinatra's eyes grew behind his mask and she winked at him.

"Elvis is dead, baby," she said. "But you won't have to wait long to see him."

"The cops are coming!" Buddy Holly yelled from his position at the door. Sirens blared and tires screeched. "Let's split." He didn't wait for his comrades and was gone before anyone could respond.

After he went, the others followed. She kept her gun

pointed at Sinatra and hitched the barrel higher. "I'll give you to the count of five then it's Return to Sender… unless you'd prefer Jailhouse Rock."

His buddies heeded her threat and fled, Sinatra wasn't far behind them. Pushing over chairs on his dash for the exit, the sirens were already piercing the air just outside. She kept her gun aimed at their backs but didn't put her finger on the trigger. Being in control of something this powerful was terrifying, giving her a new respect for what Brodie took for granted.

The room remained silent for a score of seconds. She wasn't sure she could move because her nerves were strung so tight. But when the front door swung shut with a final thump, she let the barrel of the gun fall to her side and point to the floor. The danger was eliminated. She had triumphed. But all she felt was the sudden onset of exhaustion.

One single pair of hands clapped, breaking the silence. It was joined by another pair until the room erupted in applause. The patrons were still clapping when the police came in with their guns drawn. As ludicrous as it was, she held out hope that Brodie would come in behind the cops, take the gun from her, and give her something solid to lean on. Hanging out with cops wasn't his style, but she needed him tonight.

Grant came up beside her and she was grateful that she didn't have her finger on the trigger when he touched her shoulder because the contact startled her. He pulled her into his arms after the cops surrounded them and took the gun away from her. She put up no fight, she felt so drained now that she wasn't sure she'd ever have fight in her again.

FOUR

THE POLICE SECURED the scene and questioned everyone. Zara was questioned by a detective she'd met before. That particular detective was the only official allowed anywhere near her, and a temporary black screen was erected in a shady corner of Purdy's to give them privacy. The experience of recounting the night's events and answering questions was reminiscent of the first time she'd met this detective.

After Timothy Sutcliffe's murder more than four months ago, Detective Dennis Kraft had taken her statement. On that distant-ago night she hadn't been much help because she'd been oblivious about who Timothy Sutcliffe was and why he'd been murdered.

Tonight, Kraft made no mention of that first encounter, but the special attention he paid her was noteworthy. None of his colleagues were allowed in her vicinity. Kraft stayed with her until the DA himself arrived at the scene. That such an important figure responded was a testament to the affluence of this district and to the caliber of companies whose employees were in the bar.

According to Kraft and the DA, other witness statements heralded her as a hero. The DA confirmed no charges would be filed against her, which was something of a relief because she hadn't considered the legal consequences of killing Elvis before pulling the trigger.

She'd been told to stay in her seat, behind the screen, away from the mayhem in the street out front. Kraft and the DA were still just in view near the bar and deep in conversation. But she wasn't interested in trying to eavesdrop. She was too far away to decipher what they were saying anyway. All she wanted now was permission to leave the scene.

Once the DA said goodbye to Kraft and departed, Kraft headed over to pull up a stool in front of her. Serious concern was written all over his face. From how he leaned close and held eye contact, she figured he knew she was flagging. Being a cop, he was probably used to people fazing in and out of reality and knew how important it was to emphasize every word, forcing the witnesses to follow his speech.

"The media are out front," he said. "It's just local."

She closed her eyes as she breathed in. Zara didn't have the first idea about how to handle the media and as long as she had them on her scent, she couldn't go near Brodie or the manor.

Sometimes it felt like the Greater Power was plain old picking on her. "Great," she grumbled.

When her eyes opened, he ducked to capture them with his, again ensuring she absorbed his every word. "You can't talk to them, Zara. We won't release your name to anyone," he said. She narrowed her eyes, recalling something Brodie had inferred about having a history with this individual detective. "You have to keep a low profile. Drawing attention to yourself will only bring attention to your associates. I've got Grant McCormack waiting out back, he'll take you home."

Her associates. Kraft didn't mean her CI colleague or the strangers in Purdy's. Grant gave press conferences when there was anything significant going on at CI, he loved attention and had nothing to hide. No one in Purdy's knew her and she was inconsequential enough that the young urban professionals paid no attention to her.

"Grant," she said. Kraft took her arm and stood, drawing

her onto her feet with him. "Detective Kraft, is this about—"

"You tell Raven hello from me. Let him know we looked out for you."

The lingering stare became a smile and she nodded once. He did know something about the Kindred or about Raven at least. She needed an ally today and wouldn't argue with his kindness or fail to take note that she owed him one, because she did. She didn't want to be a hero or have her picture plastered all over the newspaper. She did what she did to survive and now she just wanted to go home.

Kraft took her behind the bar through a door to a staff corridor. After a sharp right, she found herself at the fire exit. Detective Kraft pushed the release bar and held it open before handing over her purse, with the weight of the Sig inside. They shared another look, one that suggested he was as curious about her as she was about him.

Raven was an enigmatic man with secrets and a past filled with characters she didn't know. As far as Kraft was concerned, she was a woman with Raven's ear and that could be useful in many situations. Their moment of reflection passed and Kraft guided her outside with an arm around her shoulders.

Grant was sitting in the driver's seat of his idling car. The minute she got inside, he drove out the end of the alley and turned away from the busy scene. She appreciated that he didn't ask questions on the ride home. But when he pulled into the residents' parking lot at the back of her building, he parked, and turned off the engine.

Zara didn't want company, but she also couldn't be bothered arguing with him, so she let him follow her up to her apartment. It wasn't like she had to worry about Brodie lurking in the dark waiting for her, those days were long gone. Grant wasn't going to cross paths with his brother, giving her a reprieve from refereeing any battles that could break out.

The first thing she did when she went inside was to turn on the coffee machine. After that, she went to the restroom to wash her face and retrieve an ice-pack and arnica. Grant was pouring coffee when she came out and laid her supplies on the table.

He carried the steaming mugs over and put them on the table before he sat down beside her at her circular dining table. "Do you want help?" he asked as she snapped the icepack to hold it over her cheek.

"Nope."

She iced her bruises, but knew they'd had time to develop and would likely swell. Frustration and impatience were making her tense again. Keeping Brodie sane didn't include flashing the evidence of her assault in his face. If he saw these bruises, she'd have to tell him what happened. As soon as he heard the story, he'd go postal.

There was no reason for Grant to linger and she wished she'd made the effort downstairs to keep him in his car. "It's already after midnight," she said. "You should get home."

"Is it your plan to go to him?" Grant asked. She did her best not to sigh or to curse and roll her eyes. After everything that had happened tonight, the last thing that she wanted to deal with was Grant having a temper tantrum. "You're going to the manor, aren't you?"

"No," she said, elongating the word. "It's late. It would only upset him to see me like this, and it's never smart to upset Raven."

"You were amazing tonight."

Lowering her ice pack, she reached for the topical remedy, but Grant intercepted her hand. She hated it when he touched her. At one time, she had respected him more than she had respected any other person. Game Time had shattered her illusions about who he was and showed her how naïve she'd been to trust him.

Wrath swelled in her belly until her jaw clenched. "I had no choice but to defend myself," she spat out, drawing her glare from his face to his hand. "That, my friend, is how protective your brother is of his property. Take that under advisement."

Defiant and foolish, he didn't shrink. His courage grew, but she knew it was bullshit. He'd proved what he was made of when he cowered tonight. "I'm not afraid of him."

"You should be," she said, yanking her hand out of his hold. She wasn't kidding around.

Beyond how upset Brodie might be if he thought Grant was trying to make a move on her, he would be more upset by the fact that Grant had done nothing to defend himself or to fend off the attackers tonight.

She couldn't kid herself that he was in the right mental space to be interested in going after the men who had thought about hurting her. He wasn't looking after himself, so she knew he wouldn't look after her. That stark truth was emphasized by him ignoring her phone call. Brodie wasn't ready to move away from his grief, and he may not ever be. Angering him while he was being dogged by his demons would only add weight and quicken his descending spiral.

Grant didn't take the hint or offense. He stayed put and delivered his appraisal. "I think you've proved tonight that you don't need him to back you up anymore. Zara, you were impressive. Everyone else cowered and you… you were up there, doing what was right."

He twisted in his seat to face her and brushed a hand down her arm. She tried to withdraw, but he kept his hand on her elbow. "I've learned a lot recently about how to handle myself," she said. "I suppose I just clicked into that mode and did what needed to be done. It was kill or be killed."

"Sure, I understand," Grant said. "I just want you to know that I'm proud of you."

She no longer sought his approval as she had when their relationship was simply employer and employee. Validation from Brodie would mean so much more to her. But at that exact moment, she wanted to forget about what had happened tonight, to forget about the life she'd taken.

Too tired to take on another cause, she tried dismissive acceptance. "Thanks," she said and scooted away to finish up with her wounds.

Gulping down as much of her drink as she could while she cleaned up, Zara put the bathroom items back in the first aid box and came back to the table. Finishing her coffee while in a standing position was supposed to signal to Grant that she wanted him to leave, but he didn't notice it.

Still holding his own mug in two hands, and seated at her table, he observed the night beyond her windows. "This was my fault. Tonight, it was my fault," he murmured. "It was all of our faults."

Inhaling, she reminded herself that she wasn't the only one who had gone through a trauma tonight. It was likely that Grant didn't want to be alone because he was still dealing with the adrenaline that being in a life or death situation caused, but that didn't ease her frustration.

It was no longer her responsibility to coddle Grant McCormack. Any guilt she had about that quickly faded when she recalled the sound of the gunshot and the heavy weight of Art's body hitting concrete.

Grant had no one to lean on because he didn't have close friends or intimate acquaintances. But he hadn't sought companionship when he found himself alone after Frank's death, so she couldn't pity him. It wasn't like he'd wanted a bunch of people in his life that he could be loyal to and rely on. He'd gone on a vengeance spree, thinking himself superior and righteous.

Resting her hands on the back of the chair she'd been previously seated on, she saw that this moment of vulnerability might be a weakness that would allow her an avenue to probe his motivations.

"What are you talking about?" she asked.

There was only one thing that linked them 'all' and that was Game Time. But she couldn't see how the clash three months ago could be linked to a siege at Purdy's.

"I don't think it was an accident that we were in Purdy's when those guys came in. He's coming for us."

Raising her brows, she prompted him. It was late, she was tired, and she didn't feel like playing twenty questions. "He?"

"Albert Sutcliffe," Grant said and lifted his eyes to hers. Art's murderer. That name made the hairs on her arm stand up and the new awareness made her edgy. "I lost a VP and my housekeeper was killed on the same day."

"You didn't tell me that," she said.

Concern and confusion chased away her desire to be alone. The whole point of being near Grant was to get answers and he was offering them free of charge. Swerving her hips around the chair-back, she sank down into it, facing in his direction. While tragic, she hadn't given much thought to the death of the CI VP as anything more than random. Being killed by a mugger was upsetting, but it didn't warrant special interest. It certainly didn't warrant Kindred attention.

Grant's gaze became distant again and it drifted toward her windows as he pondered. What she wanted was information, an explanation, and he was dragging out each moment of this confession.

The McCormack brothers had moments of similarity, but the majority of the time they were chalk and cheese. If Brodie had something to tell her, he'd blurt it out without softening it for her feelings. If he was withholding, he'd become a wall of silence and make no secret that he was cutting her out of the loop.

Grant needed a bit more handholding when it came to getting to the point, especially about something non-work related. But his next question came from left field.

"What's it like to be with him? To be in a relationship with him?" Grant asked.

Zara hadn't expected a question about Brodie. That it came now suggested Grant had been wondering about his brother—or her relationship with said brother—for some time. Getting over her initial surprise, Zara's curiosity about the connection became suspicion. If it was no accident that she and Grant were present in Purdy's during the raid, it was no coincidence that Grant was asking about Brodie on the same night.

"Why do you ask?" she asked, interested in how he would account for the relationship between Brodie and Purdy's. "He had nothing to do with your VP or your housekeeper, if that's why you're asking."

Brodie had lied to her about the Quebec job, but she had confidence in declaring him innocent of the more recent murders. It would be difficult for him to kill when he hadn't left McCormack Manor. He was a good shot, but not good enough to defy the laws of physics.

"That's not why I'm asking," Grant said, but she couldn't trust the sincerity in his soft tone. "I want to know what he's like."

If the two brothers could get to know each other and bond then her life would be a whole lot easier. The trouble was, she knew both of them too well to expect something like that would go off without a hitch.

What Brodie was, or what Raven was, depended on who he was talking to, events, the environment, his mood, and many other factors. In fact, accounting for his personality was almost as complex as setting up a kill shot.

"You're not going to find that out by talking to me."

"You're protective of him?"

"That," she said with a confirming head nod. "And the qualities I love in him won't be important to you."

"You mean sex."

"You think I love him because he's good in bed?" she asked and to hide her smile she turned her head away.

She didn't want to reveal how deep her love for Brodie went. She didn't want to talk about his loyalty, about his devotion to a task. She didn't want to talk to Grant about her love's strength, about his awareness, about his ability to look into her and read her thoughts. Zara didn't want to reveal how Brodie had kept her safe, had watched over her, how he'd vowed to protect her and followed through to the detriment of his own life. Brodie needed her and without his intervention, she would never have realized her potential.

"Why do you love him?" Grant asked. "Why him and not..."

Thoughts of Brodie ebbed and she made eye contact with Grant again. Her boss had never declared feelings for her, he'd never made an attempt to much as get into her pants. "You don't know him," Zara said. "You can't possibly understand and what I have with Brodie is mine, you don't get to be a part of that just because you share a last name."

Brodie would probably say something similar if questioned about their relationship by Grant. Her lover was private and protective of his kin. And to him 'kin' didn't have to mean blood. Zara mimicked the sentiment because being more like Brodie was not a bad thing.

"I hope you're sure about that," Grant said. "Because

Sutcliffe won't show any mercy when he finds you."

Albert Sutcliffe had made it out of the Atlas warehouse after shooting Art. That he wasn't finished with them was something she and Tuck had discussed. Attacking Purdy's wasn't Sutcliffe's style, but all she knew about him related to his negotiations with CI while he was trying to acquire Game Time. It was possible that taking hostages and terrorizing people was his MO, he had a cult of people ready to fulfill his wishes, and he could direct them in any way he wanted.

Tuck had told her that there would be no warning, that one day Sutcliffe would come back into their lives, no doubt with a bang. But she hadn't expected him to come back into their lives while Brodie was still checked out. Brodie had gotten her through her last trial with Sutcliffe, this time she was by herself. She'd learned a lot, but not nearly enough to take on a giant and his cult on her own.

These thoughts flashed through her mind at lightning speed and all conclusions came back to how screwed she was. Back in the days before the Kindred, she could have confided in Grant and asked for his help. But her boss's motivations were all screwed up and she couldn't trust him, not like she could trust Brodie. Zara wouldn't divulge secrets about her lover or about the Kindred to the man who had been their adversary not so long ago.

The whole point of her being at CI, of being near to Grant, was to pick up on warnings that disaster might be about to strike again. This was as close to a signed neon telegram as they would ever get. It was starting all over again. The Kindred had a new mission but had no chief and no assassin.

Before panic could set in, she cleared her thoughts and tried to be pragmatic. She needed to know what Grant knew about Sutcliffe and why he had attacked Purdy's, as well as what his next move might be.

As terrifying as the prospect was, she faced the fact that whatever Albert Sutcliffe wanted, whatever revenge he wanted to exact, it was going to be on her shoulders to dig them out of the mess because Brodie had proved to her tonight that she couldn't rely on him to take care of business.

Instead of admitting to Grant that she planned to keep Brodie's secrets, she steered them back to the more relevant issue. "Start at the beginning," she said, shuffling her chair an inch closer to his. "How do you know that this is Sutcliffe?"

"He claimed responsibility," Grant said. "I got the news of the murder of my VP within an hour of finding out my housekeeper was dead. Just as I began to fear it might be retribution, he called me."

The notion was so banal it was bizarre. "Sutcliffe called you on the phone?"

Grant nodded. "He said their deaths were just the beginning." Pushing out his chair, Grant sauntered into the kitchen without invitation to refill his coffee mug. "He wants payback," he called back to her over his shoulder. "He lost his nephew and two of his men and thinks that we deliberately screwed him out of a deal. He's back to have his revenge."

A chill shot through her with the velocity of a backdraft. "Revenge? But I thought—"

"That after three months of silence we might have gotten away with it? So did I," he said, opening cabinet doors to seek something out.

She hadn't been going to say that. Sutcliffe wouldn't just pack up his toys and declare himself the loser. What she'd been going to say was that she thought Sutcliffe would come after her or Brodie first. Then again, Grant had been the point man, the man who made the deal and didn't deliver. Sutcliffe probably believed that the whole thing was a setup.

"Do you have anything stronger than coffee?" Grant asked, still hunting through her kitchen.

They weren't going to get boozed up and he was driving, so although she did have alcohol in the house, she shook her head. "I don't think that getting liquored up is the answer," she said, closing her other hand over the top of her empty coffee mug. "Talk to me, Grant. Why is Sutcliffe after you? Did you pay him his money back?"

He refilled his mug. "Of course I did," he said, coming over with his new coffee. "But it's not money they want."

"What do they want?"

Sutcliffe was using those in his cult to his full advantage, which meant any stranger could be a threat. At least she didn't have to worry about Brodie's well-being while he was locked up. The manor was a fortress.

"Sutcliffe believes we made a fool out of him and he wants his revenge," Grant said, seating himself.

There was that word again. "Revenge, but…" she said. "Who do they want revenge against? You?" If Sutcliffe put all of the blame on Grant, then it made sense that her boss was the cult leader's focus. But that made the Kindred's position murkier, would Brodie and Tuck agree to protect Grant? Did she want them to?

His silence begat her frown, but his eyes made a slow ascent to hers, although he didn't raise his chin. "Not just against me, Zara."

Being explicit wasn't required. Brodie was the one who killed Sutcliffe's kin and she was the one who betrayed the details of the deal and brought the Kindred into the game. "Against me too?" she asked.

"You were there. Everyone who was there is at risk." Sutcliffe had already killed Art. He'd killed two people close to Grant. That probably meant she, Brodie, and Tuck were next. "Three of Sutcliffe's men are dead, including his nephew, and he doesn't have the device he needs to carry out his plan."

FIVE

THE DEVICE. Revenge for the humiliation was anticipated, but if it turned out that Sutcliffe planned to carry out his original plan that meant none of the risk had abated and Grant McCormack was still a major threat. Whether Grant would be honest about his crucial role in facilitating Sutcliffe's plan needed to be tested.

"Do you think…?" she asked, but there was no subtle way to get the answer. "Is he still planning to use Game Time?"

Grant opened his mouth and took a loud breath. "When he called to claim responsibility for the murders of my VP and housekeeper, he told me that he'd give me a chance to make it better. A chance to make it right."

Zara didn't like the way panic tasted in her throat, it squeezed and contorted the inside of her chest until she almost felt like she was drowning. Their work to intercept the deal, Art's death, it would all mean nothing if Sutcliffe got his hands on Game Time anyway. Grant wouldn't stand up to the criminal, she wasn't even sure that he wanted to. If the way he was talking to her now was any measure, he hadn't learned any lessons. He'd been on Sutcliffe's side before, and she feared that hadn't changed.

If Sutcliffe came for her, she wouldn't be able to defend herself. There was nothing secret about her involvement or her allegiance; he'd witnessed her loyalty in the Atlas warehouse. She had to stay alive long enough to warn the Kindred.

Leaping to her feet, she dashed over to the windows to draw all of the curtains closed. She didn't relish severing the visual link the manor had with her apartment, but the risk of assassination was too great.

Tonight, at Purdy's, she'd killed Elvis. She'd believed it was necessary self-defense, now she feared retribution. If the dead musicians' gang were indeed Sutcliffe's men, then Brodie wasn't the only one to have taken the lives of Sutcliffe's people anymore.

Without Kindred backup, staying alive might mean bending to Sutcliffe's will. If he gave her the chance to pay him back for the slight. Sutcliffe had extended that chance to Grant. But Sutcliffe still needed the CI CEO if he wanted to get his hands on the Game Time device. To get it, Grant needed her because the original shipment was still in the Kindred's possession.

Brodie wasn't at his peak, but she could rely on Tuck. Once she explained what was going on, he would come up with a plan.

Sidelining her survival instinct, she pushed for more information. Grant could shut down at any time. "Why wait three months?" she asked, turning her back to the wall between two of her tall, curtained windows.

Her role in the Kindred had always been one of information gathering. They were all in this terrible situation together—her, Grant, and the Kindred. Last time, Grant hadn't known about her links to his brother, now he did, so she didn't have to mislead him about why she was asking so many questions.

Sutcliffe may lump the group from Atlas together as one entity. Anyone who wasn't with him was against him. If he did, she would have to act as liaison between Grant and the Kindred because the factions wouldn't be inclined to play nice with each other.

"What do you mean?"

Edging toward the table, she noticed he hadn't touched his refilled drink. "Where has Sutcliffe been?" she asked. "Why didn't he come after us straight away?"

"You remember he hurt his leg at the warehouse?" Grant asked and she nodded. "It was broken when he leaped aside to dodge the sniper's bullet." The sniper being Brodie. Although Grant's tone became accusing, she made no apology, so he moved on. "Sutcliffe had to have surgery and he developed an infection. His injuries bought us time, but he's better now and… I underestimated how fervent his followers are."

Sitting beside him again, she remained intent. "His followers?" she asked, moving the cups aside to inch toward him.

"Albert Sutcliffe is the last of his affluent family. His brother died years ago. Tim was his only remaining blood relative… Maybe some of his anger comes from that loss."

Albert Sutcliffe had been angry long before he lost his nephew. But she could understand that bereavement didn't encourage rational thinking. Brodie and Grant were not poster children for adopting healthy outlets for grief, so they could hardly judge Sutcliffe for being the same way.

One glaring fact cast doubt on Grant's assumption. "If it was payback for Tim," Zara said, "Sutcliffe wouldn't be coming after you. You didn't kill him."

Brodie killed Tim Sutcliffe, and he'd declared it in the Atlas warehouse within earshot of Sutcliffe. But getting to Brodie posed more of a challenge than getting to Grant did. Grant was active in public every day, as was she, Brodie was inside a security protected mansion.

"Sutcliffe uses his people to do the dirty work," Grant said. "I paid back the money he gave me for the product, but it wasn't enough. He's still angry, and his people are pissed off. I don't know what they're planning. But it's all linked, I can feel it."

Being on the outside must be unsettling for Grant. He'd been in control when he was selling Game Time, now he was being hunted and he didn't have the skills to defend himself.

Neither did she, but she tried to get into Sutcliffe's head to play the sequence of events in the Atlas warehouse from his perspective.

He'd arrived full of optimism because he expected to get his hands on the device he'd paid for, his plans were all coming together. Except he'd walked away with nothing, meaning his subsequent plan was shot to shit. He probably thought Game Time had been a ruse to get him into a vulnerable position so that Raven could take him out.

"They think it was a setup," she muttered to herself.

Grant reacted to her musing with annoyance. "It was a setup," he snapped. "I didn't know it. I was just duped like Sutcliffe was. But he doesn't believe me. You could've told me—"

"I couldn't have warned you," she said, though she probably wouldn't have even if she had known Brodie and the others were around. But technicalities mattered in subterfuge. "I didn't know what the Kindred were planning. I wasn't on the inside."

She might have walked away with the Kindred at the end, but she hadn't arrived in the warehouse with them. Raven's kill shots were as much of a surprise to her as they were to everyone else.

"Why not?"

Again, she did not intend to reveal the inner workings of her intimate relationship, or of the group they were affiliated to. "It doesn't matter," she said, unmoved by his annoyance because she still carried so much of her own toward him. "I did try to reason with you. I told you that selling Game Time wasn't a good idea, that the results would be disastrous. But you weren't listening. You were blinded by your reaction to Frank's death and so determined to rebel against your father." The offense in Grant's eyes made her retreat from her attacking position because she didn't need conflict in their relationship now, not when she needed him for information. "Sorry." It wasn't in her nature to condemn a person when the past couldn't be changed anyway. "Your motivation, your family... none of it is my business."

"Isn't it?" Grant asked and reached for his mug, probably

as a distraction because she could tell by his pique that he was pissed. "If you marry my brother…"

"Even if I do marry your brother, it's not like you and he have a conventional relationship, is it?"

Marriage was improbable when she couldn't get Brodie to sleep in the same bed as her most nights. But their relationship issues weren't high priority. Sure, she was hurt that Brodie had ignored her call and she was angry that he was busy wallowing while the rest of them were being attacked. But she loved him and she'd made her peace with being patient. Raven had taken his time to come clean with her when they first met. Brodie would get there. He would come back to her, in his own time.

"What else did Sutcliffe say when you spoke to him?" she asked. "Did he give you any indication of what he meant about giving you a chance to make it right?"

They returned to their neutral state. Grant didn't appear to want to fight any more than she did. "He hasn't given up on his cause. He's going to want the device from us, I'm almost sure of it. I think that giving it to him will be the only way we can prove that we weren't part of the scheme to take him down."

The gravity of that admission made her sag back into her chair. Grant delivered the line without any compunction, but she couldn't believe this nightmare was back. Sutcliffe had ideals he planned to impose on the world. For some reason, he believed Game Time was the way to make his point.

Obtaining the device had been his singular focus and he'd lost his nephew Tim in that pursuit. Pride or anger motivated this return to their lives, making him all the more dangerous to them. He'd lost henchmen and been embarrassed. Getting over that humiliation would require those he considered responsible bowing down and giving him what he wanted.

The raid tonight didn't fit with Sutcliffe's ultimate goal, which supported Grant's theory that it was for their benefit. Meaning lives had been put at risk just because she and Grant wanted to go for a drink.

"What was tonight?" she asked. "In Purdy's, why do you

think that was him?"

"It would be a coincidence if it wasn't, don't you think? Men wielding guns, threatening to kill in our presence, picking you out. It's Sutcliffe, or we have the worst luck in the world."

A coincidence, the word reminded her of something Art had said and she had to concur with Grant's thinking. "You have to find out what he wants," she said. "You have to get in touch with him and—"

"Albert needs money to support his cause, you heard what those guys said about ransom."

Elvis had referred to payment in exchange for lives. Terrorizing and injuring people just to make a buck was quite dramatic, but she could believe it of Albert Sutcliffe. Elvis had said that they planned to be there all night. Holding people hostage with the spotlight of the media trained on the event would no doubt give Sutcliffe a kick. Severe egotism was a requirement for any man who wanted to take over the world.

"Hurting people isn't the way to achieve his aims," she said, but had no faith that Grant would stand up to Sutcliffe.

Exploring the nothingness between them with his keen eyes, Grant was obviously trying to make sense of this whole affair as well. "I plan to talk to him, as soon as I can. But I don't plan to chastise him."

She hadn't expected him to voice opposition to Sutcliffe, but she hadn't expected him to admit cowardice, which led her to believe cowardice wasn't what he was express. Panic began to pulse on her larynx again. Was it simply that Grant was afraid of Albert Sutcliffe and didn't want to invite his wrath? Or was there a part of Grant that still believed in Sutcliffe's cause as he'd claimed to her he did.

Grant had received the harshest of consequences yet he'd lost a VP, and lost his housekeeper, then tonight in Purdy's he'd been robbed and shot at. It wouldn't have escaped his keen notice that she, Brodie, and the others were as yet unscathed—other than the loss of Art. Though she doubted Grant cared too much about losing his uncle, he could argue with Brodie that he too had been a victim of grief after Art was murdered.

"You need a plan beyond getting in touch with him. You

have to know what you're going to say to him, what you're going to offer in an attempt to placate him? And what if he never returns your call? Are you going to let his cult take you down?"

Grant's shoulders broadened, suggesting she'd aroused his interest. "Why do you call it a cult?"

To get a little, she had to give a little. "Because Art did," she said, sliding her hands over the surface of the table. "He told me most of what I knew about your Game Time clients."

A smile clipped onto his face that was curious given the circumstances. "Forgive me," he said, scratching a finger over his mouth in an attempt to conceal his smirk. "Sorry, it's just funny. We haven't talked about what happened and hearing that you were familiar with Art, it's… it's unexpected."

"Maybe we should," she said, realizing she had some ground to gain in winning her boss's trust again and she'd need it if they wanted to get through this.

"We should," he said, and slid his open palm across the wooden surface to finagle his fingers between hers. "We could get dinner and—"

Talking was just that for her and she wouldn't send mixed signals. "I can't," she said, withdrawing her hand to tuck it down on her lap.

"Right," he said and his eyes darted away in a show of impatience that matched his sigh. "You know, you're never going to have a normal life with him. It might be fun and exciting now, but soon you're going to realize that he doesn't fulfill you. He can't give you what you want."

Irked enough that she wanted to defend her man and her relationship, she slunk onto her feet and let her frosty stature say what she wanted to convey. With the ongoing situation, she couldn't risk alienating her boss further when there was already damage control needed. But that didn't give him the right to pass judgment on something he didn't understand, and he seemed to take every opportunity he could to do that.

"My relationship is fine, and he does give me what I want."

Grant couldn't claim to know her heart any better than she did. Brodie was the only man who had made her feel the way he did and her heart ached with the weight of grief he carried. She wasn't going to play games and start going to frequent social occasions with his brother. If nothing else, Brodie would think she was trying to get a reaction from him and that would only annoy him, as it would annoy her if the situation was reversed.

"We have to talk about Sutcliffe," Grant said. "You and I have to be on the same page. I do not want a repeat of—"

Before she could think about working with him, she needed one answer. "Do you plan to give him the device?"

"You took it from the warehouse," Grant said. "I haven't seen it since."

That answer was an evasion she wasn't going to let him get away with. "You have the ability to produce more and I'm not naïve to—"

"I have commissioned Winter Chill again," he said, rising onto his feet, wearing an expression as pissed as hers. "And I'm not ashamed of it, Zara. I still believe in—"

"Oh my God," she exhaled, having received the answer to her unasked question. She couldn't work with him. She couldn't trust him. They were still on opposing sides. "You're going to pander to him. You're going to give him what he wants."

His deep voice became authoritative and brash. "I want him to understand that I didn't motivate what happened. Why should my position have changed? I believed in Albert then and I believe in him now. I'm going to make sure that he knows that. He and I can do great things if—"

"I think you should go," she said, taking one determined stride away from him.

This conversation could go no further until she'd consulted with Tuck. She wasn't ignorant to what Grant was capable of, but she was disappointed, and the weight of that repeated disappointment angered her.

His ease became fury, but she wasn't afraid of Grant McCormack. "What are you going to do, Zara? Are you going to go running to your savior? Or are you going to make your own decisions? I don't claim to know how Brodie obtained your loyalty the first time, but I would like to think that you're working with a clearer head now, that the fog of seduction may have lifted. He made your decisions for you before, now he's out of the picture, he's not around to support you. Make your own decisions, Zara, because I believe if you sit down and think about it, you will see the merits of what Sutcliffe and I are planning… Do you remember the lunch we had after I gave you your new car?"

The hush money and the Mercedes. "Yes, I remember."

"We were happy that day, Zara. You were open and receptive. I could tell that you were warming to my way of thinking."

Brodie had just screwed her over, she was on her own, and wanted to believe that Grant was capable of more than just destruction. They had been happy that day, but she couldn't be sure now why that was. She could have been seduced by Grant's optimism and faith, and now that she didn't have Brodie at her back, she wasn't sure that wouldn't happen again. Having an ally was seductive, being alone felt cold, isolation led to vulnerability, and with her life under threat, the prospect of a partnership was appealing.

He touched her shoulders and his hands skimmed up her neck to angle her face, and when he began to descend, she froze for half a beat before inhaling and turning her head away from what could only have been his attempt to kiss her.

"Don't," she whispered. After his hands fell away, she made herself look at him. "I don't know why you want to kiss me, but it's not out of lust. You want to recruit me or maybe you just want to hurt Brodie, I don't know. But I won't let myself be used."

Resentment colored his face. "Like he used you," Grant said with the bite of anger. "That's what he did, Zara, that's why he won't connect with you now. He needed you to do his dirty work, to screw me over, and you relished the opportunity."

Whatever he might think, she hadn't rolled over on Grant easily. "I always fought your corner," she argued. "Even when you didn't deserve it. That's what five years together gets you. I won't see you hurt, but I won't subscribe to your politics just because we're familiar to each other, sir." The title was snide and enflamed his rage.

"You'll always run back to him, won't you? Next time you talk to him, don't forget to tell him I insulted you with a proposition after subjecting you to another trauma. I'm sure he'll have plenty of negative things to say about me after that."

Insulted and angry, he slid his hands into his pockets and raised his brows as though he expected her to argue. She tried not to squawk out her displeasure, but she was genuinely offended. "You think that the problems in your fraternal relationship are because of me?" she spat. "You're the older brother, you have means. You knew where he was, you could've sought him out! I didn't know he existed until a few months ago and I've managed to forge a relationship with him. What's your excuse?"

Trailing his attention down her body, he fixated on her breasts for a moment and his annoyance became something more spiteful. "I don't have your talents to distract him."

Implying that she'd used her feminine assets to wow Brodie wasn't far from the truth. What she hadn't known was that Brodie had been using her female vulnerabilities to get what he wanted.

Putting her own grievances aside, Zara took a chance to extend an olive branch by proxy. Stepping into him, she ran her fingers down the back of his forearm to take his hand.

"Does it mean something to you?" she asked, moving closer, though she knew that Brodie wasn't listening, she still felt it necessary to be discreet. "You have both lost family, do you regret not having more of a relationship with your brother?"

"Has he said that?" Grant asked. She sensed his vulnerability shining through. It was typical that Brodie wasn't even here, yet he was managing to do damage.

Sorry that she'd brought it up, she now had to confess the truth. "He doesn't talk about things like that," she said. Grant withdrew his hand. There was nothing else she could do here and she wasn't about to get into a debate regarding Brodie and his inability to express his emotions. Grant would have to get in line behind her to wait for that day.

"I have to go," he said, but stayed where he was, as

though he was reluctant to leave.

"Sure," she said. Any support she would offer him wouldn't extend into allowing him to spend the night. Human compassion brought her awareness to his solitude. She had Tuck and Brodie for support, while Grant had no one, he was all alone. "If you need to talk about Sutcliffe or anything… give me a call." Maybe that would be enough to ensure he'd keep her appraised of any actions he intended to take with Sutcliffe, but that wasn't assured.

Spreading his hands, he brought them to his face again and exhaled before he nodded. "You're a good girl, Zara."

"Do you want me to walk you down to your car?"

"I'll be fine," he said, letting his fingertips touch her cheek. "There is more that we have to talk about."

She nodded. "On Monday. Let's get over this weekend first. I think we could both use the space to clear our heads." That was half of the truth, she had to clear her head and consult with Tuck about how to move forward.

Grant went to the door and she followed him to say goodnight, accepting a kiss on her cheek before he disappeared down the stairs. When she closed the door, she locked it tight and relaxed her weight against it. This apartment was secure and she still had her gun, she was safe here. With intentions of getting a good night's sleep, she decided to call Tuck tomorrow. He would only rush over if she called tonight and there was nothing to be done this minute.

Zara examined her bruises in the bathroom mirror and made the decision to avoid the manor while they healed. Brodie might not be the most attentive guy these days, but he wouldn't miss the story her face told, and being in the mood he was, she knew he just wanted an excuse to shoot someone and more murder wouldn't help with the Sutcliffe situation.

SIX

"YOU DON'T HAVE to keep wincing like that every time you look at me," she said, smiling as she brought coffee to Tuck, who was seated on her couch.

With his arm stretched along the back, he reached over to take the hot mug from her and was already sipping the liquid by the time she came around to sit down beside him.

"You've got yourself a shiner," he said. "Now I understand why you wanted to meet here instead of at the manor. If Rave saw that, he'd track down those guys from Purdy's and take Maverick along for the ride."

Guilt softened her voice. "I killed the guy who hit me," she said.

Sleep had eluded her the previous night. Not because she was worried about Sutcliffe and his men coming to look for her, but because she had put a human being down. She had killed someone. Tuck might be impressed, and Brodie would probably be proud. But she couldn't get over the evolution of her own character. A few months ago, she could never have killed a person. These days, not only did she carry a gun, she had now used it in defense of herself.

Zara was smart enough to understand that Elvis would have molested her, and maybe killed her too, if she hadn't pulled the trigger. But concepts of compassion and morality made her modest about what she'd done. She wanted to play it down and forget about it, because she wasn't sure how to process her transformation into a murderer. Brodie would be able to tell her how he coped with taking life. She wanted to ask him about the first life he'd extinguished to find out if he'd struggled to accept what he'd done.

"Have you killed before?" she asked Tuck.

This was a conversation she should be having with her love, but she wasn't going to add to his burden. "You're not truly a part of the Kindred until you have," Tuck said. "Now you know that you can defend yourself, defend the circle. It's a shock to the system the first time. You'll get used to it."

She didn't know if he meant she'd get used to living with what happened, or if by killing more people, it would get easier to take life. There wasn't time to analyze ethics. She had to cast off her turbulent emotions and focus on what they were facing.

Clearing her throat, she tried to be objective. Working with Tuck was easy, but they were at a disadvantage being just the two of them without the input of Art or Brodie. She was so much of a rookie that Tuck was practically working alone. But she wanted to prove that she could handle this and that she could be useful. Being a part of the Kindred was a massive learning curve, but her relationship with Brodie depended on her being able to absorb and act.

"Grant said it was Sutcliffe. That he was sick and now he's well."

"We knew it wasn't over," Tuck said. She was impressed that he could hear such unnerving news while remaining calm. "But why would he come after you in—"

"I don't know. They wanted to ransom the hostages."

Considering this, Tuck nodded. "Taking prisoners forces the media to broadcast his message and lines his pockets. War is expensive," he said.

"We have our work cut out for us," she said. "Grant says that Sutcliffe hasn't changed his plans just his timetable… and I don't think that Grant is going to put up any resistance."

Tuck's concern made his brows lower and she couldn't

blame him for being shocked and angry. But they shouldn't have expected anything else. The Kindred had attempted to subvert Sutcliffe's plot by cutting him off. Without Game Time, his ability to hurt innocent people lessened. Now she could see that all they had done was delay what might turn out to be inevitable.

"Does Grant intend to fulfill the contract?" Tuck said.

Even though ratting Grant out would mean his return to full adversary status, she nodded, because hiding the truth could cost lives and he'd done nothing to earn her clemency. "He's already commissioned a new Winter Chill project."

"Where and how—"

"I don't know," she said, taking Tuck's drink from him to put both that and hers aside. "We have the original schematics, but there could have been copies. I can search the CI systems if you want me to, but I would guess Grant won't be as obvious about leaving breadcrumbs."

"He may fund it privately," he muttered and she nodded.

"He has the capital to set something up without leaving a trail. But I would like it if… maybe you could see if—"

"I'll do what I can," Tuck said. "I can try to find out where the money is being routed, but… it's possible he's split up production this time. That's what I would do. He can have the parts manufactured in certain places and bring them together to assemble the final product."

Encouraged that they were forming a plan, she could feel the heat of her blood increase. "Then that's when we need to get involved. We can destroy the device and—"

"How many times are we gonna do this?" Tuck asked, cutting her off to voice his opposition to her suggestion before she could finish the thought. "We're not gonna scare them off by tossing a couple of grenades in. We have to take a different approach…"

For the longest time, he didn't say anything and she stayed quiet, giving him peace to try to come up with a better solution because he was right. Going over the same plan again and again wouldn't work. Grant wanted to supply Sutcliffe who wanted to right the wrongs he perceived in the world using force. If Art were here, he would guide the men through making their plan. But with him gone and Brodie uninterested, Tuck had full autonomy and responsibility for whatever they ended up doing. The buck would stop with him.

"Okay," Tuck said. "I need you to tell me everything that you know, then I'm going to the manor to use the systems there. I'll see if I can track down where Grant is building the device."

"But I thought you said—"

"Knowledge is power," he said. "We're not gonna use a direct strike like we did in Quebec. I'll talk to Falcon and I'll talk to Raven—"

"Do you think he's in his right mind? I mean… will he be helpful?"

Tuck's brows came down in a disapproving frown. She hadn't meant to insult him, or to insult Brodie. But she was worried about Brodie and didn't want to add any pressure to his situation when he was struggling to cope with life as it was. The girlfriend in her wanted to protect the man she loved and keeping him in the dark would prevent him from having to face the man responsible for Art's death.

"I'm not gonna cut him out of the loop," Tuck said. "It's important for all of us to be honest. We have to be able to trust each other. We don't have the chief kicking our asses into line."

In the interests of honesty, she hazarded the question that she knew posed a risk of distracting her if she didn't admit her insecurities. "You're telling me that you're not going to take a direct strike… but you didn't tell me about Quebec either."

"I'm not lying to you," he said, tilting his head and with an open shrug, he relaxed. "I don't have any reason to. We're friends and I care about you, but… I'm not interested in getting you into bed, or worried about your judgment. What reason would I have not to tell you if I did plan to go and kill these guys, if I can even find them? Taking out Winter Chill didn't prevent the disaster, it just slowed it down. No, let them build their product. We have one major advantage now that we didn't have before."

"What's that?"

He leaned closer. "We have the original devices. If Falc is up for a challenge, or a bit of sport, we'll invite him over to reverse engineer the thing. Maybe with a bit of tweaking we can find its weaknesses and ways to sabotage it, if we have to. Like I said, I'll talk to him. Falcon is the smartest motherfucker you'll ever meet. He'll know what to do."

"It has a kill switch," she said, spurred by optimism. "I heard Grant and Kahlil talking about it in his office one time. They didn't say how to activate it. But Raven confirmed it. He said technicians spoke of one, but I don't think he knew if it was incorporated because he said it creates a vulnerability that hackers could take advantage of."

Tuck's smile came before he patted her hand. "Then we're already a shoe in. Falcon and I will be able to figure out how to take the device down."

As much as she trusted Tuck's capability, and Falcon's too—despite never having met the man—she was aware that for sabotage to be viable, they had to allow the device to be positioned and prepared to do irreparable damage, and that was a major risk. All it would take was a tiny delay or a smidge of confusion, and people could be subjected to the gas meant to kill them. But she couldn't argue with Tuck and try to coerce him into taking a safer route when no plan was set in stone yet, and she could offer no alternative.

"And me?" she asked. "What do I do?"

"What you are doing," he said. "Stay close to Grant and do your best to monitor his communications with Sutcliffe. We can't kid ourselves that he's gonna trust you like he did before, but you're still close and if he suddenly goes on a trip or has a secret meeting, we'll know to be on standby. If you can, we'll ask you to bug the office, maybe his clothes… But we're getting ahead of ourselves."

Maybe he'd noticed the look of dismay crossing her face. She still cared about Grant, despite his obvious failings, and she understood why they had to take such measures. But she wasn't sure how good she would be at planting a bug on someone without them spotting her doing it.

Tuck questioned her again about what happened at Purdy's and about what Grant had told her. Once he was clear on all the details, he bid her farewell and told her he would be in touch. Her assignment for now was to act normally. She would be happier to have an assignment that allowed her to go to the manor to try to find shelter or comfort with her love.

For now, she had to avoid Brodie, at least until her bruises faded because his mood had been so volatile that no one could predict how reliable he would be during an op or how he'd react when he found out his brother had stood by while she was hurt.

***

WORK ON MONDAY started off the same as every other day. She went about her business while trying to put the work of the Kindred to the back of her mind. The key to appearing benign was to go through the motions like there was nothing else going on in their lives.

Pretending to be oblivious became harder when she collected a contract from her printer, slid it into a leather binder, and carried it to Grant's office. All she needed was a signature and she didn't expect that there would be any cause for them to address the unpleasantness.

Except when she went into Grant's office, she saw that he wasn't as alone as she'd thought. The guest seated opposite Grant twisted in his chair to examine her and on registering his identity she froze in the doorway.

"Sutcliffe," she exhaled, and the man had the cheek to smile.

"Ms. Bandini," he said and got up. One of his legs was straight and he held a walking stick, which supported his weight. Whatever surgery or infection he'd had obviously wasn't through with him yet. At the wrong end of middle aged, his face bore many laughter lines, and his gray hair was receding, but his complexion was clear and his eyes shone with wisdom. "Grant and I were just discussing you."

"Were you?" she said and fixated on Grant, who was acting just shifty enough that she doubted their discussions had all been positive or complimentary. "What were you discussing?"

Still wearing a smile, he had no shame. "Well I wanted to kill you," Sutcliffe said. Zara had to give him points for honesty even if she hadn't expected him to be so direct. "Grant tells me that you may not be a lost cause. He explained how your infatuation with Raven has waned since the man has become a useless wretch intent upon his seclusion."

Sneering at the man who disgusted her, her reaction to his insult was snide. "I'm sure he'll be so pleased to hear that you were concerned for his well-being."

"I have a final proposition for you," Sutcliffe said, using his stick to support the couple of steps he took in her direction.

"I'm not interested in your propositions."

"Hear him out, Zara," Grant said. "Be smart, please."

Tuck had told her that she needed to stay close to Grant and that the more information they had, the better. So closing her arms around the binder, she raised her brows in acceptance of the moment and that action prompted Sutcliffe to carry on.

"I have land in a rural part of New York State," Sutcliffe said. "It's my base of operations."

She couldn't figure out why he would be confessing such a thing. Her pondering was interrupted by her realization that Grant's blinds were drawn over the vast windows. The lights were on inside the office and she hadn't considered how odd that was given that the winter sun was not close to setting. With that thought logged, she read the paranoia in Sutcliffe's hunched form and it intrigued her.

Narrowing her eyes, she peered at him. "Why confess that to me?" she asked. "You're not going to win my loyalty."

"Your boss tells me that it might be a possibility," he said. She glanced over Sutcliffe's shoulder to read Grant's beseeching expression. "And as for confessing, I did no such thing. My ownership of the compound is a matter of public record. I'm sure your colleagues already know where my group is based. The town we're based just outside of contains most of our members. It's no secret that we're there. We're not some sort of intolerant cult. We're simply a group of likeminded people who want what is best for this country."

The sales pitch wouldn't work on her and they had to know that. She wasn't going to shrug and admit she'd been wrong all along. "Why are you here now?" she asked. "How can you trust that we won't take you down? How do you think that we could forgive you for killing—"

"That was unfortunate," Sutcliffe said, but she didn't believe his look of contrition. "I am sorry that your friend had to die, but it was necessary. I had to get away without Raven and the others following me. I am imperative to my group's mission and they need me to ensure cohesion. We have some passionate members and it is my responsibility to ensure no one acts alone without sanction."

So he believed himself to be all-powerful, to have the ability to control those who were lesser than he was. Whatever this group was, Albert Sutcliffe was the one steering them all and as she looked into his eyes, she tried to decipher what was driving him. Had he gone mad? Was he addicted to power? Or was he genuinely so misguided in his own narcissism that he believed he had the ability to bring peace to the world?

"You're not going to get forgiveness. We can never forgive you for—"

"Has Raven asked forgiveness for murdering my nephew?" Sutcliffe demanded and hobbled a step closer. "Or two of my best men?"

Though he remained a good six feet away from her, she wasn't worried about him coming closer because with his impediment, it would be easy to outrun any attack he may try to wage.

"You didn't answer my question about why you're here."

"I am here because Grant has assured me he was not part of the double-cross. I am still in need of the product he provides and if he can prove himself to me then we will do business."

"And if not?" she asked. "What if this is all a ruse?"

"If it was a ruse, I could have shot him the minute he came in," Grant said, coming around his desk to move toward her. "Or called security and had him arrested." Her boss's proximity was more of a worry, especially when he took her arm and pulled her deeper into the room, thus lessening her chances of a clear and easy escape. "We have to find a way to work together, Zara. There is no alternative. Raven has lost the plot. You can't rely on him anymore. You have to start looking out for yourself and think about what best serves your interest. You can be a part of the winning side or you can lose for a man who barely acknowledges your existence."

"I'll think about it," she said, and took a step back, but Grant didn't let her go and Sutcliffe got closer still.

"How do you plan to do that when you have no new information?" Sutcliffe asked. "You have chosen a side without having all of the facts. You don't know what we do or what our intentions are. You have listened to Raven's story and that is full of holes."

"What information do you think you can give me that might sway me?" she asked. "Words are cheap and they're easily misconstrued and manipulated to suit a person's ends."

"I couldn't have said it better myself," Sutcliffe said and smiled at Grant. "You were right. She is intelligent."

Zara wasn't a genius. One didn't have to be a brainiac to know that Sutcliffe could weave a good yarn. If he wasn't so sinister, his easy, warm smile and the unthreatening air he carried himself in could probably have drawn her in. For a moment, she connected him and Tim in a way she hadn't before, Tim was charming and gracious too. Looking into Albert Sutcliffe's eyes now, she looked behind the smile and saw the pain he carried for the loss of his nephew. She recognized the ache of grief from behind Brodie's façade.

"I'm sorry about Tim," she said. Sutcliffe's smile flickered away from his face when he blinked. "I'm sorry for your loss."

Anger hardened him. "He was a good boy, who didn't deserve to die," Sutcliffe said. When that flash of anger ebbed, the truth of his vulnerability was revealed.

"We've all lost people," she said. "Don't you think it's about time we stopped killing each other? It serves no purpose except to aggravate this already fraught feud."

"We plan to stop killing our own," Sutcliffe said, returning to his smile as he reached forth to take her hand. "After we show you the truth."

That proposal was astonishing. "Show me?"

"Yes," Sutcliffe said. "You were right about words. I could talk and try to explain for the rest of the night. But you can't be sure that I'm being honest and maybe I am trying to manipulate you. But if I show you where we live and what we do, let you talk to others in the group, maybe then you will come to see the truth. All we want is a better world where our children don't have to fear for their future."

"You want to show me?" she asked and glanced to Grant, who nodded once. "You want me to come to your compound in New York?"

"Yes."

"Okay," she said and lifted her hand out of Sutcliffe's. "I will discuss it with the others in my group and if we decide that we want to—"

"No," Sutcliffe said and his smile became stern. "This is an opportunity for you, not for them. We want you to use your own eyes and make your own decisions. People in my group are encouraged to think for themselves. We welcome other opinions and debate."

That may be true, but when it came to making decisions and taking action, it was Sutcliffe who called the shots, of that she was certain.

This could be a trap but seizing her meant nothing to them. She had no useful skills and Raven wasn't a prize they wanted, except maybe to see him suffer, but he was doing that already and might not come out of seclusion even if she was endangered. There would be no way for them to get a message to Raven if they did imprison her, so he would never know that they had her.

Instead of speculating, she chose to ask outright. "What do you want from me?"

"Come with us," Sutcliffe said. "Come and see it with your own eyes."

Grant was by her side and he squeezed her arm in a way she was sure was meant to reassure her. She trusted that he didn't want her to be hurt but going to New York with them was a massive risk. Except if she didn't take the chance to gather the intelligence, she would kick herself later, and this was her Kindred role. If she couldn't use her position here at CI to get that information then she would need to be open to alternative avenues.

Brodie wouldn't be scared of this opportunity, and neither would Tuck. They accepted that sometimes risks had to be taken in order to ensure the success of the mission. And as wary as she knew she should be, she wasn't afraid for her life.

"Let me get my purse," she said. Grant let her arm slide out of his grip for her to back away toward the door.

SEVEN

AS SOON AS SHE was out of Grant's office, Zara hurried to her own office and grabbed her purse, which contained her Sig and her Kindred cellphone. Tuck had brought her a new phone on Saturday when he came to her apartment. Pulling the phone from her bag, she speed-dialed Tuck while watching her door in case Grant or Sutcliffe chose to come looking for her.

"You're lucky I answered, I was about to get in the shower," Tuck said when he picked up the other end.

"Listen to me real quick," she said, ignoring his statement. "Sutcliffe is here. He and Grant are going to the New York compound and they want me to go with them—"

"Zar—"

"It's okay. Grant won't let anyone hurt me. I will try to keep this line open when I get there," she said. Tuck had ways of doing things, the only Kindred tech she had was this cellphone, and she wished she'd made more of an effort to gather an arsenal. "Is there anything specific I should look for?"

Speaking clearly, he proved he knew how valuable this chance was by giving concise instructions. "Number of guards, number of guns, what kind of hardware they have.

Check for exits and for means of entry. We have to know if the fences are electric or if there are traps on the grounds. Try to note weak spots and any stockpiles."

"Got it."

"And Swallow," he said. "You watch your ass 'cause if Rave finds out I let you do this—"

"We're doing this for him, Swift," she said and appreciated how sincere his concern for her was. "I'll be careful."

Hanging up the phone, she stuffed it back into her purse and snagged her jacket from the hook by the door as she went past. Grant and Sutcliffe were already waiting by the elevator and she noted that they'd selected up as opposed to down.

"How are we going to get there?"

"I have a bird of my own," Sutcliffe said, and the elevator pinged to allow them entrance.

His bird turned out to be a helicopter decked out with leather seats and luxury that probably rivaled Marine One. Art had told her that Sutcliffe's family were old money, but he'd also told her that he'd lost most of his fortune through bad investments and in divorce settlements. Except he didn't look to be hurting for cash anymore.

During their flight there was little conversation, and it gave her the time to consider what enterprises Sutcliffe might be involved in that would give him this kind of means. Cults often took up crime as a way to fund the support of their people and their ideology. Noting this idea as something to flag up with Tuck, she contemplated how they could gather evidence that Sutcliffe and his band were doing something overtly illegal. They could use that as a way to get them off the grid. They could present authorities with evidence of their misdeeds and get Sutcliffe arrested.

In previous times, she had considered how the authorities might be of help to them. There was a major argument against that course of action: Tuck and Brodie were criminals. She couldn't invite that kind of scrutiny to their group. Because although the Kindred worked to take down those who meant to hurt others, their means weren't always strictly legal.

Grant took her hand as the chopper began to descend. Despite being seated in the center of the craft, she tried her best to crane her neck to see what they were going into. All she could see was a green space, circled by tall trees with a large farmhouse in the center. Picking out details was difficult. As they got lower, she noticed crops and animals, and some smaller timber structures close to the tree line.

Eventually, they touched down and the rotors kept on going. In the noise and busyness of landing, she took the opportunity to slip her hand into her purse and dial Tuck's number with hope that he would be able to listen to or record what was being said. If nothing else, he would be able to get a GPS signal from the connection, she'd seen him do that in the past. She just had to hope he was there, in the manor control room, ready to receive her signal.

Sutcliffe remained strapped in until the chopper was silent. A group of men outside rushed over and opened the doors to help Sutcliffe, her, and Grant disembark. Once they were outside, they were led toward the two-story house.

The air was aromatic. It smelled refreshing, of damp grass and tree leaves. Laughter drew her eye right and she saw children playing on a homemade obstacle course near the back door of the house. When the young ones saw Sutcliffe, they ran over to greet him. He hugged and petted them all with an affection that made her look twice. As picturesque as the scene was, she couldn't discount the possibility that the whole thing was staged for her benefit and for Grant's.

So far, she hadn't seen any weapons and everyone was dressed in civilian clothing. There didn't appear to be any sort of militia presence, which she would have expected for a group determined to right all the wrongs that they perceived in the world.

Still, she was unsettled. These people might be happy here and maybe Sutcliffe would be able to convince her of that. But as to whether or not every visible member knew about his plans with Game Time was another matter. It would be easy to raise your children in such a beautiful place, to tend animals and crops, to live as part of a group intent on looking out for each other. Just because someone subscribed to that way of life didn't mean they had nefarious motives.

It was getting dark. While she was being led inside, the women gathered the children and took them off in a direction opposite to the house. Their role in this performance was complete and they were being ushered off the stage. Zara ascended exterior stairs and went through a rear door with Grant at her back.

The space they entered appeared to be a large dining kitchen. The central table was a long rectangle and had at least twenty seats around it, so she expected to be part of some kind of meeting. Instead of being bombarded by people and by facts, everyone except Sutcliffe and one other male left the room.

Once the four of them were alone, Sutcliffe held a hand toward the lone man at his side. "This is Benedict Leatt," Sutcliffe said.

Sutcliffe sat down at the head of the table, letting out a pained groan as he did. Benedict dropped a concerned hand onto his shoulder before smiling at her and crossing to the kitchen counter. "Ben will do fine. Would anyone like a drink? Coffee or wine?"

This wasn't a social call. "No," she said, because she wouldn't trust anything that she was given to drink in this house. "I want to know why we're here. You said that we were going to get an explanation as to what your intentions are."

"Ben is one of the newest members of our group," Sutcliffe said, stretching his bad leg out to the side. "I thought you would want to meet him and maybe hear for yourself how we live."

And it just so happened that Ben was here waiting for them in the kitchen when she and Grant arrived and knew to hang back while the others were excused. On the journey, she hadn't seen Sutcliffe use a phone, suggesting this sequence had been rehearsed. The production outside was becoming less credible.

With a wide smile, Ben seemed affable, but men wore many masks and first impressions weren't always accurate. "This is the main house. We have this room and a large living space adjoining it. The rest of the rooms have been converted to bedrooms; each family who wants one gets a room."

She wasn't writing a piece for Architectural Digest. "Lovely," she said, glaring at Sutcliffe. "I don't care about how you live."

"Sure you do," Sutcliffe said, opening his arms like this shabby farmhouse was some kind of utopia. "How we live dictates our ideology, our desires. This is not a dictatorship, which I'm sure is what you believe. People are free to come and go, in fact, most of our members still have jobs that they travel to each day. The town is only a mile from here. There are bars and restaurants, a booming tourist trade that allows stores and hotels to thrive. This is a beautiful part of the world."

Lots of faces coming and going, that's what she heard. A town used to strangers, who might not mind the eccentrics who lived on the outskirts as long as they were producing reliable labor. "And when your people are there, are they watched? Do they hand over their income to you?"

It seemed that she could be as accusatory as she wanted to be, Sutcliffe wasn't biting. "Everyone who is here is here by choice," Sutcliffe said. "They believe that the way we live, the community we have, it's a safe world for their children."

"How many members do you have?"

"Staying here, over two hundred," Sutcliffe said.

She couldn't see how two hundred people could live in this one house, but Ben cleared that up for her. "There are other properties. Some families prefer to have their own space. There are cabins throughout the trees where people make homes for themselves in a safe space, where they don't have to fear for their children."

Ben had to be in his thirties. He was attractive and fit. She couldn't quite figure out why someone who appeared to have at least moderate intelligence would agree to give up so many of their personal liberties just to be a part of a cult.

Some people were susceptible to the power of suggestion and it could be as simple as that. But maybe it wasn't Ben's choice to be here. Maybe he had been coerced. "Do you have a wife and children on the property?" she asked.

Sutcliffe laughed and leaned back to pat a hand on Ben's

lower back. "He's free and single if you're interested," he said.

Her eyes widened on their own with the mortification she felt at such a suggestion. But Ben took Sutcliffe's hand from his back and gave it back to him. Although the man wore a smile, he spoke as though to a meddling uncle who was trying to play matchmaker. "I don't think that's why she came here or why she asked," Ben said, then made eye contact with her. "I'm here by choice and I'm here because I believe that what we're doing is right. Every society has to start somewhere. At the moment, there are just two hundred of us, but Albert has ideas that could bring more members to our group."

"I bet he does," she murmured, but Ben carried on without acknowledging her comment.

"We can acquire more land and build our own community that doesn't have to live in fear of crime or misfortune. To answer your question, yes, most of us hand over most of our wages. But is that any more unusual than handing them over to a landlord or a utility company? Here, we have our food and our board, we have all of our bills paid, and no one is required to work or to hand over money. Some people choose to stay here full-time, they tend to the crops and animals. They look after the children or help with other chores. Everyone contributes something because we all care about looking after each other."

This was getting a little too after-school special for her and as she tried not to cringe at what Ben was saying, Grant spoke up. "You have a council who make decisions?"

"Yes," Ben said. "Several people take part and when decisions have to be made anyone is welcome to come to the debate."

She fixed a glare on the leader. "And the device that you want from CI, where does that fit in?" she asked Sutcliffe, not pussyfooting around the elephant in the room. "You don't just want to recruit people for your utopia. You want to murder those who don't subscribe to your politics."

Clearly offended, Ben scowled. "No, that's not true," he said.

For whatever reason Ben was here, it wasn't to give her

the truth because he didn't seem to have it himself. While her scoffed amusement sounded ridiculing, that hadn't been her intention. As she folded her arms and fixated on Sutcliffe again, she waited for his admission of guilt that would clue Ben in.

"Your mind has been poisoned," Sutcliffe said and now he was the one who seemed to pity her ignorance. "Your friends have not told you the truth."

She was more inclined to believe the Kindred than to believe this man after what she'd seen of his intentions with her own eyes. "Why would you need such a device if it wasn't your intention to hurt people? Was it your people who attacked Purdy's? Why would you send them to do that if your motives truly are benevolent?"

"You're getting ahead of yourself," Sutcliffe said. "How would you like a tour? You can meet the people here and see what we're doing for them."

Ben came around the table, and when it was clear he was waiting for her to join him, she looked at Grant. "What harm can it do to go with him?" Grant asked.

Ben led her through the rooms of the house and she spoke to some of the people that they met. He took her outside and explained what they were growing. She met the children and the women. Everyone was happy. Too happy.

Her guide took her into the woods and down a path that got darker and darker as it got narrower. Zara slowed down, concerned about their distance from the house. Just as she glanced back and considered returning, there was a break in the trees, and they came out beside a large lake edged with forest. The still water reflected the moonlight shining above them.

"You're not convinced?" Ben asked, pointing to a log near the water's edge, which had been planed and smoothed into a makeshift bench. "Do you think that we're hiding some sinister secret?"

She didn't need to think. "I know you are," she said, looking out over the water. "I think that everything you've shown me has been unthreatening. It's a lovely portrayal of what an ideal society should be."

"But?"

Getting a measure of this guy could be useful, they might need an inside man somewhere down the line. "Either you're deliberately misleading me or you're being deliberately misled. I haven't decided what your role is in this. But I know for sure that Albert Sutcliffe is not the second coming here to save you all."

"I don't know much about you, Zara," Ben said. When she glanced his way, he was examining the reflection of the moonlight. "But I do know that you are affiliated with the people who killed Tim. People who dislike Albert and all he stands for."

"And you think that we're indiscriminate killers out to tear down the happiness of others?"

"No," he said and shook his head as he laughed and twisted to face her. "But I do think it's easier to be seduced by the dark side than it is to build something good from nothing. To be a part of our community, you have to be willing to put in time. It takes effort and hard work. No one gets a free ride here. Even the kids help with the land and the milking. But you get out what you put in and being a part of this… it's the most incredible place in the world. I wish you could see that."

His naivety reminded her of her own. "I don't doubt that most of the people here believe this community is the end game, that this is the point. But don't you see that this is a cult? Like so many other thousands of them that have come before, and how many of them end well? You've been deceived or you're deceiving me."

"To what end?" he asked, narrowing his eyes. "Do you think you're that much of a prize?"

If Sutcliffe could win her over, he could recruit anyone. "No, but I think that Sutcliffe believes me to be. Because if I take up your politics and subscribe to your cause…"

"What?"

The truth was so much easier than any lie. "It will damage my allies. He may even believe I'd use my influence with them in order to alleviate the pressure on his cause."

Bafflement made a groove form between his brows. "I don't understand," he said. "What do your allies give you? Do you have a similar community? Are you all pulling on the same oar for the same purpose?"

When he put it that way, she had to take her attention back to the water to figure out the answer. What did she get from the Kindred? They didn't have a utopian land where she had crowds of people invested in her well-being. At that moment, the only person she could rely on was Tuck. Yet he had been right when pointing out that although they were friends, and cared about each other, there was no vested interest in their relationship which would dictate the likelihood of any decision to go above and beyond for each other.

What she got from the Kindred was her man. Brodie. Her love. And as distant as he was at the moment, it didn't change her dedication to him. She had missed him this weekend and although she knew she was staying away for his own good, it didn't alleviate her want to be by his side. If she had been able to crawl into his bed and rest her face on his chest after the attack in Purdy's, she wouldn't have dealt with as much anxiety about taking Elvis's life, of that she was sure.

"We do want the same thing," she said. "And our ends are not nearly as nefarious as yours. What does Sutcliffe tell his recruits? Are you told to move here and take up a role on the farm and live happily ever after with a cult girl? What about the women? What purpose do they have? Are the children tools at Sutcliffe's disposal as well?"

Maybe he was curious about her, but all she read was negative judgment. "You hate him, don't you? Why is that?"

"He killed my friend," she said without any hesitation. "He sent his nephew Tim to seduce me in order to use me for his own means."

"Which were?"

Watching him, she anticipated any flicker that might indicate Ben's knowledge level. "They want a device, one built by the company I work for, CI. Grant's company. They want us to be a part of this group not because it's best for us, but because of what we can offer them. What do you do for a living?" she asked, wondering if new members were selected for similar reasons, what they could offer Sutcliffe, rather than what Sutcliffe could offer them.

"I'm a physical therapist," he said.

She tilted her head in a slow, single nod. "Medicine," she said, with exaggerated interest. "That's significant. You can offer useful skills to Sutcliffe."

"I have my own practice."

Ben might think that he was exonerating Sutcliffe. Instead he was giving her another opportunity. "And you're a business man as well, even more fruits for Sutcliffe to select from. You are a useful prize for him."

"So if I work with him and don't charge him for it, what? I'm evil? I'm going straight to hell?"

She almost wanted to spit out at the word because such a concept was so far beyond what these people were capable of. Tucking her hands over the edge of the log, she leaned forward.

"This place is not what you think it is. And I'm sorry to be the one to tell you that. But it's not."

"I thought I was supposed to be educating you about the merits of what we're trying to achieve," Ben said, and his cordial manner made her sorry for what he was going to find out. He wanted this place to be his savior, and now she would have to obliterate his illusion.

"I know that you're here to convince me of Sutcliffe's benevolence. But I have a feeling you were sent because you're as naive to the truth as I once was. Who better to convince me of his intentions than a man who believes he is nothing but good?"

"So educate me," Ben said, turning to throw a leg over the log so that he was straddling it to look straight at her.

To prevent any misconception of dishonesty, she moved into a similar position, but crossed her legs on their solid base and held her purse on her folded shins to ensure Tuck would have the clearest possible audio of the conversation.

Zara didn't worry about revealing Sutcliffe's secrets. She had no loyalty to him. Ben deserved to know the truth and maybe planting a seed of doubt would cause him to ask questions in front of others. Breaking up the cult from the inside was unlikely, but any dissension aided her cause.

Gearing up for a candid conversation, she moistened her lips. "The device that he wants from CI is meant to spread disease."

He frowned, and she took that as a signal that she'd been right about his ignorance. "Why would your company produce such a product?"

She shook her head, frustrated that he was fixating on the wrong thing. "That doesn't matter. It wasn't the original purpose for the product. That's just one of the ways it can be applied and that's why your boss, your landlord, wants it."

"Why would he—"

"He wants to cleanse the world," she said and was pleased to see that Ben looked as horrified as she'd felt the first time she'd learned about Game Time and what it could be used for.

"That doesn't sound like Albert."

"Maybe you don't know him as well as you thought."

Noise beyond the tree line stopped her from saying anything else. Either they were being listened to or someone was about to interrupt them, whichever it was, she didn't want to be hung for naysaying by the good townsfolk.

As it was, Grant broke through with a man she didn't know and they beckoned her over to say it was time to go home. Ben buddied her back to the chopper that was already warming up for take-off. Just before she parted from his side, he slid a business card into her hand.

"If you have any more questions," he called over the racket of the rotors. "Or you want to talk some more. Give me a call."

She nodded and offered a smile in thanks for his hospitality. Whether or not he knew the truth of what Sutcliffe was cooking, he had been an amiable host. So she got back into the chopper with Grant, who made eye contact as they were taking off. Powerful searchlights lit their ascent, but soon they were drifting away from the Sutcliffe compound.

It would take a while to get back to CI, but she was grateful that the excursion was ending. She was eager to talk to Tuck, she wanted to recount her impressions and her experience with Ben. After all she'd seen, she had a better idea of who Sutcliffe was, but that didn't make her any more comfortable with his motivation or his desire to harness Game Time.

EIGHT

GRANT TRIED TO TEMPT her into coming back to his apartment. He said that there were things they had to discuss. But after the chopper ride, she was exhausted and Tuck was her priority. She needed confirmation that he had heard her conversation with Ben and for his take on how they should move forward.

After giving Grant assurances that she would think about what they had learned today, she went upstairs to her apartment and didn't bother turning on any lights because the only place she wanted to be was in her bed.

Stripping off on her way through the living room, she didn't bother to pick up her clothes, or even to collect her purse from where she'd dropped it onto the floor beside her keys after locking the door. There were too many thoughts in her head, too many possibilities. She needed help sorting through them because all she felt was overwhelmed.

By the time she reached her bedroom, she was naked, and would be visible to anyone outside. The only ones who could see her this high up were those who had a camera pointing into her home: the Kindred. She was sleeping with half of those who could put eyes on the feed. They'd have to zoom in and adjust to night vision if they wanted to see anything, and she doubted Tuck was inclined to do that. He had already confirmed he had no interest in sleeping with her and was dedicated to Kadie anyway.

With a yawn contorting her features, she pushed into her bedroom and closed the door with her weight. Sagging against the door, the cool silk of her kimono tickled her back, but she wasn't going to cover herself, not when her welcoming bed beckoned to her.

Glancing to the chair in the corner, she thought about Brodie and craved the old days when he would come to her. She needed him now and hated the sore pang of disappointment that snapped in her chest every time she was reminded that she was dealing with this alone. Brodie had his own shit to process. He would take his rightful place in the Kindred chain of command when he was ready.

Berating herself for languishing in the past, Zara drifted toward the bed and crawled onto it to lie right in the middle, face down on the pillow.

"Old habits die hard."

The sound of his husky voice made her gasp and sit, pulling the comforter to her chest as she did. The room was so dark, she couldn't see much, then the lamp on her nightstand lit up and she saw her memory come to life.

Fright became delight and the weight of the world lifted from her shoulders. "Brodie," she said, unable to believe this was real. But it did appear that he was in her bedroom, standing in the corner diagonally opposite his old haunt, just to keep her guessing.

"Why am I coming to you here?" he asked and didn't sound impressed.

Even if he was mad, she'd take it. He'd come out of the manor for her. Over the last three months, he had chosen not to leave the manor for anything. Yet here he was in her bedroom. Nothing could extinguish this joy. She needed him and he was here. He'd been a recluse blinded by grief, and he was out in the world again. This could mean he was coming back to her and to the Kindred.

For a few seconds she forgot all about Sutcliffe, Grant, and Game Time. The man she loved was emerging, he was healing, and she'd underestimated what a relief it would be to her to see him make progress. This was more than a baby step; this was a massive leap in the right direction.

The light didn't offer complete illumination and until he slunk out of the corner, she couldn't see his expression. His hair was a mess, but it hadn't been cut in three months, and his scruffy face was adorned by a judgmental glare, but her insides clenched at this sight of him in her bedroom again.

"Grant dropped me off," she said, trying not to over play her elation for fear it might scare Brodie back into hiding. The realization of her dilemma cooled the fizz of happiness. She'd been with Grant at Sutcliffe's ranch, days after being attacked in Purdy's where she'd killed a man. But how much should she tell Brodie? How much truth could he take? "We've been... we got back late and... I couldn't tell him to take me to the manor, could I? And, uh... Swift and I thought it would be a good idea if you didn't... if you and I didn't..."

"He told me," Brodie said.

Another surge of relief flooded her. The last thing she wanted to do was lie to Brodie.

Dropping down to sit on the bed, he seized her chin and pulled her face into the light so he could see her bruises. For the first time in what felt like forever, his hand came around to the back of her neck and he gripped her so tight that she yelped at the pleasure it gave her to feel his familiar touch.

As happy as she was, he appeared equally pissed. "You're going to tell me how the fuck this happened or I'm going to tear apart this world until I find every man responsible."

"Baby," she exhaled and slid a hand from his chest up his neck to the coarse stubble on his jaw. "I killed him. The man who did this to me... I killed him."

The words were so quiet, she didn't know if he'd heard them until the darkness in his eyes grew to an onyx glow. Just like that, the happiness dissolved and the gravity of truth hit her full force. The moisture she'd dammed in her eyes since Friday night came out and when her face fell into his chest, he kept hold of her neck and rested an elbow over her shoulder securing her against him.

If she wasn't so distraught, she might have worried that he was going to push her away as he had done so many times in recent months. But he didn't. He held her close and used his other arm to adjust her position. She was still lost in her crying spree and didn't pay any attention to what he was doing until he laid her down.

Lifting her face from his shoulder, she swallowed and sniffed in the remnants of her upset. "Sorry, I don't know where that came from," she said, wiping away her tears on each side of her face with the length of her index fingers.

Lying on his side beside her, he smoothed the hair back from her forehead. Tearing her attention away from the ceiling, she blinked at him and saw him look at her, really look at her, for the first time in months.

Being here, beside him, made every moment of torment worth it. He was still her man and if she'd ever doubted his affection for her, all of those doubts were erased now in the way he gazed down at her, bathing her in his adoration. "If I'd known it took getting beat up and almost sexually assaulted to get your attention, I'd have done it weeks ago," she said and had meant it as a joke, but his expression lost its softness.

"Now I know the what," he said. "Tell me about the who."

Taking a deep breath, she wanted to start at the beginning and take full advantage of this opportunity to talk to him, as she'd wanted to since the crime had happened. "I had no idea," she whispered, drawing her finger around the line of his tee shirt neck. "When I pulled that trigger it was… I warned him more than once…he hit the floor and he was just… staring."

"The police were called?" he asked and she nodded.

It was a good sign that he was concerned for her liberty and for the heat that might now be on the Kindred. "They're not pressing charges, they say it was self-defense. Kraft looked after me. He got me out of there without being seen."

"Why didn't they take you to the hospital?" he asked.

"Kraft offered," she said. "But I knew it wasn't that bad. I refused to see the paramedics. Kraft told me to take it easy, that I might be concussed. I hit my head on the sink."

She touched the bump on her hairline.

"You've got a black eye," he said, grazing the edge of her cheekbone with a fingertip.

This was like the early days, them lying together in her bed, his hands arousing her with the simplest of touches. "I know," she said, closing her eyes while he stroked his fingertips on her face. "I thought I was going to pass out when Elvis punched me. If his buddy hadn't been there to hold me up, I would've been on the floor for sure."

When he stopped touching her, she opened her eyes and was wary of the darkness growing behind his scowl. "Why did he punch you?" he asked and the set of his jaw concerned her further. He wasn't happy, she just couldn't figure out why.

Being honest, as Tuck had told her was so important, she told the truth, even though it might upset him. "I told him that you'd hunt him down if he didn't let me go."

Satisfaction became pride. "You know me so well," he muttered. Laying a hand on her thigh, he ran it up over her hip and her abdomen to let it rest beneath her breast.

She had to make him see that there was no reason for him to be angry, because the man responsible for her pain had been eliminated. "Yeah, well, I saved you the trouble. When he dragged me into the bathroom and pulled his dick out, I shot him."

"Atta girl," he said, pressing a kiss into her forehead.

"I don't feel proud," she admitted and opened her hands on his chest to slide them up to his shoulders.

He curled a finger under her chin to bring her eyes to his. "You should be. You did what you were supposed to. I should've been the one to put a bullet in the bastard. I diverted your call." Falling onto his back, he pressed both hands into his face and took a deep breath that expanded his chest.

"It wouldn't have mattered," she said, reassuring him, assuaging any guilt he might feel. Doing his job, killing, didn't make him feel guilty. But he didn't have to spell it out for her, he felt responsible for Art's death. Even though it wasn't his fault, the doubt kept him questioning what he could have done to prevent the killing from taking place. "You would never have gotten there in time and there was no line of sight to the bathroom."

Rolling onto his side to glare down at her, his determination was back and it was something she hadn't seen in him since before Art died. "You think I'd have taken him out from across the street?" he sounded insulted. "Any guy who dares puts his hands on my girl gets my attention up close and personal."

His girl. God, it felt good to hear him get possessive of her. "Brodie," she whispered and rubbed her hands up and down his chest. In response to her unspoken request, he laid on his back to let her crawl on top of him to rest her head on his shoulder and caress her lips on his jaw. "Where have you been, beau? Why did you leave me?"

"Because I'm a prick," he said, twining his hands into her hair. "I forgot that there was a fight out there. I was too busy fighting a battle with myself."

His voice was clear and keen, he spoke with no equivocation, and that decisive certainty inspired her. "I would never have had the gumption to do what I did if it wasn't for you," she said. "You taught me to fight. There were twenty people in that room and not one of them did anything."

"Twenty people?"

"In Purdy's," she said, if Tuck had filled him in, he had to know some of the particulars. "Grant asked me to go for a drink. He said I had to get back to my routine. I haven't been into Purdy's since before… you know. I thought it couldn't hurt since I planned to spend the weekend at the manor. Boy, was I wrong."

Closing one hand around the back of her neck, he squeezed, holding her still while his other hand stroked her body. She felt so safe, nothing could hurt her in this place and with Brodie returning to form, responsibility left her purview. The Kindred was his jurisdiction, she was too, and her faith in his ability to protect both didn't waver.

"You probably saved the lives of everyone there," he said. They laid with each other in silence for so long that her eyes began to close as her body surrendered to exhaustion. "But you and me have got to talk about our problem."

Being that there were so many problems in their lives, she couldn't pinpoint what he was talking about but suggesting they had a private problem could spell bad news for their relationship. A blast of alarm woke her up. "Problem?" she asked. "What problem?"

Clutching the back of her neck, he pulled her up and used his other hand to grip her chin. "Don't ever hide anything from me again. It's not your job to protect me. I've seen shit like this more times than you can count. Don't hide yourself because you think the sight of you will make me lose it. Anyone ever touches you again, you come straight to me. Don't think about it. Come to me."

He didn't blink. The thump of his heart beneath hers shook her form and pumped in unison with the resolve radiating from him. "Okay," she said and had to clear her throat to rid the squeak from her tone. She wasn't scared of him chastising her. That he was angry proved the strength of his regard for her and any display of his feelings was stimulating. "I won't ever hide from you again."

Pushing her head back onto his chest, he squeezed her tight, imprinting her body onto his. Zara was so grateful to have him here. She needed his strength. Tuck had clued him in and Brodie had come here to wait for her, to be here for her when she got back. Having a mission to think about focused his mind, and Zara wondered why it hadn't occurred to her before now that a distraction was what he needed.

With his fingers tangled in her hair, he obviously wasn't as tired as her because his voice was alert. "Didn't you tell me about somebody getting killed?"

"I told you about the funeral I was going to. A CI VP was killed by a mugger," she said. "And I found out that a member of Grant's household staff was killed on the same day. Sutcliffe claimed responsibility, but it could just be a crazy coincidence and Sutcliffe's being opportunistic by taking the credit."

Intrigue slowed his stroking hand. "Recognizing a coincidence is the first step to solving a mystery," he said, easing her down onto the bed. "That's what Art used to say."

"I know," she said, sorry that she no longer had him to lie on. "Where are you going?"

He left her alone and departed the room. Propping herself up on her elbows, she prayed that he would come back to her and a minute or so later, he did. With her laptop open and balanced on his forearm, his intent face was lit by the welcome screen.

Seating himself in the corner, in his usual seat, he put the laptop on the dresser and began to type. While the computer worked to keep up with whatever it was he'd asked it to do, he looked at her still laid out on the bed.

"Why did you move your shit into the guest room back at base?" he asked without prompting, which suggested that was a mystery that had plagued him.

Getting the chance to be open and talk about their behavior over the last few weeks filled her with hope. The more they talked and were honest with each other, the easier it would be to move forward. "Didn't seem like you wanted me in your room," she said. "You were up watching TV or gaming or…" sitting in the dark staring aimlessly, which had been one of his favorite pastimes for the last three months. "You needed space and I didn't want to crowd you."

"Move your stuff back, it's still your room… even if I am being a shithead."

Self-deprecation wasn't his forte, but she appreciated the sentiment enough to smile at his effort to sort of apologize. "I never thought for a second that loving you would be easy," she said. "But I'm glad you pushed the boundaries and fell apart… if we can call it that."

"Call it whatever the hell you want," he said, turning his attention back to the laptop.

She couldn't see the laptop screen. While she was interested enough to want to go over and check what he was doing, it had been so long since she'd had him here and engaged in her presence that she didn't want to rock the boat by interrupting him. So she stayed put on the bed.

Relaxed and reassured now that she was under Brodie's control again, she hadn't discounted the idea that she may be languishing in the after-effects of some drug Sutcliffe might have somehow poisoned her with at his compound. Shifting onto her side, she closed her eyes and tried to ignore her budding headache.

"I thought you were gonna give your apartment up," he said, not done with the discussion of their relationship. She was happy to talk about it, even if she was half-asleep. With Brodie around, she didn't have to be vigilant, or cagey, what she saw with him was what she got and he'd deal with any trouble that might try to sneak up on her while she was sleeping.

"I didn't get around to it, not yet," she whispered.

"I didn't think you spent every night at the manor," he said. "And I didn't want to think that you'd shacked up with another guy… 'cause I'd have had to kill him and that would be a fucking shame for him."

"How would I have explained to him all the time that I spent with you?" she asked, tucking her hands up under her pillow, while her eyes remained closed. This weekend was the longest she'd gone without going to the manor since Art died. She was usually there at some point every day or at least every other day, to make sure that there was plenty for Brodie to eat. "And I was still having sex with you. That would be a tough one to explain to a new boyfriend too. You give me all the action I need, baby."

There was no response to her flirtation, but she didn't think too much about it. If it prompted him to come over and play with her, she was happy to be his toy. Brodie drove this relationship, whatever he wanted, he got, and she loved it when he wanted her.

"Hmm, I thought so," he said. She cracked open an eye to try and figure out what his distant tone meant, but he was no longer looking at her, he was focused on the laptop again.

"What?" she asked, intrigued. "What did you think?"

He had to hear her interest, but he remained intent on the screen and his tone didn't change. Whatever held his concentration didn't let go of him for long enough to satisfy her curiosity. "Same caliber of bullet in both crimes," he said and tapped a few keys. "Either the police work was sloppy and they haven't made the ballistics connection yet, the ballistics were inconclusive or…"

"Or what?"

"Someone in the forensics department is on the take… and we both know that's possible."

The ballistics evidence from Raven's gunshots tended to vanish. He had guys on the inside, or rather Art did, she wasn't sure how those relationships would be affected now that Art had fallen. Tuck had the ability to hack the systems and distort or destroy the evidence too.

"Can you speak to someone?" she asked. "At the police department or the forensics lab or, you know, wherever, and find out why the pieces haven't been put together?"

He wasn't as captivated by the computer now as he had been, but he was still reading something from it when he responded to her. "Maybe they have been and the police are still investigating and they don't want the outside to know their hand yet. If someone is on the take, we don't want them to know we connected the evidence."

With the explanation, her curiosity was satisfied, allowing her to relax. "Possible," she said and closed her eyes again. "So what are we going to do about it?"

"Word is, you and Tuck have already got an op running," he said. The focus of his voice made her peek at him again, this time he was looking straight back at her.

The way his hands went to the back of his head and his eyes narrowed made her wonder if he was accusing her of something. She sat up, steadying her weight on her hands behind her.

"I told Tuck what was going on," she said. "But he told me just to carry on as normal and today—"

"You went with Sutcliffe, I know," he said. The laptop clicked when he closed it, then he surged to his feet and strode to the bed. "Usually, when you have a suspicious death like the VP and the housekeeper, the first thing we would do is line up those connected with all of the victims and start crossing them off. You start with the most obvious people because nine times out of ten they are involved. If you get through the obvious, then you start looking at the less obvious. But we already know who's responsible, so we don't give a fuck if the cops have put the pieces together."

"We?" she asked and pushed up to free her hands so they could cling to his shoulders when he sat down. "Are you…? I mean… are you… back?"

"Back enough to notice that you're naked."

If she had Brodie, then she didn't need to have her private discussions with Tuck. Technically, they should talk as a group, but something else was more pressing, and it had nothing to do with business or Sutcliffe or even the Kindred. It made her heart beat faster and her skin flush. The core of her body swelled and her nipples tightened, he was looking at her, through her, and the intensity of his attention sapped oxygen from the room and squeezed her lungs.

Dragging her nails over the fabric of his tee shirt, she drove them deep. "Being this close to you and with you… looking at me like that…" she said, collapsing onto her back. "I want to have sex with you."

Except with the exhaustion of her day creeping over her, Zara wasn't sure that she was capable of doing much participating and an orgasm might make her head explode. With a feeble sob in her throat, she groaned and rubbed her hands over her face before letting her arms flop down. Brodie got up, stripped off his jacket and his tee shirt, then came down on top of her, bracing himself on his forearms.

"You've taken care of me for long enough," he murmured. "Let me return the favor."

Sliding down her body, he kissed his way south and his mouth opened over one of her breasts. When he sucked her nipple against his tongue, she relaxed a hand into his hair and realized that she wasn't as tired as she thought.

He left his task for long enough to lean over and kill the light, then came back to enfold his arms around her. "Brodie," she whispered into the night.

"Yeah, baby?"

"I've missed you."

He kissed her lower lip, drawing it between his lips and slanting his mouth for a more thorough taste of her. Exuding her pleasure in a languorous moan, her legs and arms clenched around him. But he lifted up, easing her legs apart to let himself rise onto his knees to scrutinize her naked form.

With his hands hooked under her legs, he pulled her to slide her closer to him and when he widened his knees, they pushed her thighs further apart, forcing her wider.

"How wet are you?" he asked. "You gonna take my dick now?"

Hooking one of her calves around to his back, she kept it twined around him when he bent to let his fingers sink into the cleft of her body. Using her own juices, he coated her and slid his fingers around her clit, opening and closing them to squeeze and torment her with every sculpting move.

Her body squirmed in time with the stimulation he provided. Her back arched to undulate her hips against the strength of his invading hand, which went deeper until his fingers were lost inside her. She could feel the knuckles of his liberated digits writhing and kneading against the damp pleats he'd moistened to aid him in tantalizing her.

"You like that, baby?" he asked, pushing in his fingers with punching force and sliding them out. Plundering forth, he wiggled and worked his fingers to provoke more of her natural nectar to seep over him.

"Take off your jeans," she breathed, trying to see his face through the dark night consuming them. "Please."

"I don't need to be naked to give you what you need," he growled and released her leg to loosen his jeans.

As his body sank down over hers, he pushed the head of his dick through her folds and she groaned while tightening her internal grip until he hissed. His dick was so constricted by the passage it occupied that for a good while, he didn't move. He cursed at her and tried to ease away, but she whimpered and sucked him back in deep each time he retreated.

"You are hungry, baby," he said and kissed her until she began to breathe more easily.

She couldn't deny that she'd missed having this kind of attention from him. That he'd come here to her apartment after being away from it for so long spoke to how he felt about her, to how concerned he was for her well-being.

Looming over her, he stayed still, sliding his forearms higher until they closed on each side of her head and gave her something to rest against as he stroked her cheekbones and touched her lashes. "You know, Tuck told me not to give you shit for it, but… you took a big risk today. A big stupid risk… You could've been hurt. You could've been killed. What would you have done if they didn't let you go?"

His thick cock stretched her pussy, she'd never felt so full and the sensation sent shallow, fizzling sparks to each intimate nerve. "I proved on Friday that I can take care of myself," she said, working her hips to test their connection. "I'm Kindred, aren't I?"

"Yeah, you are," he said and when he licked her lips with the tip of his tongue, she opened to try to accept him inside. But he didn't kiss her again, he elevated his pelvis until he was almost free, then pushed into her, keeping his eyes fixed on hers as he fucked her. "You're a hot, hungry little thing. You can't even breathe right. I ram my cock inside you and it becomes your whole world, doesn't it, baby? Do you want more?" She nodded and heaved in an irregular breath. "Say it."

"I… I want more," she said, moving in reaction to his quickening.

The heat and tingling pleasure that encircled the shaft he was using to gratify her began to speed up until the friction burned so hot that it spread past her hips, through her belly, and up to her overworked heart.

His skin beneath her hands grew damp and aided her in stroking his chest and his shoulders. The beat of urgency was heralded by the slap of flesh on flesh as they pulled away and joined the impending explosion of ecstasy promised by their physical fusion.

"B… Brodie!" The taste of his name on her lips was enough to unify all the factors that flooded her brain with the elements of orgasm. As she milked the load from his balls into her cervix, he swore through his gritted teeth.

His body fell in a boneless heap, half on top of hers. When he yanked her over to press their clammy bodies together, she closed her eyes and timed the rhythm of his pulse to try to marry her breathing to the thumps.

He hadn't taken off his jeans. Some things would probably never change. But that reassuring thought helped her slip into slumber, because her love for him, her dedication to this man, that was something else that would never change.

NINE

BRODIE WAS UP before her and had brewed coffee that she gratefully drank after getting out of her shower the next morning. As was always the case when she woke up with Brodie in her apartment, she was running late.

She'd forgotten to grab her cellphone, so she ran back up to retrieve it from her apartment while Brodie went downstairs to pull out his bike. She put the phone in the inside pocket of her jacket and stepped onto the concrete of the service area at the back of her building at the same second Brodie's motorcycle roared to life.

The sound stopped her in her tracks. When she looked up and saw him there on it, waiting for her, a grin burst to her expression. Rushing over to him, she took his face in both hands and kissed him so thoroughly, he must have thought they were heading up the stairs to the bedroom instead of out.

Squeezing herself close, her arms were wrapped so tightly around his neck that she held her own elbows. Still smiling, she didn't ever want to let go. "I think I just had a micro-orgasm when I came through that door. My guy is so hot." She spoke on his lips and he leaned in to kiss her again, signaling he was pleased or amused by her boast. Parting her lips with his tongue, he thrust an arm around her and jerked her body against his.

"Let's go back to base. Forget about work, baby, come on. Let's go home and get naked."

Much as she appreciated his flirting with a smile, he had nothing to prove. "I'm already yours, beau. Always."

The come on was his way of teasing and his willingness to get playful with her was another sign of his improvement. Seeing him outside, in the light of day, when he'd kept himself secluded for so long, thrilled her because it suggested progress. He was processing his grief and starting to move on.

Him in his leather jacket and jeans on the back of the bike might have had something to do with her exuberance as well. She had her man back, and when he gave her a nudge to the back and handed her a helmet from the handlebars, she turned her eyes to the heavens before she pulled it on.

If Art was looking down on them, she knew he'd used some of his magic to pull Brodie out of his funk. Tossing her leg over the bike, she wrapped both arms around him and squeezed tight when he revved the engine, not because she was scared, but because she was exhilarated. He raced away from her building at a speed she'd missed.

Being on the bike with him amplified her optimism. Sharing the night together exhibited the return of his strength. The Sutcliffe situation had distracted him from his grief and maybe shown him he needed to get back to living his life, rather than languishing in his depression.

The ride to CI took little time. With the speed of the journey, she could tell that Brodie had found some of his spirit again. He loved his bike and the freedom it gave him. This trip was a reminder of all the things he'd deprived himself of since Art died.

He drove them to the executive parking entrance of the CI complex and stopped the bike. Holding onto him for balance, she reached over to the numeric keypad to input the security code to gain entry. As she keyed it in and they sat on the idling bike waiting for the door to rise, she felt Brodie tense until he became rigid. Coming here, where there was a chance he could come face to face with Grant, was a massive step for him and one she hadn't expected him to take so soon.

When the door was up, he revved the bike hard, then navigated them to the executive parking area and pulled the bike into a space that was meant for her. She did still have her own spot, regardless of the fact that she had returned the car Grant had tried to give her, meaning she had no vehicle to fill this premium void.

Brodie turned off the engine, but he didn't dismount the bike after he helped her climb off. She pulled off her helmet at the same time he did, and he took it from her to let her toss her jet-black hair forward and shake her fingers through it. She'd tie it back when she got upstairs, but for the moment, she liked her hair being as wild as her man.

When Brodie still didn't make a move to take the keys from the ignition or get off the bike, she tilted her head. "You're not coming in?"

With a stern expression, he checked out her figure. "What's the code for the gate?"

"Three-six-two-one-six-zero," she said. His lips moved in repetition of the digits without uttering a sound. He hadn't addressed her question, and she was worried he might be shutting down again. "Brodie?"

He didn't loosen or make eye contact, but he did grab her hip to tug her near to him. "I'll come back at lunchtime. I want to check something out and then we've got to talk."

It was something of a response to what she'd asked, but she needed more than that to alleviate her worries about possible regression. If she could keep him operational, then he would have less of an opportunity to disappear back into his despair. "You could come up now," she said, trying to remain positive. "Do your research in my office?"

Part of her was afraid that if he went back to the manor now, he would never come out again and this progress would be lost. It would be like it never happened if he retreated into himself and backslid into seclusion. Coming to her apartment had shown a return to being driven, and he was right, they had barely touched on the Sutcliffe situation and she had questions.

He scowled. "No, I'm not sitting up there all day."

"Why not?"

Much as she wanted to encourage his endeavors away from the manor, she could understand his reluctance to enter the actual CI building. He probably hadn't been in it since his parents were alive. Even if he had snuck in at some time, he wouldn't want to be seen hanging around now being babysat by his woman.

But when his fierce eyes met hers, there was no apprehension in them, only anger. "Because if I come face to face with him, I'll beat him until he's bleeding from every fucking orifice and then I'll shoot him in the head."

Well that was a reason and with a head bob, she acknowledged that. He didn't have to verbalize that he was talking about his brother, that much was clear by the strength of his reaction. The last time the brothers had been in the same space, Brodie tried to choke the life out of Grant. It was true that Brodie blamed himself for not preventing Art's death, but he blamed his elder brother for putting them all in that position in the first place.

"You blame him?" she asked.

"For Friday night? I blame him for making you step up because he was too much of a pussy to do it. He should never have let anyone touch you."

The venom wasn't because of Art, at least, not all of it. His anger was rooted in Grant's cowardice and his inaction. She'd gone to that bar with Grant and he'd done nothing to stop her assault. Stroking his face, she tried to soothe him, but was overwhelmed with gratitude that this ferocious man was frothing because someone dared to do her harm.

"Beau—"

"Don't get me wrong, I blame myself too, and I'm gonna… I'll figure something out to make it right. I've put the feelers out, we're gonna find out who those bastards were and what they wanted."

Tuck had to have told him about Grant's claim of a correlation between Purdy's and Sutcliffe, but she didn't know how much detail he had. "It was more than money," she said. "I mean, they robbed everyone, sure, and they spoke about a ransom. But Sutcliffe is coming for us, beau." Fear made her tighten her grip on his jacket. She didn't want to let him go.

Brodie had killed Tim, putting him more at risk than anyone else. "I guess I shouldn't have killed Elvis so quick. I should've given him a chance to tip his hand."

If the night had played out as the masked gang wanted, the Kindred might have more information, giving her yet another reason to feel guilty over what she'd done.

"You're standing here today because you took action. You don't give a guy time to talk when he's threatening you. You did good. Aim and squeeze, same as I taught you. You're a good girl," he said, and leaned closer. "Gimme some sugar."

Brodie was more like himself now than he had been even last night. Back to his cunning, ruthless self, he told it like it was. Conceding, she met his mouth and pulled herself in close so she could feel the width of his thigh against her.

"You'll come back for lunch?" she asked. Now that he had the code, he could come and go as he pleased. Though he hadn't needed the access code when he rescued her in this space, now she understood that Tuck would have been in his ear helping him to circumvent the system.

Curving an arm around her, he squeezed her ass. "By then I'll have something to report," he said, brushing his mouth over hers.

This was too arousing, being with him, connecting with her love, after torturous months of distance ebbing and flowing. He was touching her and talking to her in such an intimate way that she didn't want to shatter this moment by walking away. He'd saved her life in this space on the same night they'd shared their first kiss. To her, it was fitting that their reconnection had brought them here.

"After work, will you come back to my apartment with me?" she whispered, kissing him twice, each a short but glorious joining.

Returning her kiss, he tightened his grip on her ass to haul her higher and closer until she relied on him for her balance. "Only if it's to pack up your things and head back to the manor," he said. "We're having company tonight."

That took her aback. "Company," she said. This was something he'd never said to her even when Art was around. Brodie was one of the most anti-social people on the planet.

"You hate people."

"Not half as much as Zave does," he said and smacked her ass. "Now get upstairs before I change my mind and drag you back to my cave."

It was a good thing that she trusted him as much as she did. Turning to walk away, she twisted to make eyes at him. He pulled on his helmet as he turned the key and revved the bike several times causing her to emphasize the sashay of her hips, provoking him to do it again. This was all foreplay, not that they needed further stimulation in the bedroom, but if it was a sign of what was to come for them then things were on the up.

***

AT WORK, IT TOOK an hour to orient herself that morning. Happy thoughts of her night with Brodie and his reversion to being keen and responsive warred with what she'd seen at Sutcliffe's camp and the possibilities that brought. Grant had wanted to come back to her apartment after their trip, he'd wanted to talk, and she'd told him that she had to think.

Before she walked into his office, she wanted to try to put her sense back into its place. Except he had appointments all afternoon, so she knew that she could only put it off for so long. She had to talk to him before lunchtime.

Giving in to the inevitable, she went through to his office. She closed the door and sat down at his desk, remaining quiet while he finished the piece of work in front of him. When his typing stopped and he closed the lid of his laptop, they made eye contact, but neither seemed sure of where to start.

"How are you today?" he asked and she nodded. It was a cliché place to start, but it was more than she'd offered as an icebreaker. "I know that we have a lot to talk about. Are you sure that you want to do this now? We could go to lunch later, get out of the building and—"

"I have plans for lunch," she said and he nodded. They could continue with the small talk for the rest of the day.

Eventually someone would interrupt them, so she got right to the point before that could happen. Turning toward his desk, she rested both hands flat on the table. "Your housekeeper was killed as was a CI VP. You were present for the attack in Purdy's. I know that you're going to tell me Sutcliffe is a righteous and reasoned man, but he's already taken so much from you. How can you still believe that?"

Although he was frowning, she read in the way his form loosened that he was pleased to be talking about this important matter. But his lips pursed and he took a breath that he exhaled through his nose before making an admission. "I can't discuss this with you," Grant said. "I don't know if I can trust you."

This was progress. At least he was being honest. "Okay," she said, opening her fingers to stretch them over the wood. They'd gone to Sutcliffe's place together, he'd wanted to talk last night and now, for no obvious reason, he was shutting down. If he'd made the decision to cut her out then that would be an interesting development and one she'd test. "I'll just go home and discuss it with my assassin boyfriend, who has something of a volatile temper."

"No," he said, lunging over the desk to catch her wrist despite the fact that she hadn't moved. "You do that and he won't miss a second time."

In the warehouse, Brodie could have killed Grant, but he chose not to. After losing Art, and with how fickle Brodie had been, Zara couldn't be sure he would be so merciful if he got the chance of a shot at Grant again and Grant had just proved that he felt the same way.

Having Brodie back boosted her confidence. "You can choose not to trust me and not to talk to me. Just remember, I'm the more merciful of your options. But even if you shut me out, Raven will still be effective at getting answers from you. Maybe more so than I will be... if you're not forthcoming, I mean."

Shaking his head in a shallow arc, his brow furrowed. "You've changed," Grant said. "He changed you."

He gave no indication as to whether he viewed this as a positive or a negative transformation, though she'd guess he meant the latter. But the idea that the man she loved had a tangible impact on her character cheered her. It certainly didn't make her want to recoil or retreat in shame.

Pride in her man and her relationship was heightened because of the last few hours she'd spent with him. She had to remember her original Kindred remit and tempting Grant to talk was a key objective. "Raven is unique and I am lucky to have caught his attention. But just because I love him, doesn't mean I can't help you."

He was quick to retort, which suggested he was emotional about this situation. "But it does mean I can't trust you," he said and let her go to sit back. "When we were in that warehouse, when you were standing between us… I hadn't seen him in fifteen years."

They were back to talking about her and Brodie, Grant had a hard-on for this conversation. For three months, he'd said nothing about her relationship with his brother. Recently, she couldn't shut him up about it. Still, if he was having issues with trusting her, she had to appear to be honest and open with him, like she still trusted him.

She nodded. "I know. He told me." Grant paused in his contemplation to display his surprise. Zara folded her arms and sat back as she arched a brow. "Sometimes he grunts out a few facts between erections."

She wasn't sure if it was disgust or surprise on his face, but Grant turned his attention to the corner of the desk that jutted between them. "I want to trust you. But I know that I can't trust him," he said. "I thought that with him cutting you out, with him being so distant, that you might have come to your senses."

So he'd hoped that she would agree with his decisions if Brodie dumped her. It didn't make sense why he would think that because she'd never been the kind of woman to need a man, or one who would contort herself into what a man wanted her to be. It just proved how little Grant knew her even after working with her for more than five years.

"If you don't trust me, why did you let Sutcliffe reveal his compound to me yesterday?" she asked, If Grant wanted to work with Sutcliffe then he should be trying to protect his possible ally.

But he wasn't shameful, in fact, he seemed proud when he rested his hands on the arms of his chair and swung it side to side a few inches back and forth, projecting nothing but ease. "He has nothing to hide and you didn't see anything yesterday that could compromise him. Did you think about what Ben told you? Did you think about what it is we're trying to do?"

"Yes, I did," she said. "But I don't think that Ben knew everything. What I saw was wonderful and everyone appeared happy. But it's easy to be happy when you only know half of the story."

Grant nodded and stood up. "If you're not going to join us, then we can't let you see any more. And I will have to ask that you return the CI property you have in your possession."

He'd become cold, and the quick turnaround made her wonder if this whole thing had been a ruse just to try and soften her enough to return what she'd taken from the Atlas warehouse. "The CI property?" she asked. "You mean Game Time, the devices and the viruses."

Businesslike, he lifted his proud chin. "Yes, that's what I mean."

"I can't do that, Grant," she said, leaving her seat and moving backwards. "If I hand over those things, you'll use them to hurt people."

"You know that we're working on building more. You're only delaying what will be inevitable," he said. "I'll give you two weeks to turn the items over."

"And then what?" If he wasn't going to play nice and was resorting to threatening her, then she was going to make him see it through.

But he wasn't going to be forthcoming, which screamed further cowardice on his part. "I'm sure you'll have come to your senses by then," he said and frowned at his desk. "I have work to be doing."

Being dismissed by him was fine by her. She'd been threatened by Grant before and it had come to naught, so she wasn't afraid now. But Brodie would be interested to know that Grant was throwing his lot in so thoroughly with the men the Kindred planned to take down.

TEN

LUNCHTIME TOOK TOO long to come, but when Brodie came into her office with his hood pulled up to hide his face, she smiled. He hadn't called to say he was coming or asked for access from security. He wasn't even wearing a standard security pass. She'd expected a phone call or some kind of communication telling her to come down to meet him in the street or parking lot, having him saunter into her office full of propriety was definitely better than that.

Impressed by his means, she smiled, pleased that he was able to access her even in this secure space. "Can I help you, sir?" she asked. "How did you get in here?"

He closed the office door and came over to her desk. Moving around the furniture, he pulled her chair out, away from her workspace, and sat on her desk right in front of her.

He stroked her tamed hair. "Someone put my fingerprint in the system," he said.

Here he was, alert and active, she'd never felt joy so potent. It was like a liberation for all of them, they were a team, figuring out this mess, adhering to priority one. On that note, she had to ask, "You're comfortable with your fingerprint floating around in CI?"

"It won't last," he said. "And it's Tuck's tech, so good

luck to anyone who tries to chase it."

"You said that you would have something to report," she said, rolling her chair closer so she could rest her arms on his open thighs. The proximity made her breathe him in and such pleasure flooded her that she let her head fall onto his leg.

"I talked to Kraft and we've got leads on all of the men who were in Purdy's on Friday. The police are having trouble tracking them down, but they all have ties to a town in New York. The town that Sutcliffe's compound is located in. Thanks to your excursion yesterday, we have the exact coordinates."

"Did you give them to Kraft?"

"I nudged him that direction out of courtesy," he said. "But I want to track these guys down myself."

She knew what that meant and when she stood up to meet his eye, she stayed in the shelter of his body and curled her arms around his torso when he grasped the back of her neck. "Do we want to go after them one by one, or do we have a larger plan to take down Sutcliffe and all of his followers?"

"That's what we're gonna discuss tonight with our guests at the manor. They'll be getting in later."

Her office door opened and she peeked past Brodie to see Grant coming in with a stack of documents. When he'd closed the door, he looked up with her name on his lips, but he stopped and dropped all of the papers when he recognized her guest.

"He… he is not allowed in this building!" Grant asserted with an outstretched arm, he pointed to Brodie with a rigid index finger. Trying to fathom how she should deal with these brothers coming face to face, she surged up and hurried toward Grant, but came up with no answers.

Brodie sauntered around the desk into the empty space between her workstation and the door. "What's the matter, bro?" Brodie asked.

Seating himself on the front edge of her desk, he reached over to snag her wrist and tugged her body into the space between his thighs. Losing her balance, Zara fell against him. He curled an arm down her back and around her opposite hip, while the other scooped her hair aside to give him access to the side of her neck.

Grant ignored the provocative behavior, but Zara wasn't as successful at ignoring her lover's overt intimacy. She had to blink a few times to try to couple her setting with the arousal caused by his kiss.

"You cannot bring guests into this building, Zara," Grant chastised her. "Your security clearance is a privilege, not a right."

"Oh," Brodie hissed, focusing on the part of her neck he'd just kissed, his hand slid down to cup her breast. "That sounded like a threat to me. What happens to men who threaten my baby?"

With a petulant huff, Grant's mouth fell open. "You better not have a weapon in here!" he asserted. "He better not have a weapon!"

Grant came nearer and she spun around to block Brodie from rising. Her love didn't let her body depart from his. But at least with her back to Brodie, she could measure Grant's reactions. "He doesn't need a weapon to hurt you, Grant," she said, trying to keep the peace between the men. "And he's only teasing. He won't hurt you."

"Because I'm family?" Grant asked.

"Because she told me not to," Brodie said, gripping her hips then sliding his hands up the outside of her waist to the sides of her breasts and back down. "I'm biding my time 'til you piss her off enough that she relaxes the choke chain… course I've got plenty of buddies who owe me favors."

"You're not going to hurt him," she said toward her shoulder, then looked to reassure Grant. "Rave's not interested in CI company secrets and even if he was, he wouldn't have to be in the building to reach them."

"Implying that you're selling company secrets?" Grant asked then frowned. "And why do you call him Rave?"

Answering that one was a breeze. "We're out of the building and we're not alone," she said, realizing how well trained she was. "Rules are rules."

Brodie's hands closed around her breasts again and he lowered his head to hum into the back of her neck. Grant's lip curled in disgust. "I didn't peg you as the type to be attracted to Neanderthals," he sneered. "And I shouldn't have to tell you not to fraternize on company time."

Without taking his face from her skin, Brodie fielded a quip that came off as more threatening than funny. "Bet if she was fraternizing with you, you wouldn't object so loud," Brodie said, squeezing and fondling her breasts in an obvious attempt to show off and make Grant more uncomfortable. "Undo some of the buttons on that shirt, baby."

Her smile was for display purposes only. Her lover's actions were stirring chemicals in her brain that oozed down through her body and the arousal was making it difficult for her to focus. Taking Brodie's wrists, she tried to pull his hands away to give herself a fighting chance of following the conversation, but he shook her grip from him and carried on groping.

"You're making her uncomfortable," Grant declared and he was right, but not for the reasons he thought. The last thing Zara would ever be was embarrassed of Brodie or his proprietary actions. Belonging to him was the greatest thrill she'd ever experienced and her pride in him was boundless.

"She knows how to make me stop if she wants me to," Brodie said, kissing her neck through her ponytail. "And no one speaks for my woman except me, so you watch your step."

Just happy that her breasts were distracting enough to quell Brodie's usual instinct to be violent, Zara let him go on kissing and caressing. "Is there something that you needed?" she asked, trying to get rid of Grant before this situation turned nuclear, which it could at any given second.

It had taken her and Tuck working together to get Brodie off Grant the last time, she wasn't sure she'd be able to separate them on her own. If Brodie decided it was time to finish Grant, he'd be able to do it in an instant.

Although he was visibly displeased and kept sneering at Brodie, Grant answered her question. "I came in to tell you that we have to go to New York this weekend."

Brodie's laugh was so rare that she probably looked as confused as Grant did when she heard it. "Nice try," Brodie smirked. "She's not going to New York." Even when he seemed to be distracted, he was aware of everything that was going on.

Sounding more huffy than superior, Grant seemed to be losing his battle with his own restraint. "You are not in a position to influence her professional duties."

Any discomfort she'd felt before at being groped by her boyfriend while her boss was standing over them, paled in comparison to the bolt of discomfort and terror that came when Brodie took her hips to move her aside. For Brodie to move her so deliberately out of his way suggested he wanted her a safe distance from whatever he was about to do. She was forgotten when he walked toward his brother, who did his best not to shrink in the face of Brodie's intimidating stature.

"My name's above the door on this place too," Brodie's baser growl made her swallow.

Even being the sole focus of this man's love, and being in a secure place under his protection, she wasn't saved from the flash of fear that the intensity of his words provoked. Soon though, the trepidation was replaced by arousal and admiration. Brodie was afraid of nothing and defended the honor of his beliefs and responsibilities no matter the circumstance. That was her man standing there between her and injustice. The environment didn't matter, the subject didn't matter, Brodie's integrity never wavered.

That being the case, she was still on alert herself, Brodie wasn't pleased and was probably looking for an outlet for the discomfort caused by his recent change in behavior. Being out and trying to return to form had to be rousing opposing reactions in him. If Brodie started a fight, this moment could change everything in a heartbeat.

Grant laughed and her eyes bulged in the shock of what his patronizing reaction would provoke. Leaping forward, she took Brodie's hand to try to hold him back, but he extricated his digits and didn't flinch, retreat, or even look at her.

"Laugh again, Saint, I dare you," Brodie said, and she curled her lower lip over her teeth in anticipation of what would happen if he did.

He didn't, but he did get rather haughty. "This company

belongs to me. You got the estate, which has my name above the door as well."

Both had been bequeathed to both boys after the death of their parents, she guessed that the decision to take one each was more of a gentleman's agreement than a formal or legal one.

If it had been Grant's intention to belittle or scare Brodie, he failed. "Except you're too much of a pansy ass to step over the threshold," Brodie said. He didn't need to laugh to ridicule his brother.

Grant's amusement vanished and the slight elevation of Brodie's betrayed that the tables were turned. After being threatened so many times and caged for the last few months, Brodie was in no state to be cornered, he'd lash out like a terrorized animal, and it wouldn't matter if the response was overkill or not. Brodie didn't do half measures.

Trying to keep the peace, because she knew Grant had the upper hand here where he could call security to take Brodie down, Zara defended her love while trying to sound as balanced as she could. If this became an all-out war, Brodie would fight to take down as many security guys as possible before he surrendered. That might lead to the police being called, but if Kraft was around, they should be able to handle that. But she didn't want them drawing that kind of attention to themselves when Sutcliffe was back on their radar. They had enough battles to fight already.

"In fairness, you wouldn't be able to cross the threshold, Grant," she said when Brodie took her fingers between his, indicating that he'd relaxed enough to shirk his violent temper. "You don't have security clearance."

It was Brodie's turn to be calm and condescending. "So here I am in your camp when you don't have a fucking hope of getting into mine," Brodie said. "Now I understand your bitch fit."

Grant was undeterred and widened a smug grin. "And what's to stop Zara bringing me onto your territory as she's done here today by bringing you onto mine. I assume she has clearance if she spends the night with you there."

Zara hadn't mentioned that she basically lived at the

manor ninety percent of the time. "I—"

"I didn't know you'd grown up to be such a comedian," Brodie said, and the men got even closer, squaring off against one another.

"It's possible," Grant said.

"It's not," Brodie said, unthreatened, though he never was. "Now are you gonna fuck off so I can feed my girl? Her lunch break's almost over."

"You cooked?" Grant sneered, not believing the possibility for a second.

"She swallows," Brodie said. Her jaw fell, but her shock was replaced by a smile when she read the slight tilt of Brodie's lips, which made Grant draw back at the same time his own mouth fell open. Whatever he thought or wanted to say, he kept to himself and just glared at both of them before he turned and stormed out of the room. He obviously felt he couldn't trump that declaration, and she would agree with him on that assumption, she had no come back either.

"You shouldn't provoke him just because you can," she said, watching her office door close.

Pulling her around to in front of him, he tugged the tie out of her hair to let her locks loose. "Who's provoking?" he asked and released her hand to unbutton his jeans. "On your knees and open your mouth."

"Here?" she asked, having never done anything sexual with anyone at work.

Brodie didn't use words, the certainty was written on his face, he wasn't going to take no for an answer. And because she was so proud of him for all the headway he'd made over the last day and night, she did as he requested and lowered herself onto her knees.

The thrill of being intimate with him here in her office was one she wouldn't forget in a hurry. The fear of being caught was nothing in the face of the arousal this public intimacy provoked. She smiled as she realized she enjoyed being an exhibitionist with Brodie McCormack. With him, she was always safe and they had to cherish these shared moments because there was no guarantee that there would be another of them.

***

AFTER SHE SWALLOWED what Brodie fed her, he slipped out without further discussion or drama, which was sort of odd because they hadn't put a plan together and she wasn't clear on what he'd done that morning. But there was still CI work to be done, so she put Kindred business to rest and got on with her day job. If they were having visitors tonight then that should mean there'd be forward momentum once they had all the information and ideas on the table.

It was nearly the end of the day when Grant returned to her office, he'd never been in here so frequently before. But he came in and stayed by the door. "I don't want him in here again," Grant said.

He was well within his rights to ask that, just as she was well within her rights to refuse him. But with tensions already stretched to breaking point, she wasn't sure how much more her relationship with Grant could take, and the Kindred still needed someone on the inside.

Taking a cleansing breath, she closed her laptop. "You have to stop seeing him as your enemy," she said without using Brodie's name. If Grant could trust his brother then he could maybe be tempted into seeing things from the Kindred's point of view. But after his earlier confession that he didn't trust her, she couldn't risk sharing any privileged information. "He's a part of my life."

"I told him that our father was a fool," Grant said, strolling farther into the room. He retrieved a chair from the corner of her office and brought it over to put it in front of her desk. She didn't often have visitors and when she did, they were subordinate administrative staff. Her furniture wasn't as luxurious as Grant's, but he didn't seem to care. "If you're inviting Brodie into CI, I can only assume that your allegiance remains with him. So you have to understand the truth. Do you remember I told you that we argued, fifteen years ago?"

She remembered. Both McCormack brothers had told her that they'd fought, but neither had admitted what it was about. "I remember."

"I don't know what either of us expected. Seeing each other again like that. We hadn't been alone since before we lost them and then when we did find ourselves alone…"

"You talked about your parents?"

When it came to history they shared, their stories were often similar. Sometimes they matched. Other times, it was easy to see how their opposing emotions colored the situation.

Recounting events seemed easier for Grant or maybe the words were just easier for him to say because he never doubted the merits of his actions or memories. "We were raised with every privilege, with the best educations, and every luxury in life. I took it for granted, but Brodie, he hated it, snubbed the life others would covet. Maybe that's why he idolized Art in the way he did, Art had adventures, he had no responsibilities. I wanted responsibility. I thought it made you somehow invincible. I worshiped my father and this company." Lifting his attention, he scanned her office, but he seemed somehow numb and didn't register or react to the environment. "We have always been different. We were never close."

Could that explain why they were so averse to each other? Why they couldn't trust each other? Maybe it did, but it also made her see that these men could never be tempted onto the same side. Their objectives were complete opposites.

After his brief moment of private reflection, Grant carried on. "I started to tell him about CI, about how well it was doing, he cut me off and told me he didn't care. He was so aloof. I berated him for being so hateful of what our father loved. Brodie gave me some spiel about how the only thing our father loved was our mother. I laughed at him. He'd been listening to too many of Art's tall tales, I was sure of it. Art idolized his sister, our mother, almost as much as Brodie idolized Art."

She gave him a verbal nudge to encourage him on. "So you argued?"

"I argued. He lashed out," Grant said with a growing scowl. "Art heard the scuffle, he came in and called Brodie off like a disobedient pup… I'll never forget the disdain on Art's face after Brodie left. He must have heard everything."

She could picture the teen McCormack's pushing each other, goading each other. Both believed themselves to be powerful, Grant in the boardroom and Brodie in combat. For years after that, they didn't see each other or doubt their goals in life. Until Grant's guardian, Frank Mitchell, died, the status quo kept the brothers apart.

Thinking of the negative aspects of their past would only increase the brothers' dislike for each other, and she didn't appreciate anyone thinking ill of Brodie. "You told me once that you thought Brodie was a hero," she said. "That his life of adventure was one you craved."

Grant didn't hesitate in his rebuttal. "Then I saw what it took," Grant said, making eye contact. "Art is dead, he's destroyed your innocence, and for what? Just to prove to me that he's better than I am? That he's right and I'm wrong? He's doing now what he couldn't do that day fifteen years ago. And without Art around to call him off, I don't know where he'll stop and I'm scared that you're going to be pulled into his destruction."

She wasn't afraid of Brodie and didn't need Grant's protection. "All he has tried to do is protect people, to stop people from being hurt," she said.

"He's killed more people than anyone else involved in this," Grant said. "He's not a hero. He's manipulated us all. How can you trust him?"

"You need to stop taking this so personally," she said. Her words startled him. She wasn't usually so bold when it came to her boss. But she was beyond pandering to him now that she knew where his loyalties were. "Sutcliffe is the villain here. He recovered from his broken leg and the first person he came after was you. He killed two people in your life. Then he chose a bar on the same street as CI, one frequented by me and other CI employees , as his first public stand. Elvis was supposed to lead those men and without him the unit fell apart, so I'd guess the men need more training. Why does he need soldiers if he doesn't plan to go to war?"

"He wants to protect this country."

Grant was adamant, but she was losing patience. "I am so sick of hearing that argument. If you want to protect this country, then go join the marines, donate money to a charity whose mission it is to save the victims of civil war and religious uprising… You don't charge in with weapons of your own and expect not to cause more damage."

"And who is going to protect the homeland when they come for us?" Grant said. "They've done it before, you know it. We can't afford to be blindsided like that again. We have to be proactive. You have to join our cause."

The rich and privileged seemed so entitled. Being right didn't guarantee victory and she couldn't ever trust Grant or Albert Sutcliffe to be right.

"I haven't made my decision yet," she said, because she would need to consult with the others in the Kindred before destroying her connections to Grant and CI.

Her boss wasn't satisfied. "What was Brodie's reason for being here?" he asked, going back to his original reason for coming to her office.

"I've been encouraging him to get out and about," she said. Brodie wouldn't relish the idea of being portrayed as weak or vulnerable. But it made sense to minimize the threat Grant might view him as, because they might need Brodie doing his thing sometime soon and he worked best with the element of surprise.

"I don't want him coming back here," Grant said, rising to his feet. He turned as if to leave, and she guessed he didn't want to address any opposition she might put up to this command.

"Grant," she said, stopping him before he opened the door. "I'm doing you the courtesy of not dismissing your request out of hand."

"And I appreciate that," he said and his curiosity made him turn back to her.

She doubted he would but wanted to even things out between them. "Will you consider the fallout? Think about the man that Albert Sutcliffe is and what the repercussions of Game Time will be if he's successful? Please, just think about it?"

He nodded. She couldn't read his expression, so she didn't know if he was simply humoring her. But she had to take any chance that she could to poke holes in his affiliation with Albert Sutcliffe. The only thing scarier than Sutcliffe and his army was Sutcliffe and his army with corporate sponsorship.

ELEVEN

GOING DOWN THE BACK stairs of CI after work, she emerged into a service alley and from there ran out to the street. Grabbing a cab, she was dropped off at the beach and walked along to the private gate where she knew her jeep would be parked, ready to take her to the house. It had been Art's way of zipping around the grounds and now it was hers.

At the house, she expected to see Brodie in the kitchen but found him in their bathroom instead, wearing only a towel around his hips and sporting a bruise on his jaw that made her inhale. That wasn't the only thing that took her aback. He'd trimmed his stubble and his hair was clipped in a buzz cut that made him look way more dangerous than he had before and she didn't think that was achievable.

Trying not to come off as the judgmental parent or the eager girlfriend, she restrained her desire and focused on concern. She wanted to know where he'd gotten his injury. "I'm hesitant to ask," she said, unzipping her jacket and leaning on the doorframe.

Unwrapping his hips, he wiped the moisture from his skin, then threw the towel into the hamper chute, which sent their dirty things straight down to the laundry room.

"Saint Grant released you then," he said, running his

fingers over his hair then spraying on deodorant.

His scowl and icy reception bothered her. She tried to keep the conversation breezy to avoid any argument he might be angling for. "I was at work. I wasn't his prisoner, so of course he let me go. And I would like to think that if I was being held against my will, you might have stuck around to help me out."

"No white horse, baby," he said, coming over, glancing at her briefly as he squeezed past her, managing to not make any physical contact.

Wondering at his aloofness, she slid her arms out from the sleeves of the jacket and followed him into the walk-in under the guise of shedding her outerwear.

She took a hanger from her part of the closet and hung up her jacket, trying to be casual as she asked about his day in the way any other couple might. "Did you get into trouble?"

"Maybe," he said, pulling on his jeans while being dismissive and distant. "But I got out, that's what counts."

He started for the door and she got in his way because she wanted to maintain the progress they'd made today and didn't want him shutting her out again. Opening her fingers on the corrugation of his abs, she stroked and pouted. "What happened? Tell me… don't think about blowing hot and cold on me and—"

Snatching her jaw, he spun her around to press her into the wall. "Get something straight, girl," he snarled. "What I do is my business, you understand me?"

After all they'd been through it was impossible for her to believe that trust was still dubious between them, so she sensed something else was at work in him. Turning her fingertips inward, she scratched his belly.

Showing strength was the only way to break through his foul mood. "Don't play games with me," she said, clenching her jaw against the force of his grip. "I stuck around through three months of your bullshit. Do you think one hissy fit is going to scare me away?"

Lowering to her level, he spoke through gritted teeth. "You don't have the first fucking clue what I'm capable of."

Her brows rose. "Don't I? 'Cause I remember standing

there when you downed two of Sutcliffe's men right in front of me. I was the one kissing his nephew when you put a bullet through his skull."

Compelling her head back, he brushed his mouth over hers. "And he's the last man who'll try it," he hissed between her lips.

That reminder of her and Tim boosted his ire until his gaze became black. "What happened, baby, huh?" she asked. For him to be this overwrought, something major must have occurred this afternoon to rile him. "Whatever you had to do—"

"It should never have happened," he growled, shoving her face away before turning his back on her. "There's no substitute for accurate and recent reconnaissance, jumping in without—"

With a short breath, she caught up with Brodie's thinking. "This is about Art," she said, resting a hand on his back to move in and press her lips to the sinews that shifted when he flinched at her comforting affection. "You think you let him down because you got yourself in a fight?"

Turning his head, she glimpsed his profile but kept on kissing because she could feel him yielding as she soothed and stroked with her hands and mouth. "He'd be so pissed that those guys almost got the drop on me," he murmured. "I was outside CI… listening to you with Saint."

She shook her head, sweeping her lips on his flesh and digging her nails into him, confusion made her frown. "What are you talking about?" she asked.

"I bugged your office," he said. "I put one in his jacket too."

The reason for their lunchtime date made more sense now. He hadn't been visiting her, not like he wanted to spend time with his girlfriend. He hadn't even been there to share information with her. He'd come up to her office to get close enough to bug his brother.

"What?" she asked, sensing there was more.

She'd have appreciated him giving her the heads up about the surveillance, but at the same time, she was grateful to him for not asking her to incriminate herself at work. Now it made sense why he'd been so eager to come up to her office at lunch instead of in the morning when he dropped her off—he'd gone back to base for supplies.

The Kindred could still see into her apartment and she'd come to see their video and audio surveillance as comforting because it kept her safe and proved to her that these men cared about her. Having a watchful ear at work just increased her protection.

"Now we can listen in any time we want," he said.

"You were listening to me and Grant? Were you worried about me?"

His frustration kept his expression hard and his body tense. "He should never have told you what he did. You don't need to know that shit," Brodie said.

"I do need to know that shit, I love you, and just because I heard the story from his perspective doesn't change how I feel about you."

Something else made him prickle, and she rubbed her cheek on his back while she waited for him to spill it. "When you talk to him it's… different than when you talk to other people."

"He's my boss," she said, skimming her hands over his obliques and around him to hold herself close.

He was being honest and didn't sound as riled, so her stroking must have worked to calm him and reconnect them. "No, it's not a professional distance. I can tell you've known him a long time… you're friends."

She couldn't decipher what emotion was carried through his voice, whether it was hurt or jealousy or anger or something else. She let her hands slide down his abs into his front jean's pockets.

"I'm friends with you too," she said, pressing her lips to his spine.

"No," he said, taking her hand out of his pocket, he moved it across to the loose opening of his jeans to curl her digits around his exposed dick. "You fuck with me."

With the way his mood had been, she hadn't thought he was interested in being friends. He wasn't the type of guy who would take the time out of his life to shoot the breeze with his buddies.

"He's pissed at me about us and wants Game Time back. I don't think he'd class me as a friend. His mood has been erratic," she said, happy to squeeze and milk his shaft. Erratic moods must be part of the McCormack bloodline too. "If you want to be my friend—"

He released a long breath. "I don't want to be your fucking friend. I'm your guy. I own you."

Kissing his skin, she let the tip of her tongue tickle him as she whispered. "I'd give him up in a heartbeat if you told me too."

"Damn right you would," he groaned.

His hips moved into her teasing hand, she was surprised when he withdrew from her crushing grip and spun around. But his motive became clear when he took a handful of hair on top of her head and rushed her backwards at the same time he forced her downward.

Pain shot through her skull when she stumbled, and the only thing that prevented her from hitting the floor was his fist tangled in her locks. But her gasp gave him the opportunity to slide his cock deep into her throat.

Although she gagged against the intrusion, he didn't seem to notice. With his palms on the wall, he pumped his hips back and forth, screwing her face without permission or grace. Zara took hold of him to try to guide the union, but he snagged her hand and fumbled for the other one to slam their backs onto the wall, so he could lock his fingers around her wrists to prevent her from moving or touching him.

"You feel so fucking good," he panted. "My dick belongs in your throat."

Pushing into her mouth over and over, she sucked and breathed concentrating on her rhythm to get him off as quickly as she could to give her stretched throat a reprieve.

The slick, thick gift of his milk hit the back of her tongue and he surged in so deep, she tried to scramble for air, but he went farther. If she wasn't used to the filth that came out of his mouth on climax, she might have blushed.

As it was, all she felt was relief when his now softening cock broke the seal it had formed to block her windpipe.

"Jeez," he said, taking time to level his breathing out, just as she had to.

Sliding his hands up to lock their fingers together, he dragged her hands up the wall, pressing his body into hers for support and urging her arms farther until they were stretched high above her head and she was on her feet.

"Five for dinner," he said, kissing her hairline. "Have we got enough food?"

She struggled to remember her name, let alone think about tonight's menu. "Food," she murmured, dragging in a ragged breath. "That's what you're thinking about?"

"We haven't all just eaten," he said, making eye contact while trailing a hand down her arm, over her breast to her stomach where he pulled up her shirt to massage her taut tummy. "Nice to know my guys are swimming around in there, filling you up."

And she liked to see that he wasn't wallowing in his grief anymore. Getting over Art's death would be an ongoing process, but it was reassuring that the severed connection had had such a profound bearing on her love. It proved his ability to feel at that depth and meant he had the potential to feel that strongly about her. Although their relationship seemed assured, she had never received any concrete confirmation from him that she meant anything to him beyond being a fuck buddy with exclusive rights.

Art had let her into this house, encouraged their relationship, and then died. She had to wonder if without Art's impetus their relationship would die too. Brodie would eventually get bored of screwing her if there was nothing more than sex between them, and then she'd have her answer. That day could come tomorrow, next week, or next year. Until he declared his feelings, she'd be in the dark.

He retreated enough to fondle her breasts, bent to kiss her cleavage, then with his fingertips on her cheekbone, he made her look at him.

"Dress nice for dinner,' he said. "You'll want to make a good impression."

Tucking himself back into his jeans, he snagged a tee shirt and left her alone. So she was supposed to dress nice, but he was dressed as he always was, so he couldn't mean that this was a black-tie affair. She'd never seen him in a suit or anything formal. After he'd issued these cryptic clues, she was more intrigued about this night than ever.

***

MAKING DINNER WAS the easiest part of the night. While doing it, she speculated about who they might be dining with. Art had told her only six people had set foot in this house since Brodie inherited it. Of those six, she only knew four: Brodie, Art, Tuck, and herself. That left two vacant spots.

The Kindred included those four and the other two aliases she'd heard were Falcon and Wren, neither of whom she'd met. Falcon's real name was Zave, and Wren's was Thad, she knew that much. She also knew that they were cousins to each other and to Brodie. Other than that, she wasn't too sure how they all fit together. Zave's special skill was hardware, Brodie had told her that once. Wren's contribution was a little murkier. But these people were important to Brodie and so they were important to her.

At regular intervals, she glanced back toward the kitchen door, expecting strangers to walk in at any minute. They never did. She had just come upstairs from the cellar with the wine when the kitchen door opened and Tuck came in.

"Hello," she said, pleased to see a friend. "You're just in time." Handing him the bottle, she pulled the corkscrew from a drawer and put it on the counter before going back to the stove to stir the sauce. "What time are the guests arriving?"

"Everyone is already here, come on," he said, putting the bottle aside with the corkscrew. Following her to the stove, he stretched an arm out to snag her shoulder before sliding it all the way around her. Urging her away from her task, Tuck pulled her toward the door.

"Where are we going?" she asked, dropping the spoon into the pot, and shuffling along beside him.

"It's time to meet everyone," Tuck said.

When they ate as a group at the manor, they always ate at the kitchen island. Apparently, this time it was going to be different. Instead of everyone coming to her in the kitchen, as she'd expected them to, the dinner party was going on elsewhere.

Tuck took her out of the kitchen, down the hallway, and bypassed the grand entranceway of the house to take her to a room tucked in the back corner of the building, right near the high rocky shore. The massive windows on the far wall of this formal dining room displayed a view of the rain and the angry sea. Brodie was staring out at the scene with his back to the room. But she was more interested in the men around the circular black table, which was big enough for ten, but only set for five.

The two men seated at the table stood up. The shorter one, who was only a couple of inches shorter, was wearing a wide smile. But the other man, whose hair and eyes were black as night, was wearing a scowl that made her shrink and search out Tuck's hand.

He patted the back of it and led her toward the table wearing a smile, which she was sure showed amusement at her expense. "You know Bess from the camera downstairs?" Tuck asked.

There was no other woman in this room, but Zara knew who he was referring to. Bess was the woman who frequently popped onto one of the screens in the main security room downstairs in Tuck's favorite part of the lair. Bess was Art's younger sister and, as far as Zara could tell, she lived in the manor's sister house. Built as the second of a pair by Grant McCormack Senior.

"I know Bess," Zara said, having had many conversations with her during Brodie's dark hours. Having someone to talk to, a friend, was invaluable. Bess was grieving her brother and didn't appear to have much, if any, female outlet.

"She's my mother," the shorter man said, coming around the table toward them.

Relaxing, she couldn't be intimidated by his ease. "You're Thad," Zara said, tilting her head to receive his kiss on her cheek.

Tuck left her side to go to Brodie, who was still staring

at the blackness beyond the window with a hand propped on the window frame high above his head. Zave gave her the once over, said nothing, and followed Tuck to Brodie's side.

"You'll have to forgive my cousins and their penchant for brooding," Thad said, putting an arm around her to look at the men she was watching. "I'm told it's what comes with superior intellect. At least that's true in Zave's case. I don't know what Brodie's excuse is."

"Physical prowess," she said and was charmed when Thad laughed without hesitation.

The three men by the window were mumbling to each other about something, making no apology for excluding her and Thad. None reacted or seemed to hear her and Thad's comments.

Thad had to be used to the snub, because he didn't even pause to await a reaction from the trio. "I understand you're making dinner," he said, and she nodded. Preoccupied by the men at the window, she wanted to know what they were talking about but was hesitant to inject herself into the conversation in case it wasn't Kindred related. "Do you need any help?"

She hadn't given a lot of thought to what the rest of Brodie's family would be like. Though if she had, she wouldn't have pegged any of them to be as jolly and approachable as Thad seemed to be.

Accepting his offer, they left the three others to their whispering and went into the kitchen where she began to prepare the pasta. Thad stirred the meatballs into the sauce and took a drip from the spoon into his mouth.

"Mm, this is excellent. It's almost as good as Uncle Art's," Thad said, stealing another taste.

She smiled and put a lid on the pot. "It is Uncle Art's," she admitted and began to uncork the wine Tuck had abandoned earlier. "It's the last of his sauce from the freezer. I supposed this was a special occasion. We don't often have guests."

"You're good for Brodie," Thad said, taking wine glasses from the cabinet to bring them to her. She poured out the liquid and seated herself with him at the lower part of the kitchen island. "I can tell that already."

"Art thought so," she said, sampling the rich red wine.

Thad had light brown hair and boyish looks, he was happy and open, and everything the rest of the clan wasn't. But he made a good first impression. "It's good that you met him and that you got to know him before…" The glow of his smile dimmed and he grew wary, like he was worried he'd made a misstep, although he probably carried grief of his own over losing his Uncle Art.

She missed Art but couldn't claim to have the same ownership over the grief the cousins shared. "He was a good man who didn't deserve to die in the way that he did." Not that he deserved to die at all. Art had the cleanest hands of all those involved in the Game Time project.

He relaxed into another smile; it was his default mode. "I meant it's good that you got to know Brodie before Art died. Zave said he's been going through a dark time but that you've stuck by him, even though it's been rough. You're a tough cookie to take on Brodie and all his shit. Though I have to say, it's understandable that Art's death hit him this hard given how close they were, they were sort of codependent, I guess you could say."

She appreciated that her loyalty had been noted by the others, but Thad was talking about things she knew and she wanted to use this chance to gain new information. "Like you and Zave?" she asked, placing her glass on the tile to leave her stool and check on the food.

He laughed. "No, I wish. I'm utterly dependent on him, and everybody knows it too."

She retrieved a serving dish and put it in the oven to warm. Hearing him declare himself dependent on Zave, without any indication of it being a reciprocal dependence, was unexpected. But it didn't upset or shame him, there was no male bravado interfering trying to cover up the truth. Thad's smile came back with a vengeance and he swigged more wine.

Zave would be a tough nut to crack, getting to know him would be impossible given that he didn't say much. "He seems…" She couldn't put words to the impression that Zave gave. "What's his story?"

"It's a long one," Thad said and as frustrating as his discretion was, it was also admirable. "What has Brodie told you about what we do?"

"Very little," she said when the truth was he'd told her nothing. What she knew of Brodie's cousins came from Bess and Art. "I know you're all part of the Kindred."

"And so are you," Thad said, raising his glass in congratulations before he became serious. "That's why we're here. Brodie needs to plan this op to take Sutcliffe down, and for the first time we don't have Art checking us all. I think we'll close ranks for a while, work closer until we're steady on our feet again."

She appreciated that none of the men would openly ask one another for help in an admission that they couldn't cope. But Brodie had to have called this meeting on the back of what had happened to her in Purdy's and with Sutcliffe. Zave and Thad had dropped everything to be here, proving that they stood by Kindred Priority One.

Having support from their corner meant a lot to her, as it would to Brodie. "I appreciate you being here for Brodie, and I'm sorry for the loss of your uncle," she said.

"We're here to make sure we don't lose anyone else," he said, picking up his wineglass and hers. "How is the food coming? Brodie will kick my ass if I'm alone with his girlfriend for too long."

Thad could do serious, but not for too long it seemed. So she shifted away from the solemn and prepped the food for serving, while Thad took their glasses and the wine through to the dining room. He came back to help her take the food and plates through to the table where she served food for everyone and took her own seat.

TWELVE

DINNER STARTED QUIETLY. Brodie, Tuck, and Zave sat down leaving an empty chair on each side of themselves, so everyone had plenty of elbow room. Thad poured wine for everyone except Zave and topped off her glass, and she was pleased to see that their new guests were much more aware of table manners than Brodie was, or Art had been. She was just seating herself after retrieving a second bottle of wine when Thad spoke to her.

Everyone else was eating, but Thad was looking at her. "So, Zara, you work for Saint Grant?" Thad asked. "I haven't seen him since I was a kid, in diapers probably, how is he?"

Grant hadn't been a fan of Art's, which she guessed extended into Art's siblings. He hadn't made an effort to get to know Brodie and had ignored his cousins. Though there was nothing stopping those cousins from trying to get into his life now. If the cousins made friends, she should get a reprieve from her covert work at CI where she was trying to wheedle information out of a boss who didn't trust her.

"I think he might appreciate a call from his cousin," she said, slurping the sauce from her fork. It was possible that Grant knew nothing of his cousins' health, just as it seemed he was in the dark about Brodie's before the Game Time debacle. "Or does he think you're both dead too?"

Thad laughed, and Zave didn't show any signs he'd heard her, or that he bothered to listen when she'd spoken. "He knows we're alive… at least, I'd guess he does." Thad turned his blank expression to Brodie. "Does he?"

Her love was distracted, but at least he answered. "Far as I know," Brodie said, reaching for his wine to clear the food from his mouth with the liquid. "You'll have to forgive Zara's tone. She's protective of her shining knight. He can do nothing wrong in her eyes."

Though he grumbled most of the words, Brodie was eloquent. Sometimes she forgot that he'd been raised in high society. Art had erased most traces of that aspect of his upbringing, but every once in a while, glimmers of it shone through his gruff countenance. After that declaration though, she wasn't in the mood to give him credit for anything.

She'd gotten over her notions of Grant's virtue long ago. "He can do plenty wrong and he has," she said, guessing that Brodie was still smarting over the conversation he'd overheard her and Grant having that afternoon through the bug he'd planted. "That doesn't mean I have to automatically think the rest of you are saints. I chose your side when it came to Game Time, didn't I?"

Thad stopped eating to lean nearer to her. "We saw Brodie all the time when we were growing up," Thad said. "Him and Zave were closer back then. Back when Zave's life was nothing but sex and excess."

"She doesn't need another history lesson," Brodie muttered, probably fed up with others educating her on his past. Art did it. Grant did it. Even Tuck had let her in on a few tidbits.

But she didn't waste her time examining Brodie's irritation; she knew what that looked like. She watched Zave, the bored man who ate his food and said nothing to anyone while managing to convey how unimpressed he was all at the same time.

She struggled to imagine how he might seduce a woman or indulge in anything. It was clear that simple pleasures weren't enough for him. Maybe he had to be coked up before he had the inclination to talk. It wasn't any lack of confidence that kept him quiet, he sure didn't look shy. He sat straight, focused on the task in front of him, and slighted everything else.

His jet-black hair and the stubble on his face didn't make him look unkempt. He just didn't seem to care much for meticulous grooming. He wasn't unattractive and she wondered if maybe women on the west coast were happy to jump to attention for a man when he snapped his fingers just because he had a square jaw and alluring eyes. Zave didn't have the social skills to manipulate a woman into bed with him that was for sure, he'd have to be willing to talk to her for that to be possible.

When no one responded to what Thad had said he released a meek laugh and carried on. "I guess we've changed since then," he said. Leaning closer still, he made eye contact, "Zave doesn't talk about those days anymore."

Brodie didn't like to talk about his personal history either. "We are not here to talk about the past," Brodie piped up. "We're here to talk about Sutcliffe, Saint, and what to do about the mess he created for us."

The mess wasn't entirely Grant's fault. Zara realized that it wasn't the time to point that out to Brodie, not while he was sitting with his brothers-in-arms wearing his game face. Zave put his fork on the table and took his napkin from his lap, signaling that he'd finished eating, even though his plate wasn't empty.

That had to be some sort of signal for Thad because he sat up straight and stopped smiling. "Where are we at?" Thad asked. "We know Sutcliffe is out for payback."

"Payback," Tuck said. "For the murder of his nephew, or because he didn't get the product he was so intent on using to kill hundreds of people?"

"Sutcliffe doesn't want to kill," Zave said, and she was so surprised by the sound of his deep voice that she almost didn't process what he'd said.

When she did, she was sort of offended by his comment because the only use Sutcliffe had for Game Time was to use it for harm. "So what does he want?" she asked.

Zave picked up his glass, swirled the water in it, and let it slide down his throat, taking his sweet time before answering her question. "Attention," Zave answered.

Thad swallowed a meatball and linked his hands over his plate. "He's right. I would agree with that. Sutcliffe only wants to kill those who don't support him. But he wants to increase his ranks in the meantime. Purdy's had to be a recruitment drive; Sutcliffe wants the world to know what he's doing in hopes that droves will show up to support him."

"Or it's training," Tuck said. "The gang fell apart the minute they lost their leader. This wasn't a squadron of pros."

She was impressed that these men had done their research. Discussions had obviously gone on without her, everyone was briefed and up to speed. Zara was just glad to be keeping up.

"So what do we do?" she asked. "Do we worry about him training his army or him getting his hands on Game Time? He can't get his hands on the device while we have it. But Grant wants it back, he asked me for it today and put me on a two week deadline." The men looked at each other, bypassing her. "Grant trusts Sutcliffe too and I think he wants to be a bigger part of whatever he's doing. But we can't trust Sutcliffe, he's already killed Grant's housekeeper and his VP. Grant could be next." Their reaction to this would be the litmus test for their views on what to do with Grant during and at the end of this mission.

"There's no evidence that Grant is his primary target," Zave said. "If he's building more devices, I'd say Sutcliffe and Saint are allies."

Grant had admitted to commissioning Winter Chill again. If that got up to speed, they could have a conveyer belt of Game Time devices rolling twenty-four, seven. But that obviously wasn't their main concern because she was the only one to bring up Game Time so far.

"So who is his primary target?" she asked, trying to gauge the stony faces surrounding her.

"We don't know," Tuck answered. "That's why we have to find out what his primary motive is. If it's revenge for Tim's death, then it's Brodie he wants. If it's the embarrassment of being setup, then it's you."

They were right. Protecting the Kindred had to be their priority, because if anything happened to them, there would be no one trying to stop Sutcliffe until it was too late. "Do you think he'll hurt Grant after he gets the device from him?" she asked because she and Brodie had protection, Grant was the little lamb trotting into the wolf's mouth. He gave all of his faith to Sutcliffe when Sutcliffe was not an honorable man.

The brooders kept on brooding, leaving Thad to respond to her. "If he's pissed at Grant for what happened in the Atlas warehouse? Yeah, he will. He never would've been in the position to lose his men and be injured if it wasn't for Grant," Thad said. "Grant sold him a Bill of Goods. Sutcliffe is probably wary about Grant's promises to deliver. Especially since Grant is working from scratch, so it's going to take him a long time to come up with the product. Sutcliffe believed that this device, that Game Time, could change the world, could change his life. The man built a dream on that idea and then it all went pear-shaped."

So he was embarrassed, dejected, and grief-stricken. Zara looked down at her plate. As delicious as the food appeared, she no longer had an appetite and so as Zave had done, she took her napkin from her thigh, put it on the table, and sat back to fold her arms.

"Okay," she asked. "So how do we placate him? We have two major problems, his desire for revenge, and his plot with Game Time—whatever that may be."

Zave made eye contact with Brodie, who then looked to Tuck. Thad seemed to be as clueless as she was and she began to wonder at his purpose. Why was he a member of the Kindred when he clearly didn't have the skill or the savvy that these other men did?

"That's where you come in, Swallow," Tuck said, making eye contact with Zave and Brodie again.

"Me?" she asked and when none of the men would look her in the eye, hers narrowed with suspicion. Her sinuses tingled and fingers chilled. "You're going to send me into the fire again, aren't you?"

Affronted, Brodie landed her in his sights. "You never

went into the fire in the first place," Brodie said. "And if you believe that you did for a second then you don't belong at this table."

She was getting impatient with the way he kept dismissing her tonight, snapping and disrespecting her. He had something to say, or he had something on his mind, and it was about time he got it off his chest or shut up about it for good. But that was an argument she would save for later when they were alone.

"Okay. But I'm going to suggest something obvious, like asking Grant or approaching Sutcliffe and you… one of you is going to suggest something ridiculous like hiring a hot air balloon and buying radioactive tracking devices that we'll shoot from a harpoon into some obscure bacteria carried in our bodies or—"

"Enough," Brodie said. "Nothing obscure."

"We're gonna take a trip," Tuck said.

"A trip?" she asked. "Where are we going?"

"Not you," Brodie said. "You're staying here."

She didn't want to be cut out of the loop, but no one questioned his deadpan command and Tuck carried on. "We're gonna stakeout Sutcliffe and find out what we can about his property," he said. "We have to find a way in."

"A way in?" she said, almost disbelieving her ears. As far as she was concerned, the idea was to uproot and oust Sutcliffe, not get cozy in his house.

"Grant is Sutcliffe's bitch," Brodie said. "He's useless to us. He can tuck tail and run. I met the fancy security guys he hired to take a bullet for him when I was outside CI listening to the bugs earlier today."

Now she knew where the bruise on his chin had come from and it annoyed her that Grant might have sent these guys for Brodie if he noticed him loitering outside. It seemed so cowardly to send others, rather than face his own brother.

Grant hadn't even told her that there were more men prowling around the building than usual, which was probably a deliberate choice on her boss's part. "He hired extra security?" she asked.

"Personal security," Brodie said. From the disgust

plastered on his face, she'd guess if he could physically spit on the ground then he would have done it. "He hired Griffin Caine."

Brodie's nemesis. Zara was surprised by that revelation and wished that Brodie had told her about it in the closet earlier when they were alone. "Just like him to insinuate himself into something like this," Tuck said.

The men fixated on her and said nothing, which made her squirm. She'd suppose that's why Brodie was in such a shitty mood and what he, Zave, and Tuck had been whispering about at the window.

"I don't care," Brodie said, breaking the silence. "As long as Caine is keeping Saint safe, he's not watching what we're doing, is he? And we don't care if he fails the mission."

The others snickered, but she was distracted by that idea, what would happen if someone hurt Grant, if someone killed him? What would happen to Sutcliffe's plot? To CI? And how would Brodie deal with losing another relative, no matter how distant the relationship was?

"You're right," Tuck said and his words brought her back to the present. "We can forget about Caine, he's been biting our heels so long I'm sort of used to it."

Brodie took charge. "We eliminate threats. That's what we do. Sutcliffe and his cult are a danger to the Kindred. We don't have to make this more complicated than that."

It made sense, but she didn't like to see that detached scowl on his face when she'd just managed to chase it away. "And you believe that Sutcliffe is going to come after you?" she asked.

Brodie wasn't the type to be scared of anything, but she could understand him wanting to take the fight to Sutcliffe rather than to sit on his ass and wait for the maniac to pounce on him. Still, she was terrified about what would happen in a direct confrontation. Sutcliffe had killed Art just to distract those that might pursue him and thwart his escape. She couldn't lose Brodie. She just couldn't.

"He's coming after you," Brodie said. He was still sullen, but on discovering that some of his crappy mood came from his concern for her well-being, her heart lightened. "That's enough reason for me to hand him his ass."

"Young love," Thad said with a theatrical sigh that earned him a glare from Brodie.

Hiding her own smile, she estimated that Thad was younger than everyone else at the table. He was the most fresh faced at any rate and seemed the most optimistic.

Ignoring Thad, Tuck was the most mission minded and brought them back to point. "We can leave in the morning," Tuck said. "Zave and I will put the gear together tonight."

Thad wasn't back to serious yet. "Get ready to get your geek on," Thad muttered from the corner of his mouth, then sloped his body toward her. "When those two get together in any room with tech, they always come up with new gadgets."

"You complaining?" Tuck asked with raised brows as he cleaned his plate. "You love playing with toys. I just made a fresh batch of chips. They're all ready for programming. What will we make them do, Falc?"

Thad was beyond caring about the mission, or the prep needed for it. He extended his arms high over his head to stretch. "I thought I might get the chance to pry some money out of you fellas," he said, straining his voice when he overextended. "I brought cash."

The others at the table snickered and she enjoyed seeing them relax into a banter with each other. "You may as well hand it over," Brodie said. "Have you ever won a poker night?"

He straightened up, exuding triumph. "I've been practicing," Thad said, not dejected by the jibe. "I got a league going at the hospital."

Her smile faltered over this new fact. "Hospital?" she asked

"Thad is a real MD," Brodie explained.

"Yeah," Thad said. "You and I are the only two with real jobs around here, Zara. We've got to carry the rest of them, teach them responsibility, you know."

Zave was impossible to get a measure of, she'd try to get more of his story from Brodie, and then try to draw some conclusions. Whereas Thad was as normal as they came, and in their bleak lives, that was something real.

While everyone was in a good mood, she probed further. "Do you live with Zave and Bess on the island?" she asked.

"My mom stays with me sometimes, when she wants to go shopping or take in a show," Thad said, propping his elbows on the table to rest his chin on his joined hands. "I have an apartment in Seattle. It's the only way I can hold down a job. And parking the chopper at the hospital everyday would be cost prohibitive."

Her intake of breath was almost childish glee because she hadn't expected that incredible revelation. "You have a helicopter?"

He appeared as happy about it as she was. "Zave does," Thad said, nodding his way. "But we both fly."

Turning her wondrous eyes on Brodie, she begged for a trip without words because her previous experience with a helicopter carried negative connotations, she'd like to try it without the threat of impending trauma hanging over her head.

Brodie sighed. "Can we fix this mess before you leave me for another guy just 'cause he has a better ride?"

Though his tone was dry, she suspected he was teasing, and so showed her teeth in a wide smile as she slunk out of her chair to creep around to him. "Baby, I wouldn't trade your ride for anything," she purred, and he accepted her onto his lap when she pressured her hand on his shoulder. "You know what seeing you on your bike does to me." Nuzzling him, she kissed his cheek then the corner of his mouth.

"Yeah, she's easy to please," he said, scooping one arm around her torso and sliding a hand up her skirt. She kept placing short, soft kisses on his face.

"How do you get the bike into the bedroom?" Thad asked.

"Who needs a bedroom?" Brodie asked, prying her legs further apart and increasing the urgency of his intemperate groping.

Taking her mouth away from his before he could take control of their kiss. She couldn't be too eager for him because if he were in the mood, he would deliver what she wanted, and not give a crap about their audience.

"While we have this many guests we do," she said, disappointed and trying without success to remove his hand from her leg. If he got where he was going, she might have to drag him away from their guests. Dinner was basically over and she had some paperwork to do. Giving Brodie and the boys a chance to bond without a female spying on them would hopefully give her love another boost of progress in his recovery from isolation. "Are you staying down here with the boys or are you in the mood for some private entertainment?"

"You can't go to bed, not yet," Thad said. "We just got here." Scanning the room, he laughed. "Though being here isn't far from being at home."

Zave's house on the west coast island was a duplicate of this one and it had to be strange to travel to a place that was identical to the one you'd departed from, even though they were on opposite sides of the country.

"I'd love to come and visit your place one day," she said, circling her arms around Brodie's neck.

"Zave's place," Thad said. "And mom would have you in a heartbeat. She loves to spoil guests."

Odd that Zave should have people in his house when he was even less social than Brodie. "So you don't have the same aversion to visitors that my man does?"

Thad laughed again. "Zave despises people," he said. "But he has regular… lodgers."

Being cryptic must be a Kindred requirement because she was confused. "Lodgers?" None of the men offered further explanation. "Is this something to do with your custom suite?"

"Right, baby, that's enough," Brodie said, boosting her off his lap and smacking her ass. "Go on up to bed. I'll come up soon."

Art gave her answers. The rest of them just gave her more questions. But one of the first things Art had taught her was not to corner Brodie in company.

There was still food on the table and these were active men, so they'd probably eat more, giving her a reprieve from clean up duty.

"Okay," she said and bent to kiss him.

Having a night with the boys would level his mood and his thinking. Passing Zave without acknowledgement, she welcomed Tuck's hand on her waist when she dipped to kiss his cheek.

"You need anything?" Tuck asked, looking her in the eye.

"No, just look after him."

"Do I get a kiss?" Thad asked.

She got as far as a smile, Brodie got to speaking before she did. "Not a chance, Wren. And none of that, 'I'm a doctor so I see the naked form all the time' either. Go to bed, baby."

It was nice that he was possessive; she just wished she knew what it meant. After Art, she gave Brodie space to grieve. Now that he was coming out the other side of that grief and had a job to focus on, Zara wasn't going to let their relationship be sidelined and that meant she'd have to be proactive about going after what she wanted.

THIRTEEN

SHE WATCHED TV in the bedroom for a while after completing her paperwork and returned some emails from Brodie's laptop, which was security protected up the wazoo. No one would be able to trace her email origin from that machine. After that, she took the opportunity to soak in the tub before wrapping herself in the blankets on the warm bed.

Zara had no clue of the time when she stirred to the taste of liquor-flavored kisses and his heavy hand resting on her pubis while his fingers massaged her clit.

"Come on, pretty baby. Wake up," he mumbled on her mouth and his weight covered her when she turned onto her back.

"Baby," she grumbled and tried to clear her throat, but his tongue coaxed its way into her mouth. Surrendering to the inevitable, she dug her nails in and returned his kiss.

"You want me to stop?" he asked, lifting his body to shove the covers out from between them.

"Even if I say yes, you should keep going."

His gruff laugh fogged the air between their mouths. He pulled her legs apart and slid a finger into her as he took his home position between her thighs. "That's what I love about you, baby, you mix it up and keep me guessing."

She kept him guessing? The idea made her freeze for half a beat. But his fingers slipped out from inside her and he pressured one inner her thigh at the same time his belt buckle clinked. Zara opened her legs for him and pushed her shoulders back in blissful anticipation of his mouth arriving on her naked body. But before she could fall into the embrace of the ecstasy he usually offered in bed, he brushed his lips across her cheekbone to settle them against her ear.

"Why are you still here?"

The whispered question jarred her from the welcome haze of sleep and hormones, and she tried to push him back enough so that she could look him in the eye to judge just how drunk he was. But he didn't stay close, and she frowned when he reared back and sat in the center of the bed.

"What are you talking about?" she asked, using her fists to bring herself upright.

Rubbing his jaw, he inhaled and his drowsy eyes betrayed that he was intoxicated. "You shouldn't be here," he said and his hand left his face to float toward hers, but before he could make contact, it fell away.

She was no stranger to Drunk Brodie. She'd met him on a night she'd feared they would never recover from—the night of Art's death. Since then he'd been a regular visitor. Sometimes Drunk Brodie just went quiet and got pensive. Other times, he got violent. Never toward her, he focused his rage on something inanimate that she had to rescue from being annihilated. Those times did lead to some rather physical fuck sessions. On rare occasions, like this one was shaping up to be, he would talk.

Any conversation about their relationship was one that she wanted to be a part of. Sober Brodie was an honest guy who knew how to keep secrets. Drunk Brodie didn't have the same filters. "Don't talk crazy," she said, tossing the bunched covers away with the intention of kneeling up, but he snatched the corner she'd just cast aside and threw it over her to cover her naked body. "What is wrong with you?"

He wasn't feeling sorry for himself or fishing for compliments, he was pissed at her and at himself. He was most comfortable being angry or aggressive, so those seemed to be his go-to places. But he'd never had a problem with her naked form being on show in his bedroom before.

"I treat you like shit," he grumbled.

"No, you don't," she said, scooting her ass down enough that she could squeeze her hand over his on the bed. "You're grieving."

His glower made him look dangerous and she wondered if Drunk Brodie was still a crack shot. "Which only makes this relationship crazier," he said, shaking his head and running a hand over his hair to clench his fist at the back of his neck. "I was a bastard before... now I ain't got nothing to keep me sane."

That he was being this honest about his insecurities made her feel closer to him. If this was going to last, he had to be transparent and prove he trusted her more than anyone, even more than the other Kindred members.

"You've got me," she said, slipping her hand up his arm to cup his face. She rose onto her knees and kissed him. "I'll keep you sane."

"And I'll drive you insane," he said.

For a quarter of a year, she'd worried about him, his health, his sanity, his eating habits; now he was proving he was putting her ahead of all those needs. The sentiment was touching, but she wasn't going to give up her responsibilities. She wanted to look after this man, to value him above everything else because when he was ready, and if he chose her, he'd exalt her welfare up into a stratosphere beyond any she could reach.

"I am not going to let you self-destruct," she whispered, trying to bolster him. "I know you're a good man."

He whipped his hand out from under hers then shifted away to sit on the far edge of the bed with his back to her. "You don't know me," he mumbled. "You don't get it... you don't get it at all."

Climbing out from beneath the covers, she crawled over to hook both arms around him from behind and then hung over his shoulder to kiss his cheek. "I want to get it," she said. "I promised Art that I wouldn't let you push me away."

An idea struck her while he was reflecting on her words.

She jumped off the bed to head for the closet, but he caught her wrist and she ricocheted back, sinking to her knees between his feet.

He was scowling. "When did you tell him that?"

"On the day we lost him," she said. "Tuck told me that he and Art talked about us, he said you lied about Quebec to push me away."

He flung her wrist out of his grip. "Nice to know you all enjoyed gossiping."

Slapping her hands onto his thighs, she straightened her legs to stand but stayed bent so she could kiss him, but he didn't return her kiss. He pushed her aside and got to his feet.

"You think I don't know you?" she asked, folding her arms, she considered him as he strode away toward the door.

He paused and his voice became clearer than it had been. "I think you have limited experience. I'm bad for you."

Considering this, she concluded he could be right, but this wasn't the first time she'd thought about what her future with him would be. She'd spent plenty of time alone with him, in bed, and here in his house. She knew his brother and his upbringing. She knew he'd killed… but she hadn't seen him in action or heard his life story in his own words.

And just like every time she'd contemplated what lay ahead for them, she came to the same conclusion. "I'm willing to take that risk," she said, eager to follow through on her idea that might shake him out of his funk. "Stay here."

She went into their walk-in closet and wrapped herself in her calf-length wool coat. Fastening all the buttons, she hurried out of the closet to join him in the bedroom again and was pleased to see he was still here. Snagging his hand as she passed him to head for the door, he followed her out of the bedroom, but his lumbering pace slowed her down.

"Where the fuck are we going?" he asked her and didn't sound happy that she'd taken them out of his room.

The house was spooky at night, but she didn't fear the shadows. This building was her nest now and the safest place she had ever known.

Peeking over her shoulder, she let her coquettish smile tempt him and she let go of his hand. "You want to play with me, baby? You've got to catch me first."

Hurrying to the stairway, she ran down the black space without confirmation he was coming after her. But he was curious and horny and he liked to be the one with the secrets, so it was doubtful he'd let her keep any of her own.

She got to the parking garage and used her fingerprint to gain entry through the internal door and to open the main garage door. While the motor was working to raise it, she ran over to the key cabinet and snagged the keys she wanted.

It was when she turned to cross to the car that the sight of him in the center of the space made her stop to catch her breath. His broad body was intimidating in a room filled with night and if it wasn't for her determination, she would fall to her knees and seduce him right here.

He seemed to have the same idea because when she strutted toward the car, he caught her and tried to pull her into his arms. "Let's go back upstairs, baby. I'm gonna fuck you so good—"

"No," she said, trying her best to stay strong. "I want to take you somewhere."

"I'm gonna take you right here," he said. Picking her up, he carried her across the room and dropped her to push her backwards over the hood of one of their vehicles. "Just bend over there, nice and easy."

Wrestling her over onto her front, he used his lower body to pin hers against the grill and rested his weight on his forearm on her back to hold her down. He loosened his belt and the descent of his zip echoed in this vast concrete cavern.

"Baby, you're gonna love this," he murmured. "I'm gonna fill you up. You're gonna take my dick deep in that pussy, you'll be branded for life."

"Brodie," she said, trying unsuccessfully to move. "Baby, I want to take you somewhere. Can we get in the car then—"

"Shut it," he snapped and yanked her coat up to find she was bare beneath it. "Well, you dirty girl. You were ready for it, weren't you? You've been thinking of my hard cock fucking you fast."

He was more than horny, he was deep in the throng of blind desire. "Always," she said, writhing against the hand he was fondling over her ass. Although she was dedicated to fulfilling her idea, she wasn't ignorant to his persistence and any time that he wanted her this much, she was controlled by her own need to satisfy his body.

With an open hand he smacked her twice, then twice more, and the joy of the burn made her suck in a breath through her teeth.

He bent his body over hers to growl his words into her hair. "You don't run away from me again. You heel, you kneel, you come. You do what I say."

The primal tone and meaning of his words sent blood to all the right places in her and she breathed his name. Logic didn't feature when they were this far into the throng of arousal.

He stopped caressing her ass and spanked her again before the thick lump of his dick pushed its way through until it impelled itself into her. The sting of his mass made her pant, she hadn't been quite prepared for his entry, but he didn't notice, he drove his way into her.

The cool metal under her cheek didn't lower the temperature of her body that was shunted forth every time he drove into her. He grunted and shoved in deeper, his engorged cock stayed in place as he rocked his hips, testing the limits of her capacity. She cried out and he continued to pulsate within her.

Grinding himself further, he forced her to take him to the hilt. Crammed so full, she yelped and gasped in a breath, but when she tried to turn, he pressed a palm onto her cheekbone and held her down, covering her eye.

"You choke my cock with your cramped little pussy," he said, working himself side to side. "You tense, baby? You're real tight tonight."

He smacked her hard and ran his hand up between her cheeks where he pressed the tip of his thumb into her ass. Wriggling up to explore this new sensation, he let it edge a little farther then grumbled an exhale of his own arousal that didn't quite become words. Dragging his hips back, he slammed into her, keeping hold of her ass as he jolted in and out of her until a minute or so later, he swore, smacked her ass, and then staggered back.

Trying to remember where she was and where she wanted them to go, Zara remained on her face with her eyes closed while she absorbed the tingles of unsated arousal.

"Baby?"

His voice was right behind her. He ran a rough hand up the back of her quivering thigh and pulled her coat down to cover her. Still on the brink of her own climax, she squirmed in the covering of soft fabric. She was tempted to slide her hand down her body to finish the job he started.

"We're going back upstairs," he said and seized her wrist, but she pulled back when he tried to tug her toward the stairway.

Even though things had gone further down here than she'd expected, she still wanted to follow through on her plan. "Come with me," she said, rounding her eyes when he turned back to look at her. The irritation on his face wasn't mirrored by his grip because when she backed away, her arm fell out of his hand.

"Where the fuck you want to go?" he asked, opening his arms.

But she wasn't going to tell him, she reversed and kept her eyes on his until she got to the car. She unlocked it and opened the driver's door and only then did he loosen in concession.

"We'll take the bike."

"You've been drinking," she said. "We're going in the car."

Ducking down, she got inside and started the engine. Before she even got the headlights on, he climbed in the passenger side door with a gun in his hand.

"What do you need that for?" she asked, aware that there were weapons stashed in the garage and all over the house and probably the grounds too.

"Don't know yet," he muttered with a shrug that moved the gun up and down his thigh. "I like to be prepared."

FOURTEEN

HE RECLINED HIS SEAT and stretched out while she navigated the car out of the garage. She drove and he locked his fingers behind his head. When she glanced back, his eyes were closed.

"Don't go to sleep," she said, prodding his thigh with a sharp fingernail next to where the gun rested. "It's dark and I might get lost."

They used the main gate so rarely that it was a possibility. But she'd spent time walking around, exploring, and was familiar with most of the footpaths in daylight. At night, the environment became much more daunting, and the landmarks were hidden by black shadows and shrouding foliage making them difficult to distinguish. The grounds were vast, driving in them was like driving in the countryside, yet they were on the threshold of the city. Living here, they had the best of both worlds.

He didn't even flinch. "As long as you don't drive into the ocean, we're fine. You can swim, right?"

Concerned that she could hit a beast and of what would come of them if she went off the beaten trail, she scrutinized the sinister shapes around them. "Are there wild animals out here?" she asked. Brodie did next to nothing to tend the grounds. The whole place was basically a natural habitat for anything that wanted to live in the woods nestled by the shielding cliff.

"Other than me?" he asked, cracking one eye open for a brief moment and putting the gun in the door well so he could twist into a comfortable position. Although he was joking, she did relax. Brodie could handle anything that came at them and he was armed, making him virtually invincible.

Zara did manage to find the gate and used the fingerprint pad under the steering wheel to unlock it wirelessly. This was the first time she had ever driven herself out the gate and her heart hammered the whole time. It was odd, but the pressure of ensuring they weren't seen and that the gate closed behind them made her think of Art.

He watched over his flock and even though he wasn't here, she didn't want to let him down. She still missed him, his guiding hand, and his help with Brodie. Art was easy to talk to and he was honest. Without him, it was her responsibility to try to cultivate that kind of openness with Brodie and she had no one to help her.

Since he was drunk and she wanted him to open up, she took advantage of him. "Have you killed anyone for free?" she asked, trying to prove to him that she wanted to be a part of every part of his life, even the parts he'd withheld from her thus far.

"Yeah, your last boyfriend," he muttered, still snoozing in his reclined seat.

"Vince?" she asked, wondering how and when he'd gotten to her ex.

He sat up and grabbed the back of her neck, drawing her attention to his glare. "I meant the fucker Tim Sutcliffe. Who the hell is Vince? What's his social security number?"

"Do I know your social security number?" she asked. Her lover was easily riled and she was learning that she didn't have to mimic that quality in order to be with him, so she remained calm, finding that was the best way to temper his outbursts. Though her actual question was moot because he probably didn't have a real social security number. Whether he did or not would remain a mystery because he was too busy scowling at her to answer. "It's not a question I ask before sleeping with a man is my point. It sorta kills the mood." She didn't even know Brodie's real name before sleeping with him.

"I'll find him," he grumbled and settled back in his seat.

She exhaled a laugh and focused on the road. "Why do we care where he is? He obviously couldn't handle me. I'm not still with him. He wasn't man enough… Are you man enough, Brodie McCormack?"

Peeking over her shoulder, she was drawn in by his tired eyes. "You are too naughty for most men," he said, reaching over to pull up her jacket so he could massage her bare thigh. "You're buck naked under that coat. You're so hot, baby, and I don't tell you that enough. I've got myself a prize."

He left his hand on her leg, but let his head fall back again so he could close his eyes. "Are you leaving early in the morning?" she asked. He nodded. She second-guessed her decision to bring him out so late because she didn't want him to be tired when he had to be focused. Except their relationship was important too, it was vital for his well-being and for the Kindred's work. "Will you let me come?"

"I left you hanging in the garage, huh? Pull over and I'll fix that right here." He bent in her direction and tugged open a few buttons on her coat, but she took his hand from the sensitive flesh near her core when his fingers tried to slide home.

With a laugh hiding behind her lips, she interlinked their fingers. "I meant will you let me come to New York with the Kindred?"

He sounded disappointed, either by the request or by his misinterpretation of it and shook his fingers out of hers. "Thad will only hang with us for a couple of days. He has a real job to get back to."

"What's Zave's story? He's sort of freaky."

"He's punishing himself," Brodie yawned, and she smiled out the windshield.

She'd asked him once why he didn't manipulate information out of her when she was tired and sex-sated, and here she was figuring out that it was the best way to inveigle information from her man.

"For what?"

Still sleeping, he looked so relaxed. She glanced from him to the road, wishing she didn't have to concentrate on driving. "He was a wild kid with a big brain and didn't take orders from anyone, no one could control him."

Which married with what Thad had said about days of indulgence. Zave certainly didn't come across as a partier. "What changed?" she asked because he was anything but wild.

His expression didn't move as he inhaled. "The same thing that always happens in my family," he said, "family tragedy. After that he became a recluse."

Most families had their share of skeletons. While Brodie and his family had been blessed with natural aptitude, they didn't have the best of luck in other areas. Having lost her own mother when she was a teenager, she understood how loss could alter a person's priorities almost overnight.

She kept driving and talking. "Thad is a happy guy, sort of like his mother. Bess is sweet."

"She's a treat," he muttered, probably getting tired of the questions.

Being out on the road gave her mind time to process and sort these new facts. "Do Zave's parents live in his house too? And I thought your dad built the twin houses for your mother?"

"He did. Zave bought the other one from my father. And his parents are dead. He has no siblings."

The family history questions were irritating Brodie because he was scowling again, and she'd need him to be in a good mood if she wanted him to open up when they got where they were going. "Just you and Grant left with that fraternal bond," she said, wondering how he'd react to that relationship while in this intoxicated state.

He sat up straight and seemed to grow alert in an instant. "Is that where we're going?" he asked, almost elated. "Oh, baby, that's a gift. Get me into his apartment while he's asleep. I'll teach him the consequences of letting my girl get hurt."

Rolling her eyes, she didn't want to encourage hostility, so a laugh became a tsk. "We're not going to punish Grant," she said.

They weren't far from their destination. From the way he examined the view with decreasing patience, she'd guess that he knew where they were going.

"White Falls," he murmured as they began their final ascent to the highest point of the coast near the city.

He said nothing else for the rest of the trip, and when they got to the top, she turned off the car and sat quietly staring out onto the inky ocean.

Brodie broke the silence. "Is there a point to this?" he asked, rubbing his hands on his thighs, lowering his gaze with renewed discomfort in his voice.

Revealing himself or any vulnerability was tough. Having made the decision to be more proactive about encouraging him to share, she wasn't going to pull back on the throttle now even if it was plain that was what he wanted her to do.

"You and Grant, you were up here the day your parents died." That much of the story she knew.

He nodded once but wouldn't focus on the windscreen. "Art brought us. We trekked up from the beach. Grant hated the whole day. He wouldn't stop bitching. It was arid, it hadn't rained for days, and… he was teaching us how to make fire and how to control it."

Treading softly, she was humbled and overjoyed that he was talking to her about such a sensitive topic. But she kept herself passive and sedate. She didn't want to scare him quiet, by gushing or overreacting to him sharing.

She took off her seatbelt and twisted her body toward his. "Art was?"

"Yeah," he said. His eyes flicked up to one side to focus on the dark mass on the water that was McCormack land. The peninsula was visible from up here, which was why Brodie had brought her here in the first place.

"The light you saw… right on the end of our peninsula? It's where the dock is… my mom had it installed to guide my dad home. He and his buddies used to go out fishing… least that's what they called it. What they liked to do was smoke cigars and talk business."

"She worried about him," Zara said, encouraged by that. Art had told her that Melinda McCormack had her husband pussy-whipped, now Zara understood that adoration went both ways.

The distance in his eyes became acute. "She was out with him that day on the boat. The light beacon was on at the dock in case they came back after dark. No one was there, at home. We were building a fire up here, but Grant was using the binoculars to try and find them."

So Art and Brodie were playing caveman, and Grant was seeking his parents, probably desperate to get home. Brodie would have been enraptured with his idol while Grant was seeking salvation.

His attention fell and there was tension in his shoulders. Her intention hadn't been to upset him. But she was gratified that he had chosen to open up to her with little persuasion. "And he saw the boat explode," she said, that much was in the papers. The boat went up ten miles from shore. Little wreckage was recovered according to the press she'd read, most of it had washed up on shore at the foot of the cliffs or on the McCormack peninsula.

He shrugged off the melancholy and settled back in his seat. "The night I brought you here was the first night I'd been back since that day. The beacon light hadn't been on either, we weren't even sure it was going to work."

It wasn't on tonight; she had only seen it on that one time. She'd spent so much time working inland on the McCormack estate that she hadn't spent any time on the other side of the house, closest to the water. Zara resolved to check out the docks and the beacon the next time she was exploring.

"It's a beautiful glow," she said because the light had been brilliant.

"Blue isn't traditionally used by mariners and lighthouses," Brodie said, more comfortable relaying facts. "But my dad chose it because it was my mom's favorite color."

Breaking the tension of the conversation was the best way to ensure she got more information from him, so she leaned closer and smiled. "Mine's purple."

His eyes softened as they flicked to hers. "Want me to change it?"

Her heart thumped, that was an almost inadvertent

admission on how he felt about her. Keeping the sparkle in her smile, she chose an indirect route. "Your dad loved her."

"Yeah," he exhaled, and his hand drifted to the door where he fingered the gun then let it go to crack his knuckles. "Why are we here, Zar?"

His impatience and irritation made him edgy, but she didn't see his intoxication anymore so she took his hand and leaned over to guide his face around to her. "Because I want to know you from the beginning, beau. There's nothing I don't want to hear."

He still looked pissed, so she knew she'd pushed him far enough tonight. She didn't want him to rebel by pushing her away. So, unbuttoning her coat, she pushed him back into his seat and climbed over to straddle his lap.

The discomfort vanished from his face and he grew cocky. "Now we get to the real reason why you wanted out of the house. You got a thing for screwing outdoors?" he asked, scooping his hands inside her jacket, parting it wide to expose her naked form as he curled his hands around her narrow waist. "You should've told me. The estate's your playground, don't ever forget it."

And he was her playmate. "This is for you," she said, sweeping her hair out of the way then pushing his forehead back and to the side so she could close her lips around his throat.

Undulating her hips against his fly, he grew to a solid mass under her stimulation with little time. "This fucking body's for me," he said, skimming his hands up to cradle her breasts.

"Yes, it is," she said, tracing her lips up to suck hard on his neck.

He hissed and snatched her wrists to thrust her back against the dash. "Leaving your mark, baby?" he snarled, wearing a glare reminiscent of the wild beast he'd claimed to be.

His arousal was her goal and she was getting him to a full steam fast. "You didn't get the full high school experience," she said. He didn't let go of her wrists but let her lean forward to splay her hands on his chest and kiss his neck again. She nuzzled her way up to his ear. "You get a girl in your car, drive somewhere private… far out of town, all alone… and take advantage of her…"

"Is this my fantasy or yours?"

She laughed while continuing to kiss his neck. "Naked under the overcoat," she said, guiding his hands onto her breasts. "I'm a walking fantasy."

"Yes, you are," he said, toying with a nipple while the other moved south to finger her. "Am I supposed to pretend you're a lily-white little virgin? Under the spell of the star football player?"

"If that's your fantasy," she whispered, riding his hand.

"That not how high school went for you?"

Grinning, she brushed her mouth over his. "I lost my virginity to the class outcast," she said, running her tongue over his lower lip then tracing her lips to his ear. "He smoked cigarettes and stole from convenience stores. He jacked cars, drove a beat-up Camaro, and dropped out of school. When he gave me his leather jacket, I fell head over heels."

"I'm stunned," he said without expression, suggesting he was anything but. Given where she was, what she was doing, and that she loved him, an assassin, it couldn't be much of a surprise to him that she was attracted to bad boys with questionable morals. Brodie took hold of her waist again; she loved the strength of his rough hands that gripped her and moved her at his whim. "How long were you with this guy before you decided you could do better?"

That was quite the question. Brodie didn't want to know about high school, he wanted to know if he was on a clock. Somehow, she was learning how to read between the lines because Brodie's questions—just like his movements—always had a purpose. If she could get bored of the high school dropout and move on when his rebellious nature became tiresome, then Brodie had to be thinking she would eventually tire of him.

Ironic that she'd been thinking not so long ago that Brodie may tire of her. Knowing her own heart and with full confidence in her staying power, she was happy to answer the question because her honest answer should reassure him.

"I never did," she said, kissing his neck and pulling up his tee shirt so she could explore his physique. "I put out then he traded me in for a younger model and my heart was broken."

It was so long ago. At the time, she'd believed she would never recover. Looking back, she almost laughed at how invested she was, her high school boyfriend beguiled her and it took her years to get over losing him.

Wearing a frown, he was intrigued by her statement, but torn toward being distracted by her body. "A younger model?" he asked, running his hands over her, up under her coat to her ass and higher then back down over her hips.

Being more specific was easy, Zara wanted him to know everything about her. "She was a D-cup," she said, rising on her knees to give herself space to loosen his jeans.

His eyes were drawn to her breasts, so she arched to optimize the view. "You have great cans, baby," he said, cupping and shaking them then giving each a kiss.

She'd never been so proud of her breasts before they gained his seal of approval. "You wouldn't trade them in?" she asked, tightening her fingers around his dick.

"Not for nothing," he said.

Brodie was a serious person, but with a naked woman on his lap he became a typical man willing to say anything in order to get some. Still, she appreciated that he took the time to compliment and reassure her because it was satisfying to know that he'd noticed. At the same time, she didn't need him to be anything that he wasn't.

Stroking her hands up to his naked chest, his tee shirt gathered at her wrists. "You know that I don't need words, beau. You give me everything I need. I'm crazy in love with you. You're my world and I'm so grateful for you."

Slanting her mouth over his, there was no time to sink into their kiss because he opened his fingers on her cheeks and eased her back. Keeping his fingers wide apart, he stroked his hands up to push her hair back from her face with his calloused palms.

"I'm an asshole," he said.

"I know."

He lost his gaze in hers. "There's nothing I wouldn't do for you."

Leaning forward, her lips brushed his. "I know that too," she whispered and dipped her tongue into his mouth.

FIFTEEN

YAWNING, ZARA STRETCHED out her body on their vast bed at the manor and smiled into the light cascading around her. Brodie slept with the blackout blinds closed, it was her who liked to wake up with the light. So if Brodie was here, there shouldn't be any sunlight, she should be waking up to a room so devoid of sunlight that a vampire would be happy to reside here.

Flattening her arm on the mattress to search behind her, she found no body in the bed with her. Sitting upright, Zara scanned their bedroom. He wasn't here. Leaping from the bed, she knew better than to look for a note or some other token of affection.

She ran to the closet, jumped into her underwear, and snatched one of Brodie's button-down shirts from the hanger because it was closest to hand. Buttoning the shirt as she ran down the stairway, she first checked the kitchen. It was empty. But the cups next to the sink were still dripping, so she took that as a sign they hadn't been washed too long ago.

On her dash downstairs to the garage, she fastened the remaining shirt buttons. When she burst through the doorway, the first thing she heard was a vehicle starting up. Panic ebbed when she saw the steel gray pick-up by the open garage door with Tuck, Thad, and Brodie there beside it.

Her sudden entrance drew their attention. "Morning, Zara!" Thad said, grinning at her legs, though the shirt hung to her knees, so she wasn't concerned about revealing too much skin.

Brodie shoved Thad's head and Tuck laughed, but Brodie was already on his way over to her.

Touching his obliques, she walked backwards at Brodie's urging when he took her shoulders. "You were going to leave without saying goodbye?" she panted.

With his eyes focused over her head, he kept walking forward. "Hush," he murmured and turned her around to crowd her back into the stairwell.

He turned her around to face him again when the door closed. "Were you?" she asked.

Lowering his focus to meet hers, he grazed her cheekbone with his fingertips. "You should've stayed in bed."

After making out like teenagers in the car at White Falls and returning to the manor to canoodle again before falling asleep, she hadn't had time to get specifics on the trip's itinerary.

"How long will you be gone?"

"A few days, a week, maybe more," he said. "We'll stay until we get what we need."

She nodded and inhaled, Art had told her that Brodie worked away a lot, so she'd known she would have to prepare to be without him. He hadn't even left the building and she was already worried. But Brodie, as Raven, had done jobs far more complicated than this one and riskier too. Loving a man in his line of work meant accepting the risks, but that didn't mean she had to be happy about them.

Without even a glimmer of a hangover, his expression was keen and his body hard. He could do this, she had faith in him, and he didn't show the slightest hint of doubt or fear.

"We're gonna stakeout Sutcliffe and his army. There's a guy out there, he's doing background for Sutcliffe. His name's Rigor, we've worked with him before, he's a game player, and a crazy megalomaniac. But if we can get ahold of the information he's delivering to Sutcliffe…"

Brodie had been doing this for most of his life. She couldn't imagine there was anyone out there he hadn't worked with. Anyone worth working with anyway.

"You can know what he knows," she said and nodded. "Okay."

Brodie shook his head, though she didn't know what he was disagreeing with, he didn't appear too happy. "I don't want you involved in that. Two things Rigor loves more than power: women and cards. He only gets to set eyes on you when he absolutely has to. You get me?"

Keeping her away from the assignment wasn't a power play; he was trying to protect her. Brodie was using Raven to put distance between her and danger. Raven had a job to do and he had to keep his head clear to do it. But for three months, Brodie had locked himself up here in the manor, and although she'd been worried for him, she hadn't realized that he'd become her crutch. Knowing where he was reassured her and now she was losing that assurance.

"Okay, you're the chief," she said, averting her gaze when her inhale sounded ragged. With his fingertips on her cheekbone, he made her look at him. In her desire to alleviate the concern etched on his face, she smiled. "Do you guys have time to drop me off at home? I can get changed in—"

He caught her when she tried to retreat backwards to the stairs. "I want you to stay here," he said with nothing but determination. "Don't go back to your apartment, stay here."

She had never been in this house alone before. Sometimes it felt like she was because Brodie was brooding somewhere in private. But his assertion that she should reside in his private space while no one else was here surprised her. "But you could be gone for weeks and—"

She tried to take her hand back, but he yanked her body to his. "Tuck showed you how to use all the systems, right?" She nodded. "You remember what I told you about this house? Tell me."

On the first night she'd come to visit, he'd invited her to stay and alleviated her apprehension before she'd voiced it. "That if I trust you, I have nothing to fear in this house."

Pride colored him and she did enjoy pleasing him. "Atta

girl," he said, brushing his thumb over the front of her chin.

He took a step back, and it was her turn to get ahold of him because she wasn't ready to lose him yet. Once he walked out of here, she'd lose the invisible cord that bonded them. More importantly, Brodie would lose it and he still needed a touchstone. "Why weren't you going to say goodbye?"

He loosened, thought for half a second, then shrugged. "I've never said goodbye," he said. "I always just… go."

No, he hadn't. Even during their first encounters, he had just slipped away—here one minute, gone the next. He hadn't said goodbye to Art, he just buried him without ceremony. Keeping himself detached was probably good for business, but not acknowledging his feelings could lead to major meltdowns as had been recently proven. And as his girlfriend, she wanted more from him than a standard colleague relationship, which was pretty much all he'd had with others until now.

Getting personal, she reminded him of their connection. "You might have enjoyed saying goodbye to me in bed."

Pushing her chest to his torso, her lips curled into a tease.

This fish wasn't for biting. "No one comes into this house," he said, coiling a strand of her hair around his index finger, watching his hand instead of her face. "Check the security log every morning and you know the lockout code?"

Guessing he was getting himself into the zone he needed to be in to do his job, she surrendered. "Treble one, zero, one."

Stroking his fingers down her face, he swept them through her hair until he had ahold of her neck with her hair tangled between his digits. He might not be using words, but his actions were intimate and she took solace in that.

"If anything happens, if we disappear from radar, go to the top floor of the south tower," he said. "You'll find what you need in there."

Under other circumstances, she would probably have gone straight to that location to snoop. But she didn't dare think of a time when she might need that information. So although she heard him, she didn't ask questions and immediately filed that detail into her brain but chose to otherwise ignore it.

"Beau," she said, sliding her hands up to his neck when he squeezed the back of hers, she dug her nails into him. "I love you."

Watching the words coming out of her mouth, he narrowed his eyes and there were three clear beats of silence. "And no other guys. Be on the end of the phone when I call."

He pulled her close and kissed her hard, then turned to walk away. She didn't expect sonnets or a dozen roses on her doorstep, but she couldn't figure out why he wouldn't reciprocate her words when his actions suggested his feelings were as deep as hers. Maybe it was just too much for him to consider when there were so many other things on the table.

It didn't matter that she was disappointed. She would keep on trying, keep on reminding him of how she felt until he returned the gesture or shut her down. Coaxing Brodie into something he didn't want to do was no easy feat, but she was committed to her man and to the love she had for him.

***

ONE DAY BECAME ANOTHER and all she could do was guess that the Kindred were safe because there was no communication from them. She stayed in the manor, as requested, and only went back to her apartment to pick up more of her stuff as she needed it.

Moving into the manor was inevitable given that it was Brodie's wish; he knew how to get what he wanted. But she found it easier and more discreet to pick up a few of her things at a time rather than taking a bunch at once.

Maintaining a normal routine was her responsibility, so she went to work at CI, did her job, and came home again. Sitting at her desk, she was counting down the seconds until she could leave to check the manor systems for signs of communication.

The intercom on her phone buzzed. "Can you come through to my office for a minute?" Grant asked through the speaker.

Zara rose and left her office to enter her boss's. He didn't usually summon her this late in the day, but she was at his disposal whenever he needed her. She drew comfort from the normality of their professional life, especially being that their personal lives were so chaotic.

She expected to go into his office to receive instructions. What she didn't expect to see was Griffin Caine, yet there he was, seated at Grant's desk like he had every right in the world to be there.

Grant stood up, wearing a smile, but she stormed over with an arm outstretched in Caine's direction. "What the hell is he doing here?" she demanded of Grant, filled with horror and anger.

"This is Mr. Caine," Grant said with faltering glee.

Switching her glare onto Caine, she was reviled to see his pleasure. "Miss Bandini, what a pleasure to see you again," he said.

He got up as if to shake her hand, but she recoiled from his reach. "Don't you dare think about touching me," she hissed.

Caine was still relaxed and that brought a foul taste to her mouth. "I'm just being polite," he said, but she wasn't fooled by his sinister smile.

Leaning toward him, she recalled their first meeting and the bruise Brodie had sported on his jaw before his departure. "Just give him the excuse," she snarled, trying to burn her hatred into him. This man wanted to hurt the person she loved the most in this world. Nothing he could say would endear her to him, just being in his presence made her feel sick. "You touch me and I'll give him that excuse."

"Zara," Grant chastised and came around the desk to grasp her shoulder. "Mr. Caine heard about what happened at Purdy's and he got in touch with me. He has extensive experience in the security industry and he is especially interested in ensuring—"

"He's interested in ensuring his own interests," she said, lifting her arm away from Grant. "You didn't think it was rather convenient that this lunatic security agent called you up and made himself available?"

"I think it's necessary for us to protect ourselves," Grant

said, closing in on her while Caine lowered into his seat, smugger than ever. "I think it's my responsibility to—"

"I'm not your responsibility," she said, furious with Grant. "If Sutcliffe wants to hurt me because I hurt him then let him. He can't get to me. I think I proved the other night that I can take care of myself."

Grant was adamant to the point of insulting her. "I am not willing to risk your safety. I don't care what you tell me about your boyfriend. He's too busy wallowing in his own self—"

"Is he?" Caine piped up, and they turned to see him fingering a pen on Grant's desk. "Is that what she told you? Her boyfriend is wallowing… why is that?"

Caine's interest in Brodie was monomaniacal. Brodie knew he was a nuisance, but to her, this man was a real threat to her love. Anyone who wanted to harm Brodie should be taken seriously because the consequences of losing him were too horrific to contemplate. "Don't you dare tell him a thing," she exclaimed at Grant. "What is your game, Caine? What do you want?"

"I thought I could be of help."

She didn't believe him and didn't want him getting too cozy. "Do you know what Rave would do if he walked in here right now?"

"I think I know better than you do, honey," Caine said, sitting back and twining his fingers. "And I know Raven and Swift are not wallowing, they're not even in the state."

"What?" Grant said, his attention snapped to her.

Caine slowly rose, swaggered over to her, and dipped to murmur in her ear. "You're wide open. I can pick you off anytime I choose."

Ducking back, she separated them and contempt spread on her face. "If you were going to kill me, you'd have done it by now. You're here because you think I'll tell Rave and that he'll be so mad he'll take his eye off the ball. You want him to make a mistake."

Caine seemed impervious to her jibes, and that riled her. Though she knew she should stay calm, it was difficult when Caine was playing with real lives, lives she cared about. "I just like reminding him that I'm in his back yard," Caine said and trailed his fingertips down her arm. "I'll be in touch, Grant."

Caine didn't address her again or say farewell. He just went to the exit and slipped out. Spinning to face her boss, she wasn't even sure where to begin in voicing her displeasure.

"How could you think to bring him here?" she demanded.

Giving Grant his due, he did appear flummoxed and it wasn't as if he and Brodie were close enough that Grant would know the intimate details of Brodie's past. But she'd learned her lessons about underestimating this man. Grant wasn't the saint she'd once thought him to be.

"Who is he to you?" Grant asked, and his curiosity made her regret her emotional reaction to Caine.

She'd painted herself into a corner, but she folded her arms and rested her weight on her back foot to consider her answer. "He's an enemy." Playing it cool now was a bit belated, but after processing her statement, Grant sighed out his own disappointment.

"Brodie's enemy," Grant stated and he was already shaking his head. "Why do you take up his cause so readily?"

"You know why," she said, because she didn't want to grind salt into Grant's wound and remind him of how she felt about his brother.

Grant turned his back on her to saunter back to his desk and it was only when he was seated again that he looked at her. "Because you believe yourself in love. You don't know anything about him."

Trying not to take out her own frustrations on Grant, she rolled her eyes upward to calm herself before looking at him again. Brodie said the same thing, and it pissed her off, but Grant saying it was like waving a red rag.

"I know more about him than you do," she said. "As this meeting proved. Griffin Caine is a parasite who feeds off the misery of his prey and he's using you as a pawn in his game, trying to provoke us."

"I don't know that Brodie would appreciate being referred to as prey."

He had no right to talk about Brodie as if he knew him,

even if he was right. "You don't care about Brodie," she said, moving across the room toward him. "You don't care about him at all. But I am telling you not to trust that man, shouldn't that be enough for you?"

"You don't realize how much damage you did to our relationship," he said, brushing a hand over the stack of papers on his desk. "Our relationship, Zara, yours and mine."

After the handover with Sutcliffe had gone so completely wrong at the Atlas warehouse, she had gone back to the manor and had stayed there for days without talking to Grant. The relationship had been damaged and she didn't trust him anymore, not since her perceived betrayal. She'd come back because the Kindred needed her here.

On the first day back, she'd shown up with suspicions that this was a ruse and had been expecting to be tossed out or to have her boss ream her out for her actions. Instead, he had groaned and rushed across his office with a pile of files. He bundled them into her arms and gave her a push toward her own office with a comment about the backlog of work.

While focusing on clearing the backlog and taking opportunities to gain Grant's confidence, she found that work soothed her and helped her forget about her woes with the Brodie situation. So she'd fallen back into her old CI routine.

Grant hadn't been forthcoming about how he planned to move forward with regards to Game Time. In fact, it wasn't mentioned at all and she didn't want to be too eager about bringing it up in case she blew her cover. She and Tuck agreed that it was a good idea to stick close to Grant, but when Sutcliffe seemed to vanish, they'd believed there was a chance that the situation was finished with.

Quelling her confrontational emotions, she took a breath. "I know that you don't trust me anymore," she said, lowering herself onto the edge of the guest chair opposite his desk. "But you have to believe me when I say that Griffin Caine is bad news."

Grant was still emotional. "And you have to believe me when I say Sutcliffe isn't finished. He orchestrated that holdup in Purdy's where you could've been killed. He has plans, and although you claim not to want to be a part of that, you are. I don't want you to be caught in the crossfire. I still care about you, Zara. You might not like the choice that's in front of you, but you have to make it. If you choose Sutcliffe, you'll live. If you don't, you'll die. I can't put it any clearer than that. Are the outcomes the same with your boyfriend?"

Brodie wouldn't kill her for dumping him or the Kindred. But he'd also protect her with his life. Grant was right not to trust her because she did not intend to consider joining Sutcliffe's cause. But for as long as she was here, she had to portray herself as unthreatening and as caring for Grant's well-being, which meant letting him believe she was open to other possibilities.

"What if he does want to hurt me?" she asked.

"Sutcliffe and I will protect you if you join us."

It was difficult to look a person in the face and lie to them, knowing all along that she didn't have Grant's best interests at heart, she tried to be genuine when they talked. All she could hope was that her guilt wasn't written all over her face. She was sure her cheeks glowed because the heat of them radiated enough to almost steam her glasses.

"I don't want to hurt you," she said "But I can't understand why you are so intent on taking up with a man who wants to hurt people. You've just stated that he'll kill me if I don't follow him."

Grant considered her for a moment, then leaned on his elbows to inch closer. "Sutcliffe's desire for the device does not correlate to his want to hurt people. He'll only hurt those who are a threat. Purdy's was about more than capital. It was a rehearsal. He needs his men to practice with live ammunition. He will place the devices in strategic locations and talk to the relevant leaders before he uses them. He will give our enemies a fair chance to change their ways before he thinks about hurting them."

Grant was talking, but she stayed calm because that was the best way to keep him talking. "Is that what he told you?"

"It's how a civilized man acts and civility is what separates us from them."

Us from them, didn't sound like they were going to war with an open mind. Sliding back in the seat, she tempered her reaction to what he was saying. "He wants to hold the world to ransom."

"Game Time is only the first stage of his plan." It was amazing to her how cool Grant was about saying something so shocking. "If our enemies do not take advantage of the warning, Game Time will be used and it will turn the spotlight on our cause, then we'll start recruiting on a much larger scale, reaching beyond one small town in America. Our soldiers will come from all parts of the globe."

Sutcliffe and Grant believed themselves to be righteous. They couldn't see that they were simply rebranding terrorism the capitalist way. "Soldiers?" she asked.

Leaning on his forearms, he seemed almost excited, but decreased his volume. "He wants to take back control. To rebuild the former empires of our wonderful nations."

Albert Sutcliffe was English, and the institution still held to old-world beliefs. It was no surprise that after being raised in privilege—surrounded by some of the oldest families in the world—that Sutcliffe had that sense of entitlement and the overblown ego displayed by the boys' club types in his homeland.

Still, she kept herself composed, like she was intrigued and open to what he was saying, not displaying how horrified and angry she was. "What will that achieve?"

"When we ruled these unruly nations there was more peace in the world than there is now."

There was more peace. It was unbelievable that any person could think that conquering and subduing a whole nation was a solution to any problem.

Talking in slow, soothing tones grew more difficult but she was getting information that would be useful to the Kindred. "So he wants to take over the world?"

His eyes closed and opened slowly. "He wants our citizens to be safe," Grant said. "And I can't say that I disagree with him. You should think about which side you're on. You should be wary; I don't know how much time you'll have. Albert isn't always a patient man."

She couldn't show anger, so she tried her best to show fear because she wanted Grant to believe she was malleable.

"How can I possibly decide?" she asked exasperated, like she was at the end of her rope. "How can I win Sutcliffe's trust if I choose his side?"

"I have reasoned with Albert. He understands, and as long as we deliver the devices—"

Her reins snapped and some of her regret seeped onto her expression, but she pulled it back. It was easy to talk about the consequences of Game Time in the abstract, but once it was out there, they wouldn't be able to take it back and the reality would break Grant. Brodie had said that his brother didn't have the stomach for murder, and here he was talking about being party to it on a grand scale.

"I'm scared that you'll never forgive yourself when you see the carnage he'll cause," she murmured, feeling momentary pity for her boss. Grant wanted to make amends, not only because he wanted to save his bacon, but also because he still subscribed to Sutcliffe's ideology. "How did you get him to relent on his desire to take revenge on you?"

Grant's expression grew hard. "We're going to work together."

"On what?"

He didn't enjoy being questioned and from the way his jaw worked, she guessed he was trying to subdue his anger. The conversation had taken a turn he didn't appreciate. "Maybe we'll work together to track down my brother."

That was a threat that scared her, but it wouldn't scare Brodie. Still, taking Brodie out of the equation wouldn't resolve Sutcliffe's resentment. It was funny how she was becoming accustomed to the idea of giving her life for the Kindred, but the thought of losing Brodie to it terrified her.

She drew her lips into her mouth to moisten them before she spoke. "You think that you can blame him for all of this?"

Bristling with his own anger, Grant wasn't great at hiding his feelings. "Can't I?" Grant asked, getting up to go to the water jug in the corner. "He was the one who destroyed Winter Chill, which limited my ability to provide for my client. He seduced you into taking on his cause… You know, you sneer at me for believing in Sutcliffe. But I would say I made my decision to support his politics with a clearer head than you did when taking up with Brodie. I wasn't clouded by puerile fantasy and obsession. I made a deliberate decision."

She wasn't insulted by the truth. "And that's what terrifies me," she murmured and got his attention again. "If this were about money, I would be disappointed, but at least there would be a chance of reasoning with you… A man like you, taking up with a man like Sutcliffe… you could destroy the world, Grant."

His optimism perplexed her. "Or rebuild it," he said, putting his water glass down beside the pitcher before he turned to look at her. "We're capable of greatness and if you were working with us—"

She shook her head and got up. "There's no way in a million years that I could persuade Raven to take up your cause."

"Pah!" he scoffed and marched over. "We don't need him, Zara. Don't you see? He's holding us back. He's holding you back. If you could just—"

"What?" she snapped when he snatched her shoulders. "Leave him and take up with you?"

"Why not? You left me for him… But I'd be willing to forgive that mistake, Zara. If you would just think about it. Just think about the possibilities… I don't want you to be left behind."

He grazed a hand down her jaw and she was ensnared by just how sincere he was, not only about the job, but in the way he looked at her. "I don't want you to do this," she said, hoping there was enough fondness left in their relationship that he might consider giving up on this for her. "If you work with us—"

Shoving away, he backed off. "I won't ever work with him… How long has he been out of state? What is it he's doing?"

"I don't know," she said because it was the truth.

"Taking life," he said, facing her again. "That's what he does. What he does is worse than anything I've done. Worse than anything Sutcliffe's done."

Maybe if they tallied up the body count today it would be, the same wouldn't be said in a few months if Sutcliffe fulfilled his plan. "But for how long?" she asked.

If Sutcliffe got his army and took up arms to achieve his misguided ends, the world would burn and it would happen indiscriminately. Game Time didn't know the women and children from the soldiers. Civilization would be dismantled, and she would know that she'd had the chance to end it and hadn't.

"You can't fight passion. Sutcliffe's faith hasn't wavered. He has made plans. The new world will arrive in our lifetime. You have to decide which side you want to be on."

"It's an impossible decision. I don't want to be hurt. But if we join Sutcliffe together… Raven is not an enemy we want chasing us."

She wasn't afraid of Brodie, and she was sorry she had to make it seem that she was. But the fact was true, Grant didn't want to make an enemy of Brodie. Taking his hand, she linked their fingers. "We shouldn't be on opposing sides. It doesn't feel right, does it?"

Grant sighed and his features relaxed enough that he appeared to feel sorry for her. "He hasn't driven that sweetness out of you… yet. Don't tread too deep into his world or that wonderful innocence that glows out of you will dim. He'll take that away from you. He'll use you and then he'll abandon you."

He might mean well, but his words proved to her how little he knew Brodie McCormack. She wished that the brothers hadn't given up on each other so long ago. It was easy for her to decide Grant was wrong and fight against him. But the man was still Brodie's brother, and Brodie had lost too many family members already.

SIXTEEN

IT WAS FRIDAY, and the idea of going to Purdy's was unappealing, but so was staying late at CI. So, in a rare show of defiance, Zara left work early. As the week had progressed, her relationship with Grant had become strained. He tried on an almost daily basis to convince her of Sutcliffe's merits. Avoiding the conversation was becoming impossible and she needed Kindred guidance on how to deal with it.

Her nerves were taut because there had been no word from Brodie since he left on Sunday. Being alone in the manor didn't scare her, but it did echo when she knocked about in it on her own. Exploring each of the rooms and taking advantage of what the manor had to offer was a poor substitute for having Brodie and Tuck around.

After getting back to base that evening, she wasted no time searching the halls for someone she wouldn't find. She wandered to the bedroom, conscious that she would spend another night sleeping alone. With a sigh, she tossed her purse onto the floor, pulled her pins from her hair, and dropped onto her back on the bed.

She wanted Brodie to be here. Turning her head, she examined the closed bathroom door and imagined it opening. Imagined seeing her guy there in the doorway, with one of the little white towels wrapped around his hips and rivulets of water sliding from his impressive shoulders, trickling down the plains of his hard pecs and onto the ridges of his abdomen. Pouting, she narrowed her lips and smiled as she adjusted her mental picture and erased the towel.

Elevating her hips, she unzipped her skirt and shimmied out of it. After she tossed it on the floor, she skimmed her fingertips over her hip to the fabric of her panties and traced her fingers over the heat nestled between her thighs.

Before she got the chance to complete her fantasy, the shrill buzz of her phone's ringtone pierced the air, and she dragged her focus from the closed bathroom door. Her disappointment at the interruption was short-lived, because she'd been waiting for a phone call all week and this could be it.

Lunging to grab her purse from the floor, she tugged out her phone and dropped the bag as she fell onto her back again to fumble with the touchscreen to answer the call.

"Hello?" She didn't mean to sound so breathy and desperate when she answered. But the flash of "unknown" she'd read on her phone could mean only one thing: Brodie.

"Hey, baby."

Sighing out a week of worry, she felt lighter and so much happier because she could hear his voice. "It's been almost a full week. I was starting to worry about you."

As confident and aloof as ever, he took a breath. "What's there to worry about? You think there's any situation I wouldn't be able to handle?"

Maybe not. But not having him near to her was enough to leave Zara unsettled. Hearing his cockiness, she smiled, Brodie was a warrior who could adapt and handle any combat situation. "Where are you? What's going on?"

He didn't waste time gushing, he got to the point. "We need you here," he said. She sat up to blink at the empty bedroom.

Brodie hadn't wanted her with them, hadn't wanted her anywhere near the op and now he was issuing not an invitation, but an order for her to attend.

"Okay," she said, twisting to let her legs dangle from the

bed. "Where?"

"Tuck has emailed your ticket. Someone will pick you up at the airport."

"Someone?" she asked, piqued by his ambiguity. "Like someone I know?"

"Probably not," he said. "The details are in Tuck's message. It's waiting for you downstairs. Pack what you need and get moving. Your plane leaves in an hour."

Brodie had a way of knowing just how to motivate her. Leaping off the bed, she cast off her clothes, while trying to maintain her link with her love. "How do you know where I am?" she asked.

"There's a tracker in your phone," he said, but she already knew that. "And there are some internal cameras."

His voice got lower and his teasing was enough for her to cast her eyes upward, then left and right. "You can see me?" She had no idea there were cameras inside their rooms at the manor, but Art had told her the building held secrets.

"You got too damn close to playing with what's mine, baby. You keep your hands off that pussy. I control your pleasure. I say when and where you get off."

She wished she'd known sooner that he was watching her when she was here in their bedroom. Knowing it now made her feel closer to him and she might have been inclined to put on a show if he was the only one watching. "You're a creep," she said, but couldn't keep the smile away from her face. "I hope your spy gear is private viewing."

Reassuring her lasted only as long as it had to. Provoking her was more fun. The mischief in his voice caused tiny firecrackers to start sparking and bouncing in her belly. He wasn't even in the same state as her and he was getting her wet. "My eyes only," he said. "Want to tell me what you were thinking about?"

Getting her turn to tantalize him, she leaned back on one hand and with the other she traced a fingertip up her abdomen and over her breast where she circled her nipple until it pinched into a painful peak. "Come home to our bed and I'll tell you every detail."

"Soon, baby," he said, humoring her. "You've got to

shift your ass into gear, there isn't much time."

Then there was no time for recreation, which was a shame because after a week without it, she needed some naked and sweaty recreation. "Why am I hurrying?" she asked, pouncing to her feet in response to his urgency. "Is there something wrong?"

"We'll explain everything when you get here. There's a window of opportunity, and we don't want to miss it."

"Opportunity for what?" she asked, hooking the phone between her shoulder and cheek so she could put her foot on the bed and roll off her stocking.

"You're Kindred. You do whatever is asked of you." He sounded angry. Something told her he wasn't riled by her question, but by something else that he wasn't revealing.

Curious, she slid her foot off the bed and conceded haste in deference to concern. "If there's something you want to tell me…"

"Just do as you're told. Dress slutty and get yourself dolled up."

She almost couldn't believe her ears. Brodie had never asked her to wear makeup. She rarely wore much, and when she did it was conservative for business functions. "Makeup? Why do I need to wear makeup?" she asked because this was an easier question than to ask why he wanted her slutty.

"You'll understand when you get here," he said. "Get a move on. Time is short."

And none of the time they did have was allocated for questions apparently because the line disconnected. She would have to trust that he'd reveal all when she got to them because she couldn't return his call, not when he'd made it from an 'unknown' number.

Rushing to the closet, she dressed and packed as he'd directed then pulled out the makeup box to decorate herself. He was lucky she had this here and it was just luck. The box had been picked up by Tuck during one of their first runs to retrieve stuff from her apartment.

She didn't have time to think twice about what she was doing. Thinking trampy, she got made up, dressed, and put her feet in a pair of spike heels that made her legs look incredible, but always hurt her feet.

The Chief of the Kindred had given her an order, and this was her chance to prove her loyalty to the team. So ignoring her nerves, she snatched her suitcase and hurried down the stairs to pick up Tuck's message.

***

SLUTTY MEANT DIFFERENT things to different people, but she was pretty confident that she'd gotten the look right because she'd never had so much attention as she did at the airport and again on the plane.

Tuck's message had included a picture of the guy who would pick her up. So when the rough-looking bearded man in the leather vest grabbed her arm in arrivals at the airport, she did her best to keep up with him and in five-inch heels, that wasn't easy.

He stuffed her and her case into the back of a pick-up and drove off at high speed into darkness. She wasn't sure what she was supposed to know or who this unkempt guy was, so she didn't try to make conversation.

He glanced her way more than a few times and she wasn't surprised. The silver top she wore hung on a string around her neck with another going across the width of her back and that was it. Her hips and midriff were on display above the skimpy, black leather skirt she wore that clung to her ass.

Brodie told her to dress slutty and told her that she was at the beck and call of the Kindred. This was the most revealing outfit she had. Brodie was going to be impressed. But she was apprehensive about what she'd have to do in the name of the Kindred that required such an outfit.

After a week without her love, she would be happy if her show of skin encouraged him to take action. But her first question would be about this stranger who'd snatched her from the airport. She'd have preferred to have Brodie or one of the other guys come to pick her up.

After driving for so many miles that civilization was a distant memory, she observed the unlit road they were on and began to get nervous until a glowing light in the distance made her frown.

As they got closer, the outline of a single-story building with a corrugated roof and a black-painted timber frontage came into view. Weeds grew out from the foundations and the parking lot was little more than compacted dirt, though that was almost impossible to see beneath the hundred or so motorcycles that were parked in haphazard spots around the area.

Bumping off the asphalt highway, her driver maneuvered the truck between two metal poles that held up a chain-link fence, which seemed to be protecting the perimeter of the whole place. A gang of half a dozen stood around just inside the fence. The driver nodded at them and they lifted their hands in greeting. This was a pleasant exchange, but she wondered how they would react if the man wasn't a friend. Or if she'd tried to come here on her own.

He drove the pick-up around until her door was parallel with the hooded entrance, though the door wasn't highlighted in any way and there was no light to welcome her near.

"Go on, he's through the back," her driver said in a gruff voice that he punctuated with a smoker's cough.

The driver rested an arm the length of the front seat when he was done hacking and she swallowed away her apprehension. She might not know this guy, but she'd rather enter this sinister place with someone than walk into it alone, especially since she had no idea if the Kindred were even here or not.

Showing vulnerability to the driver wasn't an option and she couldn't stay here all night. Calling Brodie on his Kindred number and hoping he'd pick up wasn't possible either, her cell was in her suitcase. She didn't want her lover to think her a pussy who was too afraid to enter such an ominous building anyway. She'd told Brodie that she wanted to be a part of the darkness and all that entailed, so she couldn't discount the possibility that this was some sort of test.

Grabbing the handle of her case, the driver grunted. "Leave that."

So she was to leave all of her possessions here with this stranger and walk into a building that looked like the end of the world.

Okay, she convinced herself that she could do this. In spite of the cauldron of dread swirling her guts into a heated frenzy, she thrust her shoulders back and spread her glossy lips in a wide smile. If she was supposed to be a slut then she had better start acting like one.

Shuffling to the door, she opened it and shimmied out, tugging her skirt down in the process. No sooner had she slammed the door than the truck trundled off, leaving her alone and freezing in this dark parking lot. Noise from inside carried to her, there was music and shouting. The track changed and in the brief moment of quiet, she picked out the sound of glass on glass, pool balls ricocheting, and heavy boots on wooden flooring. Okay, so this was a bar. A biker bar. Where else would Brodie feel more at home?

The men from the gate shouted and she was sure they were jeering her, but she wouldn't turn to look over her shoulder. She wanted to get inside in one piece and starting a fight outside would put Brodie in a precarious position.

The building sounded busy and if the number of bikes was anything to go by, it was packed. If Brodie was in there, she had nothing to fear. If he wasn't, she was monumentally screwed. But he would never have sent someone he didn't trust to get her.

Telling herself to get a grip, she tottered forward and with every step, she grew in confidence. This was exciting. It was an opportunity to see inside Brodie's world—rather, Raven's world.

The music got louder. She stepped onto the low square porch and grabbed the dirty door handle. Giving the long, vertical bar a tug, a hard rock tune blasted when she opened the door. The smell of sweat, dirt, and grease mingled seamlessly with the scent of alcohol. Straightening one confident leg, she strutted into the room with her head held high.

Bikers were like dogs, they could smell fear, and she wouldn't give them any hint that she was hesitant. Her driver had said through the back, so she kept moving and searched the back of the building for any clue as to where that might mean. Every table was busy, there was a crowd in a back corner, and she saw a flash of grubby green felt. The pool table wasn't her goal and she was none the wiser as to where her goal was. She didn't want to stop. Didn't want to give anyone the chance to talk to her.

Heading for the bar seemed to be a good plan, the bar man should be able to tell her where to find her party. As hard as she tried not to look at the patrons, she was aware that everyone she could see was male, heavy set, and mean looking. Taking a quick chance to scan the room, she couldn't pick out a single female.

There was a bulky guy behind the bar and she drew her lip over her lower teeth to dampen it in preparation for speech. But when they made eye contact, he nodded sideways and she saw a curtain at the back of the room, perpendicular to the optics on the wall behind the bar. He reached over the bar and around to snag the curtain, which he pulled back just enough for her to duck through.

Expecting to go into a room containing only those she knew, she came up short. To the left were a trio of low couches set around a table only a couple of feet off the floor. The five guys there were strangers to her, so she cast her eyes right to the table bearing four men, one on each of its sides. Tuck was seated at the nine o'clock position. But her eyes caught on the guy sitting at six with his back to her. That was Brodie. Her automatic smile was joined by the urge to go to him.

The space was dark and smoke hung in a clear mist spanning the room. The music from the main bar pounded, but it was muted now that there was a wall between her and it. But she'd found what she was looking for.

Creeping over to the table, Tuck noticed her and raised his brows, but the other three at the table didn't acknowledge her. The man sitting at twelve o'clock was fixated on Brodie, who didn't give any indication he was going to turn around. The atmosphere was thick, she'd walked in on something going down, and she had no idea what it was.

Brodie's hunched opponent had his dark hair slicked back and was peering at Brodie over his cards. Zara went to the table. The opponent glanced at her and his glower became a leer. Examining the tabletop, she saw chips, cash, keys, and a brown envelope in the center. Tuck and the guy opposite him had no cards, and Brodie's were facedown under his loose hand.

"If that belongs to you, I'll accept the bet," the slick-haired guy said, drawing his eyes down over her figure.

Brodie leaned back, sliding his cards toward him as he did, but he didn't lift them. A line of cigar smoke ascended from the stub in an ashtray just beside him. Having found Brodie, she didn't feel any more reassured because this tense situation was probably the worst thing she could have walked into.

Without taking his eyes from his rival, Brodie grabbed her wrist and yanked her to him. Pulling her down onto one of his broad thighs, he draped his arm around her and she scratched her fingernails against him in her own greeting because he was still stuck on the guy opposite him. She did feel better being here, seated on him, with her legs nestled in the wide vee between his legs.

Stroking a hand around her waist, Brodie's palm came around beneath her top and his knuckles grazed the underside of her breast in a maneuver that made her shiver. It had been a week since they'd been intimate and she'd missed him so much that her body was an exposed nerve ready to be stimulated by the man possessing her now.

Brodie picked up his cigar and took one long drag before resting it over the ashtray again.

"Who is she?" the opponent asked, still ogling her.

"Private property," Brodie said, tipping his head back to blow his smoke into the cloud lingering above them.

The tension in her intimate center snapped, and a buzz of excitement spread across her hips. Nerves weren't what consumed her. What she'd believed to be apprehension was arousal. Brodie was here, Tuck was on the other side of the table, there was nothing to fear. There might be five guys on the couches and two around this table who she didn't know, and the allegiances of the strangers were all unclear, but she had utter faith that if it kicked off, Brodie and Tuck would get her out of here alive.

"Nothing is private here," the guy said. "Everything you got is on this table." He raised his brows and looked at the vast pot between the two of them. There were no chips beside any of the players, everything was on the table, and she glanced up to see that Tuck was intent on Brodie. "What you gonna do, Rave? Forfeit?"

"Not a chance," Brodie muttered, setting a glare on his opponent that made her push herself closer.

"Then you got only one choice," the cocky adversary said, straightening his form.

"Okay, Rigor," Brodie said. He leaned down and angled her so he could kiss the side of her breast not covered by her top. He snagged her wrist and pulled her arm away from his neck as he jacked her up off his lap. When she was on her feet, he smacked her ass, but she didn't know what was happening, didn't know what to do. "She's on the table."

Horror fixed her eyes wide on her love. "What?"

The word was instinct and as Brodie's rival laughed, she glanced back at the door, considering retreat. "You got nothing to worry about, sweetheart," Rigor said. "I'll treat you better than your man here."

The fourth guy at the table pounced up to his feet, and Tuck wasn't too far behind, though the fourth guy got to her first. He grabbed her wrist and pulled her around the table, but she tried to resist.

"Let me go!"

"Quiet!" Brodie called out. She stopped struggling when he made eye contact with her. "You do what you're told."

She wanted to ask what happened to priority one. She wanted to argue with him, to ream him out for bringing her here just to bet her body in a poker game. But Tuck came up beside her and slid his fingers between hers. When she glanced around at the hacker, she sealed her lips. She didn't know what was going on or what they were doing, but she trusted Tuck, maybe more than she trusted Brodie because he had never once let her down.

Tuck led her around to where he had been sitting and the fourth guy came with them, as though he didn't trust her not to run. Tuck sat himself down and she went into his lap without being invited or compelled into it. Being close to her kin was the only thing that might keep her sane.

"Turn 'em, Rigor," Tuck said, leaning past her in expectation of seeing the cards each man had. For half a beat, nothing happened, and she wanted to scream at them to hurry up.

Rigor turned his cards first and no one seemed to breathe until the last one was revealed… eight of hearts, king of hearts, king of diamonds… Her vision was beginning to blur, but her lips were so dry, she couldn't pry them apart. Eight of spades… if the next one was a king… The black spade and the capital K made her throat close and with bated breath, everyone fixed on Brodie.

"What have you got, Rave?" Rigor asked, pushing back in his seat.

God, she hoped that Brodie knew what he was doing. Her nails dug so deep into Tuck's hand that she probably drew blood. She couldn't blink, couldn't breathe, she wanted her love to save her from the possible fate he'd put upon her.

"Cut her loose," Brodie grumbled and shoved up onto his feet to turn his back on her.

The strangled yelp definitely came from her. Tuck stood up and walked away, letting the fourth guy pull her over to him. He yanked her close and ran his hands down her back to squeeze her ass. Twisting as far as she could, she pushed at him and watched Brodie and Tuck retreat toward the couches. Brodie ducked and picked up a half-empty bourbon bottle as Tuck grabbed glasses for him to fill.

"What's your name, sweetheart?" the guy groping her asked and with one vice arm around her, he grabbed her face and forced her around to try to kiss her.

Dipping back, she spat out at his face, and his surprise made him stop. "That's none of your goddamn business," she hissed.

"You're community property now," the eager guy squeezing her said as he eyed her breasts. "You're gonna have a great time with me and my buddies."

"Let her go," Rigor said and curled his fingers around

her wrist. The man embracing her loosened his hold but turned to come in close at her back and hold her in place for the examination of his buddy.

"My girls behave and they get treated right," Rigor said. At over six feet and with noir hair, this guy was intimidating, but she wasn't going to show him any fear.

"You can kiss my ass," she barked. "I'm not your girl."

"You are now," he said, lowering to growl in her face. "And my men will take turns on you until you come to terms with that." He was close enough that she tried to lift her leg to knee his groin, but he caught it and thrust it down. The snarl of his anger didn't frighten her, and when he lifted his hand, she braced for the slap. But another hand appeared in front of her to block the blow, Brodie caught the wrist of her assailant before he could make contact.

"You know the rules," Tuck said from somewhere behind Brodie. She couldn't see Brodie's face, but she could tell from the glare Rigor's wore that Brodie wasn't smiling with glee. "You gotta give him one chance to win it back."

Rigor's man was still at her back, so she was stuck here and while this close to Rigor, she could smell his conceit.

"If he has something I want," Rigor said, tugging his arm away from Brodie and backing away. "He has to be able to offer me something I want to make it worth taking the risk."

Her heart worked overtime, but her lungs were starved of their fuel because she was holding her breath, praying that Brodie could get them out of this.

"I have one thing that you want," Brodie said, staying at her side, though the man at her back held both of her wrists, so she couldn't move or even turn enough to look Brodie in the face.

Rigor's eyes narrowed as his anger dispersed. "She mean that much to you?"

"If she did, he wouldn't have put her on the table," Tuck said, coming in close to the group. "You know what we want."

The men all glanced toward the table, though she couldn't be sure what they were looking at, all that she could see was a jumble of cash and items that she couldn't identify beyond their physical properties. There were keys, but she didn't know what they were for. There were papers and an envelope, nothing that she would think Brodie would value over her. Then again, she'd never thought he would put her into a pot before.

Rigor whistled and looked toward the couches. "Clear out."

The men on the couches did as they were told and bolted, leaving her alone with Tuck, Brodie, and these two other men whom she didn't know. "We talking indefinitely?" Rigor asked.

Zara was lost, these men knew what they were talking about, but no one was being explicit, so she was in the dark. "A month," Brodie said and Rigor scoffed.

"Not worth it," Rigor said, turning his lower lip out for a second.

"You know it is," Tuck said. "How many times you asked?"

Rigor lowered his chin and curled his tongue in his mouth as if considering this abstract offer that she couldn't fathom. "Three months, and I want both of you."

Tuck laughed and made eye contact with Brodie. They said nothing, and she couldn't stop peeking at every face she could see in hope for some kind of hint for what Brodie and Tuck were doing. Tuck's shoulder rose a fraction and Brodie set his sights on his opponent again.

"Done," Brodie said, but he didn't sound happy about making the concession.

"Ha!" Rigor called out. She was let go as the men all moved back toward the table. "High card wins."

Tuck gathered up all the cards and shuffled them before putting the deck on the table between Brodie and Rigor. "Winner cuts first."

He cracked his knuckles then reached for the pile of cards to cut the deck, he turned it to show a jack, and she curled her lips over her teeth to prevent herself from calling out. This was too much. Her life. Her freedom. Everything she was rested on Brodie's card being higher and the odds of that weren't in their favor.

Tuck and Brodie looked at each other, neither looked at

her. Rigor put the cards down and stepped back. "Give it your best shot, Raven… I've waited for this day for a long time. A long, long time."

It felt as though her body was frozen in a glacier, yet the thump of her insistent heart echoed in her ears. Her wide eyes were fixed on the deck and she almost didn't notice that Brodie had looked her way. After a double take, her eyes fixed on his and he didn't seem to be intending to do anything else until she did something, but she didn't know what that was.

Impatient, she just wanted this over with because she couldn't handle the suspense, but Brodie seemed to be in no rush.

"What?" she asked.

"Come here," Brodie said in a slow, deep voice.

The guy behind her had let her go but was still close. Still, when she moved toward Brodie, she wasn't prevented from going. As pissed as she was at Brodie, she wasn't going to argue with him in public because he was still the better option when it came to who she wanted to go home with tonight.

She expected him to say something, instead, he took her chin, and with his thumb pressed to the front of it, he tipped her head up. "You're a good girl."

Except she wouldn't be if she was forced to go with this crazy person who had threatened her with his men. Brodie dipped and pushed his mouth onto hers and she opened in answer to his request for her tongue, because she hadn't seen him for a week and she missed him, so her reaction was automatic.

And yet, if she was told to go with the other guy, this would be the last chance she would ever have to kiss Brodie because even after she escaped the gangster's clutches, she would never go back to McCormack manor, not after a betrayal as profound as this.

"Come on, get on with it," Rigor moaned.

Brodie wasn't great at following orders, especially from people he didn't like, and she didn't need a PhD in criminal etiquette to know that Brodie didn't like this guy. He needed something from him. But Brodie didn't savor doing business with Rigor, which made her believe Brodie enjoyed the idea of her going with Rigor even less than she did—and that was saying something.

In his own good time, Brodie stopped kissing her and turned his attention to the cards. With one hand in hers and his eyes fixed on his enemy, Brodie reached for the cards and she chewed her bottom lip as she fixated on his turn. King.

Shrieking, she bounced up and locked both arms around his neck, but she didn't get the pleasure of his mouth because he was still fixated on the man who had to be spitting fury. Tuck was already gathering everything from the center of the table into a backpack she hadn't noticed before. Nuzzling against her love's neck, she kissed his jaw.

"Nice doing business with you," Brodie said, walking backwards toward the door as Tuck finished fastening the backpack. Brodie tucked her behind him, and she went after Tuck when he began to head for the door. Brodie didn't turn his back on the room until they went through the curtain.

Then they started going faster to get through the main bar and out the front door. Tuck was already straddling a bike when she and Brodie exited. Tuck tossed keys at Brodie, then gunned his own bike out of the parking lot without looking back.

"What was that about?" she asked, when Brodie took her waist and lifted her onto the back of a bike.

"Keep it shut, we're not out of danger yet," he said, jumping onto the bike and starting the engine. She didn't have to be told to hold on to him tight, she'd done this enough times already, and the relief at being out of that dangerous situation gave him a reprieve with regards to her wrath, for now at least.

Something popped and metal tinged, the shock of it made her cling tighter to him. Brodie sped away, hunkered low over the bike and when she glanced back, she saw the men from the back room aiming weapons at them and there was a spark, then another. Brodie revved through the gate and over the bumpy road onto the concrete, then they were gone, out of the range of fire, and on their way to God knew where.

SEVENTEEN

THE ROAD WAS DARK and there were no landmarks, but they ended up approaching civilization again and when they eventually stopped, they were in the parking lot of a single story sprawling motel.

Brodie parked and got off, then took her from the bike. "Where are we?"

"Stop asking questions," he said, taking her arm to pull her toward the building.

Lifting her arm out of his hold, she took a step back. "You just bartered me away to another man," she said. "How do I know that's not going to happen again?"

Art had been impressed by her vigilance, and she wasn't going to retract her wariness until she knew what was going on.

"Because all the men in here would eat a bullet before they betrayed me," he said, lunging forward to grab her again.

Trying to wrestle her arm away, she didn't get far, especially when he snagged her other arm and pulled her body onto his. "I'll scream," she said, still trying to pull away from him. Glaring up at him, she dared him to test her.

Instead of answering her, he ducked and stole her mouth. When she tried to pull herself away, he grabbed her to force her to stay in his arms, to stay in his kiss, even when she didn't respond to him. He shoved his tongue into her mouth, so she dug her teeth into him, but that only caused him to bend and pick her up from the ground. Pounding his shoulders with her fists, her bite became a suck and when her back hit cold concrete, she gasped to inhale the breath from his lungs.

Tearing his mouth away, he nipped her lower lip. "When the fuck are you gonna learn to trust me?" he snarled.

"You're a fucking bastard," she said, hitting his shoulders again, but instead of causing pain, it made him growl. The thick insistence of his dick throbbed against her dampening core when his body pressed her against the wall in this dark space that had to be a service alley for the motel or something. She could just make out a light somewhere behind him, but she was more interested in grabbing his face to pull his mouth onto hers again.

He was a bastard, but he had to have had a plan. She did have to learn to trust him. Sometimes she struggled to remember he cared for her as much as he did, especially when he so often seemed indifferent.

Spitting his mouth from hers, she scowled at his angry expression. "Get off me."

"Too late for that," he said and relaxed his hips enough that she thought he might put her down. But with one hand between them, he freed himself from his jeans and used his dick to hook the crotch of her panties aside.

"Don't you even think about it," she said when his blunt tip probed her entrance.

"Shut the fuck up," he said and with one hard shunt, he filled her up.

With each advance, he jolted her body against the wall. This invasion was more welcome than any that had come before. His urgency and impatience to occupy her betrayed how he'd craved her and that admission by action only incensed her hormones into a deeper fury.

Fighting his mouth with her own kiss. He pressed harder and thrust deeper. Grinding her fingernails into the sinew of his neck, she surrendered to her gratitude.

So often with Brodie, her emotions were sent from one

extreme to the other. She'd been so glad to hear from him and exalted that he wanted her with him and then so nervous to go into that bar. Her emotions were all over the place, the only thing she was a hundred percent certain of was her desire to be fucked and hard by her guy.

His kiss drew back and when their eyes met, she pressed her palms to his cheeks. Her rhythmic whimpers were punctuated by the rush of air leaving her lungs each time he drove himself into her.

The friction of their rutting bodies stimulated her into a climax that made her head scrape on the structure behind her as she bucked into the bliss of his body.

Increasing his pace was a signal to her that he was building to his own release. Her slick passage burned in reaction to the abrasion caused by his bulk expanding her swollen tissues as they consumed his onslaught.

Pushing up, she caught his lip in her teeth. "Don't swear," she panted. "We have to be quiet."

His sense was lost in the flood of their endorphins, but he surged forward and bared his teeth as air hissed out of him.

Their huffing breath merged between their lips that hung only a few millimeters apart. He squeezed her ass so hard that she squirmed against the pain. But his dick was still wedged in her, so he blew out a sharp breath at her movement.

Reconnecting reminded her of their dedication and she was sorry that she'd ever doubted his commitment to her.

"I missed you," she whispered, kissing him quick. "I missed you so much, baby."

"I should've said it," he returned in a similar tone while examining the lips she smudged onto his. "Before we left the manor… I don't know why I didn't."

Skimming her hands down to his chest, she kissed him again. He might not be declaring his love now, but that he was acknowledging how he'd ignored her 'I love you' was as close as he'd come to saying the words himself. For months, she'd wanted to hear him admit his feelings, but this moment of vulnerability and the truth of his own frustration put his hesitation into perspective for her enough that she could enlighten him.

"Because everyone you've ever trusted enough to love has left you," she explained, understanding the cause of his reluctance meant she could no longer be offended by it. "Your parents, your brother, your uncle, you lost them all and you don't want to lose me."

His pelvis crushed hers to the wall so he could keep her pinned with her legs locked around him. But he freed his hands to touch her cheeks and skim them down to seize her shoulders.

The vehemence of his words made her shiver. "I'll never let another guy lay his hands on you. For the ops, we might come close, but… I'll never—"

He'd been offended by her doubt and she was sorry she'd hurt him. "I know."

"No, you don't," he said, giving her a shake. "You don't understand. I'm your guy. You'll always be safe. Always belong to me."

Any panic she'd felt in that bar had upset him because he'd sensed that her faith in him had faltered. "Should we go inside and finish this?" she smiled, rubbing her hands over him.

That they hadn't been able to contain themselves for long enough to get inside to the bed he must have been using this last week aroused her all over again. He'd wanted her so bad that he couldn't wait those extra few seconds to get inside her.

"We can go inside," he said, backing up half a step. She tugged her skirt down as he fastened his jeans and took her hand. "But we can't finish anything."

Leading her around to the front of the building, he went to a door and knocked on it, which was odd if this was his room. "You don't have a key?" she asked.

The door opened and as Brodie took her inside, Tuck walked away from the door. The motel room was large, it had two double beds and a pull out bed in the far corner beside a narrow hallway that had to lead to the bathroom. A large table in the middle of the room was covered with papers that Zave seemed to be reading. Tuck went over to a seat at the same table in front of two open laptops. Brodie was busy behind her doing something with the door, but she crept closer to the table and saw that there was a map taped down to the table surface.

"What is all this?" she asked.

Brodie came up and with a hand on the back of her neck, he urged her up to the table. "This is what we've been doing all week," he said. "That's a plan of the area."

There were stickers and Post-its on the table that said various things. She had no time to read anything, because Brodie snagged her wrist and pulled her over to seat her in a dining chair near the sofa bed. He backed up to perch himself on the end of the table and Zave rose to take up place beside Brodie. She shrank under the scrutiny of the men, Zave made eye contact and she shuddered.

Tuck finished typing on one of the laptops, then closed both the lids and came over to perch at Brodie's other side.

"Okay, I feel like I'm in the principal's office… times three," she said, tucking her hands under her thighs. "Three incredibly hot and panty-melting principals, but still… what's going on?"

"We have your first official assignment," Tuck said, all business.

"Okay," she said, scrutinizing the expressions looming over her for some clue as to what they were going to ask of her. "What is it?"

Tuck twisted to reach behind him, he shunted something aside then turned back to her and held up a glossy eight by ten inch sheet. A picture. Of a man. And one she recognized as Benedict Leatt. She glanced at Brodie, but his expression didn't change.

"What am I supposed to do with him?" she asked, reaching up to take the picture so that she could look at it more closely.

There was nothing particularly striking about the image. Ben had brown hair, blue eyes, and dimples that made him appear more cute than threatening. Wearing blue jeans and a flannel shirt, he was just as she remembered him.

"Get close to him," Zave said.

That could mean any of a number of things. She needed

clarity and tried to be calm as the possibilities flitted through her mind. "To what end?" she asked, making eye contact with Brodie. "He has information we need?"

"Access," Brodie said and his stoic form was a world away from the impassioned lover who'd just taken her against the wall outside. "The number one thing we have to find out is where they hoard their hardware, their weapons and explosives."

"And you think he'll know?" she asked, glancing at the picture.

"His name is Benedict Leatt," Tuck said. "He's the guy you met at Sutcliffe's compound."

"I know who he is," she said.

"Sutcliffe left the country on Monday," Brodie said. "He left his deputies in charge and we need to know what's going on in that house. Sutcliffe's compound is constantly occupied. We can get onto the land, but the house is too risky for us to bust into. There are proximity alarms and video surveillance."

"Not to mention the number of people he has roaming around," Tuck said, reaching back to pick up another stack of pictures, which he handed over to her. "The main house is in the center of the land. Sutcliffe's closest associates live there. But there's at least another two hundred people living on the land in trailers, barracks, and cabins."

"We can only know what they're planning if we can get some tech into that house."

"Cameras?" she asked, scanning each picture. They reminded her of the tour she'd received, though there were some images of areas she hadn't visited, such as the shot of a long single-story wooden building that looked like it could be the barracks Tuck had mentioned. The setting was unfamiliar too, so she guessed she'd been kept away from it on purpose.

"Audio would be a start," Tuck said.

She would do what they asked of her. She'd taken part in Kindred operations before and had faith that these men would keep a close eye on her. Adrenaline was beginning to seep into her system though, it was natural to be nervous, and she didn't want to let her cohorts down. "And we can't bug one of the followers?" she asked.

Brodie shook his head. "Besides the fact that the majority of his followers don't go into the main house, they don't have the access to get close enough to the conversations we need to hear. His deputies are vigilant to the point of paranoia, and they rarely leave the property."

"And Sutcliffe doesn't allow phones or internet access," Tuck said. "He has a cellphone that travels with him. So right now, there's no way for us to get in there, physically or digitally."

"But Ben has access?" she asked, returning to the first picture Tuck had handed her. "He can come and go."

"He's a level below Sutcliffe's most trusted deputies," Brodie said. "With Sutcliffe out of the country, his involvement has increased. He's only been with the group for a few months."

"Sutcliffe still doesn't trust him all the way," Tuck said. "But he likes the guy and you were right about what you said when you were talking to Ben, he is unthreatening and ignorant to most of what goes on. He's a nice guy, which was why he was the best bet to tempt you into joining Sutcliffe's cause."

Brodie nodded. "Sutcliffe enjoys making people dance before he lets them into his inner circle."

"And…" Tuck and Brodie made eye contact then glanced to Zave.

"And what?" she asked.

"Ben was tasked with tempting you, that means he'll be open to developing a relationship with you. He's still trying to impress Sutcliffe, to prove his own ability and loyalty."

Being a prize for Ben would make it easier for her to get inside. But it also meant that being inside was riskier if Ben got the wrong idea about her interest. "So Ben wants to be a part of Sutcliffe's cult and they're making him jump through hoops," she asked.

"Right," Tuck said, nodding once.

Her eyes drifted to the picture. "And so you want me to…" Horror made her thrust to her feet when she replayed what they'd said about getting close to him and developing a relationship. Could it be that the Kindred meant close in the personal sense? "What do you mean by relationship? You want me to seduce him?"

Tuck laughed and stood up to rest his hands on her shoulders. "Yeah, 'cause that sounds like something Rave would subscribe to."

Glancing past Tuck, she made eye contact with her love. "Swallow," she murmured her alias. "You want me to get close to him… the way you got close to me?"

His gaze fogged with anger and offense. "Not the way I got close to you," Brodie said. "He won't touch you."

Tuck interrupted before she could ask more questions that might rile her love further. "You have his number, you can call him and tell him you want to talk. He'll ask you out somewhere on a date, 'cause…" Tuck glanced back at Brodie. "Well, 'cause he wants to win you for Sutcliffe and 'cause you're hot."

Her eyes fell to the picture again. "Thank you," she murmured, but didn't feel flattered.

They had to have noticed her reluctance because Tuck gave her more information. "You go out with him for dinner or drinks, whatever he wants. It will be out in the open."

"Where we can watch you," Brodie grumbled.

Where Brodie had line of sight, he wouldn't take his aim away from her date. "Did you pack Maverick?" she asked.

"You bet your sweet ass I did," he replied.

"We want to know what he knows," Zave said. "Which isn't likely to be much."

Tuck added more. "But you might get the opportunity to go inside and if you do…"

"We'll cross that bridge when we come to it," Brodie said. "Ideally, you'll bug the guy and that will be it. Over."

Projecting the best case scenario wasn't Brodie's default. Tuck did his best to manage her expectations because more could be asked of her. "The problem is, we don't know when he'll be going in there. You can't bug him the night before or the week after, you know? He'd have to be wearing or carrying whatever we bugged and we'd have to minimize his chance to discover the tech."

"Okay," she exhaled. It was a difficult concept to grasp,

that she was going to befriend this man under false pretenses, she'd had a bit of practice with that at CI with Grant, but at least she'd had a previous relationship with him that she could mimic. Something else made her wary of Ben, if he was a part of Sutcliffe's group, that made him dangerous. "Is he violent?"

"He's a physical therapist," Tuck said. She knew that already but didn't know what it had to do with his ability to control his impulses.

"If you don't want to do this…" Brodie said and moved in behind Tuck.

"She has to do this," Zave said.

"She doesn't have to do a damn thing," Brodie snarled. Zara reached beyond Tuck to smooth her hand down Brodie's arm.

"I want to be a part of this. And with you guys watching out for me, nothing will go wrong."

Zave didn't give much away about his thoughts, but she'd thought the same thing of Brodie many times and she wondered if maybe that enigmatic aura was in their blood. Then again, they were maternal cousins. Art hadn't been difficult to read. Initially, she'd been sure that he hated her, but when she'd asked him, he'd been honest about his reservations.

Art had believed she was capable of saving Brodie's soul while being a part of the Kindred at the same time. As much as she didn't want to let Brodie and Tuck down, she felt the weight of Art's expectation on her shoulders. He'd wanted her to be a full member of the Kindred and had told her that she had the ability to fulfill a vital role. But to be with a man, a stranger, and to make him believe that she was not only interested in him but possibly interested in his politics as well, she wasn't sure that she could live up to Art's expectations.

"What's on your mind?" Brodie asked.

She hadn't realized she'd gone quiet, or that her concerns were written all over her face until she saw the intrigue on the faces of the men around her. "Nothing," she said, slipping her nail over the corner of one of the pictures.

Brodie grazed her cheekbone and made her look at them again. "This will only work if we're all honest with each other.

There can't be secrets."

"I was just…" she wanted Tuck to save her, but he was as curious as the other two. "I wish Art was here." Brodie's hand fell from her face at the same time Tuck took her hand.

"We all do," Tuck said and Brodie turned to walk away, which made dread seize her guts. He was probably struggling to get through this as it was, he didn't need her to remind him of who was missing.

"Do you have any questions?" Zave asked.

Clearing her throat, she left Brodie to his solitude because he wouldn't appreciate her cornering him in front of people. He didn't appreciate it at any time, but there was virtually no chance of him opening up in front of his cohorts.

Narrowing her eyes, she held the photos to her chest. "Yeah, what was tonight about?"

Tuck went over to the table and moved some things aside to retrieve the brown envelope she'd seen on the poker table. He held it up and brought it over to her. "Sutcliffe runs background on all of his prospective members," Tuck said. "He outsources it because he doesn't trust anyone and has it corroborated by at least two sources. Rigor was one of those sources."

"Rigor was Brodie's poker opponent?"

Tuck nodded. "This is everything he handed over to Sutcliffe about Leatt. So we know everything Sutcliffe does. We didn't have the time to do our own surveillance and Art would never let us run in blind. We needed something and Rigor had it, so at least we can reassure you by giving you Ben Leatt's criminal record."

"It will help you to bond with him if you know his history," Brodie said from his position facing the front window, which was covered with curtains.

Tuck handed her the envelope, but she didn't open it. "Couldn't you just pay Rigor for the information?" she asked.

"Rigor likes to play games," Tuck said. "That's how we ended up around the poker table. We didn't summon you to put you in the pot. We summoned you for the Leatt thing. We were going to have you brought back here to the motel with Zave." That would have been an interesting experience, being alone with Zave. "But as the game went on it was clear Rigor wanted blood. The stakes were getting higher and higher, he had to believe he had us on the ropes. It was the only way to get him to put the dossier on the table. He had to be so confident that he got cocky."

"And what better way to up the stakes than to put Brodie's girlfriend on the table," she said.

"The plan was always to lose," Tuck said. "Stroking Rigor's ego was the quickest way to get what we wanted. Losing the game was the goal because we knew about the double or nothing rule. You've got to give a man a chance to win back his losses with stakes that big. But that meant if he lost, we'd have to give him the chance to win it back, and we couldn't take the risk he'd win that final round."

"But you have to be able to offer him something else for double or nothing?" she asked. "What was both of you for three months about?"

"He wanted us to work for him," Tuck said. "He's been trying to get us on payroll for a long time."

"But you agreed to do it, if you'd lost—"

"I do what my chief tells me to do," Tuck said. "I'm Kindred." Brodie turned to come back to the group. "But there was never a chance of us losing."

"How can you be so sure of that?" she asked, ducking when Brodie reached for her temple, he flicked his hand and brought it around to show her the Ace of Hearts. She took it from him and blinked at the card because she had no idea where it had come from.

"It was no accident that I shuffled the deck," Tuck said, going back to his laptops.

Zave went back to his papers, and she was left alone holding the photos, the dossier, and the playing card.

"Open it," Brodie said, nodding at the envelope she held. He hunkered over a nearby duffel bag and it was then that she noticed her suitcase was there beside it. Her driver must have brought it here to Zave for her. "Read it, learn about him."

"Learn about him," she muttered, seating herself on the chair and putting her wares on the sofa bed.

"He'll have to believe that you're getting to know him,"

Brodie said. "It will be helpful if you can steer the conversation toward his interests and history. He'll believe your connection is real, which will make him more likely to trust you."

She would do what she was told and believed that these men would look after her. But Brodie's stern brow made her worry for him, so when he tried to walk away, she caught his hand. "Gimme some sugar," she whispered and hazarded a smile in the hope that he'd reciprocate. It took him a handful of seconds, but he eventually dipped to kiss her.

"Don't forget what I told you outside," he said, pressing a fingertip to her cheekbone as he crouched beside her and lowered his volume even further. "And please, baby, whatever you do…"

"What?" she asked, sensing his hesitation.

"Don't fall for this guy."

She was so surprised that her lips parted only to close again. Bringing a hand up to his hair, she combed her fingers over it. "You think I'd leave you for a cult-crazy?"

"You don't get to leave me," he said, sliding a hand up her thigh beneath her skirt. "I mean, don't feel sorry for him, because I won't hesitate to put a bullet in him. I don't care how you feel about him."

So he thought she'd sympathize with this Ben guy and might ask for mercy on his behalf if it came to it. Zara wasn't a killer by trade, but she also respected that each of the Kindred had their role to perform. If someone had to die, then Raven would be the primary candidate for taking that person out. She had to engage this guy and Raven had to erase him.

EIGHTEEN

WAKING UP WITH BRODIE was pleasant. But when she kissed him and slid her hand down the front of his jeans, he grasped her wrist and pulled her hand out of his underwear to remind her that they weren't alone. Tuck was sleeping on the sofa bed and Zave was in the bed beside them.

Her disappointment was short-lived because he picked her up and carried her into the shower where he reminded her of his loyalty. While there was other Kindred keeping guard, he relaxed his no nakedness rule and she was grateful for that after spending a week showering and sleeping alone.

Her day was spent studying up on Ben and she eventually took the plunge and called him just after lunch. Tuck was right, instead of talking on the phone, Ben asked her to meet him in a bar that night. There was so much to remember and she was terrified that she wouldn't be able to pull this off. But the Kindred guys assured her that they'd be on hand should she need backup, though none of them thought she'd need it.

Zara wasn't surprised when Tuck showed her the camera they had planted on Ben's apartment. While it wasn't easy to see inside, they had a partial view of the living room and both exits were covered. Tuck showed her this to familiarize her with the space and that was when Brodie chimed in that she would never be going anywhere near Ben's house.

But the truth was, Ben spent little time at his own apartment and the paperwork Rigor had provided showed that Ben had given notice at the rented space, suggesting he planned to move to the compound full-time.

Swift and Raven took her through what would happen when she met Ben and how to excuse herself at the end of the night. They showed her a schematic of the bar she would be meeting Ben in and pointed out all of the exits. They were nothing if not thorough. They told her she had to be fluid and flexible, and she would have to learn to improvise because they couldn't cover every eventuality. People were unpredictable and anything could happen.

The ultimate goal was to find out what Sutcliffe was planning and if he had any weaknesses they could exploit should the worst happen. For now, they wanted to know why he was out of the country and when he'd be coming back. To gain his trust and garner future information, she may have to spend a lot of time with Ben.

So she had to prepare herself for the possibility of ending up in Ben's apartment, even if it was unlikely. The more terrifying prospect was ending up at Sutcliffe's compound. If Sutcliffe came back suddenly or one of his deputies got involved and questioned her up close, she might not hold up under suspicious scrutiny.

Night was upon them and the stage was set for her to do her thing. Swift and Falcon had left the motel room to set up their surveillance position in the premises opposite the bar where she'd be meeting Ben tonight. Brodie was with her in the motel room, waiting for her cab to show up, which had been called after Swift confirmed that Ben was in the bar. While she sat looking out the motel room window waiting for her ride, she tried not to examine what Brodie was doing in the background.

A car pulled into the parking lot and honked its horn as it passed to turn in a loop at the top of the concrete space. Snagging her clutch from the windowsill, she got up to head for the door.

"Hey," Brodie said in a clipped tone and caught her arm

to draw her back. Ready for her mission, she was thinking of how to approach the situation and didn't notice the darkness in his gaze straight away. "If you let him touch you. I'll kill him."

That declaration jarred her out of the mission zone she'd gotten her head into. "What?" she asked, quickly casting aside her speculation about the future to return her focus to the present moment.

His eyes got even narrower, and she could read the killer in them. He wasn't messing around or playing with her. "I have no conscience. If I kill the guy 'cause you let him get his hands on you, his blood is on your hands."

Shock ebbed to anger and she yanked her arm away from him. If he killed Ben for no other reason than he got too close to her that was on Brodie's head, not hers. "Don't threaten me," she snapped. "I'm in charge of our sex life. If I can handle you, what makes you think I can't handle a schmuck who might try to force me?"

Grabbing her neck, he rushed her back against the wall and crouched to hiss his words in her face. "If he tries to force you, I'll blow out his kneecaps then come over there and deal with him real slow. Do you want to learn how to make a grown man cry and beg for death? I'll teach you everything you ever need to know."

Aroused by his fervent possessiveness, she elevated her chin. He loved her so much that he'd kill, not only to protect her life, but to protect her modesty too, and he didn't make false promises. Raven was a killer by trade and could put a bullet in a man just because he wanted to and he'd never think twice about it or regret the decision he made.

Brodie was her man, but Raven had killed based upon her signal and he'd do it again. Having power over life and death by proxy was intoxicating, not because she craved murder or enjoyed death, but because it was the ultimate, final power. Raven trusted her enough to give her influence over his kill decisions and knew she would never exploit him.

In the past, she'd been the object at the end of his scope, giving him something to aim at, but she never doubted his ability. Standing in target range with the barrel of his rifle pointed in her direction proved her epic trust in him. One slip, one accident, and she'd be no more. But even if she taunted him, he'd never risk her life. When he stood watch over her with his gun trained on someone maybe only an inch from her, she never worried for her safety.

Goading him, she showed no fear. "Maybe I'll let him touch me just to test your resolve."

His brows rose, but his eyes remained narrow proving he was getting riled. "You think I'm blowing smoke?" he asked, increasing the strength of his grip on her throat to force up the angle of her head farther. "Try it, baby, please. It'll be like Christmas come early for me. You remember what happened to the last man who tried to kiss you?"

Tim Sutcliffe. Albert Sutcliffe's nephew. He'd been kissing her when Brodie put a bullet in his head, and that was her introduction to the Kindred.

"You're a dirty, base animal," she sneered, but her disgust was a mask for the pulse of arousal his rough grip provoked in her.

"One who will be watching every move you make tonight, hear me? You belong to me. You go where I say. Do what I tell you to. If you dance just the way I want you to, I'll let you come home and ride my cock as a reward."

She loved it when he snarled dirty words at her, but her role was to flout his intimidation and so that's what she did. "Don't do me any favors," she said and tried to pull away his arm, but he slammed her back against the wall. Air left her lungs on impact, and she had to gasp in to fuel her lust. "Turning me on and sending me to him, is that your plan?"

His teeth clenched and he got even closer. "You better be thinking of me when you're flirting with him," he said, keeping one hand around her throat while the other pushed her hair from her face on its journey to the back of her skull. "You want him to think you want it, don't you?"

Damn, he was good. Her nerves were gone and her complete focus was on her man, who was here in front of her, holding her against this wall, proving his dominance over her in a way he knew would stimulate her. Walking into this meeting horny was the best way to convince this guy that she was interested in him for real. Men were blinded by sex and if she could make Ben believe that she wanted something more than friendship, he'd be more inclined to answer her questions.

"That is the plan isn't it," she said, trying to disguise her arousal, though he knew her too well to mistake it.

"There's only one man on the face of this earth who can stimulate you. If you need any guy to think you're horny, you better pull up some of that material I give you when I fuck you hard and dirty."

Struggling in his grip only made him hold tighter, so she went limp. "My mind's drawn a blank," she said, pressing her palm to the erection pulsing through his jeans. "Give me a refresher."

She gulped in the air that filled the void between them before the thick insistence of his tongue pried her lips apart. She was sure that they were going to get it on here in the motel room, while she was supposed to be on a date with another man, until the horn blared outside the window again and Brodie ripped his mouth away.

"I'll be there and set up before you get there," he said, kissing her again. He was going on his bike, so he wouldn't have to wait for anything inconvenient like traffic. Having him in position was her most valued security. Somehow, he knew that without her being explicit about her need to have him there watching over her. Pulling her away from the wall, he spun her to face the door and smacked her ass. "Get going before I tie you down."

Doing as she was told, she didn't look back. The cab driver was just that, but she didn't want to give any indication that she wasn't alone in this motel room, just in case. She got into the vehicle, gave the address of the bar, and then she was on her way.

The pendant necklace she wore would allow the men to see what was going on in the bar. She had an earpiece in but hadn't yet heard a whisper from Tuck or the others. He'd told her he would activate it when they saw her going in. But the reality was they couldn't communicate. She was going to engage Ben and after she did, all she would be able to do was listen when it came to the Kindred.

The glass-fronted tavern was less than five blocks from the motel, and she could probably have walked. But Brodie had insisted on a cab.

She had paid the driver and was about to enter when she heard the crackle in her ear, then Brodie's voice came through. "I'm right there with you, baby."

Opening the barroom door, she was hit with humid air and the medley of a pop song. The place was busy but entirely unthreatening. It was a light space filled with tables and pop art. It couldn't be further from the atmosphere of Purdy's. But she wasn't here to make comparisons. She was here to make a connection. So she made her way to the bar and ordered a white wine spritzer.

Art didn't have to be in her ear because he was in her head, telling her not to drink too much. She took a seat on a stool and let her eyes peruse the bar. She'd been told to seat herself in the Kindred's field of vision and to let Ben come to her. Under no circumstances was she to go to where Ben was seated. They didn't suspect she was being setup but preferred to assume that they were until proved otherwise. Seating herself and waiting for him to come to her let her be the driver and they needed her to be in an optimum spot that allowed her cohorts to see her.

When she scanned around, she noticed Ben at the end of the bar around the curve. Her pulse jacked up when he made eye contact with her. Dropping her gaze, she took a breath and looked up again, yes, he was still looking at her.

She managed a smile and then took her attention to the opposite end of the bar. She didn't want to be too eager and if she played it right, he would approach her as they wanted him to. The light inside made it difficult for her to see anything out of the large windows at the front of the building because there was nothing but night beyond them. But the Kindred would be able to see inside and that was the most important thing. With that thought, she closed her eyes and sipped her drink.

Touching the pendant on her necklace, she made a silent plea for reassurance. "We're here, baby," Brodie said into her ear and the sound of his voice made the hairs on her forearm stand up. "We can see you. Can't take my eyes off you, you're the hottest thing in the room."

Brodie was being kind by flattering her. Tuck gave her the facts. "If you go any farther into the place we'll lose visual," Tuck said.

The Kindred were in a first-floor space on the opposite side of the street. This bar was long and there was a dance floor in the back near where the restrooms were. But if this was as far as the Kindred could see then she had no intention of venturing deeper inside.

Glancing around, she was going to check out if Ben was still looking at her. Her equilibrium tilted when she realized he was no longer seated where she'd seen him before. All of her apprehension whooshed out of her and was replaced by a fear that she'd failed before she had even started.

But before she could leap up and exclaim her apologies, someone slipped onto the stool beside hers. Ben. "You're new around here," he said, and his grin made her laugh.

"Yes," she said on an exhale. "Yes, I am. Thanks for meeting me."

"Would you like to dance?"

It could just be his way of putting her at ease, or maybe he was just trying to make friends, but she couldn't think of anything she wanted to do less than dance. "Oh no," she said, losing her smile. "Oh, no, no, I don't, I mean…"

"It's okay," he laughed and pushed his drink toward hers as he edged nearer. "It's not a requirement. I just… you look like a dancer."

"Oh," she hissed in a breath and scrunched her expression. "That's only a whisker away from, 'Do you work out?' Is that a line you use on all the women you meet here?"

His smile broadened and his dimples provoked her to reciprocate. The picture Tuck had given her made Ben look boyish, but in the present, the charcoal tee shirt he was wearing revealed definition in his arms and the physique she'd initially written off as average was far more impressive up close.

"Too cheesy?" he asked.

"Just a tad."

His dimples receded and he looked her in the eye with sincerity. "I don't want to make you uncomfortable, but I'm glad you reached out to me."

She relaxed and drank again. "I've been thinking about our conversation by the lake and... I thought we could maybe... get to know each other a bit better."

His hand came toward her and she realized she'd walked into her own cheesy line. When she relented a smile, he joined in. "I hope you don't use that line on all the guys."

"I don't use any lines," she said with a tsk and a look of mock offense because their banter seemed to be relaxing them both and that was just how she wanted him: pliable. "Do I look like the type who goes trawling for men?"

His smile got even bigger and the grooves in his cheeks returned. "Hey, if I knew what that type looked like I wouldn't have spent so many nights alone recently," he said before pouring more beer down his throat.

A couple vacated a table nearer the door and so she slipped off her stool. "Well at the risk of sounding too forward, do you want to get a table?"

He noticed the vacant table too and nodded. They got up and Ben followed her to their new seats, which were nearer to the Kindred and to the exit, which for her was a double bonus. Once they were seated, there was a moment of silence and she began to squirm when Brodie spoke.

"Atta girl, Swallow, I've got a perfect line of sight." Brodie praised her for seeing the opportunity and taking it. But where her honor was concerned, she wasn't sure she trusted Brodie's trigger finger not to get twitchy. He'd never hurt her, but her date wasn't safe. All she could do was trust Swift to keep Raven reined in.

The quicker she did her job, the quicker she could get out of here and breathe easy again. "So, Ben," she said, moving things along. "How is work?"

Her brows rose as she made eye contact. Starting with the benign subject of his work life allowed him to relax. It wasn't as confrontational or suspicious as a bunch of Sutcliffe questions being her opening gambit.

He wrapped both hands around his beer glass. "My work is much less glamorous than I'm sure you think it is."

She hadn't thought physical therapy was glamorous, but she didn't correct him. Insulting him upfront would be a rookie mistake. So she prompted him to keep talking. "You must meet interesting people."

"The people are what make the job worth doing," he said. "Everyone has a story and it's a privilege to share their journey of rehabilitation with them."

"Do you have any interesting patients at the moment?" she asked and listened with as much interest as she could muster while he told her about a few patients he was working with. Both of them were dancing around the real purpose for their meeting. She would guess that he didn't want to appear to be rushing her any more than she wanted to rush him.

"People are often so grateful," he said after telling her about a third patient. "They don't realize that it's them who do the hard work. I'm just there to guide and facilitate what they need."

"You're modest," she said.

The dents in his cheeks deepened again and he glanced at their empty glasses. "Would you like another drink?"

She nodded, and he took their glasses to the bar, leaving her alone. "This isn't working," she murmured, glancing down at the table to hide her words.

"It is," Tuck said. "You've got him on the hook. You're a natural. You've just got to steer the conversation to Sutcliffe."

"Any suggestions?" she asked. She was getting better at this ventriloquist thing of talking without moving her lips. "Should I just come out with it?"

She'd said she wanted to get to know him, implying that she wanted to be friends and to be comfortable with him before making her decisions about Sutcliffe. Quizzing him on the cult and its leader seemed heavy handed. But if Ben brought up the Brit, then she could segue into her questions.

"Ask him about the future," Tuck said. "His future is with Sutcliffe, right?"

Talking about the future was a good plan, and she had

the time to think about how to approach it before he came back with the drinks. She craved the sound of Brodie's voice, but it was silent in her ear and she was preoccupied with his mood. With his grief over Art, he'd had a tough enough time of late. The last thing he needed was to watch her flirting with another guy.

"It's getting busier," Ben said, when he sat down again. "There's no space on the dance floor."

The music had gotten louder and faster, she surmised that the music got more upbeat as the revelers got drunker. Then it probably slowed down again at the end of the night, to calm people, and to give the men a chance to make a move on those they'd met.

"Do you like to dance?" she asked, keeping conversation easy.

"I like music," he said. "But I guess I just like to see people having fun."

"Is that why you frequent this place?" she asked, scanning the room. "It's welcoming."

"Yes, it is."

"A guy like you with a good job and a sense of humor. Why aren't you married?"

He laughed. "Just haven't met the right woman I guess," he said. "It's on my agenda. I'm ready to settle down. I'm getting too old for the dating scene."

"I know what you mean," she said and sipped her drink. "Is that why you got involved with Sutcliffe? You think he will help you settle down?"

He smiled and took a deep breath. Zara was glad he didn't look hesitant or suspicious. "I'm glad you brought it up. I was avoiding talking about Albert because I didn't want you to think I was trying to convert you."

Score one for her. He wanted to talk about Sutcliffe and she wanted to listen. "I'm curious," she said, thinking about what Grant had said about considering Sutcliffe's cause. But she didn't want to come across as too easy and so in a nod to her reluctance by the lake, she repeated her misgivings. "I can't deny that. I've been thinking about our conversation and… I'm worried about you. I don't know if you understand who Sutcliffe is."

"You're going to try and convert me?" he asked, and although that sentiment was extreme, his smile kept her from panicking. "You know so much about me, tell me about you. Have you been married?"

"Me? No," she said, shaking her head. "No, I come from this small little town and my friends all hooked up young. Now they have kids who go to the same schools that we went to and I… I was always surprised at how easy it was for them to settle. We've got to experience life before we can settle down, right?"

"Yes," he said. "How else can you know what you want unless you're open to new things?"

"My father wanted me to stay in town and marry the boy next door. I disappointed him by going to college instead of staying home and doing chores."

"How does he feel about your decision now?"

"I don't talk to him much," she said. "I think he'd rather pretend I didn't exist. I was the flighty one with a warped view of my position in the world."

"What position is that?" he asked, tilting his head and when she made eye contact, she was sure she blushed at his intent gaze. He was interested in what she had to say and for a few seconds she was flummoxed because she didn't want the romantic attention of this man, yet here he was being the perfect date.

Being honest was the best approach, she didn't know what intel Sutcliffe had on her and she had enough to remember without keeping track of lies about her past too. "I had grand notions of being a part of something bigger, of making a difference in the world."

"Had?" he asked, narrowing his eyes. "You don't have those notions anymore?"

Tipping her head one way and then the other, she explained. "Between college and working, I think I've finally come to realize that the world doesn't need me to save it."

"Someone has to," he said. "Don't you think the world is on a dangerous path?"

Red flags began to pop up and wave, which was a familiar

part of dating for her. Except this time, the warning lights were welcomed. They were her whole purpose for being here. "Oh, I think it is," she said, thinking about everything she'd learned since getting involved with the Kindred. "But what can I do about it? I'm just one person."

His smile was slow to creep up, but when it finally fixed in place, she knew she had him, even though the smile was caused by his belief that he'd found an open door. An avenue he could use to persuade her of the merits of his cause. "One person can make a difference," he said. "If they join forces with other likeminded people."

Ben didn't seem to have Sutcliffe's delusions of grandeur. In fact, he was one of the most down to earth people she'd ever met. By getting her to talk about herself, he was effectively doing what she was trying to, easing her into a place of security and using her history to bond with her. This was a complex dance. She wondered if he was aware of the different masks she wore behind this one she was showing him.

"And that's what you get with Sutcliffe?" she asked because playing dumb and asking him to spell it out served no purpose. She wanted him to believe that she was astute, it made her a greater asset to Albert Sutcliffe. "You think that because you all frequent the same green field that you're part of a hive? There is no community anymore, certainly not in big cities."

His vehement excitement made him sway closer to her. "Albert gives us community and we're teaching the children how important it is to look out for your neighbors," he said and she nodded. "We have the same ideals that you do. We are part of something larger, and we know it will take time, we don't expect instant results. But small changes will eventually make a difference to the big picture. We're a group that wants to make a difference in the world and that have plans to do just that."

She maintained some skepticism. "With Albert Sutcliffe as your messiah?"

"No," he said and looked at the label on his bottle. "We're not trying to save anyone's soul. We're more interested in saving the culture and freedom of future generations."

"Sounds wonderful, but unbelievable," she said, which was true. Many people wanted a safer, kinder world. But it wasn't as simple as taking up residence on some green space and singing "Kumbaya." "How did you get mixed up with him?"

"He was my patient. We met a couple of months ago. His leg was broken in an accident. We worked together to build up his balance and strength again. At first, he was just a patient. Then he started to open up to me and I was surprised by what he said."

Leaning closer, she did her best to seem as intrigued as possible. "What did he tell you?" Not the whole truth if he was claiming his leg was broken in a regular accident.

"That he was going to do something about the condition of the world. He wanted to ensure the safety of our citizens. The government won't do anything. They're too interested in protecting their political capital. But Mr. Sutcliffe wants to take control of our future. We can't be passive anymore. This is a new world. We live in an information and technology age. It's not enough to plead ignorance. No one can get away with that. We have the ability to take control of our own destiny."

He was passionate about what he was saying and she started to feel sorry for him because he couldn't understand what kind of person Albert Sutcliffe was. No doubt Sutcliffe portrayed himself as harmless and seduced followers into taking on his cause before they realized what they were getting involved in.

She sighed. "I don't know what to say," she said, keeping her interest piqued on him. "It sounds too good to be true and you know what they say about that."

"That's what I thought at first as well," he said. "But I've seen what he's building, I'm a part of it now, and it's wonderful. All he wants is to keep people safe."

"So he let you join the group? What did you have to do?"

"There's no initiation or hazing," he said with an easy laugh. "I didn't have to take a life or drink blood if that's what you think. I started by visiting, taking supplies, and sitting in on some meetings."

He was open to answering her questions and didn't seem

suspicious of why she was asking them. "So there's no pressure to just jump straight in and make a commitment?"

"No. We have a vast amount of land and we're largely self-sufficient. Imagine being able to live such a pure existence. Each person is vital to the community and we all look after each other."

Getting inside would give them the chance to bug the house. Having succeeded so far, her confidence was growing, and the prospect of venturing onto Sutcliffe land alone wasn't as daunting anymore. "It would be great to talk to more of the people there," she said.

He frowned. "I can't take you in without Mr. Sutcliffe's permission, and he's out of the country at the moment."

"Will he be back soon?"

His gaze narrowed and she widened her smile in reaction to what might have been suspicion on his face. "Are you interested?"

She nodded. "If it is a place where everyone has a vital role and lives in a society untouched by cynicism. What have you got to hide?"

"I'll talk to some people, if you want me to, and maybe we can go there together soon."

She nodded again and went back to her wine. Ben relaxed, and she was so relieved that they'd overcome a major obstacle. She wanted to find out what Ben knew about Sutcliffe's claims that he planned to protect the world.

But Tuck had already told her that Ben wasn't in the uppermost tiers of Sutcliffe's hierarchy, so it was unlikely he had specifics. Getting inside the farmhouse would let her plant the bugs and then maybe they could uncover Sutcliffe's true agenda.

NINETEEN

SHE LEFT THE BAR after making plans with Ben to talk again later in the week. He tried to get her to stay longer, but she decided that two glasses of wine was her limit when she was undercover after the second glass began to make her feel lightheaded. She gave Ben a story about being tired from the trip that involved a commercial plane rather than a luxury chopper. After that joke, he was more understanding. He walked her outside and put her in a taxi.

He seemed to be a nice enough guy, if not for his whacked out ideas about Sutcliffe. Anyone who idolized a person who gave them promises of saving the world had to have a screw loose. Yet she had sat there and listened like an innocent lapping up every word.

The motel room was empty when she got back, and she stripped off to climb into the shower with intentions of being out and ready for bed by the time the men came back for the debrief. She had just finished washing her hair when the shower curtain flew back and the shock of the intrusion made her scream.

Brodie was there, as tense as thunder before it delivered its deafening crash. She shivered in the draft stemming from the open bathroom door. He barked at her while she stood there wet with the last of the conditioner sliding off her skin. "I told you about the alarm sensors, didn't I?" Brodie's anger didn't make it any easier for her to catch up with what was happening or why he was in such a tense mood. "You're supposed to come in and set the alarm, then the rest of us knock and you let us in."

She had been told about that. Whoever was back first was supposed to set up the trigger on the door and anyone else could only get in if the person inside opened the door. "I didn't set them," she said.

There was no impediment to him or the others getting into the room, so she didn't know why he was so uptight. She hadn't locked them out then come in here to pamper herself.

He didn't loosen. "Which is why I'm pissed," he said, reaching past her to turn off the water.

She squawked and reached for the shower knob. "I'm not finished," she said, but he threw a towel at her, which she had to catch with her outstretched arm.

"Now you are," he said. "Get out here."

Pissing Brodie off wasn't going to lead to a happy fun debrief. His bad mood meant they'd catch more jibes from him than useful opinions. She squeezed the water out of her hair and dried herself before wrapping her body in the towel and departing the bathroom as per his request. Tuck and Zave were there with pizza, and she went over with intentions of pilfering a slice, but Brodie grabbed her hand and whirled her around.

"You have to call your boss," Brodie demanded.

The pizza smelled amazing and now that her anxiety was gone, she was starved. But Brodie was focused on something other than feeding her. "My boss," she said, aware that his scowl reflected the pent-up rage he was doing such a terrible job of suppressing.

She had to stay calm. She couldn't be seen to be provoking him in any way. When Brodie was wound this tight, someone could get permanently hurt. If he was just a little bit annoyed or the root of his problem came from something inconsequential, she could play with him until he released his rage in a frenzied fuck. But from the tick in his jaw and each of his huffing breaths that seemed less patient than the last, she could tell he wasn't in the mood to be played with.

"You have to tell him that you saw Ben," Brodie snapped. "He'll find out anyway if he's close buds with Sutcliffe now. If we want this to work, it has to come from you."

"My boss," she said, wondering if his refusal to say Grant's name or identify their fraternal relationship was protection or if Grant was the cause of Brodie's crappy mood. "Are we being watched or listened to?"

Turning to seek out Zave and Tuck, who were both eating pizza, she waited for Tuck to swallow and respond. "No, we did a bug sweep," he said. "We're clear."

If they weren't being listened to then that suggested Brodie was pissed at his brother. She wanted to know more but wouldn't push for specifics while Brodie was still fuming. "I'll call Grant," she said. "Should I ask for time off? I can work from here and—"

Brodie grabbed her arm and forced her around to face him again. "He can live without you for a few weeks."

"Weeks?" she said, unable to disguise her shock. "I'm going to be dating Ben for weeks? If I keep seeing him… If I see too much of him…"

Brodie's snarling expression descended. "What? If you see too much of him, what?"

If she wasn't honest, she'd just infuriate Brodie further. Her reservations would have the same effect, but she couldn't conceal them. "He'll expect something," she said.

Brodie was probably pissed because she'd been on a date with another man and that was why he'd been quiet for most of the evening. But she couldn't feel guilty about it because he had sent her there and told her that this was her job. Less probable was that Grant had somehow influenced his brother's mood, given that no one had heard from the CEO as far as she knew.

"Let him," Brodie growled.

Some of her anxiety came back. Going on a date in a public place was one thing, as was going on two or three of them. But if she ended up having a long-term association with

Ben, she'd only be able to dance around getting physical for so long.

"You're not the one standing there," she said. "What am I supposed to do if he tries to kiss me? Or worse?"

"It won't come to that," Tuck said, hurrying around the table to get in between the couple. "We won't let it come to that. We'll give you ways to get out of it. You probably won't have to see him that often. But if it becomes a possibility, one of us will step in… we'll tell him we're your overprotective brother."

Her focus switched to Brodie and she almost laughed. If someone had to step in as her brother, then it couldn't be her lover because he would be the most unconvincing brother alive. Especially since he enjoyed touching her with such propriety so often.

Returning to their first request, she sought clarification. "So why am I talking to Grant?" she said, looking at Tuck again while Brodie stormed away to revel in his frustrated fury. "If you need me to stay down here, I can tell him and he'll give me time off. But he might be suspicious if I tell him I'm seeing Ben. He already knows that Brodie is out of state, so he's suspicious about—"

"How does he know that?" Brodie snapped, whirling around to pin her in his sights. "Saint Grant been working to convert you to his cause again?"

Her own hackles were rising and she cared less about irritating her love as he seemed intent on irritating her. "He has admitted being worried about me, yes. And he has vocalized how he doesn't believe that we're right for each other."

"I told you that," Brodie murmured then regained his tension. "You had your chance to be done with me."

She wanted to scream but balled her fists instead. "I'm only telling you what he said because you told me to be honest with you."

He considered this for a couple of seconds. "You shouldn't be telling him about our movements," Brodie said, coming over to stand shoulder to shoulder with Tuck.

Tuck's head was bobbing in a loose nod. "He's right

about that," Tuck said. "You have to keep the secrets of the Kindred. We never know when it's going to be important for us to surprise someone or move in secret."

Now there were two of them talking to her like she was a fool, her adrenaline amped up. "I didn't tell him," she said.

That they were pissed at her for something she didn't do was bad enough. But for them to believe she would endanger them was even more frustrating.

Brodie sneered and resorted to cheap sarcasm. "So he just guessed?"

Zara tried her absolute best to maintain her cool. "Caine told him."

Tuck and Brodie were startled, but it was Zave behind her who exclaimed it. "Caine?"

Only with Zave's involvement did Brodie begin to calm and that pissed her off. The almighty Falcon kept his cool and that rubbed off on her love. She tried to take some subtle breaths to cleanse the anger from her system.

"He's been a pain in the ass recently," Brodie said. "He became a bigger problem when Zara came into our lives."

"He wants to use her to get to you," Zave muttered as he came into her periphery.

"Why didn't you tell me he'd approached you?" Brodie demanded of her, finding some residual annoyance.

Through steady breathing, she'd managed to lower her heart rate. Following Zave's example, she hoped being reasonable would help Brodie to reciprocate. "It was on Monday, after you left," she said. "And he didn't approach me, you know he's working security for Grant. Caine only got involved when he approached Grant after Purdy's, by the way, and fed him a story about being security who wanted to offer protection. Grant fell for it and being that it was so soon after Purdy's, he was eager to hire someone."

"Caine's been protecting you?" Tuck asked and almost staggered when he backed away and drove his fingers through his hair.

"Of course not! I told him to go to hell," she said, hauling her towel up and tucking it in again. "I told Grant to go to hell too and that's when he reminded me how bad we were for each other. Caine already knew that you were out of the city."

All of the men prickled. "Which means he knows you were at the manor alone," Tuck said and she didn't like the way he and Brodie looked at each other.

Zara hadn't thought about that fact. But Brodie had assured her that she was safe at the manor. So even if she had thought about Caine being aware of her isolation, she probably wouldn't have worried too much about it.

"What does that mean?" she asked them, but neither responded. So she got closer. "You told me I was safe in the manor."

"You are," Brodie said. "He can't get in."

"I don't believe you," she said and his glare snapped around to fixate on her. "Why would you and Tuck be looking at each other like that if that were true?"

Bending lower to pin his glower on her up close, he snagged her chin. "The manor is impenetrable. Our security isn't the weak link, you are."

That was a shock, but she wouldn't let him imply she was a liability who would endanger the Kindred… again. "Am I?" she asked, mirroring his glare. She wouldn't blink first and he should know by now that she wasn't going to wilt just because he was in a bad mood. She would only make allowances for his pissy mood for so long. Sharing a motel room left them at a disadvantage as a couple, but that wouldn't save him from the domestic. "Come here." She marched back toward the bathroom and threw open the door only to turn and see he was where she'd left him. "Get over here."

"Or what?" he shouted.

Taking the top of her towel, she raised her brows. "Or I'll drop my towel right here and then the Kindred will have no secrets, will they?"

His jaw tensed, but she didn't care that he was pissed because she was pissed. When he strode into the bathroom, she stormed after him and slammed the door, making damn clear to every unit in their block that she was mad.

Facing his fury, they stood three feet apart and his size made her feel insignificant, threatened even. But this was Brodie and she had to call him out—she was the only one left in his life who could.

"Listen to me," she said, without lowering her volume. "You and Tuck and Zave, you asked me to go out there, you asked me to go out with Ben. Nothing happened. You saw the whole thing, every minute of it. Do you want to tell me why you're pissed off when there's no way in hell you're jealous!"

"No way in hell," he repeated and ground his teeth before bending to get closer to her. Except in this tiny room, they were already in close quarters. "I can't do it!"

"You can't do what?"

"I can fuck you six ways from Sunday. You'll never have a better lover. I don't doubt for a fucking second that when it comes to sex, this is as good as it's gonna get," he said, swinging his index finger between their bodies to indicate them both. "But the talking and the laughing and the dating… I can't do it, Zar. You're never gonna get that with me."

Some of her anger dissipated and she was reminded of what he'd said about her friendship with Grant and other fights they'd had. "We've had this conversation," she said, softening in the face of the rage she knew he used as a mask for his insecurities. "I don't want normal. I don't want you to take me to bars, to ask me to dance… If we dance, we do it naked in our bedroom, in our house, where we're safe and secure. I don't want to be out in the world when I can have you all to myself. You told me that your land was my playground. We own our own tiny part of the world. It's a place where we can be ourselves and be happy. The world has nothing to offer me that I don't get from you."

He was quick to respond. "I don't know if I believe that," he muttered, backing away to sit on the edge of the bath.

She was just as fast to reassure him. "I've spent my whole life trying to find somewhere to belong, trying to find somewhere that I can be important," she said, crossing to lower herself onto the floor between his feet. She rested her forearms on his thighs and gazed up at him, wearing a smile that she could only pray conveyed her devotion to this man. "The woman I am when you look at me, she's important. I am the most important thing in your whole world and you have no idea how special that makes me feel."

They existed in this moment until he scooped his hands under her hair to cradle her face. "How the hell do you read me?"

"I love you," she answered with a self-deprecating shrug and pushed up on her knees to kiss him. "I'll do anything you ask me to, anything, because I want to live up to that image you have of me in your mind. But please don't punish me for worshiping you and following your every command. All I want to do is make you happy. I want to be important to you."

"You are."

He was calm now and soothing the beast was an achievement to be proud of. "And I don't ever want to lose this. I don't want to lose you."

He leaned down to kiss her and he smiled against her lips. "It's cute that you think you have a choice… How about you show me some of that love," he said, leaning back just enough to unbutton his jeans.

But she laughed before he freed himself and slapped her hands onto his thighs to push herself up while remaining in a perpendicular pose, so he had to tip his head back in readiness for the kiss she didn't bless him with just yet.

"You get us our own room and I'll love you all night long," she said and turned her back on him. He smacked her ass as she moved toward the door, then he was hot on her heels fastening his pants.

"Are you done with your tiff?" Tuck asked when they came back into the living space.

Paper plates on the table were lined up, each with a slice of pizza on them. This was a typical Kindred debrief.

"What's next?" she asked, seating herself and pulling one of the plates toward her.

Tuck sat too. "You're gonna call Grant and tell him you want in," Tuck said. "Tell him you've met with Ben, that you're intrigued, and that you want to shadow Ben for a while."

Squinting, she pushed deeper. "Doesn't that sound like I want to stalk Ben?"

"All we need is for you to get inside long enough to plant the bugs," Tuck said.

The pizza was good, but she kept her bites small because she had more to say. "He wants the devices back," she said.

Tuck nodded. "Zave and I have a plan for that, don't worry."

"Keep buttering up Leatt, find out what he knows about what's to come," Brodie said, sitting to enjoy his own slice. "He's not gonna make it easy. He already knows you judge him for being part of the group, he won't admit their failings."

Picking the cheese from the edge of the pizza she'd just returned to the plate, she prepared herself to make what would be a bold and unpopular suggestion. "Why don't we bring Grant inside?"

No one said anything, so she was forced to raise her gaze from the food to judge their reactions. But little was revealed because they were all frozen in time.

Brodie was the first to take a breath. "What?"

Images of Grant's face after he found out about her and Brodie haunted her. She struggled to get past his connection to Brodie too. The men were brothers and should be on the same side. If they weren't, whatever went down would only drive them further apart. "He's in danger, just like we are. He tried to protect me—"

"He left you with a guy who wanted to rape you," Tuck said. "I'm sorry, but we need skills on the team. Not dead weight."

"He has capital," she said.

"I have capital," Zave said. He didn't appear impressed. Resentment seemed to radiate from his side of the table.

Making a mental note to ask Brodie more about Zave, she knew that Art would've been more forthcoming. If they shot her suggestion down in flames then she wouldn't pursue it. But for her own conscience, she had to put it out there before they were past the point of no return.

"Is it right that we leave him swinging in the wind?" she asked. "He's family and he's got to be scared. Sutcliffe is an intimidating man."

Grant didn't seem intimidated. But even she was smart enough to be afraid of Sutcliffe because if he planned to take out droves of people with Game Time, he clearly had no aversion to murder. Part of her still wanted to believe that the man she'd worked with for five years was more than a hyped-up criminal who was too much of a coward to pull the trigger himself.

"Did he tell you that?" Brodie asked, and she shook her head. "If he wants to come to me for help, let him. Meantime, things stay the way they are."

"You don't trust him—"

"And neither should you," Brodie said, exasperated in his anger. "Has he admitted he was wrong about Game Time? Did he ask your forgiveness for what happened in Purdy's?"

Like a chastised child, she shrank and lost all interest in food. "No," she whispered and the truth was Grant was still a threat because he still wanted to support Sutcliffe and had asked her to return the Game Time devices. "If you want the truth"—she measured each of their expressions as they waited for the rest of the statement—"I'm worried that if we don't get to him first, we'll find ourselves back where we were all over again."

"What do you mean?"

Picking at the pizza, she was aware of betraying Grant all over again. "He and I… we haven't been getting along this week."

"Because of us?" Brodie asked.

"In part," she said. "But he still wants me to support him and Sutcliffe. He asked me to return the devices and the viruses."

"He asked you? That means he's still interested in doing the deal," Tuck said.

Brodie lifted both hands to the back of his head and locked his fingers. "What does Saint have to do to lose your faith?"

"No one is supporting him," she argued, leaving the table because it felt more civilized to be arguing from a standing position. "That makes him a man with nothing to lose. A man of his means… with a chip on his shoulder…"

"Which makes him dangerous," Tuck said.

From nowhere, Zave left the table and went to a suitcase in the corner.

"You're leaving?" she asked, thinking it rude of him to leave in the middle of a conversation.

"I've got business," Zave said. "Wren will be in touch."

He went out without a big goodbye, and she looked from Tuck to Brodie expecting them to be affronted as she was, but they both just looked done.

"I think I'll go and get a drink," Tuck said, leaving without further comment on Grant and she sort of felt like she'd been put in the naughty corner.

So when she fixated on Brodie she exhaled and shrugged, hoping there were some words of support coming her way, but his hands stayed locked behind his head.

"We got the room to ourselves. Want to suck the love outta my cock now?"

Ignoring her assertions didn't inspire confidence that these serious men respected her. "Beau," she said, going over to take his hands. "I'm worried about him… about what he'll do if he's angry."

He took one hand out of her grip. "You spend your whole life making excuses for him," he said, grazing his fingers on her cheek.

She sighed. "He would say I do the same thing about you," she said. "But my concerns don't come from a place of compassion. Losing Art was… it was hard on us all." He squirmed enough that she considered retreating but couldn't skirt around it any longer. "What if Sutcliffe puts a bullet in someone else at the next showdown? What if that's you or me? What if we lose each other?"

His discomfort disappeared in the face of renewed anger. "I can keep you safe. Don't you dare doubt what I'm capable of. I'll put a bullet in Saint tonight if—"

She shook her head. Brodie had not taken advantage of the several opportunities he'd had to kill Grant. Being that they were blood, she could understand his reluctance. Art wouldn't have sanctioned killing one's kin, regardless of how tempting it was.

"Like it or not, he's your brother, and all you have left is each other," she said.

He wasn't dismayed. "I have the Kindred and I've got

you," he said, curving an arm around her to haul her close. "I don't need nothing else."

Relaxing her body, she curled her fingers around his waistband. "You'd do anything for me. You told me that you would do anything."

He grumbled. "Yeah, like torture a guy slow or go to prison for you," he said. "You want me to bury myself alive for you, baby, I'll do it."

It seemed so counterproductive that Brodie wouldn't consider an alliance with his own blood when it could save lives. "You'd die for me but you wouldn't talk to your own flesh and blood?"

"Now you've fucking got it," he said, swinging her around one hundred and eighty degrees to walk her backwards toward the bed. "Who's your guy?"

She wasn't ready to just forget about Grant, nor was she ready to throw him to the wolves. But when Brodie crouched to lick her neck, she knew his mind was drifting away.

"Baby, please," she said, running her hands up his back and into his scalp. "We have to—"

Thrusting her body away from his, she bounced down onto the bed they'd shared last night. "I asked you a fucking question," he said, and the bite of anger was emphasized by the darkness coating his expression. He lowered his hands to his jeans and began to unbutton them then he tugged his tee shirt up over his head. "When I ask you a fucking question, you answer me. Who is your guy?"

The conversation was over. Period. He'd lost any inclination to humor her. "You're my guy," she said, rising to her elbows, but he grabbed her ankle and pulled her leg so high that she was forced onto her back again.

He kissed her instep and put a knee on the bed between her thighs to crawl up between her legs. "Say it again."

"You're my guy," she said. He came down on top of her and lifted her head to scoop her hair up and back to spread it on the bed above her.

"When I'm done with a conversation, we're fucking done with it."

With a grip on her wrists, he stretched her arms high over

her head as he descended to kiss her mouth, her jaw, her collarbone. The sting of suction made her gasp. Being with Brodie when he was in this kind of mood meant he'd be rough and possessive, which she loved. Except her mission required her to be clean and without signs of intimacy, meaning they'd have to restrain themselves.

"Don't leave a mark," she said and he rose enough to wink at her.

"I'll do what the fuck I want with you. You're my toy, my plaything, no one else's."

And as though to prove it, he used one hand to part her towel. As soon as her body was exposed, he began to nuzzle her breasts, licking and sucking each nipple until they were painful in their sharp need. Try as she might to coil her legs around him to pull him into a union, he kept her wrists clamped together on the bed of hair he'd spread out.

"Right now," he said, kissing her cleavage. "You're gonna open your legs so your hot, hungry pussy can swallow my dick whole. You understand me, pretty plaything?"

She muttered in affirmation, but could do little more than nod, especially when he came up to spear his tongue between her lips again.

"You gonna take my cock in deep? Are you?" She coiled her legs around his thighs, but he lifted her arms to shake her. "Tell me."

"I'm going to take your cock. I want it, beau. Give it to me."

"Greedy girl," he snarled, tasting her neck until it burned in opposition to her request.

But him taking what he wanted from her, branding her with his possession, it was his fire that stoked her that made her want to glow as bright as he made her feel. Their passion for each other was inextinguishable, and this was what they both needed.

Brodie was still recovering from his seclusion. They were thrown back into the deep end and already their relationship was being tested. Brodie had to know that he was her priority, especially after having been on a date with another man tonight.

"I'm hungry for you," she said, trying to tug her arms free so she could levy up to bite at his lip. But he shoved her onto the mattress, pinning her arms with the weight of his forearms clamped down over her, and a cold laugh echoed from his throat.

"I'm gonna fuck you so hard, baby," he said, scraping his teeth on her chin then kissing her lips. "You won't move for a week. You won't be able to breathe. You'll feel me inside you with every step you take."

Oh, God, he had a way of taking her sanity until she couldn't breathe past the need to be sated. "I already do," she exhaled and he let her steal his mouth.

Stretching her arms higher, he shifted one forearm over them and held her down. With his freed hand, he traced his palm down her side and pressed his hand down between them. His fingers began to wheedle their way through the moisture her body produced in anticipation of receiving him. Each slide of his fingertips, each press of his knuckle, enticed her further. But frustration made her draw her lips into her mouth, away from his because focusing on the motion of their kiss was becoming difficult.

"It's too much," she exhaled and writhed up against his hand that was still playing in her juices without entering her. "Please, Brodie."

"Please, what?" he asked, wearing a wry smile that was fully aware of her torment.

"I need it, please…"

Massaging her entrance, he dipped his fingers into her opening and pushed down with the pads of his fingertips. She yelped and he took the opportunity her parted lips gave him. Removing his fingers from her, he took them upward to coat her lips with her own juices then, without a word, he came down to kiss her again.

"Taste good?" he asked. She managed to nod while desperately trying to tempt his mouth again. The heat between them was humid and thick, their mouths were so close, his reluctance was a tease and she whimpered. "Answer me."

"Yes," she cried. "Yes, it tastes good."

Any reminder of her arousal was torture, she wanted

fulfillment, wanted him to satisfy her, yet he was taking his sweet time. "You want to worship me," he growled against her mouth. "You've got to pay your dues."

Anything he asked of her, he'd get. He'd tormented her body enough that her sense was dulled and she was high on the chemicals their physical connection drenched her in. The weight of his arm relieved its pressure and the ache in her limbs foretold of bruising, but she could only focus on breathing. He kissed her chin, her throat, and sucked each breast, but didn't slow his journey. Dipping his tongue into her belly button, he dragged it down her abdomen, through the line of hair that signaled his approach to her core.

Licking her clit, he tongued her labia aside to suck the moisture from inside her and the sting made her snatch for his head. She was close, too close for him to be playing foreplay games, but the heat of his amused breath came when he released the pressure. He knew exactly what he was doing. Pushing into her clit with the tip of his tongue, he flickered over it and raised his hands to her breasts.

The pinch on her nipples was like a switch connected to orgasm and she reared up into his mouth with a yelp. Her body hadn't relaxed again and her eyes were closed in the spasm that still racked her body. But his mouth was gone from her center. He grabbed ahold of her hips and spread her legs wide with his own, then pushed the head of his dick into the well of juices eager for him.

She was almost sobbing as he pumped in and out of her because she was still in the grips of the crest of climax and his frenzied motion took her over again. She couldn't think or breathe, all she could do was feel the girth of his cock stretching and sating her.

It forged in deep, bleeding moisture from inside of her to hasten her love's journey to his own peak of pleasure and when it came, she didn't try to quiet him or restrain herself. She screamed out his name and swore in time with him because he'd just proved his worship of her body and in this minute that was all she needed from him.

TWENTY

ONCE THEY WERE FINISHED pleasing each other's bodies, Brodie went out to get supplies and to find Tuck, giving her the chance to call Grant. She had a feeling that Brodie left her alone because he'd known she would want to be to make the call. She did feel more comfortable making this call without an audience, and it had been on the tip of her tongue to say she was going out for a walk to talk to Grant when Brodie said he was leaving. He didn't say that he didn't want her out this late alone and distracted by a phone, but she got the message and didn't argue.

It was late, but she didn't mind risking a call to Grant on his cellphone and as it turned out, he answered on the second ring.

"Zara?"

"Hello, Grant," she said, noticing how eager he sounded. "I'm sorry for the late hour."

"No, I was about to call you," he said. "I spoke to Albert and arranged a meeting. He wants to see both of us."

Ideas rushed through her, had Ben told Sutcliffe about their meeting already? Was Grant the one trying to get her inside with Sutcliffe? Or was Sutcliffe using her faux receptiveness as a trap?

"Both of us?" she asked. "But why—"

Grant was excited about this, it was in his voice, and it helped her to understand why the Kindred didn't want him in their ranks. Once he made up his mind, he had obstinate blinders on. It didn't matter to him that Sutcliffe was going to kill people, Grant wanted to be at the cool kids table and he saw Albert Sutcliffe as the man.

"He's in London this week," Grant said. "He gets back into the country on Friday night. The meet will be on Saturday. I need you to be there."

Grant needed her to be there? Or had Sutcliffe requested an audience with her? "Okay," she said, fixating on the door with hopes that Brodie would come back. As it turned out, she needed an audience after all.

Grant didn't notice her hesitation, which was good, but her suspicion plagued her. "We're going to meet at the Grand. In the conference room, in private."

"I can be there," she said. "I'm out of town. I was going to ask if I could take a few personal days. The calendar this week is light and most of the meetings—"

His excitement morphed to anger in an instant. "Are you with him?" Grant demanded. "Zara, I—"

Squeezing her eyes closed, she sat on the bottom corner of the bed. "No," she said, and it wasn't a lie. She was alone in this motel room. Though the scent of her lover and their joining still permeated the room. But Brodie's essence didn't count as a real presence, no matter how it affected the ambiance and her hormones.

"I saw Ben last night. I'm doing what you asked… I'm thinking about it."

A few moments of silence made her hold her breath. "Zara," he said and the tone in his voice was one of pride and gratitude. "Of course, take all the time you need. Talk to Ben. Maybe visit the compound and come back in time for the meeting with Sutcliffe. You can deliver the devices to us as a show of compliance… Albert will be pleased."

"I'm not making any promises," she said, because she didn't know how this meeting would affect Kindred plans, and also because jumping on board with too much haste might appear suspicious.

"Yes, sure, okay," Grant said, but his pace had increased and it was obvious he was jumping to the best case scenario. "Yes, take time to think. Thank you, Zara. Thank you for giving this real consideration."

He signed off, and she was still sitting on the bottom corner of the bed looking at her phone when there was a knock at the motel room door. Crossing to check who was on the other side, she disarmed the makeshift warning system and opened the door to let the men in, while staying behind it. Tuck and Brodie came in and while they were setting up the security again, she went back to her perch on the bottom corner of the bed and considered what Grant had said.

"Did you talk to him?" Tuck asked. She nodded, before tossing the phone toward the pillow.

She took a deep breath. "He's spoken to Sutcliffe and confirmed that he's in London. Sutcliffe wants to meet in the Grand."

"Meet you?" Brodie asked, coming over to sit on the bed opposite her.

Tuck sauntered closer too and rested on the table to fold his arms. "That could be risky."

"I don't think so," she said, having had the time to ponder Grant's enthusiasm, she'd decided it wasn't a bad thing. If he was ruled by emotions, then he wouldn't look too closely at her motivation for so suddenly switching loyalties. "He wants to meet Grant and me. Grant wants me to bring Game Time to prove my sincerity."

"When?" Brodie asked.

"Saturday," she said, watching the men make eye contact.

"That's enough time," Tuck said, reassuring them both before pushing away from his seat to round the table and sit at a laptop. He spent a lot of time on computers, he seemed to prefer them to people.

Brodie continued the interview while Tuck typed. "What else did he say?" he asked.

"I told him I had met with Ben. He encouraged me to meet up with him and to go to the compound."

"That's good news," Tuck said, glancing over the top of

his laptop. "We want you in there. Now you can use Grant's suggestion."

Tuck was happy with the news, but Brodie wasn't looking at her, he was fixated on the floor and his frown worried her. "What is it?" she asked when he didn't say anything for a while. "Grant was thrilled. He was flattered that I took his advice. He wants me to consider what Sutcliffe is doing."

He made eye contact. "How thrilled?" Brodie asked.

She wasn't used to putting a measure on someone's mood and there was no gauge that might help her. "Eight out of ten," she said, hazarding a guess with a loose shrug.

The answer seemed to intrigue Brodie more. "That you were meeting with Ben? Did he ask what you talked about or how you felt about the guy?"

"No," she said. Brodie's questions deepened her concerns. "What are you thinking, beau?"

She counted three breaths before he answered. "I don't know," he muttered and got up to go to the sofa in the corner. While he was putting his thoughts into order, she gave him some space.

"I'll make some coffee," she said. Tuck was still working and Brodie was thinking. They should all get some sleep if they wanted to be fresh in the morning. But she was beginning to realize that most Kindred work took place at night, so she would have to get used to burning the candle at both ends.

She made the coffee and took her time to read what information the Kindred had compiled on Sutcliffe's group and the folio was concerning. Most of what the Kindred had observed led to the conclusion that Sutcliffe was building an army, just as Grant had said, and a well-equipped one at that. It proved that she'd been right about her visit to the compound. Sutcliffe had set up the wonderful appearance of idyllic living that was only half the story.

Pictures of men with guns at the gates, hiding in bushes, and strolling around the perimeter showed them in army fatigues and heavy boots. These men were strong and trained, she could tell that just by how they stood and the resolute expressions on their faces.

She was sitting on the bed with her legs stretched out in front of her. Stifling another yawn, she went back to the beginning of the stack of glossy photos, deciding to go through them again.

"You've been sitting there staring into your coffee for half an hour," Tuck said. She looked up to see that he was twisted in his seat, craning around to observe Brodie who was still sitting in the corner on the couch. "Are you gonna share with the group?"

Brodie put his cup aside and rubbed his hands on the front of his thighs before he took a long breath, sat back, and linked his hands at the back of his head. "Don't you think it's strange that Sutcliffe and Saint are so eager to have Zara back?" he said. She put the photographs on the bed beside her to cross her legs and listen as Brodie continued. "She screwed them over, right? As far as they're concerned, she was the one who orchestrated the double cross in Atlas. If it wasn't for her, Sutcliffe's men wouldn't be dead, he wouldn't have broken his leg, and he would have the device he needs to execute his grand plan."

Worry joined her understanding that he was right and she wondered if he knew he was freaking her out. "I can hear you," Zara said, linking her fingers together. Her lover didn't acknowledge her. When Tuck glanced around at her, his serious face made her sit straighter. "Wait, I don't understand what you're saying."

"I'm saying that this is all wrong," Brodie said. "We're used to having Art thinking about the background, about the motivations and how our enemies end up doing what they do."

His lesson of life without Art had been harsh. But he'd learned it when Caine jumped him outside the CI building. Art had been his safety net, thinking about the things that Brodie didn't have to. Now Brodie was learning that his safety net was gone and he had to come to these conclusions alone.

Vaulting onto his feet, Brodie was more ready for action than slumber. "We're being played."

With a sideways nod at Tuck, Brodie began to stride toward the door. After a few quick swipes at his keyboard,

Tuck was up and moving into Brodie's wake. She leaped off the bed.

"Wait!" she exclaimed, making the men stop less than three feet from the exit. "You can't say something like that and then leave. What does that mean? We're 'being played', are we in danger?"

Her love and their colleague weren't concerned, but panic was making her shiver. "You're Kindred, you're always in danger," Brodie said.

If she hadn't been so perplexed, she might have been encouraged by her lover's return to cryptic. When they first met, everything he said and did was of the cryptic variety. But whatever conclusion he'd reached while sitting on the couch pondering, it meant something had to be done by him and Tuck. She was being excluded.

"Where are you going?" she asked, scared that they could be off to do something dangerous. "When will you be back? What can I do?"

"You're gonna lie down and go to sleep," he said, moving toward her.

Such a mundane suggestion took her aback. "I can't do that." His fire was extinguished and calm took its place. She envied his confidence. The closer he got, the more his eyes softened. When he seized the back of her neck, he touched her face, and some of his peace seeped into her.

"I'm done being angry about losing him," Brodie said. Art. He was finally confessing the truth of his grief. "All that's got me so far is a battered girlfriend and a bruised ego. He'd kick my ass if he knew how long I'd spent feeling sorry for myself. The Kindred comes first. What's priority one?"

"We look out for each other," she murmured, fixated on his certainty.

"That's right, and you've proved your commitment to us by keeping everything together while I was busy boozing. It's not gonna happen again. The Kindred Chief doesn't get the luxury of downtime. I've had my head up my ass for too long. It should never have gotten this fucking far. But it has, so I need to get us out of it."

She couldn't see Tuck because Brodie's body blocked her

view, but she could feel his smile and his relief, because it had to be as tangible as hers. As tempting as it was to make a joke about never sleeping with her boss, she thought the better of it because her other boss was Brodie's brother.

If he was excluding her, he had his reasons. She had to prove her confidence in him. "I trust you to come home safe," she said. "But is there anything I should know?"

"This is a game and I've finally figured it out."

"Will you clue the rest of us in?" she asked.

"I'll clue Swift in," Brodie said. It seemed unfair that the hacker was let in on the secret while she was kept in the dark. But Brodie would have his reasons, and they wouldn't have anything to do with a lack of trust. "It's not that I don't trust you."

"I know that," she said with a smile as he'd just read her mind. "Worrying about you has become something of a habit."

Every day for more than three months, her life had been dedicated to making sure Brodie had everything he needed. Her concern for his well-being was engrained, and she wouldn't want it any other way. Having him as such a dominant part of her thoughts empowered her and it lightened her other woes because Brodie was a monolith and she finally had him back.

"I want you to get your beauty sleep," he said, wrapping his fingers around the section of her hair in front of her shoulder. "Because I need you thinking tomorrow. You're gonna make that Ben bastard fall for you so hard you'll have him begging for table scraps."

He didn't lose his confidence, in fact Brodie smiled. Zara forgot to breathe for a second and glanced around to check she was still in the right reality. "You want me to—"

"Just show him those big browns that get me hard, baby, flutter those sexy lashes… He won't be getting his hands on you. Right now, I gotta go."

Kissing her quick, he spun to head for the exit Tuck had prepared for them. "But…" she stuttered, taking an aimless step. "What—"

Brodie stopped in the doorway to look at her once more.

"Sutcliffe has an army and to fight them, we'll need one of our own," he said and went out into the night, closing the door on his statement.

Brodie had purpose and seeing him invigorated was encouraging, yet he'd told her to sleep. Excitement made it difficult for her to relax and it was frustrating to know only half the plan. Somehow, that unknown paled against the realization that Brodie was back with her. Raven was back at his peak. Sutcliffe wasn't going to know what had hit him.

TWENTY-ONE

"I THINK YOU OWE ME."

Friday night, in the bar with Ben, Zara's attention had been drifting, but it snapped back to him when he made that statement. The audacity of his smile prompted Zara to think he was making a joke. But she wasn't in much of a joking mood.

The place was alive with people and the music was energetic. Raven and Swift were at their posts opposite the vast glass façade, and she was safe. But she was still in the dark as to what Brodie had meant about them being played. Brodie and Tuck whispered with each other or went out and left her alone. They were cooking something up and she didn't know what it was.

"I owe you?" she asked.

Ben was still smiling, he held the neck of his beer bottle and pulled it closer. "We've seen each other every day. We've talked all about my life and Albert's, tonight I'm supposed to take you over to the house."

They'd talked earlier in the week about her want to go back to the compound, and he'd promised to take her tonight. She wasn't wild about the visit being nocturnal. Especially given that her Kindred cohorts couldn't keep eyes on her there. They'd been watching since she'd met up with Ben in the bar, but they wouldn't witness what went on inside the compound where there was no external line of sight.

Keeping her anxiety to herself, Zara didn't want the men to think that she couldn't handle the job. They might not be present to view her every step in the Sutcliffe house, but she would be carrying audio and visual equipment. If she got into trouble, they'd get her out.

Brodie had assured her that he'd blast the place off the face of the earth before he'd abandon her if she needed him. Recalling her love's vehemence helped her to return Ben's smile. Ben didn't make her nervous. He was a physical therapist who clearly had no idea what Albert Sutcliffe was capable of.

Her anxiety came from her mission. She had to plant bugs at the Sutcliffe house. She had to find out the location of the cult's arsenal. Tuck found records of equipment and ammunition being bought, yet they hadn't seen deliveries to the house. They'd been unsuccessful in locating any hoarding site using their original ground and aerial observations.

As if tonight wasn't stressful enough, tomorrow she had to travel back to her apartment and prepare for her meeting with Grant and Sutcliffe, where she was supposed to hand over the device the Kindred had been keeping hidden for months. She wasn't worried about her safety. She was worried about letting down the people who were relying on her.

Playing it coy, she averted her eyes. "What is it that you think you want from me?" she asked Ben.

"I feel like I don't know anything about you, Zara," he said as he swayed closer. "How did a girl like you get mixed up in this?"

Over the course of the week, they'd talked about their lives, but she'd rather cover old ground than confess the whole truth. "I've worked for Grant McCormack for five years. I know all of his business dealings."

"And you always subscribe to his ideology?"

"No," she said.

This conversation was edging into dangerous territory. "You said that Albert killed your friend," Ben said and she wondered if he was testing her. "But your friend killed his nephew."

This suggested he'd been talking to Sutcliffe about her. "You think this is a game of tit for tat?" she asked, lifting her glass to squeeze her straw between her lips. "My friend did what he did because he was protecting me."

"Sutcliffe said you loved him, that he got into your head."

Any news on Sutcliffe's thoughts was welcomed, but it wasn't pleasant to know they'd been discussing her personal life. "He did," she said, examining the grain of the tabletop. "In the way a lover does."

Softening her tone, she fluttered her lashes at him and leaned closer. "That's it, baby," Brodie said into her ear. "Show him that smile. Use your assets, Swallow."

Initially, she'd been surprised that he was giving such commands, but every time he murmured in her ear, her sexual awareness peaked. Brodie aroused her with his words out here in public, just like he did in their bedroom. These meetings served as foreplay that always eradicated her anxiety of overthinking the next step.

Brodie guided her, giving her permission and instruction, using her to get what he needed from Ben. She was a tool that gave him leverage. But he rewarded his instrument when he got her alone and their passion was given release.

She widened her eyes and did as her lover told her to. Folding her forearms onto the table, she pushed her upper arms tighter around her bosom and was amazed to realize that the more she amplified her cleavage the more relaxed and therefore malleable, Ben became. These little maneuvers had been working all week.

"It's getting late," Ben said, dragging his admiring attention upward. "Are you ready to get out of here?"

With a nod and a coquettish smile, she rose from the table and let him help her on with her jacket. "Are we going straight to the compound?" she asked, allowing him to take her hand as they left the bar.

Brodie wouldn't be happy that Ben was touching her. But that Ben thought he was allowed to take these small liberties suggested to her that their plan to seduce him had worked. "Yeah," Ben said. "It will be quiet tonight."

Quiet tonight meant nothing to her because she didn't know how busy the place usually was. But she got into his truck with him sparing a brief glance in the direction of Brodie's position.

"We're gonna be right behind you," Brodie said as Ben started his truck. "We'll still hear every word."

But Brodie wouldn't have a line of sight. They'd found positions of weakness in the defenses, Zara knew because she'd heard the guys talking about it and the map laid out on the table in the motel room showed where those weaknesses were. If they had to get to her, they would. But they wouldn't risk exposure by sneaking onto the property because they didn't need Sutcliffe and his people strengthening their defenses.

The journey was short and when they got to the gate, it was open. There were no men or guns around either, meaning this was another staged event for her. There were some lights that she could make out through the trees here and there, but she didn't see people or homes. In comparison to the drive through McCormack land, this drive was short. The house was lit up, but still, there were no people.

"Where is everyone?" she asked when Ben parked his truck and came around to help her out.

"Like I said, it's late," Ben said, keeping hold of her hand as he led her up the grand front stairs to the doublewide door. When she'd come here with Grant, they'd gone in and out the back, now she had the privilege of using the main entrance.

The L-shaped hall had stairs to the right. To the left was a long corridor, which led to the kitchen, and had doors leading off it. Having had the tour, she knew which of these rooms were communal and which were bedrooms. But that didn't make her lower her guard. Anyone could be in those rooms lying in wait to harm her.

Ben didn't try to take her through any of the doors. With his hand still in hers, he took her down the corridor and into the kitchen at the back of the building. It was no longer the homely room that it had been before. When Ben stopped by the vast table, she knew he was awaiting her reaction to what lay around them.

There were no guns. But the table was covered with other items, flashlights, heavy boots, camping equipment, and dehydrated food. A couple of hunting knives were secreted beneath a tackle box, which made her wonder what was inside, she doubted it had anything to do with fishing.

"Wow," she said. "Are you planning a trip?" She walked away from him, around the head of the table, trying to catalog what was laid out.

Being careful to look out for weapons, as Tuck had advised her to do the last time she came here, she was surprised not to see any. Though in truth, the lack of hardware was noteworthy. This was another carefully choreographed scene that she was supposed to happen upon. Sutcliffe was letting her see what he wanted her to see and no more.

Touching an item here and there, she ran a fingernail along the table and with a deliberate push of her fingertip beneath the tabletop, she affixed the audio bug Tuck had given her. It was larger than the ones they put in their ear because it needed its own power source. But she did her best to stretch as far under as she could without appearing awkward. Brodie and Tuck had made her think it was no big deal, but as soon as she stepped away from the device, she began to sweat. Now there was evidence on the premises that she was a mole and not interested in Sutcliffe's cause.

"We keep a regular check on inventory. We wouldn't want to run out of anything we might need," Ben said, gripping the back of one of the wooden chairs that stood around the table.

"Inventory," she muttered and cast her eyes around to the papers stuck on the wall of the kitchen perpendicular to the back door, again, these hadn't been here the last time. She didn't have much of a memory for maps, but the one just below her eye level was interesting. There were street names she recognized, this was a local map, yet it was hand drawn. "This is quite a sight to see."

Raven and Swift had been quiet in her ear. They'd told her the range of the audio and visual equipment that she wore was around a mile. In her judgment, the road she and Ben had driven from the front gate was long enough that they would be pushing those boundaries.

"Swift's patching in."

The sound of Brodie's voice in her ear made her draw in a breath that Ben had to hear, but she sighed it out in a deliberate attempt to allay any suspicions he might have about her sudden show of relief.

Trying to appear overwhelmed and impressed, she ogled everything she could. "This is so much information, how do you keep track of it all?"

Ben came to her side. "No one knows every piece of information. We keep track of our own little corner and everyone works together as a team to make sure nothing gets missed," Ben said.

"Take a step back," Brodie said in her ear and while touching the line of her necklace to keep it steady, she did just that, and took the chance to look upward.

The pendant had a camera in it, but she wasn't sure it was picking anything up. The bug under the table would allow the Kindred to keep track of her conversation because it was more powerful than the one in her ear. But she needed them to be able to see what she was seeing. Swift was good and might be able to piggyback his signal on the planted bug, making it act as a relay. If that didn't work, they would have to make a decision to either get closer or back away. If they chose the latter, valuable intel might be lost, so it would be up to her to remember what she could.

"What's this one?" she asked Ben, touching the local map with a fingernail. Brodie had told her to leave as few prints as possible.

But if Sutcliffe wanted her fingerprint all he would have to do is ask Grant for it. The CI doors were all secured with fingerprint recognition technology, so her print was on the CI system. Still, she did what she was told and used her newly manicured nails to do the touching for her.

"That's our storage facility," Ben said, coming even closer to her side to examine the map with her. "Mr. Sutcliffe likes to be ready for any scenario. If for any reason we had to split up or leave in a hurry, we have supplies there that could help us find a new place to settle."

Playing dumb, she glanced at him. "Why would you have to leave in a hurry?" she asked and curled a fingertip around her necklace.

"I'm with you, don't you worry, baby," Brodie said into her ear, and she smiled.

The smile made Ben relax, which was good because he'd probably share more. But her expression was meant for her love. She needed his reassurance because being alone this deep in enemy territory was unsettling.

"Mr. Sutcliffe is a thorough man," Ben said, putting a hand on her shoulder. "He looks after his people. You know, I'm glad that you're going to meet with him tomorrow night. I hope you'll join us… soon."

Join us. That was a joke. Tuck had briefed her and Brodie that afternoon and she'd been shocked to hear that there had been an epidemic of hostage situations all across the northeast. None were big enough to warrant major national coverage. Most were written off as simply robberies and the cash was no doubt funding Sutcliffe's cause. The calling card at each scene revealed the truth to those who knew it. "4 Tim" was written, scratched, or scorched into walls or furniture at each scene.

The other Kindred were fueled by this news that Sutcliffe was carrying out a war at home, against his people, rather than one abroad. But they also voiced concerns that these raids could be rehearsals for something bigger that could be coming if Sutcliffe got his hands on Game Time.

Zara heard something else when Tuck was recounting the details of the stick-ups. Tim was in the forefront of Sutcliffe's mind and his nephew had become a martyr to the cause. Beyond the fact that suggested anyone who was killed as a result of Sutcliffe's misguided mission would be elevated to martyr status, it also meant these people held a grudge.

Grant had told her that Sutcliffe wanted revenge and when she heard Tim's name was being used as a beacon at each scene, her concern for Brodie ratcheted up. He would be a prize. Anyone who could take down the man who had taken down Tim would be a hero, but she wasn't interested in being widowed. Brodie told her to use her fear, just like she used her anger to achieve results and it surprised her just how effective that was.

Turning her body toward the covered wall, she did her best to scan it with her pendant, though she had no confirmation if her effort was useful. "Do you remember I told you that Sutcliffe wanted a device built by the company I work for?" she asked and Ben nodded. "I told you that its purpose is to spread disease. It's meant to kill people. Doesn't that concern you? You've dedicated your life to medicine, to making people better. How can you be a part of something that intends to do harm?"

"Stop trying to recruit him," Brodie grumbled in her ear.

"He'll be reporting back to Sutcliffe and he can't think that you have doubts," Tuck added.

Both men were right, so she moved closer to Ben again and took his hand. "I just want to know that you're in all the way before I join the cause. You're my friend. I'm going to need your support. Albert and I have a rocky history and Grant is my superior. I'll need someone to hold my hand if I'm to be a part of this."

His eyes became drowsy and he slid his free hand across her shoulder toward her face, she didn't like it but she couldn't scream and run away. For one thing, Brodie would want to know where the dude's other hand was and he'd spill all the blood he had to in order to find out. So while still smiling, she caught his hand before it could get to her jaw and glanced away. Playing it coy, she made brief eye contact, then looked away again.

"We shouldn't... you know," she said. "Get too close. Not until we've spoken to Sutcliffe about it." Nodding, she blinked up, fluttering her lashes, she waited expectantly for him to concur and with a sigh he did.

"You're right," Ben said.

Brodie's mood soured. "You've got sixty seconds to get out of there before I come in." And blow the whole op, though Brodie didn't say that.

The deep growl in his voice betrayed his anger and she

wasn't going to test how long he could hold on to his restraint because she'd never known him to maintain any reserve.

"I should go," she said. "I wanted to come here, to see the place again, but… I feel like I'm trespassing on something private, you know? I don't want Sutcliffe to think that I'm going behind his back."

"He knows you're here," Ben said.

Zara had figured that, from the arranged set to the influence he had over his people, Sutcliffe controlled everything. "Did he ask you to report back?"

"Yes," Ben said with a deprecating laugh. "But I think he asked the wrong man. I don't think I could say a bad word about you." That was a nice thing to say, even if this guy was a sociopath, which he would have to be to subscribe to Sutcliffe's ideology.

"Thirty, twenty-nine, twenty-eight," Brodie said into her ear, making the hair on her body spring up.

Urgency made her want to run, but she had to keep her cool if she wanted to prevent suspicion. "Thanks for tonight," she said and edged past Ben. "After tomorrow night, everything in my life will change."

"It's worth it," he said, moving with her as she left the kitchen to walk up the hall.

There wasn't a second to spare. She took Brodie at his word. He and Tuck could get in here, but if they did it would destroy everything they were working toward. The only thing they'd achieve was killing the guy that was pissing Brodie off and that did nothing for their long-term goal.

"I'll take you home," Ben said, opening the front door for her.

"It's a beautiful night," she said, looking at the sky as she descended the stairs. Her statement was as much for Brodie as it was for Ben. Telling him she could see the sky would hopefully halt his countdown. "I think I'll enjoy the walk."

"I brought you, I have to take you home," Ben said, putting an arm around her shoulders to direct her back into the truck.

It might be a gentlemanly thing to do, though it would probably have been more chivalrous to offer to walk with her than to coerce her into a vehicle. But the lights she'd seen on the land coming in might belong to something she wasn't supposed to see. They wouldn't want her wandering around and possibly getting lost, or claiming to be lost, and stumbling onto something Sutcliffe would declare as classified.

She wanted to walk so that she could try to see the things she wasn't supposed to and because she didn't want Ben taking her back to her motel. But she caught a break when he agreed to drop her off at the taxi stand near their bar. He put up no fight and was preoccupied, so she figured he was keen to get back to report to Sutcliffe.

A man so eager to please a superior had something to prove. A man who resisted intimacy with a woman until he had the say so from another man had an inferiority complex. Leaving Ben's truck, she compared her date with her love and knew her tastes could only be satisfied by a man motivated by his own will.

The first cab pulled into the taxi stand less than thirty seconds after Ben disappeared around the corner. But she chose instead to walk the route back to the motel because it was a nice night and she didn't want to be sitting in the motel room alone waiting for Brodie and Tuck to return. Walking killed time.

Tonight she'd accomplished the mission she'd been assigned and despite spikes of anxiety, she'd succeeded. Now her thoughts turned to the following night. Sutcliffe wouldn't be as easily fooled. Grant wanted Game Time back so he could hand it over to Sutcliffe and she was to stand up and declare her allegiance to their cause.

Zara wasn't so confident about succeeding, but Brodie would be with her, he'd have Maverick trained to protect her. Even if she messed up big time, her love would be there to catch her if she fell.

TWENTY-TWO

"WHAT'S THE MATTER WITH YOU?"

Coming back to the manor had been a short-lived relief. There had been no time to relax and enjoy being home. The Kindred were preparing for her meeting with Sutcliffe, and the plans made her nervous. But as distracted as she'd been, she had noticed Brodie's perpetual frown. Initially, she'd discounted it as his determination. He wanted to have a clear head, to be in the zone for the mission. But it had stayed etched on his features even through dinner.

Tuck was downstairs in the control room, he'd made his departure after they'd eaten and she wasn't surprised he was uncomfortable, Brodie had become increasingly surly throughout the day.

"I could ask you the same thing," she said in response to Brodie's question as she gathered up the dinner plates and took them to the dishwasher. "You've been snapping all day."

"Not at you," he snapped. She discarded the dishes to turn around and look at him. He was sitting at the kitchen island where they always ate when they were doing it as a group and still his frown cast a shadow over him.

"Is it Art?" she asked. "Are you thinking about the last time we did this?"

The Grand had been the venue of her first unofficial Kindred mission. It was the hotel Grant had used to demonstrate the capabilities of Game Time. Raven had kept her in his gunsights but had Swift and the chief to back him up. Now he was running the op alone with only Swift at his side.

"No," he said and didn't offer anything else.

"It's okay, you know," she said, tiptoeing back toward him. "Art was with you through every mission. He's always been with you. It can't be easy not to have his voice guiding you."

"That's not it," Brodie said, gulping the last of the water from his glass. Pushing it away, he left his stool and came over to pick her up and sit her on the island they'd just eaten at. "It's you."

Pleased that he wasn't just shutting her out, she remained open to what he might say. "What about me?" she asked, caressing the width of his arms. "You think I'm going to screw up?"

"I think you rely on me and I think that last night I let it go too far."

He was holding her neck but scrutinizing her chest. He had too much intimate experience with her chest for her to believe he was genuinely distracted by it, so she had to assume he was resisting looking her in the eye.

"You mean with Ben. Nothing would've happened. I didn't let him touch me."

"That's not what I mean," he said. "I would've come in there. I would've razed the lot if I had to get to you. If you needed me."

Smiling, she knew she'd been right not to doubt his assertions. "I know that. I heard you and I know you mean what you say. I got out. We were fine."

His eyes drifted to hers in time with his hand sliding through her hair past her ear. "We weren't fine," he said, tracing his fingertips on one cheekbone, his other arm came around to squeeze her close to him. "I underestimated what it was to have my girl in the field... You went into that compound and all I could do was watch."

Brodie had never trusted a woman enough to bring her to the manor. In fairness, he hadn't brought her here, Art had been the one to let her in and with that concession, she'd slipped into the Kindred ranks and into Brodie's heart.

"If I'd been uncomfortable, I wouldn't have gone," she said.

But he wasn't appeased. As he squinted, his lips parted. "You think that you're hiding your nerves, but you're not. You've got balls, baby. But I see it when you're freaking."

She hadn't been expecting that revelation. It was natural to be nervous when facing danger, but she tried to stay as focused as the men in the group. Brodie was usually so in his own head that she didn't think he noticed her mood.

Tracing her fingernails back and forth on his neck, Zara relented honesty because denials would only reinforce the truth he'd discovered. "You've never said anything."

"Because what do I know about comforting a chick?" he asked.

"If you're that worried about me holding my nerve, why do you let me go into the field?"

They considered each other. The longer she sat here without an answer, the more tempted she was to fill the silence. But she'd bet that's what Brodie was counting on, her need to speculate, so she sealed her lips, curling them around her teeth. Her brows slid up and with that subtle sign of expectation, he dropped his thumb to her chin and pushed it down enough to tempt her into letting her lower lip pop out from her mouth.

"After this," he said. "I'm leaving the country."

Alarm and terror made her tense. "What?" she said and grabbed his wrist to remove his hand from her face. "Why? Where are you going?"

Shaking his head, he was frowning again. "I'm too in my head here," he said. "Cabin fever, I guess."

Brodie and Art spent the majority of their lives overseas, and it had taken a trip abroad to help Brodie get over the grief of losing his parents. So she could understand why he thought a vacation was a good idea. But Brodie didn't leave the country just to relax, he went to work.

Dampening her selfish objections, she took a breath. "Do you have a job?" she asked, trying her best to be understanding. It had taken her all this time to get Brodie to look at her again, and just when she thought they were making progress, he was declaring his intention to leave her.

Art had told her about their excursions and how often Brodie wasn't home. At the time, she'd been smart enough to see that the chief was trying to explain that sometimes she'd have to live without Brodie at her side and she'd thought she could do it. But worrying for him, and for their relationship, was a difficult habit to break.

"No," he said, taking hold of her hair. "But I'll find one."

That she didn't doubt, but as her attention moved to his chest, she wasn't quite sure how she was supposed to respond. Should she wish him luck? Encourage him to leave when she would never be able to pin him down on when he'd be back.

"Are you taking Tuck?" she asked, because at least if Tuck were with him, she would have some reassurance that he had backup.

"No," Brodie said. "He has his own issues to work through. Time on his own will be good for him. He needs to get himself neck deep in trouble before he'll realize he screwed up."

That was an unusual and ambiguous statement. "Screwed up?" she asked with renewed intrigue. Tuck was the most efficient member of the Kindred, and she'd never seen him make a mistake. He didn't let his feelings get in the way of the job like the rest of them could be accused of. "I told him to go and get some TLC from Kadie."

"He broke up with her," Brodie said, watching her lips again.

Her mouth fell open. She'd spoken of Tuck's girlfriend and he'd never confessed that. "When?" she asked.

"Right after Art."

That was months ago and Tuck had let her talk about Kadie as though she was still a part of his life. "Why did he do that?"

"Screws with a guy's head, losing a member of the team like we lost Art."

Thinking back over their conversations, she remembered that Tuck had commented on how if he'd taken the bullet Kadie would never have known. "Man," she exhaled and relaxed her weight onto Brodie. Her arms slid around him until she clasped her own wrist at his lower back. "He broke up with her because he thought it wasn't fair on her to be waiting for him and because he could be hurt and Kadie would never know what had happened to him."

"Maybe," he said. "We'd have taken care of Kadie if anything happened to Tuck."

"Did you tell him that?"

"Kinda," Brodie said. "He looked after you when I was off the grid, didn't he?"

"He did," she said.

Tuck and Brodie weren't the types of men to open their hearts to each other. But Tuck had told Brodie about dumping Kadie, it was a sign they were closer than she had given them credit for.

"I'd have felt better about you going away if you were taking someone with you," she said, breathing in his scent. "What about Zave?"

"Zave's not much of a spotter," Brodie said and the heat of his mouth warmed her hair. "You think you're up for the job?"

It hadn't occurred to her that Brodie might ask her to go with him. But as she slid out of his arms to look up at him, she didn't read any doubt in his features. "You want me to go abroad with you?"

"You've always wanted to go, right?"

Her smile spread, but she was speechless. He'd listened, he'd considered, he'd cared, and he'd chosen her. "What happened to not making any plans past tomorrow?"

His scowl was sarcastic. "You doubt the team? You think someone's gonna fuck up?"

She smiled. "No," she said, but her faith was stronger than his.

"If you don't want to," he said, but from the way he leaned away, she could tell he was teasing her.

Grabbing handfuls of his tee shirt, she hauled him back

and climbed up him to steal his mouth. "I'd go anywhere in the world with you," she said, coiling her arms around his neck and squeezing herself close. "I love you, Brodie McCormack."

"Yeah," he said while sucking in a breath. "And that scares the shit out of me."

Some of her exuberance waned. "Why?"

"Because every time you leave my side you're in danger. When you were out there at Sutcliffe's and out of range… I couldn't cover you and if that fucker had hurt you, I wouldn't have gotten there quick enough."

Nothing he'd said so far suggested he was wild about having her in the field again. During this mission, her confidence had grown, and she didn't want to fade into the background again. Being a part of the Kindred was as humbling as it was invigorating. These men trusted her and she wouldn't let them down—if Brodie didn't yank her. Without Art here, Brodie's word was the one everyone else followed.

The joy from a moment ago cooled to confusion. "You're saying you can't work with me?"

"I'm saying…"

The way he trailed off and glanced upward intrigued her. She smoothed a hand up his throat, curling her fingers to rasp them through his stubble.

"Beau?"

With a rough exhale and a glare, he confessed. "I'm saying I was jealous."

"That I was with a man I have no interest in?" she asked.

His stern eyes weren't playing when they landed on hers. "The jealousy was irrational. But I carry a powerful weapon, sweetheart. I hurt people for a living. Jealousy riles me, which clouds my thinking and I act without thinking when I—"

"No one got hurt."

He took a few seconds to compose himself. "As long as I can see you, we're fine," he said. "We'll just have to keep that in mind during future missions."

It would be hard to control his volatility, it was something she hadn't even tried to do. If she was going to be a part of the Kindred then he would have to learn that he couldn't always be in control of her. Although, it was flattering that he lost his senses over her. It might be primitive, but these suggestions of his feelings always heightened her own.

"You want to watch me every minute of every day?" she asked and smiled because that might be quite hot, though the idea was probably more alluring than the reality.

"Keep you in my line of sight at all times? Yeah," he said and his frown finally relaxed. "I think I might do that."

Having him and Maverick watching over her movements would make her the safest person on the face of the earth. "I have to go shower and change," she teased, sucking her lower lip into her mouth to moisten it, only to let it slide out again with more ease as her saliva lubricated it. "Do you want to start now?"

"Yeah," he said and one corner of his mouth rose. "And don't forget you've gotta follow your superior's orders."

She couldn't say no to anything he told her to do, superior or not.

TWENTY-THREE

"I'VE GOT THIS," she muttered to herself and rested a hand over the purse she had slung across her body.

Walking toward the Grand Hotel, Zara wasn't as self-conscious about talking to herself as she had been the last time she'd been on this sidewalk. Maybe that was because this time her words were for her rather than the men in her ear.

"Looking good, baby," Brodie said and she smiled. "Your legs look fucking hot."

"Thank you," she muttered, trying not to let her glee spread to her expression because grinning like an idiot would probably be more conspicuous than talking to herself.

"They'll look sexier with my head between them later."

"Rave," she whispered, sure that her blush was making her face luminous.

"If you get back what you give, she can earn her name," Tuck said and she could only conclude the teasing was a way to relax her.

"She earned that months ago," Brodie muttered and Tuck laughed. "There's no bird called a spit."

A laugh escaped on a breath as she pulled open the door to the Grand lobby. "You got an eyeball on them?" she asked.

It took no time for the men to refocus on business. "The

blinds are half closed, but yeah, they're in there," Brodie said, sounding serious now that the game was upon them. "Where am I?"

"With me," she whispered and pressed the elevator call button.

Again, she held onto the purse that was across her body. She'd intended to get dressed up like she had the last time she'd been here, that was until Brodie reminded her there was no party and no one to impress. So wearing a short gypsy dress that was approved by Brodie, she had plenty of room to move if she had to make tracks in a hurry.

According to Brodie's instruction, if she had to run, the first thing she was to lose were the shoes. Now that he'd admired their effect on her legs, Zara would bet his opinion on that would've changed.

She'd suggested wearing flats, but that might have been an obvious safety net. Brodie preferred the spike heels and had explained how to push the point through the eye socket into the brain. The act would eliminate any threat but would probably make her lose her lunch too. From her sneer, he'd guessed how disgusting the idea was to her. Her love had reminded her that he was her chief and if he told her to do it, she had no choice.

The more casual dress allowed her to wear a larger purse and Brodie had allowed her to take her gun. But that wasn't why she kept touching the purse. Inside were the keys to the van she'd parked a block over. The van that had been secreted in a storage locker for a month before she and Tuck had moved it to a separate unit on McCormack property.

They'd lost Art protecting this device. They'd hidden it to stop it from falling into the wrong hands and now she was supposed to just give it away.

The Grand elevator came and she stepped inside to select the conference room floor. "Are we sure about this?" she asked as the doors closed, giving the men the chance to revise the plan.

"Shit," Brodie hissed and the suddenness of his exclamation made her jump.

"What?"

"They closed the blinds," Tuck said. "It's okay, we still have the neck cam."

The necklace camera was the same as the one she'd worn at the compound and was becoming part of her regular jewelry routine. "You want me just to shoot him?" she asked, but it was unlikely Sutcliffe would allow her to get her hand in her bag to pull out her gun then put a round into him before he took her out himself. If she got a gun into that room, she had to assume that the others did too.

"No, the meeting is here because it's public," Brodie said. She was heading to a private room, but the hotel was public. "Someone will hear the shot and we don't trust Saint."

At the pre-brief, they'd sat in main security and the men had explained to her how the bustling hotel in a busy part of town was a difficult place to commit murder. Even from Brodie's position, it would draw too much attention to their group. It was Kindred protocol to do their work when people were alone or in a deserted area. As she thought about it, she realized that was what had happened to all of the men she'd been present to see die by Maverick. Tim. Quebec. Sutcliffe's men.

The plan was to let Sutcliffe take Game Time with the belief that he'd transport it to the arsenal. They had a low-quality image from the map she'd seen in the kitchen of the Sutcliffe compound, but Game Time would be taken to the most secure storage area, where the most destructive weapons would be kept. That was the location the Kindred had to identify and the reason for her taking this risk.

"Give them the keys and get out," Brodie said. "Fast as you can."

Zara had never considered hanging around just to shoot the breeze. But Brodie had told her about his struggles when she was in the Sutcliffe compound and out of his range. While there wasn't quite the same distance between them at that moment, there was a tormenting barrier to him keeping her safe.

"Copy," she said and strode along the corridor.

"Don't knock," Brodie said. "Gives them time to take aim. Stay to the side."

She didn't like any of these statements but expressing her apprehension would make him abort the op, she was sure of it, and she hadn't gotten herself hyped up for nothing. She was doing this. Doing as Brodie told her, she stayed near the wall and opened the conference room door without knocking. A beat of nothing passed. She'd betrayed her presence, so she had to enter, but her heart was hammering as she did.

Slinking around the doorframe, she saw Sutcliffe and Grant on the couch, neither had a weapon drawn, in fact, they were both smiling. "Miss Bandini!" Sutcliffe exclaimed and put a glass of dark liquid aside to stand up and cross to her.

Zara left the door open, just in case, but he came all the way over and took her hand to shake it vigorously. Maintaining his hold on her, he pulled her into the room and over to the couch where there was a decanter and an empty glass on the end table.

"We were just discussing your turnaround," Sutcliffe said and pulled her onto the couch to sit between them.

"I can take it blind," Brodie murmured as Sutcliffe went to the end table to pour her a drink.

With the men on the couch, Brodie could picture the room and take the shot if he had to. But there would be zero room for error. The blinds could affect the bullet trajectory, and she was in the center seat, where Sutcliffe had put her and as she glanced at Grant's smile, she wondered if they'd put her here on purpose as a shield for both of them.

After the Atlas warehouse, they had to be wary of a sniper, especially being as she claimed to love one. "I brought the product," she said, opening her purse.

Grant's smile faded as he watched her put her hand inside. Instead of seizing it, she slid her hand beneath her weapon and was reassured by the weight of the cool metal on her knuckles. She'd killed with this weapon once before and if she had to, she would do it again now.

Pulling out the van key, she held it up toward Grant, who opened his hand to receive it. "It's a black van, one street over."

"How did you get it?" Sutcliffe asked, coming over to give her the glass of liquor. "Wasn't it under Kindred protection? They wouldn't have handed it over without a fight."

She took the glass but didn't drink. Whether it was just alcohol or contained a drug, she didn't want anything slowing her reflexes and Art's warning about hard liquor remained with her. She'd been a part of the Kindred for a short time and every word of advice she'd been given thrummed through her mind. All of it was useful. The others were trained and experienced. She was the rookie.

"It was no trouble," she said.

"Raven has been out of the picture," Grant said. Zara was surprised to hear him answering for her. "Zara has been abandoned by her previous allies."

"Typical," Sutcliffe said, seating himself beside her and retrieving his glass from the table. "You were used, my girl."

She wasn't used. Nor was she his girl. She could practically hear Brodie grinding his teeth together, he'd be using all of his restraint not to take the shot right this minute. What Sutcliffe knew about Raven's identity was unknown. But if Grant was trying to butter up the Brit then there was a chance he'd told the truth. Regardless, she wasn't going to reveal any secrets.

"Ben told me that you were at the house last night," Sutcliffe said. "Can we assume that we have your loyalty now?"

"Ben has been a good friend," she said. "He's a good man."

Sutcliffe made eye contact with Grant on her other side. "We want you to move to the compound."

That request was unexpected, but she tried to hide her shock. "Move?"

Discerning as he drank, Sutcliffe lost his humor and became pragmatic. "Our pace will only increase now that we have Game Time," Sutcliffe said.

Looking from Sutcliffe to Grant, she was surprised to see the certainty Grant was exuding. "Your pace?" she asked.

"We plan to hit a high-profile target," Sutcliffe said.

They couldn't know that she was worried. Hiding her fear took all of her restraint. "I thought the point was to protect our people," she said, hating that this turn of events was making it difficult for her to think straight. "If you plan to hurt—"

"It won't be in this country," Grant said.

It was on her lips to exclaim her surprise. This was a room for revelations. The closed blinds were only a few millimeters thick, but she'd never felt so far away from Brodie as she did at that moment. They wanted her on Sutcliffe land and they planned to turn Game Time around quickly, meaning there was a chance it would never be stored on US soil, they could have a plane waiting for it.

"When?" she asked.

Getting answers wasn't as easy as asking the right question. "You'll be given more information when you're settled in. When will you join us?"

Recognizing opportunity was another Kindred requirement. "Now," she said. She couldn't delay if she wanted to ensure Game Time was monitored.

"Excellent," Sutcliffe said and took one of her arms while Grant clutched the other.

They helped her onto her feet and she put aside her glass to go with them to the door. Glancing back at the blinds, she hoped the others understood her reasoning. There was nothing that Brodie and Tuck could do to protect her after she left the conference room.

"I'm coming, baby," Brodie said and she could hear movement in his tone. Background noise suggested he was running down an echoing stairway.

"No," she said. Grant paused, but Sutcliffe kept on moving. "You don't have to pull me. I'm coming. I want to come to the compound. I want to be a part of what you're doing."

Sutcliffe didn't let her go. But Grant did. "Are you talking to me?" Brodie asked and the slight pant in his voice made her swallow.

"Are you sure?" Grant asked, which gave her leave to answer Brodie.

"Yes," she said to Brodie. Grant and Sutcliffe stopped inside the stairwell they'd brought her to. Making eye contact with Grant, she was still talking to her lover. "You'll stay with me?"

"We're on it," Brodie said. "Don't take the earpiece out. We'll lose contact until Swift and I catch up. But we're there, okay? And if you need to start shooting, do it."

This was her commitment to the Kindred. None of the men she'd met would request rescue on being given the chance to experience the inside of the enemy lair. Sticking close to Game Time might be the only way to keep track of it.

"You want me to?" Grant asked and she nodded. She didn't mean with her, like with her, but if he stayed on the compound too, then at least she'd have one person to voice her concerns to if she had them.

Making it clear she didn't mean anything intimate, she managed a demure smile. "If Albert has enough rooms?" she asked and turned to Sutcliffe, who was peering at her. He wasn't convinced of her allegiance, and that made her wary. But until he gave her cause to believe she was being setup, she wouldn't show her hand. "What about the product?"

Blinking innocent eyes at the two men looming over her in this dark stairway with its gray walls and steel staircase, she couldn't let them think that she was worried about her safety. She had to make them think that she trusted them. After Brodie's confession that he could tell she was nervous even when she tried to hide it, she was doubting the strength of her game face.

"You want us to kill it?" Brodie asked in her ear. She was struggling to blank her expression while listening to the Kindred's Chief, who had to be rearranging priorities and plans fast.

She was getting better at holding two conversations at once. She didn't get the sense that Grant or Sutcliffe thought she was talking to someone other than them. "We can't leave something so valuable on the street," she said.

"We'll have men pick it up and bring it to our storage facility."

"Good," Brodie said.

Grant took her hand and Sutcliffe began to head down the stairs with her. Grant wasn't too far behind. The limp that had made Sutcliffe seem impaired was lessened today. There was no stick. Although he favored leaning on the banister, she would guess that he could move if he wanted to. The severity of his injury had been another illusion.

"We're not gonna kill it until we know where it's going," Brodie said in her ear.

She could no longer respond but read between the lines. While she hadn't been privy to the particulars, she knew that Swift and Falcon had taken the thing apart and she'd been told that they could destroy the device remotely. But if they did that it would also destroy the tracking technology that the Kindred had secreted into the device.

"Your limp is better," she declared to Sutcliffe because she wanted Brodie to know that Sutcliffe had more ability than he'd revealed. "Did Ben help you with that?"

"Ben has been my physical therapist for months," Sutcliffe said, taking them out of a door and along a corridor that led to a rear entrance. There was nothing fancy about this escape route, and she would guess it was a functional space meant as a fire escape or staff access.

A car was idling in the alley they emerged in and she was put inside. Grant and Sutcliffe remained outside for a few seconds. When Grant came in, the first thing she saw was that he was no longer holding the van keys. They had to have been handed off to someone who would take the device to where Sutcliffe wanted it.

"How long will the drive take?" she asked Sutcliffe when he and Grant got into the back of the town car with her.

"Less than an hour," Sutcliffe said. "We're going to take the chopper from CI, the same as the last time."

Well at least it was a journey she knew. It would take Raven and Swift some time to follow her, but she wasn't as nervous as before. She had a weapon, and Sutcliffe had proved he wanted her alive as he hadn't taken advantage of the many previous opportunities he'd had to kill her.

***

SPENDING THE NIGHT at the Sutcliffe compound hadn't

been as horrendous as she thought. She was given a private room and left alone. Once settled, she had tried her best to sneak out and listen to the meeting going on in the kitchen, but she'd only been on the stairs for a few seconds before she was happened upon by a Sutcliffeite and had to claim to be looking for a bathroom.

All night she'd listened in hope of getting something in her earpiece. At some point, she'd fallen asleep and when she woke up, she was dismayed to see that the earpiece had come out of her ear and begun to disintegrate. But by then the sun was streaming through the window and someone was knocking on her door.

Breakfast was had outside with dozens of people coming and going. The sheer number of people meant there was a lot of food, but there was plenty to go around. Having committed robberies to fund the operation, Zara wasn't surprised that they were well-supplied. Although everyone was smiling and laughing, she counted a disproportionate number of men to women, the army was out of uniform, but no less obvious.

"Do you want to change clothes?" Grant asked, coming over to sit beside her.

The sunshine was pleasant, but she was suspicious of everyone and struggled to relax and think of this as an average picnic. "Clothes?" she asked. She'd poured coffee for herself and refused food and had only drunk the coffee after witnessing several other people pour from the same pot and drink without issue. She'd even gone so far as to switch her mug with someone else's, just in case the mug itself was somehow tainted.

Grant was smiling, which in itself made her uneasy. "Albert and I want to show you something today."

"You want to show me something," she said. She was unable to pass up the chance to gather intel, but she didn't want to wander too far from here because the Kindred would have expended all of their resources trying to get to her. They'd be tired, and she needed them at their peak because there was a chance she'd need them in a hurry.

"Where?" she asked.

"Not far, it should only take an hour or so."

"Okay," she said.

Her fingertips touched the warm white gold of her chain and she wondered where Raven and Swift were at this moment.

"That's beautiful," Grant said, picking up her pendant.

Under normal circumstances, she wouldn't want him touching her or her accessories, but her reluctance was heightened as he examined the piece. She was terrified he might notice the camera secreted beneath the stone.

"Thank you," she said and took it from his fingertips to look at it herself. She'd looked and never seen the camera, but that wasn't the point, she needed to get it out of his grasp because the longer he held it the more anxious she got.

"It's the same as one my mother used to wear. Did he give it to you?"

The unexpected question brought her up short. "Why do you want to talk about him?" she whispered, putting the necklace back in place then folding her hands over the purse in her lap.

"It's important that I know," he said. "He could have planted something in it or—"

That might sound sensible, but she knew it wasn't the whole truth. "Is that the reason?" she asked.

"I know you have a gun," Grant said, glancing down at her bag. "I know he gave you that… Are you having second thoughts?"

"No," she said. It was disconcerting how convincing she was, but the single word was said with such conviction that she had the confidence to frown as she looked him in the eye. "Why am I here if you don't trust me? Why would he plant devices in gifts he gave me?"

"To know where you are at all times."

"Even if that's true," she said. "Sutcliffe said that this land was his and that knowledge was public. If Raven wanted to know where this place was all it would take was an internet search, wouldn't it?"

"You're still defending him," Grant said, peering closer.

Sliding down the bench of the long picnic table, she began to bring her legs out from beneath it. "I'm not defending him. I'm offended that you doubt me. You told me to think about joining Sutcliffe. You asked me to give you the benefit of the doubt. I do it, and now you're trying to poke holes."

"I'm worried about you," Grant said. "Not about Sutcliffe. He can take on anyone who tries to come after him."

"Then you have nothing to worry about," she said and stood up, but he grabbed her arm before she could get away.

"Do you still love him?"

The question was proof Grant wasn't interested in her motivation for practical reasons. "Grant," she said, hunkering down into a crouch. "You're the one who told me how bad he was for me. You're the one who wanted me to walk away from him because you said I could never get what I needed from him… But if you're asking me if I hate him, no, I don't. What I'm doing here, I'm doing because it's smart. It makes sense to be on the side that's going to win. Like it or not, Sutcliffe is a clever man with the ability to talk others into believing his sermons. That gives him power."

"And you're attracted to that?"

"I'm not attracted to Sutcliffe. But being part of something bigger, something epic, yeah, I'm attracted to that."

Apparently, that was what Grant wanted to hear, because he relaxed and nodded. "Okay. Back to my original question, do you want something new to wear?"

"No," she said as much because she didn't want to get naked in a place filled with people she didn't trust, she couldn't be sure that there wasn't a camera in her room watching her every move. "If there's something I need to see then I want to get there. I want to see it. I want to prove to you and to Albert that I can be trusted."

"Okay," Grant said, coming out from the picnic bench to stand by her side and once again take her hand. "Let's go."

TWENTY-FOUR

THE JOURNEY TOOK LESS than an hour, just as Grant had said. She'd been given the option of showering and changing, but she didn't take it. She kept fidgeting with her necklace, which gave Grant and Sutcliffe an excuse to look at it, so she tried to leave it alone.

Swift should be tracking her position. The camera wouldn't function if the Kindred were too far away from it. But the GPS tracker was patched into Swift's computer and should work no matter the distance. She hoped.

While getting ready to leave the compound, she'd dragged her heels to give more time to the Kindred. They wouldn't be able to get into position until after she arrived because they weren't sure where they were going. But this was it, this was what they wanted, to know where the arsenal was. It had to be destroyed before they could think about attacking the compound.

Sutcliffe and his people had had a lot of time to practice maneuvers and to stockpile munitions. The Kindred needed to even the odds if they wanted to take Sutcliffe and his people out of the game for good.

Zara had expected a storage facility like any other. But when they drove off-road and bumped along a dirt track before hitting gravel, she grew nervous. There were no overlooking buildings. There were no buildings at all. Even the trees had thinned out to practically nothing. The gravel and exposed scene meant it would be hard for anyone to sneak up. A large concrete bunker with a corrugated roof appeared behind the rise of a hill. This was a custom-built place and probably private land too. It might even be booby-trapped.

A chill of awareness made her concentrate on her breathing. She would be out here. Alone. With Sutcliffe and Grant. Brodie had told her murder was best committed in private and she'd just become the calf at the slaughterhouse.

"Why did you choose somewhere so remote for storage," she asked. "How will you be able to make it here in a hurry if you have to?"

"Our concern is not protecting the estate," Sutcliffe said from the driver's seat. "We don't expect to fight a war on our own soil. This is separate from our compound because it's safer. There are some dangerous things here, and we wouldn't want any accidents to harm our people."

So he was worried about the children playing with guns and bombs. She'd be more understanding of that if he hadn't shown a blatant disregard for civilians in other places. He'd said he was going to use Game Time against those who wanted to harm western society. But had no finesse about doing it. Sutcliffe had no concern about taking out innocent women and children after planting the Game Time device and running away.

The practicality of his plan stumped her. "You're going to take these things overseas?" she asked.

Sutcliffe pulled the truck up to the bunker, facing the door, and he left the engine running. "Why don't you have a look for yourself?"

If she looked, she might be able to ascertain just how big Sutcliffe's war was going to be. But that information wouldn't help her if he intended to let her see and then to put a bullet in her. Clarity would join her in her grave and she would never be able to report back to the others.

Grant put a hand on her purse, he'd let her keep it close so far, but now he held out his other hand, and she knew he was asking for her weapon. As opposed to handing it over, she lifted the strap of her purse over her head and put it on the seat. Whether Sutcliffe knew she had a gun or not, she wasn't going to take the gun out of its hiding place and give it to someone who might use it against her. She put it on the farthest side away from Grant and he nodded, indicating that he was satisfied.

They all got out, and Sutcliffe gave Grant a key, which he moved forward to use on the bunker. Sutcliffe stayed behind her, setting her more on edge. Either he was going to kill her or he wanted her to think that he was going to. Neither option screamed trust.

Grant bent to unlock the door, which was little more than a padlock on a strip of steel, though there were sliding bolts at the top and bottom too. "No one knows this place is here," Sutcliffe said. "Our property is safe."

She hadn't asked, but he was probably just making sure she knew how alone they were out here. Grant took the padlock out of its loop and pocketed it before lifting the door up. The shutter rattled loudly as it rolled into place above their heads and Sutcliffe nudged her forward with a hand on her shoulder until she was inside.

The space was large enough for them to stand in, but specifics were hard to see in this darkened place. There were wooden crates, metal boxes, and army green tarps covering larger items in a corner. So much for getting a look at their capabilities, she couldn't see one specific item.

"It's all packed ready for shipping. We have our own transport planes and access to a private airstrip at both ends of the journey," Sutcliffe said. "You can see that we're well-equipped. Our war is going to—"

A sharp rush of concentrated air preceded Sutcliffe's silence. She recognized the sound of death meeting concrete from when Tim had fallen on the pavement in front of her. Whirling around, she saw Brodie coming out of the shadows by the door, inside the unit.

"Thank God you shut him up."

This came from behind her and Grant sauntered up at her side. "One down, one to go," Brodie said, switching his aim to Grant.

Letting her eyes fall to Albert Sutcliffe's lifeless form on the floor, Zara wanted to breathe a sigh of relief but had no idea what his death would mean to the others at the compound. Would they disband? Or would this just strengthen their resolve?

Still looking at Sutcliffe, she decided that death was never pretty, even when it was deserved. "You killed him?" she said.

This hadn't been a part of the plan, but there had been no plan for this. The Kindred hadn't known she was going to Sutcliffe's compound after the meeting. Yet they'd regrouped and somehow got to this bunker before she, Grant, and Sutcliffe did.

Brodie had been lying in wait inside, he couldn't have been outside because there was nowhere to hide out there and no one had come in behind them. She was so grateful that he was here. She felt better being close to his watchful eye. But because there was no plan, she wasn't sure how she was supposed to receive him. As a lover? Should she pretend to be caught betraying him?

"Thank God, somebody had to," Grant said, and she turned to frown at him.

He'd been kissing Sutcliffe's ass, singing his praises, and now his idol lay on the floor of his own secret bunker bleeding onto the concrete, yet he was smiling as if all was right with the world. Could Grant have sized up the situation and switched allegiances so quickly? If he had, then he was much more tactically minded than she'd believed him to be.

"You're happy that he's dead?" she asked.

"Sure, it's all part of the plan, right?"

What plan? She had no idea what he was talking about. "Plan?"

Coming to her side, Grant squeezed his fingers between hers. Anytime he'd held her hand in the past, it was never in such a familiar way. It was impossible that he just happened to do something so familiar when they were standing in front of her lover.

She frowned at their linked fingers. "What are you doing?" she asked, but when she tried to free her hand, he constricted his hold.

"She's chosen me, not you," Grant muttered, losing his smile as he faced Brodie.

Oh, so he was going to gloat that she'd abandoned the Kindred. She assumed that this would be when the truth came out because Brodie knew she hadn't chosen Grant. But she waited for Brodie to tell Grant that. He was obviously here as part of a plan and she didn't know what it was, or what her role was yet.

"Do you think so?" Brodie asked and his fixed black stare remained on his brother.

"Yes," Grant said. "You showed up right on time, right when she said you would."

Zara was confused. She hadn't said any such thing to Grant. Brodie didn't say a word and his stoic expression gave little away. His arm remained straight, and his aim at Grant was true.

Brodie wasn't playing, that gun with its silencer was no toy. "Let her go."

"Do you think I forced her to be here? I didn't. She's chosen my side. You abandoned her, so she abandoned you."

His triumph was odd given that Sutcliffe had just been killed. Even if it was true that she'd chosen Sutcliffe, he was no more. "I didn't—"

"You are predictable," Grant said, sidling closer to her, probably in an attempt to appear casual, but he was using her as a shield just as he had the previous night in the hotel. "You did what she said you would."

"What?" she and Brodie asked at the same time.

Grant's swagger increased. "She told us that you would follow her, that this was the place you were looking for," Grant said and kept on talking before she could exclaim a denial. "Of course, only she and I knew Sutcliffe was your real target. But we needed him dead." He laughed and pulled her into his side, so he could link their arms. "Killing is what you do, that's what she said. Pulling the trigger for us kept our hands clean."

Outrage sealed her throat. "What shit are you talking?" Brodie growled.

"We needed to get rid of Sutcliffe, but Zara and me, we're not killers." Technically, she was. She'd murdered Elvis in self-defense. "I wouldn't ask her to dirty her hands for the cause. But we needed Sutcliffe out of the way."

"Out of the way for what?"

"For me to take over," Grant said and his smile returned. "You got played good, brother. She makes an excellent double agent, doesn't she?" Was Grant suggesting that she'd betrayed the Kindred and led Brodie here on purpose? Grant laughed.

"You're full of shit," Brodie said.

"How do you think I knew you would be here?" he sneered and Brodie's eyes flicked to her.

No. The smoke of suspicion crept into Brodie's gaze, and she exhaled. He couldn't believe Grant; he just couldn't believe that she would betray him the way Grant was implying. Grant was trying to poison the minds of the men who trusted her, and there was her love, gun in hand, looking at her like he might believe his brother.

Trying to move away from Grant, she inched toward Brodie, who was about ten feet in front of them, right by the open door. "B—" the click of the hammer being pulled back on Brodie's gun made her stop. "What are you doing?"

But the question was answered by actions, not by words. His straight arm moved in a short crescent and stopped only when the gun was aimed square on her.

Grant was all pride and glee. "She screwed me over and Art was killed. You shouldn't be surprised that she did it to you too," Grant said.

The bastard was taking pleasure in this, and she wanted to smack his smarmy face. None of it was true. He wasn't just telling Brodie that she was subscribing to someone's cause, he was lying about her setting the Kindred up like she'd adopted his vendetta.

As he still wouldn't free her arm, she mollified herself by glaring at him. "Why are you doing this? I didn't say any of those things to you. Why are you lying?" she asked Grant and tried to pull his arm away from hers, but his fingers dug deep. Still trying to liberate herself she turned to Brodie. "Don't you listen to him. I would never lead you into... I would never ask you to kill. I—"

"Isn't that why you called him at Purdy's?" Grant asked. "That was the last straw for her. She mopped up after you for months and when she needed you… where were you? It's okay, Zar, it's over. He knows the truth now. You've done the right thing. You'll be at my side as we finish what Albert started. That's where you belong, you know that. You belong with me."

"You set me up for this…" she whispered at Grant. "I trusted you and—"

"You don't have to lie anymore," Grant said, explaining away her reaction. "You're free. He deserves to be double-crossed. He's a killer, pure and simple. He's good at doing the only thing he knows, just like you said."

Zara had never said that either. Grant was playing them both, destroying Brodie's faith in her because he wanted to ruin the people who had sabotaged him. Grant was malicious, having orchestrated this whole situation, and he had no shame about it. Brodie was her only hope, except he was the only one with a gun and it was pointing straight at her.

"Baby," she whispered and took a step toward him.

"Stay there," he said, strengthening his arm. When it was clear that Brodie was heeding Grant's confident words, Grant loosened his hold on her. But it was pointless now, Brodie didn't want her to move and she knew how efficient he was with a weapon.

She wanted to run away from Grant, toward Brodie. But that gun was a terrifying barrier between them. "Don't do this," she murmured. "Don't listen to him. You know I would never—"

"Do I?" Brodie asked and the ice in his gaze froze her heart. With one reverse step, he got closer to the door. "You're both gonna stay where you are… You're welcome to each other."

Moving backwards, he kept aim on her until he got into the open and sidestepped. Zara intended to run after him, but Grant snatched her and held her back. "No!" she called out and tried to fight Grant off, but it was too late.

A bike roared to life and Grant released her, she got

outside in time to see Brodie zipping away from the bunker on a dirt bike that moved fast across the gravel and into the distance, then he was gone. Stuck with Grant and Sutcliffe's corpse, fury balled her fists and she spun around to storm back inside just in time to see Grant examining one of the metal crates.

"What the hell was that?" she demanded, ignoring Sutcliffe's prone form to get near her boss. "I didn't tell you anything about Raven. I didn't tell you we could lure him here to murder Sutcliffe just so you could get yourself promoted! You lied to me! You made me believe that you wanted me to be a part of this. That you trusted me—"

Grant wore his own fury. "Welcome to the club, Zara! I trusted you, and you ran off to fuck my brother! You sold me out."

Grant kicked the crate and spun toward her; his anger made him forget everything else in the place.

It became so clear to her. "You didn't think you could get me," Zara muttered. "You used me... You... this was payback. All of it. You didn't want my trust. You wanted to set me up."

Grant's self-satisfaction shone. "And that you so readily accepted Sutcliffe's offer told us that you were still working for Raven, that you were going to betray me again," Grant said. "Don't stand there acting shocked and hurt. You came to the compound and pretended to entertain the idea of an allegiance because you planned to betray me—again! All I did was play you at your own game, Zara."

She couldn't be angry because he was right. She was on the side of the Kindred, inside CI, close to Grant, all because it was supposed to get them information about Grant's plans. She'd completely missed that he planned to get Sutcliffe out of the way and take over. But as she glanced around at the dead body, she saw it so clearly.

Grant was a powerful man. CEO of a multinational. Billionaire. Men like him didn't work for anyone, and they were even worse at taking orders. Somewhere along the way, Grant had gone from being complicit to craving authority. It could have happened when he saw what Sutcliffe had built, maybe he wanted to be exalted by the cult.

"What makes you think that they'll let you take over?" she asked, still looking at Sutcliffe. "Are you just going to saunter back to the farm and tell them Sutcliffe is taking a nap and left you in charge? How long do you think they'll accept that for? Sutcliffe was their leader and—"

"He was ridiculously inefficient and slow. It won't take them long to see that things are better under my leadership."

Grant wasn't the man she thought he was. When she turned to look at him, his egotism disgusted her. "Under your leadership. What about the company, Grant? Are you just going to abandon CI while you take up your position as supreme leader?"

"The company gives us the tools we need. War is a business and just like running a multinational, if it's led by the right team of people with the right acumen, it's impossible to lose."

"You told me this wasn't about money," she said, backing away from him when he encroached upon her. "You told me this was about ideology."

"Everything's about money," he said and some of his enthusiasm turned to a sneer. "Or sex. You proved that."

Brodie might doubt her but she couldn't doubt him. "You know, it doesn't matter whether he trusts me or not," she said, taking farther small steps of retreat. "He's still going to take you down."

"I don't think so," Grant said, taking the padlock out of his pocket. "The loss of our parents crippled him. Losing Art sent him back to square one. And now he's lost the woman you claim he loves, he'll turn right back into a hermit again. He's nothing on his own. He's easily broken."

She wouldn't believe that. Grant had played a cruel game with her, and maybe it was one she deserved to lose. But she wouldn't agree with him disparaging her love. "If he loved me, then he wouldn't have believed your claims, would he? By your own admission, he's incapable of love. So all you've done is strengthen him. Now he has more hate for you and hate for me. Pissing Raven off always has consequences," she said, and nodded at Sutcliffe. "Look what he did to the last man who pissed him off."

Grant stopped to look down. "He won't be able to get to me."

The upper hand was returning to her. "If Sutcliffe's people accept you, maybe he won't get to you quickly. Your little game might have fucked with Raven's head and broken us up. Maybe you're pleased that I got what I deserved. But there's one thing you haven't achieved, one thing you can't steal."

"What's that?" Grant asked her but was unconcerned.

Free and joyous despite the rift Grant may have caused, she still had hope. "My love for him," she said and smiled. "You can fight a thousand wars and raise an army of a million. You can stamp your feet and demand to get your way, but Raven is not alone. Day or night, no matter what you do, I will always belong to him."

And while Grant was building up another red-faced fury, she bolted to the truck Sutcliffe had left idling and sped away as fast as the vehicle would take her. As soon as she was too far away for Grant to catch her, she stopped to take her purse from the backseat so she could call Ben to tell him what had happened. Although she put the gun in Grant's hand and omitted all reference to Raven.

Her goal was to cause as much mayhem and dissension as she could before Grant got back and spun his own yarn. That he was marooned in the middle of the field would help, because although he probably had a cellphone, he would have no one to call for help. With Ben on the case, spreading the news, she dumped the truck, wiped her prints, and caught a cab to the airport.

TWENTY-FIVE

SHE HATED EVERY SECOND of the journey. In her desperation to get home, she counted every second, especially the ones where there was some sort of delay. If someone so much as stopped in front of her to tie their shoe, she had to dampen her urge to scream at them to get out of her way.

If Grant wanted to cause more trouble, then he could get back before her and be in her apartment. But he had a cult to usurp, so she doubted he'd be chasing her down. There was nothing more for him to win. He wanted to bust up her relationship with Brodie as payback for their association and it was possible he'd succeeded. But stepping into Albert Sutcliffe's shoes would be enough of a job to keep him busy for a while. Zara didn't think it would be as easy as Grant seemed to think.

Sutcliffe had spoken about being valuable to the group to ensure cohesion. After she'd killed Elvis, cohesion fell apart. Without Sutcliffe's direction, she'd guess that most of the group would disband—the innocent ones at least. Bringing together so many type A personalities, as Sutcliffe had to build his army, would lead to clashes now that the position of leader had become vacant.

The flight was bumpy, but she was too distracted to care.

Then the cab she'd jumped into outside arrivals got stuck in traffic. So by the time she ran up the stairs to her apartment, she was tired and annoyed. Thinking about what had happened in that bunker for too long drained her senses. Grant had set her up, which she was raging about. But it was the look on Brodie's face as his brother wove his magic that broke her heart. Every time she pictured it, tears came to her eyes. Her man had hurt enough, he didn't deserve to be played with for nothing more than sport. At least when she'd betrayed Grant it was for the greater good. Grant did what he did in that warehouse just because it was fun.

Sticking her key in the lock of her apartment, she closed her eyes for half a beat and prayed that she'd find hope inside. The apartment was dark. It was cold and nothing moved. She locked the front door, threw her purse onto the floor, and marched straight to the bedroom. There were no lights in here either, but she didn't have to search the corners, he was lying right there in the middle of the bed.

She couldn't pick out his expression, but from his pose with his hands linked behind his head, she could tell he wasn't here for a fight.

"What took you so long?" Brodie asked her. Her smile came after her tongue pushed into her cheek. "Get your sweet ass over here."

Zara was shaking her head when she ran over to throw herself on top of him, but she grabbed his face and kissed him ten times in a row before she spoke. "I hate you, you know that?" she said and kissed him again. "I guess you didn't close the door on us after all."

"I had you going," he said and snatched her body to roll over and tuck her under him. Her dress was off the shoulder and loose enough that he could just pull it down out of his way. But after exposing her breasts, he gave them a brief look then kissed her mouth.

Brodie loved to kiss and when the urgency of his tongue heated hers, she mumbled and took his jaw into both hands to separate their mouths before things went any further. "What was the point of that? Why did you leave me there with him?"

She'd been terrified that her relationship with Brodie had been irreparably damaged by Grant's antics. If Brodie was still looking for a way to push her out of his life, Grant had given it to him. Each extreme had warred within her, which was why her journey was so taxing. She'd convinced herself Brodie was going to cast her out of the Kindred, then swung back to the other extreme that the whole thing was an elaborate ruse, and he did trust her.

"I guess you gave him the riot act after I left," he said, brushing his nose over hers and kissing her cheek then her chin before he pressed his lips to her mouth.

Pushing him up, she still didn't understand. "What did you expect me to do? Was this all part of your evil plan? Can you explain to me what—"

His loud exhale was as frustrated as it was resigned. He had to have known she'd want answers. "You knew I'd be here, didn't you?"

With his arm around her, he relaxed onto his back. He picked up the ends of her hair that hung down her back and let them snake between his fingers. She moved onto her side and laid her hand over his heart. "I hoped you would be. I told Grant that if you loved me, you wouldn't have believed him… I was on the plane when I realized I meant it. We've been through so much and… I don't want trust to be an issue for us anymore. I couldn't get home fast enough. I had to know."

He admired her. "If I was here, that meant I love you. If I wasn't, we were over?"

Saying it so plainly brought back old worries. Looking at him, she couldn't picture her life without him at the center of it. "It would never be over," she said, sliding down the bed to rest her head on his shoulder, but he kept picking up and dropping her hair. "I told him I would always belong to you. A woman can't love a man like you and then go back to Regular Joe's, it's just not… it wouldn't be possible."

"What's a guy like me?"

Pushing her hand onto his sternum, she levered herself up to make eye contact with him again. "A guy who's intense and assured and bold. You're quick and you're smart and you love me more than a hundred men love their wives."

His brows rose as his head tipped in her direction. "And I'm the one who's assured?"

"Deny it," she said, wearing a grin. Pushing both hands onto his chest, she climbed over to straddle him and rub her lips gently, side to side on his. "Deny that you love me."

His voice got lower, making it more intimate. "You think I can't lie about how I feel?" he asked, splaying his fingers on her back to take as much hair between them as he could when he slid them upwards and locked both around the back of her neck.

She squinted. "Would the lie be that you loved me or that you didn't?"

"I don't know. If you need a check on my emotions, I guess you'd have to ask my old lady."

"She says it's true," Zara said and he accepted another kiss. There was still business to talk about before they could get busy. "I called Ben."

"Figured you would," he said. "What did you tell him?"

She sat up on him to stroke his torso, watching the motion of her hand as she did. "That Grant killed Sutcliffe and wanted to take over. I took Sutcliffe's truck from the bunker, stranding Grant. I figured that would buy some time because Grant would have to walk back to the road. There are no phone lines at the compound, right?" He nodded. "How did you get to the bunker before us?"

"Easy, we had everything we needed. Swift just needed time to clean up the map image we got from your camera."

Touching the edge of the pendant that was still around her neck, she closed her fist around it. "Is he still recording?"

Brodie half shrugged. "Probably, but it's on backup at the manor. We can get there before him."

That raised another question. "Swift's not at the manor?" she asked.

Seeing Brodie open and relaxed was such a treat. He'd come so far, and she was proud of him, just as Art would be.

"He cleaned up the image of the map while we traveled there last night and when Game Time stopped moving, we knew we had our target. Zave was already in town with the chopper, so the journey didn't take long. Security wasn't up to much at the bunker. Sutcliffe was relying on it being a secret. If you beef up security too much then you draw attention to yourself. Sutcliffe wouldn't want attention on his weapons stash. Picking the lock took seconds and then we unloaded everything."

That was an impressive operation. "You unloaded everything? What does that mean?"

One of his hands slunk down her body to squeeze her ass. "It means all the boxes and crates you saw there are empty."

She'd been terrified when Sutcliffe's supplies came into focus. All those boxes and crates suggested that he'd planned for a massive mission. Knowing that the Kindred had cleared him out alleviated some of her fear. "Does that include Game Time?"

With a single nod, he erased her remaining worries. "That includes Game Time."

They had to have been working all night, breaking into each crate, removing its contents and then staging the place to look like nothing had been touched. It was genius. "How did you and Swift do all of that—"

"We had help," Brodie said. "Remember I said we needed an army? Rigor and his men helped us clear the place. We let them have some of the lower level stuff, the rest Zave brought back with me in the chopper. In the end, it took three trips. The chopper was waiting for me with the final load after I left you with Saint."

"Which brings me back to my first question? What was that all about? How could you have a plan in place when you didn't know what Grant was planning?"

"I had an idea," Brodie said. She brushed her cheek on his when he switched his focus to the window.

She didn't want him to withdraw now, so she kept caressing to soothe him. "Tell me."

"In the motel room, after your meeting with Ben. I said it didn't make sense, right? Putting myself in Grant's place, I wouldn't trust you, not after you screwed him over in the Atlas warehouse."

Opening her mouth, she breathed in to argue, but there

was no other way to put it. She wouldn't blame Brodie or the Kindred for what had happened, or for losing Grant's faith. As it turned out, he wasn't the type of person she wanted to be allied with.

Deflated, she changed the tone of her interruption. "Go on," she said, letting the air out of her lungs.

His lips tilted like he'd read and was amused by her thought process. "Swift and I talked about it that night, after we left the motel room to meet with Rigor. The guy was pissed after that poker game, but he's smart enough to know a good deal when it finds him. He got arms and cash, and he'll get a whole lot else if everything goes our way. Grant was gonna screw you over. There was no way he'd trust you. I'd have told you that when you decided to go back to work at CI, if you'd asked me. The way he let you back in was just too easy."

Back then she couldn't ask him to so much as pass the salt because he was too distracted. Thinking again, she wondered if she'd been wrong to mollycoddle Brodie the way she had. If she'd forced him to listen, forced him to help, maybe he'd have found his way out of his funk sooner. "Swift and I spoke about it."

"Swift doesn't have a brother, and Saint has always been that way, he holds grudges. Since we were kids, he couldn't keep friends because as soon as he didn't get his way he sulked. That's probably why he held onto the argument we had about our folks when we were teenagers."

Grant wasn't the only one to hold onto that, the brothers' relationship was already in tatters and after that, neither of them had made any attempt to patch things up.

"You could've just told me to walk away," she said. "You didn't have to sneak out of the motel room and make secret plans with Tuck."

"Saint would never have hurt you, look at what happened today, he thought he conned me into coming to that bunker to kill Sutcliffe because Saint wouldn't get blood on his Italian loafers. He doesn't have the stomach for it. That's why he needs Sutcliffe's army. If I thought he was gonna hurt you, I'd have yanked you. As it was, he needed to win, needed to defeat us and today he did."

She was still confused. "So you were just playing fair? You hurt him. I hurt him. So we let him hurt us back."

"He's not looking at you anymore, is he? You got away clean, and he's smug."

Grant wasn't focusing on her; he was trying to ingratiate himself with the cult. If Brodie had ignored Grant's claim that she'd betrayed him, he'd be even angrier and even more likely to focus his wrath on them.

"You were protecting me?" she asked. "You let him think he won because as long as he thinks we're not together, he's satisfied."

"As far as we're concerned, yes."

"You were protecting me?" she said and her love for him swelled.

He didn't even register that what he'd done was a big deal, but it was to her. He'd foregone battling egos with Grant to make sure she was safe. "It's my primary mission, baby."

"Beau," she murmured, but had no words for how humbled she was. It wasn't every man who would let his opponent claim a win just to protect the sanctity of the heroine.

Still, he was nonchalant. "Don't worry," Brodie said, rolling her onto her back again. "He'll know by the end of this that we conned him again. We just need this window."

He began to descend to kiss her, but she stopped him. "For what?"

"For the grand finale," Brodie said. "Swift is still out there, he and Rigor's men are causing hell at the compound. Scaring the shit out of people and shaking some trees. It should be enough to scare off the women and children."

Saving innocent people was a plus, but the non-innocent people would raise hell. "But the men will mobilize," she said, not sure that she liked this plan because it put people she cared about in harm's way.

"With what? We have the majority of their arms… and with Sutcliffe gone…"

"It will be mayhem," she said and let him kiss her while she sorted through what these developments meant. The weapons were gone, but they probably didn't know that until they showed up to retrieve them from the bunker. There was a chance that the men were so busy fighting amongst themselves that no one had taken charge yet. Grant didn't have their confidence, he was just a random suit who had recently shown up, he hadn't proven himself to anyone, didn't have their faith.

Ben would have told everyone her version of events, and now that everyone thought she'd fled for her life after witnessing Grant murder their leader, there would be fear and tension in the ranks. Brodie was good, he'd come through, he'd thought about how to play this beautifully and it was all the more impressive that he hadn't come up with the full plan until they were in that motel room.

Breaking their kiss, there was something she had to know. "What made you figure it out?"

His glower almost made her smile. He wasn't pleased that she'd interrupted their bonding. But he grumbled and answered her question. "Grant was obsessed with our relationship. Then he found out you went to Ben about Sutcliffe. You didn't confide in him, you went to Ben. Art and I already knew Grant had the hots for you. It didn't make sense that he would be happy for you to be chatting it up with Ben, a practical stranger, and yet he was thrilled to hear that you were talking to him. Why would he be happy about that? Why would Sutcliffe have a private meeting with you when the last time you three were in a private space he was shot at?

"I don't know how much Sutcliffe knew about Grant's mistrust of you, but I'd bet he knew something, that's the reason he let you live, just to see you destroyed… Which was why today Sutcliffe's time was up. Grant wouldn't have the balls to hurt you, but Sutcliffe would, and after he found out that we emptied his locker, he'd have used you to get to us."

Sutcliffe needed to be disposed of and Raven didn't waste time with conversation. He had a job to do and he did it. If he hadn't, Sutcliffe could have held her hostage until he got his supplies back. "It wouldn't have worked," she said. "I—"

"It would have," Brodie said with a nod and stroked her hair from her face. "I'm not a cop or a government official. I don't have any 'no negotiation with terrorists' protocol to follow. I'd have done every single thing he told me to do. I'd have killed. I would've fought in his damn war. Hell, I'd have set Game Time up myself, even if it meant killing millions. I'd have made Swift work for him, and Falc, and Wren. I'd have handed over all of our resources and let him put me on a leash."

She couldn't imagine anyone as strong as Brodie bowing to the threats of another. Confusion made her frown, but he was still relaxed. "Why?" she exhaled. "He was a monster. You don't believe in his cause. How can you be so sure that you would—"

"Because I love you more than a thousand men love their wives," he said and the confession made her heart stop. "There's nothing I wouldn't do to keep you safe."

Even if it meant sacrificing himself and everything he stood for. Her lip wobbled, so she tucked it into her mouth and let her teeth clamp down on it. A tear slid from the corner of her eye and skidded down her temple to her ear. "You said it."

"Yeah," he said in a murmur complementary of this intimate moment. But his tone quickly became its usual abrupt self. "I fucking said it… now are you gonna put out?"

Spreading her arms, she wrapped them around him and forced his mouth onto her. He loved her, he'd said it, and she had no doubt that he meant it. Just as she was sinking into their kiss, relishing the taste and texture of his warm mouth as it responded to hers, he slid his clasping hands from her knees down to her ankles at his ass. Holding her ankles and with her shins resting on his forearms, he reared up, taking her body with him as he left the bed.

"Where are we going?" she asked, squeezing her legs on either side of his ribs, keeping her hands on his shoulders for balance.

He didn't respond and carried her in this elevated place to the corner where he turned and sank down into his chair and lowered her onto his lap. Wearing a smile that split her face, she ran her hands over his hair.

"You want to be my fantasy?" he asked with a snarl in

his voice that made her body spasm around his.

Coming in for a kiss, he grabbed her chin to push it aside so he could lick and suck on her neck. "I should put my stockings on," she said.

Watching her breasts move as breathing grew more difficult for her, his voice got deeper. "I got all I need right here."

Pulling her dress farther down her body, he took hold of each breast, giving each some tough love before he rammed a hand down between their bodies, beneath the coiled fabric of her dress, which was bunched around her hips. He pressed the pad of his middle finger to her clit.

The pressure was enough to make her whimper and she wriggled against it, trying to tempt the digit inside, but he moved it away each time it got close. Removing his mouth from her neck, his hand then snaked around to the back of her neck, and while she worked herself against the finger he had under her dress, he pulled her forward to bury his face in her hair over her ear.

"I know what you want, baby," he mumbled into her locks. "What do I want?"

"You want me to ride you, here in your chair," she said and slowed the movement of her hips so she could rise up enough to unbuckle his jeans. His dick sprang out, making brief but potent contact with the juices he'd smeared through her folds and she stroked him with her fist, running her thumb up over the crest of his urgency to coat him with the pre-come seeping out of him.

"Why do I want that?" he asked and curled his fingers to take a handful of her hair, enough that he could pull her back to make her look at him.

"Because your plaything has to say thank you," she said. "To show appreciation to my chief."

"Good answer," he said. From the way the corner of his mouth twitched, she knew she'd amused him and that wasn't the answer he'd been expecting. "Say pretty please, pretty baby."

"Pretty please," she said, gasping in before he yanked her forward to shove his tongue into her mouth. He sucked on her tongue and squeezed her breast, brushing her tight, sensitized nipple with his rough thumb then pinching it between two fingertips to roll and tease it until the pounding in her belly almost made her climax.

Holding onto his cock, she lowered herself, and without asking what she needed, he slid farther down in his chair until he was in the perfect position for their joining. With her knees on either side of him and her lower legs trapped between him and the arms of the chair, she descended farther and let the tip of him find its way into her passage. Brodie wasn't interested in waiting. As she breathed through every second of the excruciating pleasure his dick gave her, he thrust up, slamming himself into her.

Zara hadn't been expecting him to do that, she thought she was driving, but that was probably his reminder that he was always in charge. Still with their mouths frozen in a kiss, she breathed through the sensation that made her body feel like it was about to split in two.

"You don't get to tease me," he said. "I tell you to ride it, you damn well better do it right, baby. Show my cock you appreciate it or you won't get a second chance to prove yourself."

His arms moved under hers until his forearms were supporting her weight and she began to move, slow, then as her legs adjusted to their lack of space and her knees found traction on the solid arms of the chair, she got faster. Brodie didn't blink. He kept his dark, intense eyes fixated on hers. As her core got wetter, her bouncing increased.

He didn't crack a smile, didn't offer words of encouragement, he just looked at her and there was something in the way he examined her that increased the potency of this joining.

"Brodie," she whispered between huffed pants. "Baby, I need to—"

"No, you don't," he said. "Not yet. Work harder."

Her legs were tingling and weak, her body was sweating, and yet the searing pleasure that burned inside the space his cock occupied made her want to please him, she wanted him to have this same measure of mania.

Brodie loved her, he'd given his all to protecting her, he'd murdered for her. With renewed energy, she pumped herself up and down on his dick, squeezing her muscles around him on every descent until his jaw worked in a clench and she knew she had him.

"Oh, you fucking bitch," he said, releasing the words on a pained exhale.

He didn't want to climax yet. He wanted to be in control and to give her permission when it was time to come. He'd done it before, and it drove her wild, which always gave him pleasure. But both of them were a little out of control tonight and he wasn't as able to keep his horses reined.

Snatching her neck, he pulled her forward and stuck his tongue into her mouth, making her stop. Orgasm beat through every bone and she clenched so tight around him that his seed exploded into her, but instead of the usual curses, he just kissed her deeper and didn't stop until both had ridden the wave all the way to shore.

He kissed and stroked her. "Pack your shit," he said, tracing his fingertips down either side of her spine.

Zara didn't want to move and the ticklish itch that thrummed through her from his hands was an electricity that she wanted to savor for a while. "I'm tired, can we sleep here?"

"No," he said and got up, dumping her out of his lap and onto her feet.

Her dress fell off her body and warmed her toes. The sudden change of position sent blood back into her lower limbs and they began to tingle. Brodie was already storming past her. He pulled a sports bag from the closet and opened drawers to stuff whatever he found inside into the bag.

The odd action perplexed her. "Most of my things are at the manor," she said, sitting back in the chair they'd just had sex in to bend over and rub her legs. "There should be enough there to—"

"I called a realtor," he said. "Your place is gonna be on the market next week."

Zara stopped rubbing, but didn't sit up, she wasn't sure how to react to the news that he'd taken control of her abode. If any other man had done it, she might have been offended, but Brodie was different from all other men and it was encouraging to have the reminder that he had returned to his former arrogant self.

As heavy-handed as the gesture was, it was so decisive and such a clear indication he wanted her at the manor full-time that she smiled and relaxed into the seat, pulling her knees up with her to tuck her feet over the front of it.

"You called a realtor?" she asked. "I hope you didn't do it from the manor. The Kindred have rules about calls to outsiders from there."

"Yeah, they do," he said, slamming the drawer to turn and face her. "I told Wren to call. I don't make phone calls like that."

Brodie didn't make phone calls, other than that one to her. "I guess I'll need to find a new place to live then."

He wasn't in the mood for teasing. "It's time for you to be where you belong."

As appreciative as she was that he was making his intentions clear, she had to be sure he knew what he was getting himself into. "You know now that Grant thinks he broke us up, and after what I said to him today… I won't be going back to CI."

Brodie wasn't discouraged. "I wouldn't have you there anyway and we've got plans to see the world, baby… I'll show you shit that will blow your mind."

She didn't doubt that, he could blow her mind while they were sitting together in her bedroom and Brodie knew spots on the globe that few people had seen. The possibilities were endless. She had a first class tour guide to show her the world. Experiencing these beautiful places would be made more thrilling because she'd be sharing them with the man she loved.

"Okay," she said, touching the pendant that still hung between her breasts. "It will take me a few hours to pack up—"

"Bring anything essential that's left here," he said. "Zave and I had to bring the last of Sutcliffe's cache to the manor. You know that's the safest place in the world. But we can't leave Swift out there with Rigor and his men for long. We have to get back. Zave is waiting at the manor to give us a ride."

So it would be a matter of dumping her things and leaping onto the chopper to get back and help Swift. She was disappointed that there wasn't more time. She'd been 'on' constantly for days and the exhaustion was taking its toll. But this wasn't over yet and the situation wouldn't pause for her to rest up and get her bearings again.

"I know you're tired," he said, tossing the half-full bag onto the bed. "If you want to stay at the manor, you can. Swift and I will finish this."

"No," she said, making herself stand up. Brodie was a determined individual who completed a mission no matter what, and she wouldn't give the Kindred less than her absolute best. "If you need an inside contact, I'm the only one who Ben has seen, the only one who he might trust. If there are any more innocents there someone will have to get them to safety while the rest of you clean up."

Clean up was her way of saying taking out anyone who posed a threat. "Timing is crucial," Brodie said. Coming to her, he stole her hand and pulled her over to sit on the bed with him. "We've set this up so we can get what we need while there's mayhem. They don't have a leader, there will be in-fighting and mistrust. We have to get in there, remove any weapons, and make sure no one wants to come back."

"How will you do that?" she asked. "How can you be sure that even if you burn every hut and kill every crop—"

"Because that place is Rigor's payment. Him and his men are moving in and they'll protect it."

Rigor didn't seem to be a rational guy, she didn't like the idea that they were handing him power, especially when he'd just gotten a hoard of weapons too. "Isn't that replacing one dictator with another?"

"For the most part, Rigor and his guys are low level criminals. They talk a good game, but they don't persecute and suppress innocent people. The only thing they're hiding from is the cops. Chances are they'll turn it into a drinking den, a makeshift casino, whatever, they won't be planning a war. Rigor just isn't that motivated."

From what she'd experienced of Rigor, she'd say Brodie

was right. That he'd shot at them after he lost the poker game didn't seem to be any kind of issue and she had to ask why. "He shot at us, are you okay with that?"

He ran a hand up the front of her bare thigh. "Everyone had too much to drink and tempers ran hot. Rigor hates to lose," he shrugged. "Wouldn't be the first time someone's taken a bullet for winning a hand."

She could no longer say that Brodie was the one who lived in a different world from everyone else because she was now a part of that world as well. She'd been shot at, seen men die, and become a murderer herself. Her initiation into the Kindred certainly seemed to be complete.

After this was done, there would be plenty of time to rest. She'd started this mission with the Kindred, and she was determined to see it through to the end. "Tell Falc to get the chopper ready, we'll be out of here in five."

She didn't ask more questions; her chief had given her an order and she'd just learned tonight how sexy it was to follow the orders of the man she loved. Packing up the last of her important things, she shoved everything else into a box in her office and then they were running down the stairs of her building to get to Brodie's bike out back.

There had barely been time to dress let alone shower or think about grooming. But if Brodie was right, they needed to get the drop on the compound now or the window of opportunity would close. Zara didn't know how this would play out, but it was clear. This was going to be over tonight.

TWENTY-SIX

THEY MET TUCK at a bar less than a mile from the Sutcliffe compound. Zave had stayed with the chopper, which they'd landed in a field without permission. Zave didn't seem to be the type to get his hands dirty, yet he was completely aloof about flying them here, there, and everywhere, even in spite of what the plan was. His conscience couldn't run too deep. But based on what she'd seen so far, his bravery was negligible.

On approaching the small, single story concrete structure, she saw only shadows in the high windows and little light. A notice on the battered wooden door declared the premises closed and from the neglected fascia, she wasn't sure this bar was ever open. It looked abandoned yet looked to be in better shape than the biker bar Brodie had summoned her to. So it could go either way.

Alone, she and Brodie walked through the entrance. There was no music or noise that would indicate fun, so she guessed the place served a purpose for them and their allies tonight that had nothing to do with drinking and dancing.

Brodie hadn't said anything since they left Zave, so she guessed he was getting into his game head and when he took her hand, she was startled. The gentle intimacy wasn't his style, if he wanted to claim or touch her, he grabbed her neck or pulled her body.

Inside, Tuck was with Rigor and a bunch of other men whom she didn't know, though she recognized some faces from the biker bar. Brodie squeezed her hand but didn't look at her. He might have been trying to console her in this intimidating situation, but she thought that was unlikely.

When the dangerous looking men, who she assumed were affiliated with Rigor, spotted their physical connection few hid their surprise. Brodie wasn't consoling her. He was marking her and highlighting her significance to him. Tonight wasn't a night for playing, and she doubted few would try flirting with her, but she was the only woman here.

There was no time for them to explain their relationship to these people. He wanted to get straight to business. Most of the tables had been pushed into one corner of the hardwood floor, giving the lower ranked men space to loiter, while those who made the decisions stayed together. A map was spread out on a large central table, just like in their motel room, and that was where the men congregated.

These men had been working hard and Brodie needed an update before the final push. Tuck acknowledged them with a nod, then turned to the table when she and Brodie got to his side. "We've still got guys out there," Tuck said. "They're holding the perimeter. We flushed out everyone we could."

"How?" she asked and Tuck glanced at Brodie.

"There was already confusion 'cause Ben told them Sutcliffe was dead. So we went in and confirmed it, most ran as soon as they figured it was true. There's a bunch of guys holed up in the house. We exchanged fire outside, but as we suspected the majority fled. We followed and found them at the bunker. After they did a weird ceremony and buried Sutcliffe like he was some kind of deity, they started to load their trucks. Didn't take them long to figure out the crates were empty."

"They split?" Brodie asked.

"Most of them," Tuck said with a nod.

Using the map that the more important men were fixated on, Tuck talked about the perimeter security and the four cult men guarding it.

"We used FLIR to confirm it," Tuck said. "These four guys are the last ones protecting the perimeter. Everyone else is in the house battling to take the lead. The perimeter is wide open, it's too much for these four guys to guard alone. We can ignore them and go in anyway, but then they're at our backs, so I'd suggest—"

"Won't take me long to get rid of them," Brodie said. He and Tuck exchanged a calm look. "Then we go in."

Tuck, Brodie, Rigor, and three of his men were crowded around the table and in this fully lit space, she got more details of Rigor. He was as shrewd and as shifty as he had been in the biker bar. But his eyes were clearer, he was listening and contributing as the three main men discussed what to do with those in the house.

"Anyone who has ideas of taking over is inside," Tuck said. "If I was inclined to take bets, I might let them alone in there and see how long it takes for them to kill each other."

Brodie was intense when he frowned. "We don't have that kinda time, I don't want them to get the chance to regroup or call back those who have run. This is it. This is our chance to neutralize the threat for good."

Sutcliffe was dead. His nephew was dead. There was no bloodline to take up Sutcliffe's mantle. Those who were on the compound looking for a good, idyllic life would have run as soon as Tuck and Rigor showed up, dressed in black, as they were now, telling the cult that their leader had been murdered. Women wanted to protect their children, husbands wanted to protect their wives, those left were those in the army Sutcliffe had built.

Even then, most of them would have tucked tail and ran when they found out their bunker had been raided and their supplies ravaged. There was little left to fight for when the man with the plan was gone. Sutcliffe was the brains and the money. Rigor had done his homework on many of Sutcliffe's men and was a wise ally for the Kindred. They had no need for Sutcliffe's land, but they couldn't leave it empty, that would raise questions and leave opportunity for anyone who might look to move in. People like Grant.

Thinking of Grant, she wondered where he was now, and where Ben was too. "Do we know who's in there?" she asked because she hadn't heard any names yet.

"At least twenty men, maybe as many as thirty," Tuck said. "It's hard to get a read, but we're still listening in, the bug hasn't been found yet."

"What about Grant and Ben?"

Her concern wasn't for their safety. If anything happened to Grant, she couldn't claim he'd been innocent. Any harm that came to him he'd invited. In typical arrogant fashion, he'd believed these people would turn to him as their new savior when he put himself up for the job. As it turned out, he wasn't the only man with an ego working with Sutcliffe, apparently the Brit attracted that sort of follower.

"They were both seen going inside," Tuck said. "But it's chaos and pulling out individual voices is tough. Most of the time, they have meetings in the kitchen and they end up screaming over the top of each other."

"Has there been any indication of a secondary site or a backup bunker?" Brodie asked, remaining at her side. The heat of his arm against hers was reassuring and standing here with him, absorbing his strength, made it easier for her to keep a clear head.

"No," Tuck said, looking back at the map. "Doesn't mean that there isn't one. Just that Sutcliffe didn't share that information with anyone."

"Or whoever he did share it with isn't talking," Rigor said.

"Okay," Brodie said and backed away from the table, giving Tuck the space to roll up the map. "I'll take the guys at the rear out first, I'll circle back, eliminate the guys at the front then we surround the house."

"You think it's smart to just walk up through the front?" Rigor asked, separating from Brodie and Tuck to join his own men.

"We don't skulk," Brodie said. "This is an assault, and we've got to be willing to lose people. Anyone who runs, let 'em go. If they want to come back at us later, let them. I don't think one little fucker with a BB gun is gonna come after your people or mine on his own later."

The men chuckled, displaying just how cocky they were about their abilities. Brodie was right that anyone who ran away was unlikely to cause them much trouble because they simply wouldn't get close enough to the Kindred or to Rigor. But an all-out assault was risky and she could understand Rigor's hesitation.

An image of Art's last moments bled into her thoughts. That was how quickly it happened. Sutcliffe's shot was deliberate, but it was as possible that a stray bullet could catch them unawares. Brodie wouldn't let her be part of the advance and that made sense because she didn't have the combat skills of the others.

While Art was bleeding out, time took on a new pace. Her mother had left her. Art had vanished too soon. And she wouldn't be there to care for her love if something went wrong at that house. She was still staring into space when the men laughed and all began to move, before Brodie could get too far, her arm leaped up to catch him.

"Wait," she said. He stopped to frown at her because everyone else was moving toward a door at the back of the room. This was obviously going to happen now. "I don't want you to go."

His aloofness became tension. "What?" he said, turning to face her. He came closer as his frown became a deeper disbelieving smile. "What the hell are you—"

It was pathetic and not her role tonight, but she was scared she might lose him when she finally thought that their future was secure. She had to share her fears with him. "It's dangerous. The sniping at a distance I can handle but… I'm willing to lose other people or to give my life for you. I'm not willing to lose you."

He blanked his expression and took a breath. "You said that you wanted to be a part of the darkness. That you wanted to be a part of what the Kindred do."

She nodded and hated that her eyes were beginning to blur. "I do. I do. But…" Focusing on Brodie's grief had allowed her to sideline her own. She hadn't known Art for long, but she'd cared for him and watching a good man die had damaged her. It had reopened the wounds that made her recall what losing her mother was like and seeing how it affected Brodie traumatized her. "I won't be either of those if something happens to you, will I?"

"You'll always be Kindred," he said, taking the back of her neck in one hand and touching her cheekbone with the other. "Even if Swift and I don't make it out, Falcon will—

"I don't want Falcon," she said, whispering her petulance. They were alone inside now; vehicle engines came to life out the back signaling the other's departure. "I want you.

"I have to go," he said, straightening his body. "I've got to go to work and I can't afford to be worrying about you while I do it. Stay here."

"But…"

"If we need you to negotiate, we'll call."

His hands fell away from her body and he backed away then turned to beat a retreat out of the rear door, making no secret of his anger. His hard expression chastised her because he didn't need her pulling this kind of shit when he was getting into the zone. She could chase after him, could make a fool of herself and of him in front of men who respected and feared him. But if she did that, he'd resent her for making such a scene.

"I love you," she murmured.

Whispering the words to an empty room consoled her, but that feeling didn't last long. The room got quiet quickly. Too quiet. The bar was closed and the front door was locked, so she didn't have to worry about anyone looking for a drink. All she could do now was wait.

TWENTY-SEVEN

POURING HERSELF A MEASURE of liquor, Zara shut off the lights, so as not to draw attention to the premises because she didn't want to argue with anyone who rattled the doors. She didn't know much about how long it took for a sniper to do his work, but they weren't far from the compound, so the troop would have arrived.

She finished her drink then laid down on one of the wooden benches that lined the far wall of the room. By now, Brodie would have taken out the men in the rear and probably the men at the front as well. If he had a vehicle then the drive would only take a few minutes. They would only use vehicles to get up the path to the house if they wanted to announce their arrival, otherwise they would be sneaking in on foot and it would take longer.

Brodie had been right to ignore her concerns. What else could he have done? The mission had already started. He couldn't have walked out back to face the men who were gunning for a fight to tell them that he'd changed his mind and was going to sit here on his ass because his girlfriend decided to pitch a fit.

She wanted them to take their time and get it right, so as not to lose any men. But she also wanted them to hurry up and get it over with, so she could relax and stop worrying about her love. Selling her apartment, giving up her job, traveling the world with a marksman, she couldn't believe her life had become so unrecognizable. But she wanted a life with Brodie more than she'd ever wanted anything.

Smiling, she sat up and scrutinized her empty glass. Brodie was capable. He would get this job done and then they could concentrate on loving each other for a while. He might be an unconventional choice, but Brodie gave her everything that she needed.

Bold, brash, and domineering, she couldn't claim to have changed the man, but if he changed for her then he would no longer be the man she fell in love with because Brodie always thought he knew best and that was just how she liked him.

A noise at the rear door made her look up. If they were back already that must be a record, they'd been gone for less than an hour. Pushing her glass to the center of the table, she rose to her feet and began to move toward the door. She hadn't heard any vehicles, but they were so close to the compound that someone could walk or run here.

If someone had fled the scene, it could be an indicator that something had gone wrong. Picking up speed, she was ten feet from the door when it burst open, and she skidded to a halt.

"You're a lady who likes her liquor."

The night outside hid his features, but she recognized the build and the tone of that self-satisfied voice. "Caine," she said. Her purse was on the bar and she thought about running for it when he took a step forward to reveal the glint of his own pistol.

"Care to come in for a drink?" she asked, taking a step back and opening an arm toward the bar. If he came inside and let her go behind the bar, she could get her gun.

"Another time," he said. "There's somewhere you need to be."

It couldn't be a coincidence that he was here. Though if this bar was owned by Rigor or his men, Caine could be here to loot their supplies or maybe he knew something about the building that she didn't. "Oh yeah? Where am I supposed to be?"

She expected a smart answer, but his words weren't spoken for amusement. "The scene of the crime."

"What the—"

"Come with me," he said and pushed the door open with his back, keeping the gun on her. Glancing toward the bar, she wished for her purse and considered making a run for it. "You can try and do something stupid, but you know I'll get a shot off before you get to where you want to go. I'm here to retrieve you because I've been watching Swift and his dumb friends all day."

"You like to watch, don't you?"

Caine had first introduced himself to her while watching Raven and his progress in stopping Grant from first selling the Game Time device. Then he'd come into her life again through Grant after watching her at Purdy's during the assault. Brodie was locked in his seclusion then, and Caine had deduced her importance to the younger McCormack. Without his usual subject available to stalk, it seemed he'd promoted her to pole position.

"I'm pretty damn good at it."

"Everyone has their strengths," she said. "Like Raven, he loves to watch a man suffer and he never forgets a debt." If Caine hurt her, Brodie would be set on getting his revenge. After today his calendar would be clear for a while, especially if she was gone. How ironic would it be if she got herself killed after claiming Brodie would be safer staying here?

Caine kept his aim on her. "I'm the king of holding a grudge and proud of it. Now come on, sweetheart, let's pay lover-boy a visit."

"Fine, let me get my purse," she said and managed two steps toward the bar, but he leaped forward.

"I don't fucking think so, get your ass over here now or I'll put a bullet in your pussy and watch you bleed slow." She stopped. "There's more than one way to kill a guy. How you think he'd like fucking the mangled mess I'll leave him with?"

Caine had been a nuisance and she hated him because he dogged Raven, constantly nipping at his heels, dragging him down, distracting him from business. But she had never heard

Caine be so evil or make such threats, certainly not about her. Art had said Caine would only put a bullet in her if Brodie was there to watch, now she wasn't so sure about that. He could put a bullet in her then drag her bleeding body through the streets and dump her in her agony at Brodie's feet.

Caine wouldn't last long after that, but she wasn't certain enough of the guy's sanity to test his resolve. "Okay," she said, trying to stay cool in an attempt to keep Caine calm. "Let's go."

Leaving the bar, Caine walked behind her and she considered her options. Except there weren't many. The street was wide and clear, if she tried to run, he would get a shot off before she could get to the other side of the road or to safety. This was also a remote part of town and this was the road out of it. No one lived out here, there weren't even any cars she could try to flag down.

The walk didn't take long, and when they turned into Sutcliffe's estate, she expected to see activity. But there was none. She didn't see a soul or hear anything but nature. Whatever was going down, it had to be happening at the house.

Engaging him in conversation might get her some answers. "You do know Raven is armed," she said, but he poked the gun barrel into the back of her shoulder to keep her walking up the path toward Sutcliffe's house.

They were most of the way up the dirt road that led to the main house. She hadn't expected it to be so quiet. The calm was eerie. Caine came closer to her back, but the gun stayed against her shoulder. Having a gun pointed at her wasn't as scary as she thought it might be. It was scary, but logic kept her fear to a minimum.

Caine didn't want to kill her. He'd had the chance before. He could have put a bullet in her and left her at the bar for Brodie to find. For now, she was safe, but the chance she'd stay that way would fall dramatically when they got to the house. But Brodie was in there and confidence in her guy helped her maintain composure.

Caine wasn't much in the mood for talking after they left the bar, he hadn't tried to engage in chitchat, and during their previous encounters he'd always enjoyed the sound of his own smugness. Either he was worried or he was anticipating the need to focus.

Getting him to talk might help to distort his thinking. If she could distract him from planning or thinking about the next step, she might put the Kindred at an advantage. "Surprising the Kindred isn't smart, especially when the first thing they'll see is you pointing a gun at one of their own. Does Grant know about this stunt?"

"We don't know each other well, Swallow," he said. "I love the alias by the way."

And she wasn't going to spend time quizzing him on how he'd figured it out because that was probably what he wanted. His life was dedicated to stalking Raven and had been for years. If Caine hadn't figured out a way to get new information she'd be unimpressed. "Your point?"

"This kinda shit isn't my style. I'm way more subtle."

Subtle like he had been when he descended on her in Purdy's to threaten Raven. Yeah, subtle, she almost laughed. A further truth struck her, if this wasn't his move and he was working for Grant…

"Grant wants me here?" In danger's way or as a pawn to manipulate Brodie? "Why?"

"Thought he had it all worked out with the double cross. About now he's hearing from your lover-boy that it didn't go as he thought."

Grant had figured out that she and Brodie were still in cahoots and Brodie would take pleasure in filling in the blanks for his brother. "Where do you feature?" she asked. "Or are you just playing lap dog?"

"When he figured out the bunker was empty, then people started dying, and he found the compound in mayhem. Grant suspected your man."

As he always did. When anything went wrong in Grant's life, he always blamed his younger sibling.

"He told me to find Raven," Caine said. "Imagine his surprise when I told him Raven was with you in a dive bar plotting with the men who'd attacked the farm and probably emptied the bunker. Kudos on that by the way."

"All Raven."

"I figured."

The time for conversation passed and neither said another word because the house had just come into view. Although there were lights on, she saw no one outside and no movement behind the curtains. Instead of going through the grand front door, Caine poked and prodded her with the gun to take her around to the back, which led straight into the kitchen where those present were no doubt congregating.

"Up the steps, move!"

Zara didn't like how Caine hung back as she clutched the exterior banister and hauled herself up. She still couldn't hear anything coming from inside, so she had no idea what she was about to stumble into and scaring whoever was in Sutcliffe's kitchen could be her final act.

Those inside were already edgy because of everything that had happened in recent hours and she suspected that self-preservation was what kept Caine in a rear position. If anyone was twitchy and the back door suddenly opened, they may act on impulse rather than rationale.

Leaning as far to the side as she could, she turned the handle then splayed her fingers on the wood to give the door a shove. It swung open and male voices began to shout, but no one took a shot.

"Go," Caine said, at her back again with the gun barrel pressed into her waist.

Drawing her lips into her mouth, she straightened her back and took a breath in through her nose before she stepped over the threshold, pushing the door fully open as she did. The scene inside immediately made her tense. Grant stood to the right, in front of the wall covered with papers, with Benedict just behind him.

There were men beyond them in the lower part of the L-shaped room, significantly, none of them were standing, all she could see were bodies on the floor. Grant sneered at her, but she didn't examine him for long, she looked right to where Brodie was standing with Tuck at his side to her left. Rigor was near the door that led to the long hallway, which would take them to the front door, but he was crouched next to a bleeding man, the one she remembered from the bar.

The long table that had once been central, was on its side, shoved against the counters. All of these facts were alarming by themselves. But before she looked into anyone's eyes, she fixated on the large, scary gun in Grant's hand.

"What are you doing?" she whispered.

"What does it look like, Swallow?" Grant spat out. Caine shoved her and when she stumbled, Brodie lunged forward to try to catch her, but a gunshot made him freeze and her scream, as she fell to the floor. "Don't you dare touch her!"

Pushing onto her hands, she took stock and her heart began to pump again when she saw Brodie was still on his feet. There were holes in the walls, so she guessed the wide shot was a warning.

"She doesn't need to fucking be here," Brodie said through gritted teeth. Despite their eyes being locked, there was no softness. All she read was blind anger.

"Doesn't she?" Grant asked. She turned to see him waving the gun around, definitely pleased that he held court. "I think she does, given that she's the reason we're all fucking here!"

His volume grew with every word. "You can't be that angry," she said.

"Lies! Lies! Lies!" Grant exclaimed and stormed over to crouch beside her, pointing the gun into her face. "I gave you everything, Zara Bandini, and you threw it all away to take up with my murdering brother. What is it he has? Huh? Did he give you your dream career? A salary that let you live in luxury? Did he?"

He was unhinged and she didn't dare move in case she angered him further. "I appreciate everything you did, Grant, but—"

"No!" he said and pressed the gun barrel into her shoulder. Brodie's heavy footstep came toward her, but Grant surged back to his feet to point the gun at Brodie again. "You're not going to play the hero, brother! You're the villain."

"Is this about revenge?" she asked. "You want to hurt us so bad that—"

"You are insignificant," Grant barked. "Get up!"

Doing as she was told, she slowly got her feet beneath her and began to rise to full height. "If you don't care about—"

"I'm tired of your lies! And you need to be taught a lesson," Grant said. "You lied to me about your association with this Neanderthal, you betrayed me just to get into his bed. You hid your connection to him, hid your love." Being a CEO, his ego was healthy and he was used to people sucking up to him. He was also used to being on the inside, making the decisions, and it was obvious he couldn't handle that power being taken away from him. "Get over there beside him!"

Grant's fury fogged his intention, but she didn't trust his stability. Neither did Brodie. Because as soon as she reached his side, he twisted his body to put her behind him. She didn't fight or shun his protection. She just wished that she could offer him the same security. Staying a few feet behind him, she edged out enough that she could see Grant glaring at them with disgust.

Brodie had figured it out, that Grant could never have accepted her back into his life after she chose her love over her boss. This had been a ruse from the beginning, only this time, she was the victim of the subterfuge. "You directed them to me," she said, realizing what had happened at Purdy's during the assault. "You were with me and you signaled them, didn't you? They didn't pull me up because of my phone. You told them I'd be there with you and that I should be singled out. Why did you do that?"

"To draw him out," Grant said, pointing at Brodie. "Because of Art, he'd gone too deep for us to reach. I wanted him out in the open. After the murders of my people, Sutcliffe called me, told me I could make it right. He wanted Game Time and he wanted Raven, which suited me. I wanted both of you punished."

"So you set it up to look like I'd screwed Raven over to break us up? That was your master plan?" She struggled to see the committed and harmless man she'd worked with for five years. Losing his guardian, Frank, had taken its toll on him.

But her betrayal, her affiliation with Brodie, somehow that screwed him up more.

"The plan was to kill him, but Sutcliffe was okay with punishing you both first. It was your sordid affair that caused us to lose Game Time."

Brodie had killed the cult leader and spared his brother. Her love didn't hesitate to do the job while others were dicking around having their own fun. "Neither of you banked on him pulling the trigger first," she said.

Grant wasn't defeated. "Ultimately did me a favor," he said. "I wanted him and Sutcliffe dead, so I could take over here."

"Why?" she asked. "How could you hate your own brother so much? He was protecting people."

"Because he took what didn't belong to him!" Grant exclaimed with an ire that made his eyes water. "Just like he always does. He's so entitled, he storms in and steals whatever the hell he wants and doesn't give a damn about the damage he causes."

Rigor was seated on the floor on the other side of Tuck, but the man with him was lifeless. Tuck and Brodie blocked her from harm, and didn't appear to be effected by Grant's words, but Zara was dumbfounded. She had never seen Grant so emotional. She had no idea he cared so much about Game Time.

Brodie revealed that Grant's emotion wasn't connected to the device. Her protecting wall of a man inhaled. "You wanted her," he sneered. "We always knew it."

"I had her! She was mine," Grant insisted.

Zara wasn't a toy in the sandbox that they were fighting over. She was a person. She and Grant had never been romantically involved, not even close. But she had been his employee for half a decade. He'd confided in her, trusted her with everything professional. She had a relationship with Frank Mitchell before he died too. She had been part of the CI machine, an intrinsic part. Being Grant's executive assistant had given her power in the firm and she'd enjoyed wielding it, she liked being valued by him and being indispensable. Then Brodie had come along and shot it all to pieces.

She didn't blame Brodie. He had been trying to save lives, just like Art was, and they'd convinced her of that so thoroughly that she hadn't considered backing Grant's side. Now she could see how that devastating betrayal affected him more than she ever could have projected it would.

Brodie, Art, and her were a unit working against him and that had only pushed him closer to Sutcliffe. Whatever the cult's ideology, Zara had a feeling it didn't matter. Grant was broken. He wanted to lash out and punish those who had humiliated him. This wasn't about getting revenge for Sutcliffe. This was about Grant getting his revenge.

Grant had set this up from the start and somehow convinced Sutcliffe to go along with it. There was no need to have such an elaborate plot for Sutcliffe to get revenge on her or to acquire Game Time. Grant wanted to turn her and Brodie against each other. He wanted to see her ousted by the man she'd fallen in love with after Grant convinced his brother that she was a double agent. Grant hadn't considered the fact that Brodie returned that love, or that he would trust her, despite his brother's assertions.

Grant had once told her of how Brodie was incapable of love, how he used people and cast them aside. Grant had believed his own words and concluded that it would be easy to eviscerate her and Brodie's relationship.

As the puzzle came together, words slipped out of her. "You didn't think he could love me," she whispered and with one step, she began the journey toward her lover's side. "You thought he'd cast me out. Maybe you thought he'd kill me. You didn't for one second consider that he and I might talk to each other. That he might give me the benefit of the doubt… You didn't think he could love me."

"He can't," Grant spat, and his expression grew more hateful. "When he's finished with you, he'll turn his back on you."

Sliding a hand up Brodie's back, she received no acknowledgement from her love, but she didn't need one. "He's never turned his back on anyone. His loyalty is absolute. You said it yourself, when you tried to badmouth his father, he defended the man. You've turned your back on everyone.

You chose not to honor your mother's wishes, you chose Frank when she wanted you with Art. You disrespected Art by belittling and ignoring the lessons he could've taught you.

"When your younger brother didn't bow and capitulate, you chose to ridicule and ostracize him. You know that Frank wouldn't agree with the path you've chosen since his death, so you don't even honor his memory... Then there's me." Exhaling, she inched closer against Brodie until his body supported her weight, but she kept her eyes on Grant, resting her cheek on Brodie's upper arm.

"What about you?" Grant asked.

"I disagreed with you. I had the audacity to tell you that what you were doing was wrong. You ignored me. Tried to cajole me. And carried on anyway, even when I said no to you. It's funny, now that I think about it... I love Raven because... he's the exact opposite of everything you are. I used to admire you. But beyond the fancy suit and the shiny car, you're more broken than all of us. You just refuse to admit it. You're broken, Grant, and you've shunned anyone who might have the inclination to help you."

"She did the right thing joining us," Brodie said. "You were gonna hurt innocent people, Saint."

"You shut up!" Grant screamed and his arm sagged an inch while he frowned at his brother. "You took everything from me, took Zara, made her lie to me, you took Art, and today, you took Sutcliffe and everything he built."

Finding the bunker empty must have been another knock to his presumptive ego. He thought he was winning, going higher, then Brodie and his crew proved to be one step ahead. "We can talk about this," she said, stepping away from Brodie and lifting her hands to try to calm Grant. "Please, you don't have to—"

His anger strengthened his gun arm. "I won't be made a fool of again," Grant said, and regained some composure. "But I am reasonable."

She didn't trust the humor in his voice and glanced at Brodie, but he was watching his brother. "Reasonable?" she asked, willing to do almost anything at this point.

"I will allow one of you to live and I'll let you decide

which."

That didn't leave much room for negotiation and the burn of tears made it harder for her to breathe. Standing here, so close to the man she loved, caught in the web created by her boss, a man she'd once trusted, made her chest constrict. If he expected to cause more conflict between them and have them turn on each other, he wouldn't be satisfied.

Groveling wasn't beneath her. She'd do anything to save their lives. "Please," she said, willing to beg for mercy. Art's death had proved just how quickly one curl of a finger around a trigger could steal life. Panic fueled her desperation. "I'll never see him again. I swear to you. We'll walk out of here and I will never see him or talk to him. I won't have any contact, I promise."

She'd rather know that Brodie was alive without her than dead because he loved her too much to let her go. Giving her life for his would be an easy choice for her to make. But after witnessing the torment he suffered at losing Art, she couldn't burden him with the loss of her life too. He'd have no one to bring him back from that.

Her pleas received no answer from the bully before them.

Her love snubbed her appeal and took control. "Put a bullet in me," Brodie said.

She shrieked. "No! No, please, Grant!"

"Don't have much to live for if I don't got my girl, do I?" Brodie said.

He remained tense with his eyes trained on his brother and she wished he would turn and look at her because if he did, she might be able to get through to him. Losing his parents and Art, coupled with his previous assertions that he wasn't good for her, Zara couldn't exclude the possibility that Brodie would welcome death.

"Beau—"

"Quiet," he said and didn't flinch.

Caine was just inside the door and was watching the events like they were a theatre performance. He leaned back against the doorframe and a smile bent his lips. "This is fucking good entertainment."

"Murder isn't in his blood," Tuck said and looked at her before turning to Grant. But his words weren't reassuring when Grant was the only one holding a weapon. She searched the floor and saw that there were other guns scattered around, her hope was snatched when Tuck caught her looking. "They're all empty. He's the only one with a clip left. The coward hid and used everyone else as shields."

Human shields. The man she'd worked alongside for five years was a monster. "Oh my God," she breathed.

"If murder is in his blood then it's in mine," Grant snarled. Brodie's form vibrated with taut fortitude. "Get over here or I'll shoot him." Grant swung his aim to Tuck. "Then I'll shoot her." He moved the gun past Brodie and onto her.

Tuck stepped up. "By the time the round hits me, Rave will have that weapon from your hand and if he won't put a bullet between your eyes, I'll do it."

Usually she would guess it wasn't a good idea to tell the guy with the gun the plan. But Grant was enough of a coward that the warning might prevent him from shooting. She didn't want Tuck to sacrifice himself either, she wanted them all to walk out of here alive, but that was looking decreasingly likely.

"Good thing I have backup," Grant said. "Ben?"

Up until now, Benedict Leatt had stayed quiet in his position behind and to the right of Grant. Now he reached behind him and produced a gun, a reserve weapon that no one had known was there.

"Ben," she pleaded as tears cascaded down her face. "Please, don't do this. Why would you follow Grant? You barely know him!"

Grant scoffed. "Wasn't so difficult to convince him your lover was the one who murdered Sutcliffe when he found out he killed Tim too."

That was one truth they couldn't refute, not when Sutcliffe would have pinned Tim's murder on the enigmatic Raven too. Ben knew her friend had shot Tim; he hadn't known that friend was also her lover.

"Come over here," Grant said and Brodie took a step.

"No!" she cried out and grabbed Brodie's arm. Grant could only want him closer to shoot point blank. Grant wouldn't want to risk aiming wrong, he wanted to look in his brother's eyes as he delivered the death shot.

Twisting toward her, Brodie turned his back to Grant to curl his hand around the back of her neck. "Close your eyes, baby. Let me go and turn your back. You don't need to watch this."

She shook her head fast and more tears coated her cheeks. "I won't let you go. Without you I… I can't breathe."

"You follow orders, Swallow," he said but his severity didn't compel her to comply.

Digging her nails in deeper, she couldn't release him. "I love you," she said, drowning in his determination because this wasn't a decision she could support.

"You'll be taken care of," he said and as he peeled her fingers from his flesh, he glanced to Tuck.

Putting her hand into Tuck's, Brodie began to back off and Tuck took her shoulders to turn her away. She sobbed as she lost her view of Brodie. Tuck pulled her downward and she was happy to collapse into a crouch while he held her. Before she could drag in a breath, the distinctive bang of a gunshot made her scream.

A body hit the floor. She whirled up and around, rushing forward at the same time, and came up short against the solid barrier of Brodie's back. He wasn't dead. Relief lightened her body, but it didn't slow her tears. Lifting his arm, Brodie curled it back to snag her body to haul it against his and it was then that she saw the body on the floor: Grant.

"Oh my God," she gasped and hid her face against Brodie who was squeezing her tight.

"Why did you do that?" Tuck asked. She peeked out to see that Ben was holding the smoking firearm.

He'd shot Grant. From the awkward way Grant was lying with the gun skittered away from his fingers, she could only assume he was dead. The threat was gone so she was relieved, until she saw whose boots were beside the weapon. Caine ducked down to pick it up and his conceited pleasure made her nauseous. They couldn't appeal to him for mercy.

"Ben?" she asked, although when she tried to move away from Brodie, he yanked her back to him. "You didn't believe

Grant when he…? When he said Raven shot Sutcliffe?"

The only reason Ben would have to shoot Grant was if he was protecting her or the Kindred. Except when his brow lowered, the glare he wore wasn't one of camaraderie. "Albert Sutcliffe had his share of enemies, Grant McCormack did too. You have no idea how deep this goes." She couldn't believe it. He was more furious than Grant had been. "My superior has their own plans."

Rigor stood up now and in spite of the blood staining his clothes, he came to their side. "I checked you out, you motherfucker, you're a nobody."

"You've only known Albert Sutcliffe a few months," she said, having believed they'd met when Sutcliffe was rehabbing from his Atlas injury. "You didn't even know Tim."

"Intriguing, isn't it?" Ben sneered. She'd never seen him look so wicked. Moving until his back was against the wall, he turned on Rigor. "Bet you didn't look too hard, did you? You found out about my practice, my work with Sutcliffe, that's all legit. You don't know the half of it."

The past wasn't as crucial to her as this moment was. "What are you going to do, Ben?" she asked, putting her hand into Brodie's back pocket then curling her nails into the denim beneath her palm. Getting rid of Grant hadn't solved their problem.

"I'm giving you thirty seconds to get the hell out of here," he said and she was so surprised, she gaped. "I've got work to do and I'm on a clock. You need to get the fuck out before I start shooting… You can have the place back when I'm done."

"You're abandoning the compound?" Brodie asked.

"Want to ask questions? Or do you want to split before I change my mind and finish you all?"

Caine was still smiling but pushed open the door and gestured for them to exit. They didn't need another invitation. With a sideways nod, Brodie indicated to Tuck they were leaving. He held her tight as they slipped out the exit with Tuck and Rigor in their wake. Brodie got them around the house but didn't go on the road.

He snatched her hand and pulled her a few feet into the

trees, then stopped short. At first, she didn't know why. Tuck and Rigor rushed past them and pulled open the doors of a black jeep almost indecipherable in the thick night and dense environment.

Brodie shoved her into the back, then jumped in beside her. Rigor started driving before the door was closed. They bumped as they drove toward the road and Brodie grabbed her neck, but it wasn't a sign of affection. He shoved her face down into his lap and then turned to glance backward before bending to take something from the floor: Maverick, his rifle.

"You see anyone?" Tuck asked.

"Stay down," Brodie said to her and turned to kneel on the back seat, positioning the rifle on the backrest to aim it out the back. He didn't fire any shots but kept his eye on the scope, which would give him a better view of what was going on behind them.

She began to push up, but Brodie shoved her head back down without ever taking his eye away from the sight. "Rave?" Rigor asked, colored with worry.

"We're clear. Keep it moving," Brodie said, maintaining his position.

Curling into herself, she lay on her side on the backseat and closed her eyes. Grant was dead. But they were free. Brodie had lost another family member, a man she'd helped drive insane. She feared that Brodie could return to his grief. Right now, he was focused and heroic, but she had no idea what the future would hold for them and the Kindred.

TO BE CONTINUED...

Thank you for reading this tale!
If you can, please take the time to review.

~

Ask your local library for more Scarlett Finn novels!

~

For all things Scarlett Finn
check out:

www.scarlettfinn.com

BOOK THREE

Being the sniper's sight... opens more than her eyes.

CUCKOO

Kindred Book Three

SCARLETT FINN

OUT NOW!